FIFTH VICTIM

ZOË SHARP

ISIS
LARGE PRINT
Oxford

First published in Great Britain 2011
by
Allison & Busby Limited

Published in Large Print 2011 by ISIS Publishing Ltd.,
7 Centremead, Osney Mead, Oxford OX2 0ES
by arrangement with
Allison & Busby Limited

British Library Cataloguing in Publication Data
Sharp, Zoë, 1966–
    Fifth victim.
    1. Fox, Charlie (Fictitious character) - - Fiction.
    2. Bodyguards - - Fiction.
    3. Kidnapping - - Fiction.
    4. Detective and mystery stories.
    5. Large type books.
    I. Title
    823.9'2–dc22

ISBN 978–0–7531–8912–2 (hb)
ISBN 978–0–7531–8913–9 (pb)

Printed and bound in Great Britain by
T. J. International Ltd., Padstow, Cornwall

For David Thompson of
Murder By The Book and Busted Flush Press.
Damn, you're going to be missed . . .

CHAPTER
ONE

The only thing more terrifying than fighting for your life is fighting for someone else's.

Especially when you're losing the battle.

On my knees in the warm sand, I gouged at the reluctant earth with a driftwood shovel, with both hands and my every breath. And the more I burrowed, the more the sides of the hole folded in quietly to meet the void. I knew then, gritted in the face of defeat, that there was only one way this was going to end.

Badly.

Pig-headed, I ploughed on, seeing nothing but the next scoop of sand that rushed in, mocking, to fill the last insignificant hollow. Dig, twist, throw. *Dig, twist, throw*. Up and out into the coastal wind, over and over, while my mind stamped and cursed and wailed silently inside my head.

How could you let them take you? Why didn't you run? Why didn't you fight? And — more bitter, more self-indulgent — an almost childish cry: *Don't you think I have enough damn blood on my hands?*

I'd lost a principal two winters previously, had watched her die, helpless, only metres away. Might as well have been light years, for all the use I'd been to her then. But that was better than this agony of grim expectation, of not knowing life from death one way or the other. I was overwhelmed by a sense of waste and dread, so strong I feared the stink would always linger.

Dig, twist, throw.

Just ahead of me, one end of the shallow pit was marked by an upright length of pipe. Ordinary grey soil pipe, about forty mil in diameter, like any plumber would install for the drain of a sink or a shower. Before I'd begun my ragged excavation, it had stuck a hand's breadth out of the ground, protected from the elements by an upturned plastic bucket. Now I could see half a metre or more before the pipe disappeared into the sand beneath.

I stopped digging and scraped around it carefully with cupped hands, creating a protective moat and driving granules deep under my broken nails as I did so. And, all the while, I had visions of someone watching this frantic rescue from a safe distance and laughing at my attempt to exhume what might so easily turn out to be nothing more than a false thread laid into empty ground. I resisted the temptation to grab and rive, just to make sure the other end really was attached to something. Because if it was, and I yanked it free . . .

To come this far and face failure, so close to the finish, would be worse than never finding the bloody burial site in the first place.

I heard the swish of footsteps approaching fast across the loose surface behind me, but didn't stop, didn't turn.

2

Dig, twist, throw.

"Charlie!" Parker's voice, hoarse against the ocean breeze rippling up the beach. I glanced over my shoulder then, in time to see him rip off his jacket and tie, bunching himself to jump down into the hole.

"Don't," I said, gasping with the effort of speech. "We don't know what the box is made out of — how much extra weight it will take — and I'm lighter."

Parker must have seen the desperation in my eyes. To his credit, he didn't point out that he was stronger, fresher, and could probably clear the grave a hell of a lot faster than I could.

Instead, he squatted near the open end of the tube, cocked his ear close for any sound of movement below, any sign that we were not too late. I could have told him I'd already tried that and hadn't come away reassured, but I saved what little breath I had left for the ground.

"Hang on in there," he shouted downwards, paused. Silence. "If you can hear me, we got you. Help's coming."

I kept my head down and my thoughts to myself.

Dig, twist, throw.

"They should have thought of this hours ago," I muttered. "Where the hell *are* they?"

"On their way," Parker said, but his face was white.

He scrambled round to the side of the pit and began clearing the sand I'd already raised, levelling the ground, kicking it away to stop it sucking back into the hole. It suddenly seemed that I'd made much less progress than I'd thought.

I prayed our gravedigger hadn't favoured the traditional depth of six feet under. By my reckoning, every extra foot was another half a ton of fill to shift. I'd attended enough funerals over here to know that the modern American trend was to go down only four feet, then encase the coffin in concrete to make it solid enough to be driven over, and not rise in a flood or be raided by scavengers.

If that was the case, we were all fucked.

Dig, twist, throw.

And then, at last, I thudded into something solid yet strangely hollow, jarring my arms hard enough to make me grunt. I dropped the driftwood and scrabbled at the sand, fingers meeting roughened timber. I battered down to the surface, found cheap chipboard, like you'd use to board up a derelict house.

A spurt of renewed anger flushed through me at this crude vulgarity, as though bird's-eye maple with rosewood inlay would have made it any better. I snatched up my driftwood again and attacked the remaining sand, sending it up and out of the hole like flung hail. Even Parker stepped back in the face of it.

By the time it was half cleared, the outline spoke for itself. Not a simple rectangular box but a long taper towards the end furthest from the pipe. Parker, higher up, realised the significance first. He began to swear, soft and vicious under his breath.

I have utterly no concept of what it's like to be put underground in something that's so obviously shaped like a coffin, still alive and scared out of your wits.

Still alive? I bloody well hope so . . . or why bother with the pipe?

I swept the last film of sand away and stopped, panting. The lid was held down with screws around the outer edge, already beginning to corrode with the salt. They were spaced at irregular intervals, as if whoever had built this monstrosity had been in a hurry, and careless about the details.

I fumbled in my pocket for my Swiss Army knife, wrenched out the screwdriver attachment and went down on my knees, hand slapping hard onto the surface.

"Hold on," I yelled in a voice not quite my own. "Hold on!"

Parker slithered down behind me, his own pocket knife out. I met his eyes and saw my own tightly clamped emotion reflected right back at me. Then I was bending close to the first screw head, blowing away the grit so the tool would bite hard enough to turn.

A faint scuffle of noise reached my ears and stopped my breath. I froze, glanced up at Parker, hope flaring until I saw his eyes. He shook his head, and I realised it was just a clump of sand dropping back into the pit to scatter with cruel deception across the exposed wood.

A sudden image reared up, vivid enough to stun, of another reaching out to me, unable to make himself heard or gain anyone's attention, trapped in a soundless, wordless, motionless nightmare. Everything seemed to lurch under me. I put a hand up onto the damp sand to steady myself.

"You OK?"

I blinked. The vision was gone. Parker's gaze was concerned, but his voice was tight. He understood, empathised even, but this was not the time to start unravelling on him.

"Yeah," I said, and bent to the task.

We went as fast as we dared, which must have seemed appallingly slow if you're trapped in your own premature grave waiting for release. I worked along one side, Parker along the other, from the head down, clambering over ourselves in the confined space like some macabre game of Twister. One screw loosened after another until my forearms and wrists were screaming and the blisters bled.

The lid was too thick to bend — thick enough to take the weight of both of us without a bounce. We probably could have driven over it, even without a concrete casing.

"That's the last of them," Parker said. "Get clear. I'll do this."

"No chance." I shoved the knife back in my pocket, stilled when he caught my arm.

"Charlie," he said quietly, "you've done enough."

But I hadn't, and we both knew it.

Expressionless, he nodded as if I'd spoken, released me and stepped back. We grasped the lid together, braced ourselves, and heaved.

Dig deep, twist, throw . . .

CHAPTER
TWO

I liked the Willners right from the off, and in some ways that made it all so much worse. Far easier to protect a principal if you can be objective about the exercise — ambivalent, even. Dedication to duty is one thing, but emotional investment is the way madness lies. And if not that, then certainly a spectacular burnout.

Still, by the start of that summer I was probably heading for both.

It was the first week in May when Parker Armstrong drove me out to Long Island for our initial consultation with the formidable Caroline Willner. I remember her fixing me with a piercing eye and asking the million-dollar question.

"So, Ms Fox, are you prepared to die to keep my daughter safe?"

Despite the intensity of her gaze, her voice was little more than calmly curious.

My answer mattered to her, of course it did. But her attempt to hide that fact behind a cool facade was revealing. It made me more deliberate in my choice of words than I might otherwise have been, facing a wealthy potential client for the first time.

"If it comes down to it, yes," I said. "But I'd rather we didn't have to find out."

She raised an eyebrow at that, lifting her teacup. Beside me on the sleek leather sofa, my boss twitched in sympathetic response.

We were sitting in the huge living area on the top floor of the Willners' ultramodern house in the Hamptons, with plate glass windows offering a widescreen view of the shoreline. Below us, beyond a stark white security wall, the Atlantic surf rolled in all the way from North Africa. Caroline Willner had been sitting with her back to the glass when we were shown in to meet her, leaving us to be overawed by the open vista. She clearly did not share our concerns about the potentially uninterrupted field of fire.

"What Charlie means, ma'am," Parker said smoothly, "is that close protection is all about anticipating trouble — keeping the principal out of danger in the first place. Dying on the job is considered a failure in our line of work."

Even as he spoke, he realised what lay beneath and behind the words. His eyes flickered across to mine.

Charlie, I'm sorry . . .

Forget it.

If Caroline Willner noticed this silent apology, she gave no sign of it. The woman opposite was no doubt used to people hesitating around her. She had the steely demeanour of someone who took no prisoners, suffered no fools. The crow's feet radiating from her eyes and the lines ringing her neck showed she had the self-confidence to reject surgical intervention as the years

8

advanced. Her hair was unashamedly silvered, but cut in a style as severely modern as her home.

An interesting mix of defiance and pride that would not, I noted, make her accept advice easily, particularly when it came to matters of personal safety. Such people tended to confuse caution with cowardice, and react accordingly.

Parker had given me the background on the drive out from the office in midtown Manhattan. That she was rich went without saying. You don't own beach front property in Suffolk County and scrape by on your uppers. The money came from investment banking and was largely of her own making. Since her divorce from some minor branch of the German aristocracy, though, she was no longer entitled to call herself Countess. I took in Caroline Willner's fiercely upright posture and wondered if that rankled.

"And have you ever failed?" she asked now. She spoke with that New York old-money clip I'd come to recognise.

"Yes."

The baldness of my answer — or perhaps the truth of it — surprised her. She covered by taking another sip of tea from a cup so delicate it was almost translucent. There was a smear of lipstick on the gilt rim, but none seemed to have come away from her mouth. It wouldn't dare.

Her pale-blue eyes held mine with a certain arrogance, awaiting my elaboration. I said nothing.

"But you didn't die."

I returned her stare blandly. "Not entirely."

She nodded, disengaging for a moment as if checking with some internal database, nodded again slowly as the figures tallied when she hadn't quite expected them to.

So, she had done her homework on us.

Or on me . . .

Parker and I sat side by side, holding our own cups in which the liquid had already cooled beyond comfort. We waited, unfazed by her brief silence and not rushing to break it. Clients of Caroline Willner's status moved at their own speed. When it came to judging the pace of their mood, Parker was an expert.

He was a quiet man, not overly tall, not overly muscled, a chameleon who blended perfectly with whatever company he kept, without ever losing the essence of himself in the process. His prematurely grey hair gave him an air of maturity that inspired confidence in any client, belying a face that could turn surprisingly youthful when he smiled. And sitting here, in this exceptional house, he looked relaxed and quite at home.

Eventually, Caroline Willner said, "Dina came late in my life. By that time, both my husband and I did not expect to be blessed, and then . . . we were." A brief smile, almost rueful, but affectionate. Then she glanced up and it was gone. "An unfortunate side effect is that I have always felt a generation removed from my daughter, Mr Armstrong. My focus has been on my work and I regret that while Dina was growing up I probably did not pay her as much attention as I should have. We are not as . . . close as I would like."

Caroline Willner sat very still as she talked, only her face showing animation. She looked from one to the other of us closely, checking for censure. We were careful to show her none.

Her hands were folded in her lap and now she straightened her fingers, absently inspecting the rings on her right hand. Habit rather than vanity, although I'd escorted enough precious gem couriers to know that the emeralds she wore must have cost well over twenty thousand dollars.

"Has she been in any trouble?" Parker asked, neutral.

"No!" Caroline Willner's head snapped up, but her gaze slid on past. "Just a few foolish games. Drinking, partying, that kind of thing. She's young and she's fallen in with a crowd who are something of a bad influence. I never know where she is or who she's with." Her eyes settled on mine again, more resolute. "I'm hoping that is something Ms Fox's presence will rectify."

A flutter of movement beyond the glass caught my eye. A girl on a big muscular white horse came bounding along the surf line, the horse's gait snatchy through the knee-high water, neck flexed against taut reins. I had the impression he was more than a handful, and his rider's decision to go paddling had been taken more in an attempt to regain control than for pleasure.

"If I'm to take this job," I said mildly, "it will be on the understanding that I am not the girl's gaoler, nor your spy. I can only suggest, not enforce. And I can't protect her if she doesn't trust me."

Parker shot me a warning glance, but if anything Caroline Willner looked faintly gratified, as if having someone who would stand up for her daughter — against any detractor, regardless — was a personal vindication in her eyes. Proof that she had made the right choice.

"You're close to Dina's age," she said. I was nearer thirty than twenty, but naturally I let that flattery pass. "And you're British, well-spoken. It gives you, if you'll forgive me for saying so, my dear, a sophistication not often found in someone of your . . . professional background. I hope she will take note of you, at least."

I considered telling her that if she was looking for a role model for her daughter, she had best look elsewhere. My own parents had been at times both shocked and disappointed by the way I'd turned out. But then Parker asked, "Is Dina close to her father?" and the moment passed.

Caroline Willner shrugged beneath her beautifully cut jacket. My own black wool business suit — the most expensive thing in my wardrobe that didn't contain Kevlar — suddenly seemed like peasant garb by comparison. So much for my worldly air.

"My husband and I separated when my daughter was eight," she said tightly, as if forced into group therapy against her will. "He returned to Europe after the divorce. There has been no . . . regular contact since."

She rose, turning away from us and smoothing down her dress with an unconscious gesture that reminded me of my mother. Dignity at all costs. There was a large canvas on the wall to my left, a huge bold splodge of abstract colour exploding diagonally across it like multicoloured blood spatter. She moved over towards it and, after a moment's apparent absorption with the brushwork, twisted back, poise almost masking the tension.

"So, can you protect her?"

Parker put down his cup. "We can certainly do our best — and our best is pretty good," he said with a faint smile. "But you have to appreciate, ma'am, that preventing kidnappers who are well prepared, well financed and highly motivated is almost impossible without the kind of restrictions on your daughter's lifestyle that she would find unacceptable. All we can do is minimise the threat — make your daughter no longer seem like a soft target."

"Make them look elsewhere, you mean?" She gave another quick frown, not liking the idea of passing the buck.

"If we can liaise with the authorities, study the reports on the previous kidnappings, and get a handle on the way these people operate, maybe we . . ." His voice trailed off, then turned sharp. "Mrs Willner?"

"The authorities know nothing of any of this." Another stern stare. "I was assured that the discretion of Armstrong-Meyer could be relied upon absolutely."

"It can." Parker stilled, eyes narrowing. He knew as well as I did that only around one in ten kidnappings were ever reported, but that didn't mean he had to like it. "You should be aware that there has been considerable success in apprehending kidnappers inside the United States — far better than in many other countries around the world," he said flatly. "I would strongly advise full cooperation with local and federal law enforcement agencies."

Caroline Willner inclined her head, almost graceful. "What I feel about the matter is irrelevant at this point, Mr Armstrong. My family is personally unaffected." She aimed a level stare. "I should very much like that state of affairs to continue."

"Nevertheless, a number of young people have been kidnapped — young people of extremely wealthy parents with homes on Long Island — over the past year," Parker pointed out. "Keeping it under wraps can only make things worse."

"Nobody likes admitting that they gave in to extortion," I agreed. "And if the victims were not precious, they would not have been taken."

Caroline Willner did not appreciate being ganged up on. Her spine stiffened. "In the kind of social circles in which I move, involving the authorities would generate bad publicity that is something to be avoided at *all* costs." She glanced at me again, something calculating in her face now. "If word of this had gotten out, it would be open season."

"There have been — what? Three so far, I believe you said?" I asked dryly. "The first of which was the middle of the last summer and the last was only a few months ago. I rather think it already is."

"I am not saying I condone the decision of the people involved to handle things without the intervention of the authorities, Ms Fox, only that I can understand the reasons behind it." Faint colour lit her

14

cheekbones. "That is why I am taking these steps to avoid the same fate befalling my daughter."

"Of course," Parker said. "The final decision in such an eventuality would be yours to take."

She straightened, regal, her voice remote as if this was a business deal in which she only had marginal interest. "So, do we have an agreement?"

Parker glanced across at me, but I shook my head. "That's up to your daughter," I said. "I can only protect a principal with their willing participation. If she's against the idea, or obstructive, and refuses to take sensible precautions, then I can't hope to do my job."

Caroline Willner flipped back the sleeve of her jacket and consulted a wafer-thin wristwatch. "Dina should be back momentarily," she said. "Why don't you ask her yourself?"

CHAPTER
THREE

I stood in the lee of the security wall and watched Dina Willner wash clods of salt-laden sand from the white horse's legs and belly. The animal delicately sidestepped the gush of the hosepipe with much snorting through distended nostrils, making a production out of it.

Dina was a slim girl, not much more than my height, and she seemed to handle him a lot more confidently on the ground than she had done while on his back.

Strictly speaking, white horses were referred to as "greys", but such a dull term didn't do justice to his haughty magnificence. I detected Spanish blood in the thick-crested neck and long sloping shoulder, pedigree temperament in the clearly delineated veins standing out through his coat. And if perhaps he wasn't the most prudent match for Dina's equestrian skills, I could understand, once she'd set eyes on him, how it would have been hard to settle for anything less.

As he scraped and stamped amid the spray, shoes ringing on the concrete pad that lay beneath the high wall, I briefly considered offering to hold his bridle, but quickly kept hands and thoughts to myself. I wasn't yet officially in the Willners' employ, and horse slobber, as I knew from my youth, would require dry-cleaning to remove. The white horse was producing enough froth around the metal in his mouth for me to imagine he'd been gargling with Alka-Seltzer. He distributed it freely with every temperamental shake of his head.

I had introduced myself as Dina rode up the beach to the house. Or rather, as soon as I'd stepped out of the gate in the wall at her approach, she'd smiled and called out brightly, "Hi! You must be the bodyguard."

So much for keeping a low profile.

She was wearing a loose white blouse and a black felt hat with a wide brim and a flat crown that matched the nationality of the horse a little too carefully, I felt. Her hair was dark, pulled back into a ponytail that hung between her shoulder blades. And she had on a pair of pearl drop earrings. I wondered briefly what kind of person wore such expensive looking jewellery to go riding on the beach?

There didn't seem to be an answer to her question that wasn't inane. I slipped on my sunglasses against the glare of sun on the water and said, "Did the way my knuckles drag on the floor give it away?"

For a moment she looked startled, then flashed a quick grin and dismounted, landing lightly in the sand. She looped the reins over her arm and elbowed the horse aside, not unkindly, when he tried to rub his sweaty face against her shoulder.

"I'm Dina Willner — but I guess you knew that already."

I shook the gloved hand she offered and murmured my name in response. She had a firm grip, backed by composure and the cool self-assurance that seems to come naturally to the offspring of the very rich. All too often, I'd found, brattishness and stroppy tantrums were bundled in as part of the package, but Dina's gaze was frank and refreshingly open in its appraisal. She led the horse up onto the hardstanding near the gate, and pulled out the retractable hose.

"When Mother said you were a girl, I wasn't sure what to expect," she admitted, suddenly doubtful. "You don't *look* like a bodyguard."

"I wouldn't be much use if I did."

A stock answer to a stock question. Parker usually wheeled me out when the client was looking for a more discreet level of security. There were plenty of guys on his books who really *did* look like they could drag their knuckles, and they had their time and place.

"But . . ." She paused, face clearing. "I hadn't thought of it like that. You're right, of course — this will be much more fun."

Less like having a babysitter, you mean.

She flicked me another sideways glance as she played water over the horse's tendons. "So, are you . . . armed? Right now?"

The weight of the 9mm SIG sat neat and snug in its Kramer holster at the small of my back, but the wool suit had been carefully tailored to mask the outline of the gun. I smiled blandly. "If I did happen to be carrying concealed," I said, "and I told anyone about it, then technically it wouldn't be concealed anymore."

"Ah . . . I suppose not." The horse shifted again, bored now with this game. Dina shut off the water and let the hose reel wind back in. I obligingly held the gate open and the pair of them went through, Dina walking by the horse's shoulder. They both had a long purposeful stride.

Inside the gate was a pleasant shady courtyard containing the horse barn. It was a building about the size of a small bungalow, with a sliding door at one end and far enough from the house not to bother either set of occupants with noise or smells. When Dina opened the door, the air-conditioned gloom revealed a row of ornately constructed loose boxes down one side. Even the horses over here were spoilt rotten.

"You're not offended that I asked, I hope," Dina said over her shoulder as she led the white horse into the nearest stable, pivoting him round to unsaddle him. I stood in the open doorway and watched her deft movements, impressed as much by the fact that she was doing this herself as by her competence. "I've never had my own bodyguard before."

"That doesn't mean you get to dress me up and put ribbons in my hair."

She laughed out loud at that and the horse gave a surprised snort as if in agreement. "You're funny. We're going to get along just fine." She slipped the bridle down the horse's long nose and rubbed his ears. "Just fine. Aren't we, Cerdo, hmm, boy?"

"Cerdo?" I queried. "Isn't that Spanish for —?"

"'Pig' yes," Dina agreed, eyes dancing. "He has some long fancy name in his papers, but sometimes he can be real stubborn, so it seems to suit him."

She gave the horse a final pat and came out of the stable, carrying his paraphernalia with her and clipping

19

a chain across the opening. She paused in the wide central corridor, still holding the saddle in her arms. I wondered if her devotion to horse riding extended to cleaning tack and mucking out.

"So, when do you start?" she asked. "Or have you already?"

"I think that's rather up to you," I said, neutral. "And your mother, of course."

"Of course," Dina echoed. "But she wouldn't have sent you down here to meet with me if she didn't approve, so I don't know what you said to her, but congratulations — you obviously passed the test." And for the first time there was a tinge of resentment in her tone.

I deduced "mother" was not an easy woman to live with, never mind live up to, so I took a gamble and said easily, "Well, I didn't wipe my nose on my sleeve and I managed to drink my tea without slurping it from the saucer, so I suppose she realised I was house-trained at least."

It paid off. The lines of strain flattened out of her forehead and the quick grin was back, making her seem very much still a teenager. A pretty girl who lit the place up when she smiled. I guessed she hadn't yet learnt to adjust the intensity. If she was this unguarded around boys, I thought privately, I would certainly have my work cut out fending off the hordes. Whether they had ransom on their minds, though, was quite another matter.

"So, I guess Mother's told you about the kidnappings," she said. "I mean, everybody's behaving like nothing's going on, but you have to know, don't you? Otherwise, how can you try to stop them?"

"There doesn't seem to be much *to* know at the moment." I paused, wondering if she was tougher than she looked, and decided she'd be better with the truth now rather than later, however unpalatable. "But to be honest, because none of the victims have gone to the police or the FBI, there isn't much can be done to stop these people."

"Oh . . . you mean they could just go on and on doing it for ever, and *never* be caught?" She seemed astounded by the idea. I supposed that unless you've been personally touched by violent crime, your views are formed by the cosy propaganda of the TV cop shows, where the good guys always triumph before the closing credits.

I shrugged. I'd already disconcerted her enough, by the looks of it, without adding that the decision to keep things under wraps meant the perpetrators were indeed likely to go on making comparatively easy money until it couldn't be covered up any longer.

Until somebody died.

As an illegal earner it was less risky than robbing a bank, but just as profitable. More than half a billion dollars a year disappeared into kidnappers' pockets around the world, and the annual number of victims was rising rapidly. The relatively few kidnapping cases in the States was down to the high detection rate, a moot point in this case. *Rich parents who would do anything to avoid bad publicity — I bet they can't believe their luck*, I thought. *What reason do they have to stop now?*

Still frowning, Dina put the saddle down onto a shaped wooden rack and laid the bridle across it. She swept off the hat, loosing her hair at the same time, and ruffling it distractedly back into a style mine never seemed to achieve after being flattened under a bike helmet. This despite the best efforts of my hairdresser, who'd talked me into a chin-level bob that had proved surprisingly durable otherwise.

"So . . . what will you need for me to do?" she asked at last, trying for her previous nonchalance. "I mean, I assume you don't want me to hide in the basement or anything silly like that. Otherwise, there wouldn't be much point in having you around, would there?"

I shook my head. "We'll go into details later, but the basic rules are just don't go anywhere without an escort — namely, me — and vary your routine. If you drive yourself to work, don't always take the same route. That kind of thing."

She laughed. "No worries there — I'm taking a year out. Mother tells people I'm 'considering my options', which sounds so much better than 'bumming around with horses', don't you think?"

The white horse, piqued by no longer being the centre of attention, had shuffled forwards until his broad chest was hard up against the chain across the stable doorway. He stretched his neck towards us, ears flicking like radar, and grubbed at Dina's sleeve with his lips. She reached out absently to scratch his nose.

"Do you ride him on the beach at this time every day?" I asked.

"Usually — before it gets too hot. But they wouldn't try for me then, surely?" Her voice was shocked. "What about Cerdo?"

I shrugged again. Kidnappers had been known to shoot bodyguards, boy- or girlfriends, employees, dogs and innocent bystanders, in their quest to secure a valuable hostage. A horse would present few problems. Besides, all they had to do was turn him loose on the sands. It wasn't as if he'd be able to pick them out of a line-up afterwards.

"Best not to go out alone, then, just in case."

Her smile was less confident than it had been. "That's only a problem if you don't ride."

I thought of all those years spent Pony Clubbing back at home in rural Cheshire. "I'm a little rusty, but I'm sure it'll come back to me."

The door at the far end of the barn opened and Caroline Willner walked in with Parker Armstrong beside her. His eyes flicked straight to mine. I gave him a fractional nod, saw his surprise and relief only because I knew him well enough to discern it.

"Ah, *there* you are, darling," Caroline Willner said. "You have not forgotten we have the senator and his wife coming to lunch, I hope?"

"Of course not, Mother," Dina said in a slightly drawling voice she hadn't used with me, but she made no moves to go and change, which I assume was the motive for the reminder.

There was a long uncomfortable pause during which time the only noise was the circular whirr of the ceiling fans inside the barn and the rush of surf from the beach. Even the white horse seemed to be waiting, still and expectant, to see who won this minor stand-off.

"Well, I see you two have gotten acquainted," Caroline Willner said carefully at last, and I wondered why she didn't want Dina to know what this meant to her. I glanced at the girl, caught her slightly mulish expression and realised it was all power plays between the two of them, had probably been that way for years.

"Of course," Dina said, her tone airy as she pulled off her leather gloves. "Charlie was just telling me it would be dangerous to go out riding alone." A slight exaggeration, but close enough for me not to contradict her. "So, I guess she better start soon. I can't leave Cerdo standing idle for more than a day or two. You know how wild he gets if he isn't exercised."

Caroline Willner's only response to this veiled double-edged threat was an enquiring glance in Parker's direction.

"If you've come to a decision about needing close protection for your daughter," he said, non-committal and diplomatic, "then it would be prudent to have it in place as soon as is practicable."

Caroline Willner didn't quite sigh, but it was pretty close. Her gaze flickered over me with less warmth than she'd shown upstairs, as if I'd fed her daughter's fantasy rather than squashed it, as she'd hoped. "Very well. I'll leave the arrangements to you, Mr Armstrong."

24

She had already begun to turn away, focused on her impending lunch party no doubt, when Dina's voice brought her up short.

"In that case, Mother, there's every reason for me to go to the regatta party next weekend," she said, very clear, her triumph almost — but not quite — under control. "Don't you think?"

Caroline Willner turned back, frowning, and I realised that Dina had lured her into check, playing a game I wasn't aware of, by rules I didn't understand. "I —"

Parker came to her rescue with a suitable line of escape. "We would have to assess the risks, of course," he said. "What kind of a party?"

"Oh, it's a friend's birthday, but it's also a kind of big celebration." Dina smiled, that bright open smile she'd given me at first sighting, down on the beach. "For the victims of the previous kidnappings. They're all going to be there, so if Charlie really wants to find out what happened to them — so she can try to stop the same thing happening to me — well, what better place to start?"

CHAPTER
FOUR

"You OK?"

It took me a moment to focus on Parker's voice. I swivelled in the passenger seat and realised we were driving through Queens, the chic elegance of Long Island far behind us in favour of cheap high-density housing. I'd never quite got over how much wiring seemed to be on view in American cities, the buildings festooned with it as though wearing their blood vessels on the outside of their bodies.

"Yeah, I'm OK," I said, leaning back against the headrest. Ahead of us, a passenger jet was pulling out of LaGuardia and lumbering doggedly skywards. I could sympathise.

I was tired, I recognised. The kind of bone-deep utter weariness that long-term stress produces. But I kept on going through the motions, treading water, marking time.

Waiting.

We were in one of the Lincoln Navigators Parker favoured as general runabouts, heading back towards Manhattan where Armstrong-Meyer had its prestigious offices. I wondered briefly how long Parker would keep the "Meyer" part of the name intact, without the man himself to back it up.

From behind the wheel, my boss flicked me a brief speaking glance. His eyes were hidden behind Ray-Bans, but I didn't need to see them.

"If you're not sure about this job, tell me now and I'll assign someone else." To his credit, there was nothing to react to in his matter-of-fact voice. Sympathy was the last thing I could cope with.

I lifted my head. "I thought you didn't have anyone who fitted the bill." That was how he'd persuaded me to go out to the Willners' in the first place. Not that *persuaded* was quite the right word, but neither was bullied. Cajoled — that was more like it.

Anything to take my mind off Sean Meyer.

"I don't," he agreed candidly. "Mrs Willner specifically requested a female close-protection officer, one who was young enough to get on with her daughter. Apparently Dina developed a crush on one of the house security guys last fall, and she doesn't want a repeat performance."

I raised an eyebrow at that. The guy who'd answered the door to us this morning was obviously more than just an ordinary flunkey, and when Caroline Willner had suggested I go down to the beach to wait for her daughter's return, I'd seen at least two other bulky members of staff who had the unmistakable carriage of ex-military men. No doubt they had their share of war stories, calculated to impress someone as impressionable as Dina. Had I ever been that young at twenty?

"What about Gomez?" I said. "She's closer to the daughter's age than I am. OK, she lacks a little experience, but her instincts are sound."

"I need her for Paraguay." He smiled faintly. "You could trade with her if you like, but I kinda assumed you'd want to stay close to New York for a while."

I dredged up a smile of my own. "Yes . . . thank you."

It didn't matter that I knew I could be back from just about anywhere in the world in less than twenty-four hours. A lot could happen in a day. Or, nothing could happen at all. Not for one day, not for a hundred days. Three months, one week, four days of suspended animation.

Parker sighed. "It's OK, Charlie," he said gently. "If I was in your position, I'd want to stay close, too. I just thought . . . you need to work. At least the farthest this kid is likely to travel is up and down the east coast, from one party to the next."

I swallowed and stared sightlessly at the scenery flashing past beyond the tinted glass, feeling disconnected as a ghost from the lives outside. I'd stopped trying to tell myself that it could all be so much worse, because deep down I knew that wasn't true anymore. Concentrating on a job — any job — had to be better than the wretched loneliness of my own thoughts. For a while this morning, out at the Willners' place, I'd felt almost . . . normal.

And the prospect of a temporary change of scene, of living in, somewhere that wasn't silent and filled with empty spaces, had definite appeal. At this point, I might even class it as essential.

I took a breath, made a conscious effort to divert my brain into more productive tracks. "What's your take on this birthday bash Dina's so set on?"

His hands relaxed very slightly on the wheel. "Could be she just wants to show off the pretty new toy her mommy bought for her."

My lips twisted. "Ah, that would be me, then — this season's must-have accessory."

"Yeah, something like that." He flicked me another glance as he changed lanes around a slow-moving bus. "Whatever her reasons, you can't fault the logic of her argument."

"In favour of going, you mean?"

He nodded. "Without any official reports, we're working blind. Anything you can learn about what happened to the other victims might make the difference to Dina being taken or not."

I fell silent. Since I'd joined Parker's outfit I'd worked family protection details numerous times. Usually in places like Mexico or Columbia, where prevention was always better than the alternative. There, it was a toss-up whether the hostage would be returned alive, even if the ransom was paid. And if it wasn't, well, less than a quarter of hostages in Latin America survived rescue attempts, and only a tiny fraction of kidnappers were ever caught. If the ransom was large enough, a whole rake of people could be included in the pay-off, including local police officials.

But this was not some dusty South American backwater. The parents must have known the odds of detection and capture were far better here, that by keeping silent they had, in effect, given the kidnappers a licence to continue their deadly game. So, what were they so afraid of, that it was worth risking their children's lives?

"Is it coincidence, I wonder, that all three families paid up without going to the cops?"

"Might be, but I kinda doubt it," Parker said. "Which means they were targeted very carefully. Somebody knew they had the available cash and the inclination to pay up clean and fast."

"An inside job, you mean?" I murmured. "And if they all had the kind of general security Caroline Willner employs, you'd need pros to make the snatch in the first place. Disgruntled ex-employees perhaps?"

"Maybe. I'll check it out. Finding a common link between the victims is our best lead to tracking down a multiple kidnapper."

I gave him a long level stare while he pretended to be absorbed in negotiating traffic. "Either I'm supposed to be protecting Dina or playing detective," I said mildly. "Which is it, Parker?"

"The two objectives are not mutually exclusive." He allowed himself a fractional smile. "You may think you hide it well, but lack of exercise is sending you as stir-crazy as that horse of Dina's."

I paused a beat, then said, "Even if I do go with her to this regatta thing she mentioned, I've no authority to question these other kids. They may still be traumatised, not want to talk about what they've been through."

Every kidnap victim reacted differently, but all too often there was guilt at the sacrifices made by the family, resentment at their own helplessness, and an overwhelming general sense of fear at going out and doing normal things again. Feelings that could last for weeks or even years after the event. Some former hostages never fully recovered.

"Sure," Parker said, and there was satisfaction in his dry tone. He had me hooked, and he knew it. "And that's why they're all turning out for a birthday party aboard a million-dollar yacht, huh?"

I opened my mouth and shut it again, acknowledging defeat. "Good point. Well made."

"I thought so." He smiled out loud then, creasing the corners of his eyes and taking years off his face, and added casually, "Mrs Willner wants you on duty first thing tomorrow morning."

"Fine," I said. "I had nothing else planned."

"You were organising logistics for Paraguay . . .?"

"All in hand. I emailed my report to Bill Rendelson before we left this morning."

"That was fast work."

"Ah well, I try constantly to disappoint Bill with my unexpected efficiency." It was better than admitting I didn't sleep much these days, either.

Parker sighed. "You don't have anything to prove, Charlie," he said quietly. "If anyone ever thought you were just along for the ride, they kinda revised that opinion a long time ago."

31

"Even Bill?"

"Even Bill," he agreed gravely.

Bill Rendelson ran Parker's office with an iron fist inside an equally iron glove. Invalided out of active duty after the loss of his arm, his only pleasure now, it seemed, was in dissatisfaction with the rest of the staff — and me in particular. I'd only seen one brief flash of humanity from him, gone so fast it might have been a trick of the light, never to be repeated since.

But if I'd been about to comment, it was cut short by Parker's cellphone ringing from its hands-free cradle on the dashboard. He had, of course, switched it off while we were at the Willners' and the calls began to pile in now.

He talked on the phone almost constantly for the remainder of the journey onto Manhattan Island, swapping easily from one subject to another, going over itineraries without pause for thought or recollection, smooth, unflustered and professional. An ideal boss.

He'd proved an ideal friend, too, over the past three months, when the shock and pain and all-consuming sense of loss had sometimes threatened to overwhelm me. Sean was, as Parker had once pointed out, my soulmate.

I expected Parker to go directly to the office in midtown, but to my surprise he continued north, eventually pulling up outside the front entrance of my apartment building on the Upper East Side.

Strictly speaking, the building was Parker's — or some wealthy relative of his at any rate. It was in a prime location and should have been financially way out of reach, but the heavily subsidised rent had been another of the incentives that lured Sean and me to New York in the first place.

As I reached for the door handle, Parker put his hand up suddenly and I stayed put, waiting for him to tie up the last call. The Navigator sat idling by the kerb, sporadic traffic passed, the sun came and went behind high cloud. An elderly lady, wearing a huge amount of make-up and swaddled in furs, tottered by dragging a small shivering hairless dog by its diamanté-studded collar and lead. She was a regular fixture of the neighbourhood and I'd never seen her without the fur — or the dog with any — even in the height of summer. Life with all its oddities, staying the same and moving on.

After no more than a minute or so, Parker hit the End button and removed his sunglasses.

"Sorry about that," he said. "Look, Charlie, I want you to keep in close contact on this one. If you need help, call me — day or night — OK?"

"O . . . K," I said slowly. "What are you not telling me?"

He shrugged. "You know as much as I do."

"So why the fuss?"

"I'm worried about how you're holding up, that's all," he said at last. He put his hand on my arm, lightly, saw my surprise and lifted it away again. "You're looking tired, Charlie. You should get some rest."

"I will — later," I said. I opened the door and climbed out, glanced back to find him still watching me, narrow-eyed. "After I've been to see Sean."

He smiled briefly, put the car into gear and drove away, and as I watched him go I wondered what he'd *really* been about to say.

CHAPTER
FIVE

When I walked into Sean's room, he was lying on his right side in the bed, with his back to the doorway.

"Hi, it's me," I said softly. "I brought you coffee."

He didn't respond. It was warm in there and the sheet was rumpled around his waist. Above it, I could see the steady rise and fall of his ribcage as he breathed, the bones forming a series of ridges under the skin like sand along the tideline.

He was thinner than he'd been at Christmas, the visible shoulder angular and pointed where once it had been as sleekly clad in muscle as Dina's white horse. Just as graceful, and just as dangerous to underestimate.

I stood in the doorway for a moment, gripping the frame and uttering the usual silent prayers. That this time it would be different.

It wasn't.

Carefully, as if afraid of waking him, I moved round to the other side of the bed. He had always been a light sleeper, almost catlike in his reflexes, but his face was soft in total relaxation. I reached out a hand, hesitant, and stroked the pale skin of his upper arm. Under my fingertips, I felt a little quiver of response and I watched his face minutely, as I always did. His eyelids, with their ridiculously long dark lashes, remained resolutely closed, as I had known they would. But, inside my own chest, something twisted.

Sean's coma had lasted since his near-fatal gunshot injury in California, a hundred days ago. After the shooting, he'd been airlifted to the Los Angeles County/USC Medical Center. The surgical team there had spent seven painstaking hours removing the shattered fragments of skull from his brain and repairing the damage caused by the path of the single 9mm round. It had been a glancing blow rather than full penetration, but that had been enough.

In the several weeks that followed, it was to LA that Sean's mother had briefly flown to weep with quiet dignity by his bedside. A calm, sad woman who'd known her share of grief, she'd talked of Sean in the past tense as if he were already lost to her.

My own parents offered to make the trip but I'd refused — to, I suspect, their secret relief as well as my own. My father might have retired from his own speciality as a consultant orthopaedic surgeon, but he would have cut to the heart of the medical jargon with a little too much clinical precision for me to stomach back then.

The doctors had been initially dubious that Sean would survive at all, but he'd defied their gloomiest prognoses. He'd responded well after surgery, to the point where they were able to remove him from the ventilator and allow him to breathe unaided. Sometimes he reacted to touch, moving under my fingers, and sometimes to speech, turning his head towards the sound of my voice.

But he didn't wake up.

The fact that the guy who'd shot him had been caught — that *I* had caught him — was no consolation, I'd found.

As soon as Sean was stable enough to travel, Parker had chartered a private flight and brought him back to New York, to a specialist neurological rehabilitation centre where they were experienced in dealing with long-term coma patients. Here they fed him, kept him hydrated and gave him passive physio to keep his joints in working order, even if his muscles were wasting. I'd been coming every day since then.

I flipped the lid from the coffee and put it down on the side cabinet, close enough for the aroma to reach his nostrils, and dragged the visitor's chair closer to his bedside. Out of habit, I glanced at the cardiac monitor, wired to patches on his chest. I was no medical expert, but I'd grown to know the rhythms of his body well enough to recognise there had been no change.

Sean's hair was longer than he would probably have preferred, falling dark and straight over his forehead. I pushed a lock of it back from his temple, revealing the narrow scar that streaked back into his hairline from the corner of his left eyebrow. If he continued to wear his hair in a style less military to the one he'd always favoured, I realised, it was likely people would hardly notice. The surgeons had made a neat job of putting the pieces back together. Time alone would tell how much was missing on the inside.

A nurse appeared in the doorway, a motherly figure in brightly patterned scrubs. Nancy. She lived across the river in New Jersey and enjoyed the reading time offered by her daily commute. Her husband was in the construction industry and she had two sports-mad teenage sons who drove her to affectionate distraction. I'd come to know a lot about Nancy.

"Hello, Charlie," she said, her voice slow and musical, as always. "It's time to turn him."

I helped her shift Sean onto his back, his limbs slack under our careful hands. He had to be moved every few hours to prevent sores and Nancy was often the one who did it. She had a gentle touch and bottomless compassion and it seemed to me that if Sean made one of his apparently random physical responses — a twitch or a turn of his head — it was for Nancy that he moved most often.

She rearranged the sheet low across his stomach, checking the monitor patches were still firmly attached, and the gastric tube that disappeared into the wall of his abdomen. Initially, they had fed Sean using a nasogastric tube down his nose and through his oesophagus, but that, I was told, could lead to complications. As soon as it became obvious this wasn't going to be over quickly, they'd inserted something more permanent, through which puréed food could be squirted directly into his stomach.

The thought of it did little for my own appetite. When Sean finally awoke, I thought, refusing to consider another outcome, he would be about ready to kill for a taste of the daily coffee I brought to tempt him.

Nancy smiled serenely and departed. I tucked my fingers into Sean's open hand and began to tell him about my visit to the Willners, about the recent kidnappings and Dina's apparent glee at my employ. I sought his opinion, unvoiced, on the wisdom of Dina going to the party she was so keen to attend, and reported Caroline Willner's own hesitation over the same event. And all the time I wondered if doing this was for his benefit, or my own. Sean always had been a good listener.

"These three kids who've been taken so far all live on Long Island, at least part of the time," I said. "I say 'kids', but they're late teens, early twenties, but so far that's all we know. I suppose this party is a good opportunity to look for patterns, but at the same time, there's the risk that if someone is watching them — working security for one of the families, maybe — am I exposing Dina to danger by agreeing that she go? We don't know how the victims were selected, or even how they were taken. They can't remember much after the initial abduction, apparently, which probably means some kind of pre-med relaxant, like we used in California for that cult extraction — remember?"

I paused. Sean's head seemed to rock a little in my direction. Involuntary, no doubt, as most of his movements were, but it still felt like he'd reacted with discomfort, as if trying to warn me of something. I'd read about coma victims who were actually locked into their paralysed bodies but totally aware of everything going on around them, screaming silently into the void, sometimes for years. Like being buried alive.

Bearing that in mind, I looked for meaning in every gesture, however pointless they told me that might be.

Sighing, I let my thumb stroke the back of his right hand. Without animation from within, his skin felt different, alien to the touch. And I remembered, with splintered clarity, every moment we'd spent together. Sean was everything I'd ever wanted, even before I'd known what that was. He understood me better than I understood myself, and he would have understood, better than anyone, how this slow limbo was crushing me from the inside out.

"I need you," I said out loud. It sounded stark and craven in the quiet room.

Gently, I let go of his hand and stood up. I shrugged into my jacket, picked up the cooling coffee from the cabinet.

"Last chance," I murmured, waggling the cup slightly. Sean didn't stir. "Maybe tomorrow, hey?"

I walked out of the room and along the corridor, resisting the urge to look back.

We'd talked about death, in a roundabout kind of way. We couldn't do the job we did without the subject coming up and being faced in advance. Sean had always said, calm and casual, that when his time was up he wanted to go clean, fast, and know nothing about it.

Well, two out of three ain't bad.

A sudden dazzling image exploded behind my eyes, the way his head had snapped sideways from the bullet's impact, the slash of blood, the instant drop.

40

It didn't give any comfort that he'd gone down in the line of duty, as he would have seen it. Doing his job. Hesitation had never been a possibility with Sean and it seemed that to hesitate now would be to let down everything he'd stood for. So if it came to it, I thought fiercely, then yes, I would die to protect Dina Willner, as her mother had asked.

And maybe I'd do it just a fraction more willingly than I might have done, a hundred days ago.

CHAPTER
SIX

"Isn't this just to die for?"

Dina opened the ring box and turned it towards me. Inside was the biggest, ugliest yellow diamond I'd ever seen. It looked like nicotine-stained glass and cost the same as a car.

I held up my unadorned hands with the fingers splayed, and shook my head. "I'm the wrong person to ask about jewellery," I said evasively. "But couldn't a ring as a birthday present be . . . misconstrued?"

She coloured slightly, snapped the box shut again and handed it back to the eagle-eyed sales assistant. "You're right," she agreed. Her eyes drifted indecisively across the glittering display cabinets. We'd been into a dozen similar high-end stores so far on this street alone, and all that dazzle was starting to give me a bad head.

"The party's the day after tomorrow. I just wish Mother had given in earlier, then I would have had more time to find something suitable," Dina said. She sighed. "Tor's *so* difficult to buy for. I mean, what do you give the guy who's got everything?"

Recognising that Dina was clutching at straws on the ideas front, I refrained from the old joke about penicillin. Torquil Eisenberg, whose twenty-first birthday celebration was the cause of all the fuss, was the son and heir to a vast transportation empire. Eisenberg Senior, so I understood, owned a large percentage of everything that flew, drove or floated with a bellyful of bulk goods, from crude oil to car parts. There was rich, and then there was Eisenberg rich. I took a wild stab that suggesting some aftershave and a pair of socks was probably not quite going to cut it.

"You've seen the necklace Tor's mother has, of course — the Eisenberg Rainbow?" Dina said now, undeterred by my silence. "All these rows of beautiful diamonds — different cuts and colours. Not just white, but some are pale pink, or deep blue like sapphires. It's priceless, and utterly fabulous."

She sighed, as if — by courting Tor's favour — she might get to wear it herself one day. I'd seen news photographs of the jewellery in question. To me it looked as fake as something from a cheap Christmas cracker, but I thought it best not to say so.

"What's he like — Torquil's father?" I asked instead as we walked back out into the sunshine. I checked the passers-by out of habit before we crossed the street and I blipped the locks on Dina's Mercedes SLK. "Have you ever met him?"

"Mr Eisenberg?" Dina looked blank for a moment, then shrugged. "A couple of times. He's OK, I guess," she said, and heard the doubtful note in her own voice. "Well, he *can* be OK — when everything's going Tor's way. Which is kinda weird, because from what Tor says, he's hardly ever around."

So, money can't buy you everything.

We climbed into the car. I fired up the engine to let the air con disperse the heat that had built up inside the cabin, and found Dina watching me.

"Why did you ask?"

My turn to shrug. "I'm just surprised, that's all," I said, "that he's putting on a big birthday bash for his son when there've been these kidnappings. You would have thought he'd be wary of conspicuous displays of wealth — go out of his way to make his son seem a less attractive target."

She laughed. "From what I hear, Tor hasn't had to ask twice for anything since he was about six years old," she said wryly. "Can you imagine what would happen if his twenty-first birthday party was cancelled because it might be risky?"

"He likes taking risks?"

"He wrecked his first Ferrari when he was sixteen. He's into skydiving, snowboarding, you name it," she said. "If it's dangerous, Torquil will do it." But where there should have been a certain amount of respect or admiration in her voice, something more heartfelt took its place.

I checked the mirrors and slid the Merc out into traffic. "You don't like him very much, do you?"

"I —" She flicked me a telling glance and lapsed into glum silence for the next couple of blocks before finally admitting, "It's not that. He just doesn't know when to stop, you know? Like, it's not funny until someone gets hurt."

"Yeah, and then it's hilarious," I muttered, glanced across and caught her frowning. "So, why are you going to all this trouble over his birthday? Your mother obviously didn't want you to go, and you've admitted you don't really like the guy . . ."

"It's not for Tor— ," she began, biting off whatever she'd been about to say next. "Oh, never mind!"

I wasn't being paid to be easily offended so I just shrugged. "OK."

We drove on in silence, with Dina staring pointedly out of the window. It was the first hint of discord, of temperament, she'd shown in the three days since I'd been assigned to her.

Dina swam every morning in the heated outdoor pool on the lower terrace, while I made a show of apparently lounging around, keeping her company. At varying times we rode out on the beach — Dina on the showy white Cerdo, and me on an elderly chestnut Quarter Horse that had apparently been her previous mount.

Dina had been friendly and chatty enough, without actually revealing much of herself to me, nor enquiring too deeply in return. She seemed most interested in my riding skills, acquired in my childhood and not used much since.

Apart from that, she'd shopped, and gone to hairdressing and beauty appointments, all with me firmly in tow. I'd done my best not to crowd or irritate her and it had seemed to be working fine 'til now. When she'd lunched with her mother at a fashionable restaurant, I'd excused myself to the adjoining bar area and kept a discreet watch over the pair of them from there. If body language was anything to go by, they ended the meal in excruciatingly polite disagreement over something. I didn't ask, and Dina didn't tell. We didn't have that kind of relationship.

And today, she'd quickly accepted that I was not going to act as her own personal pack mule, not that she'd bought much so far. Certainly nothing suitable as a birthday present for the thrill-seeking only child of a billionaire.

I checked my mirrors again before changing lanes, indicating late before our turn-off to flush out a possible tail. There had been no hint of anything so far, but it did no harm to be cautious.

Our destination was a shopping mall that seemed to stretch as far as the eye could see in all directions. My heart sank at the prospect of a long afternoon's continued dithering, but when I parked up near the main entrance, Dina made no immediate moves to get out.

"I'm sorry about . . . before," she said in an awkward rush. "But, you see, there will be other people there — at the party. People I kinda like . . ."

"So, putting up with an evening of Torquil's dubious sense of humour is the price you're prepared to pay."

"Yes . . . I guess it is." She gave a wan smile. "Doesn't make it any easier to choose a gift for him, though."

So, her earlier dreaminess had been strictly for the necklace. I sighed. "From what you've said, it sounds like you can't hope to buy anything that's going to impress him, so why not get him something quirky instead? Something that will make him smile. It doesn't have to cost a fortune."

She stared at me like I'd suggested she dance naked in the streets. "Like what?"

I resigned myself to yet more shopping and nodded to the mall looming ahead of us. "Let's go and find out, shall we?"

CHAPTER
SEVEN

In low heels and an all-purpose evening dress, I leant on the balcony rail of the yacht club and stared out across the glittering lights of the harbour.

When Dina had said the birthday celebration was taking place at a regatta, I'd envisaged sailing boats of some kind, slim and sinuous. What greeted me instead was a collection of floating gin palaces, halfway to cruise ship size, bobbing fatly, gleaming and self-satisfied in their allotted mooring spaces, like prize pigs at a trough.

Below me was a wide outside terrace area overhanging the water, strung with fairy lights and bordered by waist-high glass panels, presumably to stop the more enthusiastic partygoers tumbling into the murky depths. There were currently about thirty or forty of them down there, doing their damnedest to put that to the test.

Our host for the evening, Torquil Eisenberg, was at the centre of things and working a little too hard at being the life and soul of his own party. He was a thin geeky kid with a long neck and prominent Adam's apple above the bow tie of his white tuxedo. I guessed, in different circumstances, he would have had buck teeth and sticking-out ears, too, but Daddy's considerable riches had fixed what it could and showered him with money in the hope of taking your mind off the rest. If he was into the extreme sports Dina had mentioned, it hadn't helped convert his stringy physique into anything immediately impressive.

It took me about ten seconds after meeting him to decide I didn't like the kid. Dina had handed over her beautifully wrapped gift with studied casualness, like his reaction didn't matter to her. He tore his way through the brightly coloured paper and ribbons and looked suddenly nonplussed when he came to the manufacturers' logo on the box.

"Victorinox?" he said blankly. "What's this?"

"Why don't you open it and find out?" I suggested.

He managed to open the box itself and found, nestling inside, the most comprehensive and expensive Swiss Army knife in the shop, bristling with attachments for every occasion. After she'd chosen it, Dina had gone back to the jeweller's and had six words neatly engraved along the side of the casing.

FOR THE GUY WHO HAS EVERYTHING

Torquil stared for a moment longer and I could have sworn I caught the slightest twitch at the corner of his mouth, then he looked up and it was gone, replaced by an indifferent contempt.

"Is that it?" he demanded, dumping the gift into the hands of a flunkey and elbowing his way towards the next hopeful bearer.

Dina tried to affect a blasé pose in response, but I saw her quickly bitten lip and wanted to slap his legs for him. Sadly, such an action was not part of my remit, however much personal satisfaction I might have derived from it.

The party had been going for about three hours by that point. Torquil had made a showy arrival by chauffeured Bell Jet Ranger, touching down on the yacht club's private helipad, and been swept into a huge marquee on the lawns for a short but concussive set by a moody rock group. I initially had them pegged as a particularly good tribute band and only realised, when the lead singer nearly punched out the birthday boy for making a grab at his favourite guitar, that they were actually the real thing.

The catered meal that followed defied belief, from the massive ice sculptures on the tables to the vintage champagne freely available. Then it was on to the yacht club itself and the partying had started in earnest. What it had all cost was anybody's guess.

Now I sipped my ginger ale on the rocks slowly, as if it were whisky, and looked for trouble.

There was general perimeter security in place, a load of guys built like American football players, squeezed uncomfortably into dinner jackets and bow ties. Not bad as a gatecrashing deterrent, but with neither the agility nor the experience, in my opinion, to prevent an organised, well-orchestrated attack. They'd given my evening bag a cursory search on the way in, but had completely missed the SIG hidden beneath the back of my short jacket. I hadn't enlightened them.

If I'd been trying to guard Dina against potential assassination, the rear terrace of the yacht club would have been a nightmare to control and contain, even with a full team. Open on three sides, brightly lit against the darkness, the exposed location offered too much concealment on the far shoreline for a sniper, with too easy an exfil once the job was done.

As a possible ambush site for kidnapping, however, it wasn't nearly so attractive. Anyone approaching from the water would be clearly highlighted all the way in to the lower landing stage, and the only landward exit meant climbing the short flight of stairs to the balcony where I now stood. From here, I could keep a watching brief on my principal without cramping her style, as per my instructions.

And Dina seemed to be following hers — for the moment at least. She stayed in plain sight and kept tight hold of her champagne glass at all times. The three kidnap victims so far had all been slipped something to make them compliant, I'd pointed out. They could have been injected — any exposed muscle would do the trick — but there was no point in taking chances that the drug had simply been palmed into their unguarded drink.

She had shaken off her earlier embarrassment without, I was interested to note, entirely blaming me for its cause. I had a feeling Torquil would have been determinedly unimpressed with anything she might have given him, and at least the Swiss Army multi-tool I'd suggested was a fraction of the price of that yellow diamond.

After a few minutes of self-pity, she'd shaken herself out of it, agreed with my assessment that he was an ungrateful little bastard, and made a firm decision to enjoy the rest of the party as best she could.

I remembered Caroline Willner's quietly murmured last words before the limo had collected us from the house to bring us here.

"Take care of her for me."

So far, so good.

I caught movement behind me, shifted a little to see a young man step out of the bar, and recognised him as one of the many guests I'd seen earlier. He moved forwards to lean on the railing a couple of metres away. We nodded to each other. I kept my face blank to discourage small talk, but made a mental note of him, all the same. Sandy hair, medium height, thickset but light enough on his feet for it to be athletic muscle rather than junk food. He dressed like money was not a problem and probably never had been.

I checked him out under cover of taking a drink, but his eyes were on the group below, where Torquil was refilling the champagne glasses of two giggling girls. They both had a lot of blond hair and tanned skin on show, and could well have been twins.

"A regular Prince Charming, isn't he?" said my companion, as if reading my thoughts. I glanced across, surprised. His accent was classless English, with just a hint of American inflection in the way he asked the question to suggest a long stay here.

"I'm barely able to contain my lust," I agreed dryly.

He laughed, a pleasant uncontrived sound, accompanied by a flash of teeth. "You say that, but half the girls down there would crawl over broken glass to be the one he takes home tonight."

"Really?" I murmured as I watched Torquil drape his arm across the bare shoulders of another girl, leaving it there just a little too long before moving on. I didn't miss her exaggerated shudder and pulled face behind his back. *If they really think so little of him, why are they all here?* "What's his trick, then? Can he breathe through his ears?"

In the middle of taking a mouthful of drink, my companion spluttered and came close to choking. I kept my eyes on the throng, double-checking Dina's location and too wary of deliberate distraction to come to his immediate aid.

He recovered enough for speech, wiping his mouth on a folded napkin. "English, right?" he said. "Where are you from?"

"Here and there," I said. "London latterly."

"I've been out here five years. Was at Oxford before that. Nice to hear a familiar accent." Something had sharpened in his gaze. "And here I was, expecting just another boring evening."

I cursed inwardly. If I'd smiled sweetly and made some vacuous comment, he would have soon ignored me. As it was, his patent interest was an inconvenience at best, and — if anything went down and he was overcome with stupid ideas of chivalry — it could turn into a serious handicap.

"I'm Hunt, by the way — Hunt Trevanion," he said then, moving closer to offer me a tanned hand. He was older than I'd first thought, maybe approaching thirty rather than twenty, which gave him ten years on the average age of the crowd.

I touched my fingers to his briefly, not letting him get a decent grip even if he'd been so inclined, and said, coolly offhand, "Trevanion? Isn't that a Cornish name?"

He shrugged. "Is it? I've never done the whole family history thing." He eyed me, assessing. "Have I seen you around before? At the tennis club, maybe?"

"I don't think so. I'm Charlie — I came with Dina."

I had insisted that my new principal introduce me simply as a family friend, which she had done without undue awkwardness. Popping up out of nowhere with a claim to be bosom pals, I'd found in the past, led to too many difficult questions.

"Dina?" Hunt said. "Oh, yeah, I know — down there in the orange number? She's a sweet kid."

I thought of the hours Dina had spent earlier this afternoon, trying on what seemed to be every single frock in her substantial wardrobe. In her quest for the right air of alluring sophistication, she'd finally settled on some designer gown in apricot silk which I'd privately thought was too old for her. *A sweet kid*. Not exactly the effect she'd been aiming for.

It was so much easier, I reflected, to be restricted in choice to my one all-purpose evening dress. When I'd bought it, I'd been largely influenced by the fact that it was dark enough for blood not to show too badly, was machine-washable, and made of some stretchy synthetic material that not only allowed a reasonable degree of movement, but was also apparently impossible to crease. Anything else was a bonus.

"So, why are you lurking up here instead of mixing down there among the bright young things?" Hunt asked now, ignoring my best attempts at cold shoulder. He wasn't good-looking in any conventional sense, I thought, but there was something attractive about him, even so. The more he spoke, though, the more I realised there was something a little off about his speech cadences, as though he was trying to cover some kind of regional accent. There were only so many rough edges, I considered, that an Oxford education could polish off.

I sipped my fake Scotch. "I might ask you the same question."

He grinned and shook his head. "Oh no. It's not me they've come to see."

It clicked then, that when I'd seen him earlier, his arm had been around a petite black-haired girl in what I hoped was a fun-fur coat, who'd been treated like she was something special. Although, in a crowd of minor celebrities, that didn't narrow it down much. The Eisenberg name, it seemed, had brought them all out of the woodwork.

"Oh yes, the girl you came with," I said vaguely. "She's famous, isn't she?"

Hunt grimaced into his drink, almost a reflexive twitch. "Infamous, more like," he muttered. "Poor kid."

"You don't mean . . . she was one of the people kidnapped?"

He looked up sharply. "Who told you that?"

"With that kind of a reaction? You did."

A flicker of distaste crossed his features. He drained his glass. "Nice to meet you, Charlie, but if you're just after gossip for the tabloids . . ."

CHAPTER
EIGHT

I stared at him, then said mildly, "Hey, *you're* the one who started chatting *me* up, remember? Not the other way round. And Dina's mother mentioned the kidnappings, that's all. She's worried that the same thing might happen to her daughter. You can't blame her for that."

Hunt hesitated for a moment, then his shoulders relaxed a little inside the well-cut jacket. "Yeah, well. OK then, fair enough," he agreed at last, casting me a still-dubious glance. "Yeah, Orlando was the first victim."

His eyes drifted to where the girl in question was standing at the centre of an admiring circle that included both Torquil and Dina. For once, Torquil seemed content not to be the focus of attention. Dina hovered on the outskirts, not quite included — or excluded, either.

I briefly wondered why she hadn't pointed out Orlando to me as soon as she and Hunt had arrived. Getting useful information out of the previous victims was supposed to be one of the main reasons for us being here. We would, I determined, have words about that later . . .

Because it was always easier to start with a question to which you already knew the answer, I opened with, "How long ago did it happen?"

Hunt's gaze turned suspicious again, but it must have seemed a reasonable thing to ask because he said grudgingly, "Last July."

Ten months ago. "She's doing well to be here, then," I said. "It can't be easy for her to feel safe coming out again."

"Yeah, she's quite a girl," Hunt said softly. "But they grabbed her from home, so I don't think being *outside* is the issue." He waved his empty glass towards the darkness beyond the lights. "Besides, it looks as though old man Eisenberg has laid on plenty of security around the place."

I debated on telling him the guardian gorillas weren't up to much, but decided that would raise too many questions — not least of which was how I could tell.

"I'm sure you're right," I said instead. "It's scary, though, don't you think? I heard three people round here have been held to ransom over the last year. I mean, aren't *you* worried?"

"I'm not rich enough to be worried," he said with candour. "My folks are well off, don't get me wrong, but hardly in the same bracket as Orlando's people."

"Or Torquil's?"

He laughed at that, his former amusement seemingly part-way restored. "Nobody is quite in *that* bracket."

I asked him what line of business his family was in and, with that easy flash of teeth again, he told me they'd made their money in the music business, which seemed to cover a multitude of sins.

I would have asked more, but at that point Torquil bounded onto the bottom step below us and clapped his hands for silence, which he achieved with a speed that must have gratified him. Someone even turned the music down a notch.

"All those of you lucky enough to have gotten a special invitation, we're moving this party up a gear and onto my father's yacht," he shouted. "The rest of you — you've had your fun, now go home."

There was a smattering of laughter, as though he'd said something funny instead of merely downright rude. Torquil grinned at their confusion and continued up the staircase, leading one lucky lady by the hand. It wasn't hard to recognise the tiny figure of Orlando being pulled along in his wake. She was barely five feet tall, slim to the point of undernourishment, in a floaty kind of a dress that was not far from being a nightgown.

Behind the pair, the crowd jockeyed for position and an undignified scramble developed, as if proximity alone would convey favour. Dina was among them, I noticed, but it was hard to tell if she was making the running or just being carried along in the crush.

As Torquil reached the top of the staircase, his eyes glided over me totally without recognition, then flared when they landed on Hunt.

"*There* you are!" he said with a mix of annoyance and relief. "Where are the others?"

Orlando disengaged herself and moved to Hunt's side, wrapping herself around him like a cat. Despite what he'd said about her comparatively settled state of mind, she was clinging to him for more than physical comfort. Hunt ignored Torquil's question long enough to smile indulgently down at her. She blossomed under his gaze.

Sean, I recalled starkly, had made me feel like that. Although we had not been able to show it much in public, it had still been there.

Torquil opened his mouth again, but it was Orlando who tore her eyes away from Hunt's to say calmly, "They might come, or they might not. It kinda depends on if they have something better to do."

She had a cool, clear voice that carried. Certainly, those hurrying up the steps on Torquil's heels heard it and there were one or two audible gasps, and then a giggle.

The birthday boy's head reared back — shock or anger, it was hard to tell. And as the initial jolt passed, his mouth twisted into a sneer. He rounded on the people behind him, glaring furiously. There were enough smiles among the eavesdroppers to tip annoyance over the edge into full-blown temper. Did *anybody* like him, I wondered, watching their faces? Clearly not.

And Torquil must have seen that, too. Whether it came as a surprise to him or not was something else.

"Oh, just get the hell away from me — all of you!" he cried suddenly, taking a step towards them and jerking his arms as if to scare birds off a lawn.

60

It was unfortunate that Dina reached the top of the stairs just at the moment Torquil's tantrum exploded. Propelled from behind, she had no option but to keep moving. She stumbled, reached out blindly and caught hold of the sleeve of Torquil's white tuxedo in a completely reflex attempt to save herself from falling.

Her champagne glass was still in her hand as she did so, and the remaining contents splashed up and out in a pale arc. The majority of the liquid landed, inevitably, across Torquil's chest. Enough spattered onto his face to make him flinch, and the involuntary reaction seemed to piss him off all the more.

There was a moment's stunned silence, then someone sniggered. It was infectious, and within seconds everyone was either laughing or making too obvious attempts not to. If Torquil had possessed an ounce of class, he would have laughed with them.

But he didn't.

Dina recovered her balance and put a hand to her mouth to try and mask a sound that was half gasp, half moan. Torquil's wiry body was actually quivering. I caught the expanding rage in his eye and shifted my weight, fast.

"You stupid, clumsy, little, *bitch*!" he got out, his voice rising to a breathless howl. Dina cringed, and Torquil's straightforward anger turned into something much more dangerous. He moved forwards, arm rising as if to strike.

I stepped in under his wild swing and grabbed his wrist, whipping his palm down and round into a rotated lock that brought him up short with my body blocking the action from most of the onlookers.

He briefly tried to resist. I tightened the lock and, almost to my surprise, he had the sense to freeze before I was forced to dislocate his wrist. I guessed it had more to do with saving face than pain. Our entwined hands were jammed between our bodies, mostly hidden in the folds of clothing. If he didn't struggle, they were likely to stay that way.

I butted my shoulder against his chest and met his furious gaze from a lot closer than either of us would have liked. From that distance I could tell he plucked his eyebrows to stop them meeting in the middle.

"Don't spoil the party," I murmured. "And don't make me spoil it for you."

His instinctive first reaction was scorn, followed swiftly by the knowledge that the torsional pressure I was applying to his hand was slowly but relentlessly forcing apart the bones of his forearm. He was involved in enough dangerous sports to know what physical damage felt like. I don't think I was prepared to actually break his wrist, just to prove a point, but for a moment I wasn't sure about that, and neither was he.

"All right!" he managed through his teeth, loathing me with his eyes.

I let go abruptly and moved back, keeping between him and Dina just in case he got brave again. He went instinctively to cradle his injured hand, then realised how that would look and let it dangle.

When I glanced across, Hunt had drawn Dina aside and was looking slightly bemused by the whole episode. Dina herself had turned as pale as Torquil. Orlando's face was expressionless, as though any hint of violence caused her to shut down.

"I'm so sorry," Dina said. "It was a complete accident. I'll have the jacket dry-cleaned, of course."

Torquil tore his eyes away from me long enough to stare at her like she was something he'd stepped in. Into the buzzing silence came the thump of boots through the bar leading to the balcony and two of the bulky security men finally elbowed their way through. They were both out of breath.

"What's the problem, Mr Eisenberg?"

"There's no problem," Torquil said at last. He jerked his head towards Dina. "But see she leaves, right now." His eyes flicked over me, very quickly, as if he was afraid of what he might see in my face. "And take your . . . friend with you."

I retrieved Dina from Hunt with a nod of thanks for his care, putting my arm around her shoulders. She was shaking.

"Come on," I said quietly as the security loomed beside us. "I'll take you home."

She allowed me to guide her silently through the stares of the bar, and down onto the wide wooden jetty that led towards the exit gate into the parking area. I glanced at her face as we went, and found her eyes were dry but hollow with misery.

"It's all over," I said, aiming to comfort, but the effect was not what I expected.

Something like a sob rose in her throat and she whirled to face me, hands clenching in frustration and anguish. "Oh, Charlie, how *could* you?"

CHAPTER
NINE

"I'll never be invited to anything *ever* again!" Dina moaned. "He'll tell *everyone* what you did and nobody will even *speak* to me."

I waited for her outrage to subside, then said carefully, "Don't you think you're maybe overestimating how popular Torquil is?"

She threw up her hands. "What's being popular got to do with anything?"

I felt my eyebrows climb, heard the trace of acid creep into my voice. "Would you rather I'd just let him hit you?"

Her eyes skated away from mine. "He wouldn't have," she said, but it wasn't me she was trying hardest to convince. She stared glumly at the sparkling toes of her evening shoes. "What am I going to do now? They'll all be laughing at me."

I regarded her for a moment. "So, encourage them."

That snapped her head up. "What?"

"Make light of it," I said. "Make a joke of it. Tell everyone he should be bloody grateful you were drinking champagne and not red wine or he would have looked like an extra from a Tarantino movie."

She tried to look scandalised but couldn't sustain it. I caught the distinct edge of a smile curve her lips, quickly squashed. The gesture reminded me of Torquil himself, when she'd given him the engraved Swiss Army knife. What was it about being rich, I wondered, that made these people so determined to be miserable?

We plodded on towards the exit gate, Dina stepping carefully over the gapped planks in her high heels. Behind us, Torquil's two heavies followed at a suitable distance, just to make sure we really did vacate the property.

The sound of a vehicle pulling up beyond the security fence had me instantly wary. I put a cautionary hand on Dina's arm.

"Slow down," I murmured, eyes on the new arrival — a stretch Lincoln with the usual limo-black tint on the glass, riding low and heavy. From it, four obvious close-protection guys emerged with the care and technique needed for debussing from an armoured personnel carrier in a hot zone. To my mind, it was way over the top for the situation, calling unnecessary attention to the occupants, but they certainly made the existing gate security look like monkeys. Maybe that was the point.

After a long pause, during which time they stared hard at anything that moved, and at quite a bit that didn't, one nodded to the others. The rear door of the limo opened again and a couple climbed out. They were both in their late teens or early twenties, and dressed to kill.

Alongside me, Dina gave a gasp. I guessed without being told that these two were the other kidnap victims, whose possible non-arrival had caused Torquil such anxiety. They were ushered through the gate without the usual checks and strode towards us along the planking.

The boy was short, almost squat, with dark curly hair and Mediterranean heritage written in the olive skin and the facial bones. He had on a dark dinner suit with the bow tie undone and he kept one hand in his pocket as though he'd practised the brooding-yet-casual look in the mirror before he came out.

The girl wore a voluminous sable coat, together with a wide-brimmed hat and sunglasses, even in the dark. I waited to see if any of this would cause her to trip and fall into the water, but she negotiated the jetty with practised ease.

Dina froze, giving a fairly good impression of a deer in the headlights. It was only when the couple neared us that any flicker of recognition passed across the boy's face at the sight of Dina. It was followed by a hint of contempt, and he would have swept right on past us, had the girl not stepped round him and grasped Dina lightly by her upper arms, air-kissing her on both cheeks. I suddenly saw her profile in the light for the first time, and I realised with shock that I knew exactly who she was.

"Dina, honey!" she said. "Surely you're not leaving already?"

Yeah, Dina. Let's go. Let's go right now.

My attempts to will my principal into a course of action proved a failure. Dina stepped back with confused surprise on her face at the unexpected warmth of this welcome. She threw a quick glance in my direction, as if afraid of my reaction. "Uh, well, I —"

"Oh, but you *can't* go now," the girl said firmly, linking her arm through Dina's and steering her back in the direction of the yacht club. "Not when this party's just about to get interesting."

I was pretty sure I knew what constituted her definition of *interesting*, and was equally positive I didn't want to stick around long enough to make sure.

The boy gave an impatient shrug. "She wants to leave, let her go, Manda," he said, dismissive.

"It's not that," Dina said quickly, voice rising. She snatched another look at me and disengaged herself with obvious regret, swallowing. "Look, I'd love to stay, honestly, but maybe this isn't a good time. Torquil and I, we had a-a falling out over a glass of champagne. I tripped and he kinda ended up wearing most of it . . ." Her voice petered away at their blank expressions. She straightened her spine with a determinedly carefree little smile. "Lucky for him I wasn't drinking red wine, huh?"

Manda's eyebrows rose far enough to appear over the frames of her designer sunglasses, then she let loose a big grin that belied the cool appearance. Even the boy stopped scowling for long enough to look briefly amused.

"Priceless," Manda drawled, glancing at him sideways. "I told you we should have gotten here earlier, Ben-Ben."

The boy did not look like he enjoyed being called "Ben-Ben" in public. "We're here now, aren't we?" he said. "Where the hell's Tor? I need a drink."

Right on cue, I felt the planks bouncing under our feet as someone came hurrying along the jetty. I turned and saw Torquil had emerged at the far end, near the yacht club, and was approaching as fast as he could without actually running.

"Manda! Benedict! Great to see you!" He was trying desperately for casual, but the stress of relief came across all too clearly in the pitch and timbre of his voice. He swallowed, said more normally, "Glad you could make it."

"Hey, Tor," Manda said, offhand. "How could we miss your little party?" She reduced all this extravagance to the level of having half a dozen kindergarten tots round for a slice of cake and a cup of flat lemonade. And just as he began to look crestfallen, she hit him with, "Dina was just telling us all about your silly little spat."

Torquil flashed me a look that was part hate, part fear, but pure poison. I stared right back, keeping my face bland, and he wisely refrained from comment.

Manda eyed Torquil for a moment longer, expectantly, then turned to Dina. "Come on, let's go aboard Tor's little boat and find Ben-Ben a drink before he *dies* of thirst, and then you can tell us all about it."

69

"No!" I would have objected myself, but it was Dina, to my surprise, who dug her toes in first. She realised it had come out too stark and softened it down with a smile that held genuine regret. "I'm real sorry, Manda," she said hastily. "But I don't want to spoil Torquil's birthday, so we'll —"

"Oh, that's so sweet of you," Manda interrupted. "Well, honey, our limo's still here. Tell you what, why don't the three of us go find somewhere to have a drink? Tor won't mind if we skip out, I'm sure."

But it didn't take an expert in body language to tell that Tor did mind. He minded like hell.

The two security men he'd sent to escort us out were hovering with their mouths open, unsure what to do next. The other partygoers who'd received their special invitations had emerged from the yacht club and were closing fast on their way to the Eisenberg liner, with Hunt and Orlando in the lead.

Torquil must have known that for Benedict and Manda to leave now, so soon after arriving and with Dina so publicly in tow, would be the ultimate humiliation. He only had one realistic option, but that didn't mean he had to like it.

"It would spoil the party if you left, Dina," he said, with an almost credible attempt at sincerity. "Stay." I'm sure it was only shock that made her keep him waiting for a response, but he flushed at her silence and added through clenched teeth, "Please."

"I . . . er . . . yes," Dina said faintly. "Of course. Thank you, Torquil."

He glared at her. "Don't mention it," he said, his tone ominous. His gaze swung to me. "But your *friend* still needs to leave."

CHAPTER
TEN

There was a long pause after Torquil's last statement. It was eventually broken not by Dina but by Manda, who threw her head back and began to laugh.

"Oh Tor, honey, that's just priceless," she said, indicating me with a languid wave. "But there's no way *she's* going to walk out of here and leave Dina behind to your tender mercies." It was the first time she'd acknowledged my presence.

Torquil subjected me to a rapid scrutiny as if afraid he'd missed something obvious. His mouth opened and closed a couple of times before he finally had to admit defeat. He knew the joke was on him somehow, but he couldn't work out what or how. "Why the hell not?" he demanded.

Manda laughed again as she removed her dark glasses. I caught the brief flicker of her eyes and realised she'd been waiting for the crowd to arrive. She wanted an audience.

Some things never change.

"Because, honey, that's not how professional bodyguards behave, is it, Charlie?" she said, loud enough to carry. "And I ought to know, huh?"

If I'd been hoping for anything else, it was too late now. In my peripheral vision I registered shock in varying degrees. There was no point in denial. Suppressing a sigh, I agreed gravely, "Yes, Amanda, you ought."

Her face twitched. "It's Manda," she said sharply. "I haven't been called *that* for years."

Two years, certainly. Two years since Amanda Dempsey had briefly proved the bane of my life, trying to protect her old-monied family from threats largely manufactured by their own wilful teenage daughter. Caroline Willner's fears for Dina, by comparison, were mild and unjustified.

I jerked my head towards the limo. "I see you've progressed from sneaking out over the castle wall at night."

"Yeah, my trust fund finally kicked in."

I nodded slowly. "How is your father these days?"

"He's dead," she said with a ripe satisfaction, and when that failed to elicit the expected response, she added reluctantly, "Natural causes, I'm sorry to say. The old bastard had a stroke."

Well, you've been doing your best to bring that on since you were fourteen.

"I'm sorry."

"Don't be," she said with spirit that held more than a touch of bravado. "I'm not."

Benedict made an impatient noise in his throat. "Sorry to break up the touching reunion," he said acidly, "but are we gonna stand around here all night, or are we getting on the damned boat?"

Torquil jerked out of stasis. "Yeah, uh, let's go aboard." He brushed past me without eye contact and shook his head briefly to the two gorillas. They shrugged and turned away. Manda determinedly took Dina's arm again.

With Torquil in the lead, we followed him along the network of jetties, through another security gate, and approached what must have been the largest and most luxurious vessel in the place. I let out a low whistle under my breath. With an unblemished dark-blue hull, white upper decks and tinted glass, the superyacht's huge superstructure was raked back so that it seemed to be moving at high speed even lying graceful at its berth. It screamed of money and class.

The yacht must have been the best part of three hundred feet long. It was wider than a house. I counted about four separate deck levels, plus a helicopter pad. Every deck had big sliding glass doors that opened out onto private balconies, and most had a jacuzzi or a hot tub. Even by Long Island standards, the whole thing was a monstrous display of wealth.

As we neared it, the yacht suddenly lit up, underwater neon turning the surrounding water into an ice-blue glow and sending any aquatic life scattering. Deck lights blazed. There was an audible intake of breath from those approaching, and Torquil turned to catch the reaction. It must have been all he hoped for, because he treated us to a wide smile, the first sign of genuine pleasure he'd shown all evening.

Short of grappling hooks, the only way to scale the endless smooth sides of the yacht was via the lower deck area at the stern, presumably for diving or swimming — although why you'd want to get into the nasty old sea when there were so many private swimming pools on board was anybody's guess.

Two crewmen wearing an approximation of naval officers' white dress uniform were standing by to help us along the short gangplank. A gently curving staircase led to the next level, a pool deck, with yet more discreet neon under the water and flanked by sunloungers. I took one look at the acres of teak decking on view and was glad my evening shoes did not have the kind of spiked heels that would leave a trail of damage. Nobody else seemed to bother.

More crew appeared with trays of canapés and drinks, their faces carefully blank to the revelry winding itself into full swing around them. The yacht boasted a sound system with external speakers that must have had half the harbour reverberating to the beat. After about ten minutes, I began to wish I'd brought the ear defenders I normally reserved for visits to the gun range.

It was the kind of party where several people were bound to end up flinging themselves, shrieking, into one of the pools before the night was out — either fully clothed or completely naked, take your pick.

Nobody seemed to bother much about that, either.

I tried to keep a careful eye on Dina without gluing myself to her side, although the yacht had been designed with the privacy of its guests in mind. Every deck had its own personal sun deck, none of which were visible from the others. I was only too aware that things could very quickly get out of hand.

As standard operating procedure, I'd already identified myself to the ship's captain, pointed out my principal and asked for notification if anyone tried to take her off the yacht without me in attendance. By his reaction, this kind of request was not unusual.

Still, she was my responsibility, and she didn't need to be taken ashore in order to be taken advantage of, so I ended up doing a constant roving sweep, no mean feat on a boat that size. Dina, apparently oblivious, danced with various people on the pool deck, sat and chatted to others in the thickly carpeted main salon area below. If her earlier experience with Torquil and the glass of champagne had unsettled her, she gave no sign of it. I saw nothing to alert me that she was in danger.

I suppose it was inevitable, sooner or later, that I'd run into Manda Dempsey again as I prowled round the decks. I was up near the slim pointed bow, far enough forward to have a glimpse onto all the balconies and where the volume of the music was less combative. She stepped out of one of the open sliding doorways and made a beeline for me. At first I thought it was purely coincidence, but I quickly realised she'd sought me out. I put my back to the guard rail and waited. She stopped a couple of metres away, took a sip from her champagne glass and said at last in a cool voice, "I always wondered if I'd end up meeting with you again, Charlie."

Smiling to take the sting out of it, I said, "And I always wondered if you'd end up in gaol."

She continued to regard me for a moment, her body swaying to the pulse of alcohol or music, I wasn't sure which. Then she smiled.

"That's what I always liked about you. You were so damned unimpressed by this kind of thing," she said, nodding towards the magnificent yacht laid out behind us. "I may have despised my father and the sycophants with which he surrounded himself, but at least you were never in awe of him." She laughed. "You once told me, if I hated him so much, to stop taking his money and go make my own way, do my own thing."

Her *own thing*, I recalled grimly in the face of this charm offensive, had included seducing a gullible boyfriend into an attempted hit on the old man. It hadn't worked, and the Dempseys' flat refusal to do anything constructive about their only child had been one of the reasons I'd asked to be taken off the job. A decision I'd never regretted.

"Nice to see you took my advice to heart," I said dryly. "Trust fund, didn't you say?"

She smiled again. "From my grandparents. So, technically, I *did* listen to you." She took another sip of her drink. "I wanted to let you know that you were a big influence, though I guess it didn't seem like it at the time."

I waited for the flash of guile, but saw enough apparent sincerity to deliver a cautious, "Thank you."

"You're welcome," she responded. A girl with looks that were striking rather than pretty, with dark hair which — now she'd discarded the hat — I could see she'd had cut sleek and stylish, feathered in around her neck. The dress probably cost more than my entire annual clothing budget, and she wore it with the careless elegance of someone entirely used to such expense. "I've done some growing up over the last couple of years," she said, almost rueful. "About time, huh?"

"You were kidnapped," I said, recalling the fortress-like parental estate, made even more secure by the installation of the electronic surveillance equipment and sensors that I myself had overseen. They should not have been able to get within a mile of her.

I cursed the sketchy reports, the lack of official investigation, and asked, "How did they get to you?"

Manda's lips twisted. "Too easily," she said. Her eyes flicked across to me. "I was almost home. It was late, dark, and there was something in the road. I thought maybe someone had hit a dog, so I stopped and — just like you always told us not to — I got out of the car." She shrugged, her smile turning wan. "I don't remember much after that. Apparently they had me for four days. I kinda lost track of time."

She moved alongside me and rested her forearms on the polished mahogany capping rail. She leant out over it slightly, staring down into the artificial blue glow beneath the hull. "My father once told me I'd had everything I could ever wish for," she said quietly.

"I remember." At the time, she'd flung back a furious denial. Told him that, on the contrary, she'd had everything *money could buy* and if he didn't understand the difference, there was no point in her trying to explain. There had been more swearing and raised voices to it, but that was the gist.

She straightened, turned so her back was to the rail and gazed at the ongoing party with a cynical eye.

"I guess you don't appreciate what you have, until there's the chance of losing it all," she said then. "Not just your lifestyle, but your life."

"They threatened to kill you?" I said, keeping my voice absolutely level.

"Oh yes," she said with a bitter smile. "They told me in great detail what was going to happen to me if the ransom wasn't paid. And if my family went to the police, involved the authorities in any way, I'd suffer because of it."

I thought back to the rebellious teenager I'd once known. "I can't imagine you took that lying down, Manda."

"Oh, I tried to fight back, and after they beat me, they sent photographs of the bruises to my family," she said. Her voice was devoid of emotion, as though retelling a mildly interesting story of things that had happened to someone else. I'd used it myself as a natural defence mechanism. "For every delay, they said, they would . . . mark me. Somewhere permanent. Somewhere it would show."

"And did they?"

She gave a shrug. "I was lucky," she said. "My family paid."

CHAPTER
ELEVEN

With very little prompting, Manda told me the story of her captivity and release. It didn't take long. She had seen or heard nothing that would help to identify her kidnappers. She thought there were three or possibly four of them. They had been of similar size and weight, had spoken with no discernible accent, never used names, and had worn shiny chain store sports clothing and gloves and masks at all times.

In other words, they were professionals.

She recounted the tale with a dry wit, and a lack of self-pity or exaggeration that I found intriguing.

"How much did they demand for your return?"

"One million." She said it casually, as though it was too small a sum to be worth mentioning. "Wired direct to an account in the Caymans." She shrugged again. "My father had been dead six months by then. The trustees eventually agreed to pay half."

Half a million dollars. Cheap, by heiress standards. Not much to split between three or four perpetrators, for four days of high tension and no doubt months of planning leading up to that. Perhaps that explained why they'd found another victim comparatively quickly.

"Benedict was taken not long after me," Manda said, matter-of-fact. She had her hands wrapped around her bare arms, gently rubbing her own skin as if for comfort as much as warmth, but the night had begun to turn chilly so I couldn't read too much into it. "I didn't know him then. We didn't get together until afterward." She smiled. "Not many people understand what you went through, unless they've been there."

"Was he taken by the same means?"

Manda shook her head. "Not really — car trouble. He'd gotten a flat and called OnStar assistance, and he was waiting for them to arrive when they grabbed him."

"He'd called out help to change a wheel?" I queried, unable to keep the surprise out of my voice entirely, but Manda just gave me a wry glance where the old Amanda would have sulked.

"His folks gave him a tricked-out Cadillac Escalade on these huge chromed wheels," she explained. "He said it was a two-man job, taking them on and off. And it was kinda dark, and raining."

Another roadside ambush. I made a mental note to be particularly vigilant when Dina and I were out in the car. I'd arrived at the Willners' place on my motorbike, a Buell Firebolt, and I'd been using whatever was in their garage since, like Dina's Merc. Maybe I'd call Parker in the morning about using one of the company SUVs, which had a certain amount of non-standard reinforcement in the bodywork and chassis, and run-flat tyres.

"Did his kidnap follow the same pattern as yours?" I asked now.

"If you mean did they threaten to kill him — slowly and painfully — if the police were called in?" she demanded. "Then, yes, it did."

"And the amount they wanted was the same?"

Another head shake, harder this time. "This time, they wanted two million." She saw my reaction and added with a surprisingly resentful edge, "That amount is loose change to the Benelli family."

"And how much did they get?"

She gave me a cool straight stare. "Two million."

"They paid up the whole amount, just like that?" This time I didn't bother to hide my disbelief. Such a move was not only practically unheard of, it was also unwise and possibly downright bloody dangerous.

Unless . . .

Manda was watching my face. She levered upright abruptly and began to turn away. "No. It wasn't *just like that* at all."

I heard something quiet and brittle in her voice, took a step after her. "Manda, what —"

"Hey, Manda, what's the matter — you don't love me anymore?"

A figure had appeared from one of the brightly lit doorways and was standing silhouetted against the light, with a glass of champagne in one hand and the other still stuffed into his pocket. Benedict's usual studied pose.

"Of course I do, honey," she called, almost bringing off a relaxed drawl while at the same time shooting me a warning glance. "Charlie and I were just catching up on the bad old days."

Benedict sauntered across the deck, looking darkly handsome and completely aware of his own animal magnetism. He draped the arm with the champagne glass around Manda's shoulders.

"Come," he commanded, giving her a narrow-eyed pout that, to my mind, made him look both sleepy and grumpy. Never two of my favourite dwarves. Each to his — or her — own.

I would have expected her to laugh off this display of machismo, but Manda gave me a vague smile and allowed him to lead her away. I watched their departing backs and wondered what the hell had been so different about Benedict's kidnapping that his parents were prepared to pay up, in full, an amount that was four times what had been accepted before. And why Manda was so wary of talking about it in front of him. Not for the first time, I cursed the lack of investigation that had taken place into these crimes.

Shrugging off the irritation, I checked the time — a little after two — wondering when I could legitimately insist we pack it in. The night still classified as young, if this lot were anything to go by. I began to feel correspondingly old.

The watch was a cheap-and-cheerful model I'd bought to navigate by on a job in California. Sean had given me a beautiful Tag Heuer when we'd first moved out to live and work in America, twelve months before. The day they flew him back to New York, still in his coma, I'd put the Tag away in a bedside drawer and decided only to get it out again when he was awake to see it.

I'd hoped to have been wearing it again long before now.

I sighed, glanced up at the deck where Dina had been dancing a few minutes before, only to find she was no longer in plain sight.

Swearing under my breath, I headed for the nearest staircase that curved around the superstructure to the upper deck. Nothing.

Working in a logical pattern, I began a sweep of the yacht, checking cabins and walk-in lockers as well as the more crowded areas. It was amazing, the kind of places I found occupied for clandestine reasons, but none of the fumbling encounters I interrupted involved Dina — willing or otherwise. The minutes ticked by, and my anxiety level rose with each one.

Finally, I found Hunt, lounging on one of the built-in sofas that lined one of the smaller sun decks, playing with his iPhone.

"Where's Dina?" I demanded.

Hunt looked up sharply, apparently taken by surprise at my approach. The heels were not only low, they were quiet, too, and the fact he had the phone's earpieces in place hadn't helped.

He slid the whole lot into his pocket before uncrossing his legs and rising from the sumptuous cream upholstery with an elegant smile. "She's having a heart-to-heart with Orlando in one of the staterooms, I think," he said. "Did you want her for anything in particular?"

I gritted my teeth. *Yeah, so I can do my job.* "I just need to know where she is, that's all."

84

"Relax, Charlie." His tone was gently chiding, as though I was taking all this much too seriously. "She said if you came looking for her, to tell you she was OK but wanted to talk privately, and you were to just chill out and wait for her."

"Nice of her," I said shortly, "but that's not how it works."

He moved in front of me, still affable. "Do you really think a kid like Dina is a likely prospect for a kidnapping?"

"Was Orlando considered at risk?" I asked quietly. "Were any of them?" He didn't answer. I sighed. "Dina's parents are not exactly on the poverty line, and she's twenty — hardly a kid anymore. She's a legitimate target, and it's my job to see that she stays safe." I started to turn away, mind already on finding the staterooms, when Hunt's question stopped me dead.

"Have you considered that she might not *want* to feel safe?"

"What?"

"She might not want to feel safe," he repeated. "Her father lives in Europe — Vienna, I think. Dina was supposed to go and stay with her old man for the summer to get her out of the way, but she's refusing. You didn't know," he added flatly, seeing my face. "So, how exactly are you supposed to protect her, Charlie, if they haven't told you what's going on?"

"Good question," I muttered, already on the move. "When I find *that* one out, I'll let you know."

I went below. The first familiar face I encountered there was the last person I wanted to bump into again that night.

Torquil.

I was rushing along a plushly carpeted internal corridor when he came out of a cabin just ahead of me, pulling the door closed behind him. He gave a kind of start when he saw me, face colouring furiously as recognition flashed in, and he muscled sideways as if intending to block my path.

"I'm in a hurry and not in the mood," I said tightly. "Which stateroom is Dina in with Orlando?"

His head jerked with shock and I suddenly realised how my question might be misconstrued. *Give me strength!*

"I believe they're only talking. But I need to find Dina," I explained. Still he hesitated, but when I checked his face I saw indecision rather than obstruction, and tried a more reasonable approach. "Look, Torquil, I'm sorry about what happened earlier, but I'm sure you've had enough bodyguards of your own over the years to know how we respond to a perceived threat."

For a moment I thought he was going to sneer, then he grinned at me, all sunny like a little kid distracted from a grazed knee with a lollipop. "Yeah, I'm . . . um . . . sorry, too, I guess," he said, surprising me utterly with the apology.

"Don't worry about it," I said blankly. "Do you know where they are?"

He took a breath, let it out. "Come on. I'll show you."

Naturally distrustful of this sudden change in behaviour, I kept half a pace behind him as he led the way along another short corridor. If my bearings were correct, we were working our way towards the stern of the yacht. We passed through an open salon area with an oval ceiling, beautifully inlaid with different coloured hardwoods, and a curved bar at one side. The only large vessel I'd been on before this was an Irish Sea ferry and it really didn't compare. The art on the walls here was genuine, and didn't look cheap, but I was in no mood for admiration.

Eventually, Torquil stopped outside a pair of double doors and jerked his head. "You wanna do the honours, or shall I?" he asked with a grim smile.

I shrugged. "It's your boat."

Torquil forgot his supercilious demeanour for long enough to grin at me again. I just had time to wonder why he was enjoying this so much before he grabbed both handles at once, flung the doors wide, and strode in.

If Torquil had been my principal, I never would have allowed him to go first, but he wasn't, so I waited half a beat before I followed.

Our arrival was greeted by a moment's immobile silence and I flicked my eyes across the whole scene. Inside, the stateroom had every convenience, from its own private sun deck beyond the wall of tinted glass, to a huge oval four-poster bed carved from some semi-precious timber. On the wall opposite was the biggest flat screen I'd seen outside a multiplex cinema.

But the people in the stateroom were not there to use any of those facilities, it seemed.

87

There were three of them — Orlando, Benedict and Dina. They sat in the curved easy chairs, which were grouped around a low coffee table set with lilies to perfectly complement the decor.

Orlando gave a startled gasp when Torquil made his grand entrance, and couldn't stop the dismay from passing across her features shortly afterwards. Benedict shoved his fist in his jacket pocket so fast I didn't catch what might have been in it. There was a buzz about them both that sent prickles of apprehension racing across my skin.

Dina was jazzed, eyes glittering. She stiffened at the intrusion, but there was a reckless challenge in every line of her body.

"Charlie!" she said, shock making her voice haughty. "I told you to wait."

"That's not your order to give," I snapped. "What the hell are you doing in here, Dina?"

She brought her chin up stubbornly. "That's none of your business."

"It is when you sneak off without telling me where you're going —"

"I left a message!"

"Not good enough." I moved closer, saw the size of her pupils, the excited jitter she couldn't quite hide. "What have they given you? What have you taken?"

"Nothing! And how dare you speak to my friends like that!" Her voice was an outraged squawk. "How *dare* you?"

I whirled on Benedict. "What did you try to hide so fast when we came in?" I demanded. "Because if I find you've given her anything, I'll have you arrested as a dealer, and I don't give a damn who your family is."

"Charlie . . ."

I ignored Dina's sharp protest, holding Benedict's gaze. Eventually, he got to his feet, slow and insolent.

"It's not what I've got that I'm *trying to hide*," he bit out. "It's what I *haven't*."

And with that he took his hand out of his pocket, fingers spread, and with a cold ripple down my spine I discovered exactly why the Benelli family had been prepared to pay up all that ransom money without haggling.

CHAPTER
TWELVE

"They cut off the little finger of his right hand," I said. "Straight through the knuckle of the first joint. Used a meat cleaver or something pretty similar, and no anaesthetic."

Parker winced. "Nasty."

"Yeah, but apparently the worst thing is that Benedict was reputed to be quite a talented classical guitarist."

My boss let out a long breath. "Well, I guess that's the kinda thing where you need all your fingers."

I shrugged. It was uncharitable of me, but I couldn't help it. Benedict had taken on a distinctly martyred air after he'd done his big reveal of the missing digit — more so after Manda had come rushing in to comfort him. I'd been on the receiving end of more than a few daggered or reproachful looks.

But I remembered Bill Rendelson, who was missing his entire arm, and my initial sympathy for Benedict's situation rapidly dissipated. Bill might not be the easiest person to get along with, but on the whole I preferred his general bad temper to Benedict's "woe is me" attitude.

Dina, needless to say, had barely spoken to me for the remainder of the evening. The party had finally wound down at about 4a.m., and by the time we arrived back at the Willners' place, the sun was on the rise.

I saw Dina to her room, where she slammed the door smartly in the face of my murmured "goodnight". I suppose that was only to be expected.

More in hope than expectation, I'd called Parker's cellphone. It went straight to voicemail, which wasn't a surprise, either, but was still a disappointment. I recognised that I needed to talk as much as make my report, that on previous jobs I would have been able to call Sean, any time, and he would have been there for me. Instead, I left my boss a brief precis of the night's events, including the details I'd learnt of the road ambushes used to grab both Manda and Benedict. I knew that he would immediately suggest upgrading Dina's transport to something more substantial without me needing to put in the request.

Anticipation was one of Parker's qualities.

I wasn't quite so appreciative of his efficiency, though, when he turned up at the house a little after eight the following morning. He called when he was less than ten minutes out to warn me that he was personally bringing over one of the agency Navigators. It just about gave me time to scramble out of bed and take the world's quickest shower. Dina, I'd been reliably informed, was more than likely to sleep in until noon after partying half the night, and I confess I'd been quietly hoping for the opportunity to do the same.

As it was, Parker was already in the open-plan living area, sipping tea with Caroline Willner, when I made a belated entrance with my hair still wet, in khakis and a hastily donned shirt, both chosen more for proximity than style.

Parker had forsaken his usual line of immaculate dark suits. To blend in on a Saturday morning, he was in jeans and brown leather deck shoes, and a polo shirt in a pale washed-out shade of blue. Caroline Willner passed a critical eye over my own appearance, made her scrupulously polite excuses, and left us to it.

Wary of prying ears among the staff, I took Parker down to the garages, which occupied the entire ground floor area at the front of the house. He'd pulled the Navigator into an empty bay, next to Dina's Mercedes. There was also a Range Rover, a couple of anonymous vehicles the staff used to run errands, and a little bright-yellow Mazda two-seater convertible. I'd recognised it as an MX-5 from home, but over here it was called a Miata instead. Caroline Willner had described it to me as her personal toy, with just the suspicion of a reckless smile hovering round her mouth. I'd found space for my Buell in a quiet corner, and not used it since I'd arrived.

Parker handed over the Navigator's keys and I examined all the usual areas that might be vulnerable to sabotage, following protocol rather than demonstrating a lack of trust. He watched me without comment. And while I worked I gave him the full information, as it had come to me, about what had happened to the previous victims of the kidnap gang.

"I'll check out their stories, as far as I can," he said when I was done. "But without any official paper trail, there won't be much I can confirm." He paused. "You said you have some history with the Dempsey girl. That going to cause you a problem?"

"I don't think so," I said. "She seems to have grown up a lot since I was working for them."

"But she still told everyone at the party what you are. If the connection between the victims is the circle they move in, you've been made."

"Maybe. But it doesn't stop me doing my job, Parker." I paused. "Did you ask Caroline Willner about trying to talk Dina into going to stay with her father?"

He nodded, frowning, and turned a slow circle as if admiring the gleaming paintwork on the Miata, but I saw the flick of his eyes and knew he was pinpointing the two CCTV cameras that monitored the garage area.

"What's the set-up here?" he asked.

"Video but no audio, monitored live off site, and recorded to hard drive via an Internet link to the security company's own server. Local cop response time is eight minutes."

He smiled very slightly, in such a way that I realised he already knew the answer before he'd asked the question. He was just checking that I knew it, too.

"She confirmed, but was evasive," he said then. "Tried to pass it off as some kinda short vacation."

"But you didn't believe her?"

"No." He gave a slight smile. "She was too tense. There was clearly more at stake than just a battle of wills between the two of them."

"Ah." My turn to frown. "Is it just that she doesn't believe she's in real danger, or that she doesn't want to leave her horses, I wonder?"

"That you might have to ask Dina — when the two of you are speaking again," he said gravely. "Meanwhile, stay sharp. Don't forget that the first girl, Orlando, was snatched from the family property."

I nodded. "And her parents are rolling in it, by all accounts, so their home should not exactly be a soft target."

"We already know these guys either have very good intel, or they're real pros," Parker agreed. "But some folk are remarkably careless with their own safety. Until the worst happens."

"Yeah well, Orlando and the boyfriend, Hunt, certainly left with some pretty heavy security in tow. Could you put out some feelers in the industry — find out how much of it was put in place *after* the kidnap? It would give us a better idea of what we're up against."

"Of what *you're* up against, you mean." He watched me for a moment, the kind of narrow-eyed stare Benedict could only ever aspire to. "You need backup, Charlie, you let me know."

"I will."

He held the eye contact a beat longer. "Sean would not forgive me if I didn't take real good care of you while he's out of action."

"I don't need taking care of, Parker," I said gently, touched but strangely discomfited by the pitch of his gaze. "Have you . . . been to see him?"

"Went yesterday, right after his scan —"

"Scan?" I interrupted. "What scan? He didn't have anything scheduled or I would have been there. Do they think . . .?"

Unable to finish forming the words of wretched hope, I turned away, moved across to the Buell and ran a hand over the smooth acrylic tank. Whoever habitually kept the Willner cars gleaming had gone to the trouble of wiping the dust off the bike, I noticed absently.

When he spoke again, Parker's voice was much closer behind me than I was expecting, and perhaps because I couldn't see his face, I heard the hesitation in his voice more clearly. "Look, Charlie —"

"Just tell me, Parker."

He sighed. "The consultant ordered him up for another CT scan yesterday," he said at last. "Apparently his physical therapist has been growing kinda concerned about some of his responses."

"Concerned how? About what?"

"His brain activity," Parker said flatly. "I'm sorry, Charlie, but . . . they think it may be slowing down."

Slowing down. You mean he's dying?

My shoulders went rigid. When I made a conscious effort to relax them, it seemed my self-control went at the same time. I let my chin drop, stifled a kind of half gasp, half sob, and felt Parker's hands on my arms. He

95

turned me back to face him and ducked to get a good look at the misery I couldn't hide.

"Do *not* give up on him," Parker said with quiet ferocity. "Whatever happens, Charlie, we'll get through it. You're not alone in this."

I took a steadying breath and stepped out from under his fingers. He made no moves to stop me, letting his hands drop.

"Yeah," I said with a shaky smile. "I know. Thanks, Parker."

"I'd tell you to be careful on this one, but I know you will be anyhow," he said. "Apart from that, how're you finding things here?"

"OK," I said carefully. "I thought Dina and I were getting on pretty well — until last night. I'm waiting to see how she behaves when she wakes up. If she's still not talking to me, you might have to use Gomez for this after all."

Parker smiled more fully then, as if glad to be back on safer ground. It made him look younger, too, despite the old gaze. "According to Dina's mother, you're the only one she'd trust to get the job done and not give a damn who you rode over to do it."

"Ah." I recalled with discomfort the reckless comment I'd thrown at Benedict Benelli the night before, about how if he turned out to be peddling drugs to his friends, I'd take him down regardless of family influence, and the ripples it was likely to cause. "I don't suppose she qualified that at all, did she?"

Parker made an amused sound in the back of his throat, too dignified for it to be a snort. "She likes you well enough and thinks you're doing a fine job, Charlie," he said. "Someone offers you the moon, don't ask for the stars as well."

I would have remarked on the exaggeration of that statement, had it not been for the fact that we both knew he wasn't talking about Caroline Willner.

Sean was still alive — for the moment. I tried to tell myself that anything else was a bonus.

CHAPTER
THIRTEEN

I sat on the old Quarter Horse, whose name was Geronimo, and watched Dina cantering in decreasing circles on an increasingly het-up Cerdo. We were in the Olympic-size all-weather outdoor arena at the local riding club, where Dina took the white horse every week for private lessons in equestrianism.

The instructor was a tall, well-built Australian called Raleigh, who seemed to take delight in pushing horse and rider to the point of explosion. They'd been trying to perfect a difficult dressage move, canter pirouette, for the best part of an hour, so far without satisfying Raleigh's exacting standards.

To my mind, Dina hadn't attained nearly enough willing submission from her horse in order to achieve the lightness and balance required for the movement, so each attempt rapidly degenerated into a hauling match. I reckoned Cerdo was consistently ahead on points.

But I kept such an opinion firmly to myself.

Raleigh turned and caught me watching. "Taking a breather already, hey?" he demanded. "Let's see you try it, then, Pom."

I gave him a bland smile, ignoring the vague insult, and nudged Geronimo forwards. First into an ambling trot — not his best pace — and then into a collected canter around the outside edge of the arena. Although I hadn't been on a horse seriously since I'd left home as a teenager, riding out with Dina on the beach every day had rekindled those half-forgotten skills. In that respect, it was very much like riding a bike, as well as giving me aching seat bones for the first few days.

This was our second time under the stern scrutiny of Raleigh. Dina told me that his nickname was the Wizard of Aus because of his ability to turn out first-class competition riders in a very short space of time. It seemed to me that his reputation was rather more important to him than the kind of gradual progress that Dina and Cerdo needed to make together.

I kept that one to myself, also, but I'd made a point of riding just a little more sloppily than I was capable of in front of Raleigh. I'd found out very quickly in this business that nothing gets a bodyguard fired faster than showing up their principal in public, particularly at any kind of sporting activity. Obviously, that did not include anything involving firearms or martial arts. If your principal thought they could outshoot or outfight you, they also tended to think they could do without you. The best plan was not to accept that kind of challenge in the first place.

We were riding with English saddles, which were not as armchair-like as their western counterparts, and it was clear that Geronimo was more at home in less formal attire. Now, I neck-reined the Quarter Horse in a fast tight circle, feeling him squat down on his ageing haunches as he spun round like we were roping a zigzagging steer.

As expected, Raleigh yelled, "Jeez, Pom, call that dressage? Useless!" and turned his attention back to Dina.

I let Geronimo fall back to a walk and patted his sweating neck as I scanned the area near the arena. The riding club consisted of a smart collection of horse barns built around a central courtyard, surrounded by white-railed paddocks and a substantial cross-country course that ran for the best part of a mile.

In the yard, there was even a clock tower with a weathervane on top, tubs of well-tended flowers evenly spaced along the neatly swept concrete, and a café with tables arranged along an open balcony for a view of the arena where we practised. I ran a critical eye over the few spectators, but none of them rang any alarm bells.

Adjacent to the outdoor arena was an indoor one of similar enormous size, for use in bad weather. A far cry from the muddy farmyards and patchwork buildings of my youth.

It had rained lightly during our previous visit, and Dina's lesson had taken place indoors as a result. From a security point of view, I would have preferred the same again, but Raleigh told us it was already in use. I thought about making an issue of it, then just shrugged. Dina and I had still not regained our earlier easy relationship after the party, and I knew that she would consider any insistence on my part as showing her up in front of her mentor.

Something else to be avoided.

Besides, in light of the previous two ambushes, I was more worried about being tagged while we were en route from the Willners' house to the riding club in the Navigator, which was considerably slowed down by having a horse trailer on the back. Making aggressive evasive manoeuvres with such an unstable cargo would be impossible.

I didn't like the arrangement, and said so, at which point Dina dug her heels in, much as she was doing now. Cerdo didn't appreciate it any more than I had.

It was late morning and the day was nearing its hottest hour, but that alone wasn't enough to cause the sweat to cream into lather where the reins rubbed against the horse's arched neck. He gave off waves of agitation in the lash of his tail, the uneven stamp of his gait, the laid-flat ears and white-rimmed eyes.

He couldn't have given any more warning of impending trouble if he'd hired a giant neon billboard in Times Square.

Eventually, after another barrage of scorn from Raleigh had translated its inherent tension into Dina's seat and hands, Cerdo threw in the towel.

Or rather, he used a couple of squabbling birds as an excuse to leap sideways towards the middle of the arena and drop his outside shoulder. Dina, unbalanced by his sudden swerve, didn't stand much of a chance. She went catapulting off into the sand at his feet and the horse shot off loose for a victory lap, tail streaming out behind him like a banner.

Abandoning finesse, I booted a startled Geronimo into action and was by Dina's side in moments, almost sliding the poor old Quarter Horse onto his rump in his anxiety to obey my instant go-stop commands.

Dina was floundering on the ground. I jumped down alongside her and ran my hands quickly along her limbs, despite her gasping protests. All her bones were the shape they were supposed to be, and she gave no flinches of pain anywhere.

Just winded, I concluded. *Wounded only in pride.*

I sat back on my heels, saw that Raleigh had managed to recapture Cerdo, who was looking more frightened than triumphant by the success of the ditching operation.

Dina scowled in his general direction, although to be fair she might have been pulling a face at her instructor as much as her horse.

"What did I tell you?" she muttered. "Lives up to his name, huh?"

I put out my hand to help her to her feet and murmured quickly, "He's confused and frustrated, Dina. You're pushing him too fast and he doesn't understand what you want. Have you come off him before?" She shook her head, watching as Raleigh walked the horse back towards us. "Well, he's just scared himself as much as you — look at him. Take five or ten minutes just to walk him round and reassure him that he can trust you again, otherwise that's not going to be the first time you bite the dust today."

She threw me an entirely disbelieving look as she slapped the loose sand off her clothing, but when Raleigh brusquely ordered her to get back up there and do it again, she looked him firmly in the eye and said she wanted to give the horse a breather to resettle him.

Raleigh shrugged as if to say the meter was running and it was up to her how she spent the remaining time, but agreed more readily than I'd been expecting, giving Dina a leg-up into the saddle and watching them walk away on a loose rein. Maybe he, too, had realised they'd been getting nowhere. Somehow I doubted I'd get him to say so out loud.

"Go easier on her," I said to him, keeping my tone light to offset the words. "They both need a bit more confidence in each other before they aim for greatness."

The Australian gave me a calculating glance, then went back to studying Dina, walking large circles at the far end of the arena. She was leaning forward to stroke the white horse's neck and was talking softly to him. Cerdo had started to relax, his stride smoothing out and one ear flicking back and forth to listen to her.

"Shame it's not you on that horse," Raleigh said, keeping his own voice low. "Got some great potential."

"Oh yeah? I thought I was a useless Pommie bastard," I said dryly.

"I was talking about the horse," he said, back to arrogance, but there was a smile lurking behind his eyes as he looked down at me. "And you *are* bloody useless — when you're deliberately not trying."

103

I didn't answer that, just said, "I'll put Geronimo away, if you don't mind? I think the old boy's about had enough for today."

He waved me away, his interest lost. We were only a short distance from the gate out of the arena and I didn't bother remounting to get there. Raleigh did not offer me a helping hand back into the saddle, in any case.

As I reached the gate, one of the army of teenage girls who seemed to hang around the riding club just to be near the horses appeared and offered to walk Geronimo round for me to cool off. "So's you can watch your friend ride."

Dina was still slowly circling, watched by Raleigh who seemed content, for the moment, not to interrupt.

I thanked my wannabe groom and climbed the wooden steps to the café balcony, peeling off my gloves and riding helmet as I went. The latter left me with worse hat-hair than any bike lid ever did.

When I reached the small balcony overlooking the arena, there was only one person in occupation. He was sprawled at the end table, with a large coffee, an expensive sleek cellphone and an extreme-sports magazine on the surface in front of him. His style of dress leant very much towards urban, rather than rural — baggy jeans and a huge warm-up jacket and baseball cap, which would have looked great . . . if he'd happened to be a black teenage rap star.

He looked up with a grin at my obvious consternation. The last person I expected to see here. Or wanted to see anywhere, for that matter.

104

CHAPTER
FOURTEEN

"Hiya, Charlie," Torquil said. "Surprised, huh?"

His voice was almost a taunt. I made a point of looking round very carefully before I moved in his direction. He took that as the insult it was intended to be and fidgeted with the insulated band round his coffee while I bought a cold drink from the serving window.

"Yeah, I'm surprised," I allowed at last, taking a seat at his table without waiting to be invited and angling my chair so I could keep an eye on Dina at the same time. "You alone?"

Now it was his turn to make an exaggerated show of looking around. "Looks that way." He faced me with a sly grin. "Why — you wanna go somewhere?"

I sat back in my chair and took a long swig of cola straight from the can. It was cold enough for condensation to have formed on the outside already.

"You normally have a two-man detail covering you twenty-four/seven," I said, sidestepping the question. "One stays with the car, but the other should be all over you like a rash. Where is he, Torquil?"

"Maybe I sent them home." Torquil shrugged. "Maybe I just got fed up with having someone looking

105

over my shoulder. All. The. Damn. Time," he said, the precision of his words making a lie of the apparently light tone.

I glanced around, keeping it casual, and saw a big short-clipped man in jeans and a casual jacket that he wore unzipped. The man was loitering by the edge of one of the horse barns, alert, balanced, and watching me with slitted eyes.

I put down my drink slowly and gave him a slight nod, letting him get a good look at my empty hands. He tensed, then nodded back, one pro recognising another. I saw him relax, but wasn't sure if it was because he'd discarded me as a possible threat, or thought I might be prepared to lend a hand if things went bad.

He must have known that the latter was unlikely, though. Bodyguards, by their very nature, had to be utterly single-minded about their field of responsibility, or chaos would ensue.

Torquil, catching my nod, followed its direction and scowled at his bodyguard, shooing him away with an exaggerated flap of his hand. He was not, I surmised, the easiest principal to protect. When they were young and arrogant, they sometimes seemed determined to do half a potential kidnapper's work for them, defying precautions and creating a perfect window of opportunity.

Out in the arena, Dina had gathered the white horse together again, but this time the pair seemed a little less combative with each other, as if that brief flash of equine temper had cleared the air. They had a long way

106

to go, but I thought I detected the beginnings of trust between them.

I turned my head, realised Torquil was watching her intently with a faint frown, like he was trying to work out how a conjuring trick was done.

"You ride?" I asked.

He took a moment to drag his gaze back to me. "Horses?"

I suppressed a sigh. "Considering our present location, what else?"

Torquil dipped his head to leer over his designer shades at the girl groom who was walking Geronimo round in the yard for me. She was probably fifteen or sixteen, with blond hair in a plait, and she was wearing skin-tight jodhpurs that left remarkably little to the imagination about the nature of her underwear. "Well, I guess I could be persuaded to . . . mount up."

"Thoughts in that direction will land you in gaol," I said dryly, but the comment provoked a weary laugh.

"You think?" He shook his head. "You don't know how things work in this country, do you?"

"Why don't you enlighten me?"

Torquil sprawled back in his chair, as if he couldn't believe I seriously needed to ask such a dumb question.

"My old man has more money than God. Don't ask how he made most of it. Hell, even *I* don't ask how he made most of it," he added, as if he and his father had conversations about high finance all the time. He grinned. "But the long and the short of it is, money don't talk — it *sings*. And, when it does, everybody dances." He leant forwards, elbows on the table, the smile dropping away. "And that means I can do, or have, anything I want, and nobody will lift a finger to stop me. *Capiche?*"

I waited a beat. "How very boring for you," I said, letting my voice drawl.

Torquil looked momentarily surprised at my lack of proper intimidation, and then he laughed out loud, a proper bark of amusement. "I *like* you," he said. "I don't know why, 'cause you're a bitch, but I really do like you."

"Thank you . . . I think."

He held my gaze for a moment longer, then turned his attention back to Dina. Beyond the waist-high kick boards that edged the arena, she had managed to coax Cerdo into a creditable canter pirouette to applause and cries of "Way to go, Dina!" from Raleigh.

Any moment now, I thought cynically, *he's going to suggest a group hug*.

"I wouldn't put that untouchable status to the test as far as she's concerned, if I were you," I said quietly. "She's well protected."

"I kinda like *her*, too," Torquil said. "That was a cool gift." And as if to prove it, he reached into a pocket and dragged out the Swiss Army knife Dina had given to him for his birthday. He fingered the engraved casing, looking almost unsure of himself. "I thought I might invite her to dinner. As a thank you and an apology. You think she'll come?"

I thought of Dina's comment before the party, that Torquil was the price rather than the object of going. It was not part of my job description, I decided, to vet my

108

principal's choice of date unless they posed an actual threat.

All I said was, "A little early in the day for that, isn't it?"

"Depends." Torquil checked the encrusted Rolex that swamped his wrist. If he ever fell into deep water wearing it, it would pull him to the bottom so fast his eardrums would burst. "I know a place does great seafood in Miami," he said, almost diffident. "And Dad's just bought a new Lear 85."

"Nice choice," I said sedately. His expression turned slightly mulish, as if he'd been hoping for more surprised admiration of his father's executive jet. I put my head on one side, asked in mild tones, "How do you live with such certainty? Once you've had everything — done everything — how will you even bring yourself to get out of bed in the morning?"

Just for a moment, something flitted across his face. It took me a moment to recognise it as panic and I realised he'd already reached his boredom saturation point. He was a week past his twenty-first birthday.

At that moment, his cellphone began to vibrate and emit the theme from *Mission: Impossible*. Now why didn't *that* surprise me? Torquil snatched it up immediately.

I tuned out his mumbled phone conversation and watched Dina instead. She was walking Cerdo in a cooling-off circle around her instructor at the far end of the arena. Raleigh was talking animatedly, mainly with his hands, and Dina was nodding seriously, a buzz of

109

excitement about her. At least she hadn't reached the same plane as Torquil. Not yet.

It was a testament to the newly attained state of relaxation between horse and rider that the sudden clatter of hooves on the concrete yard didn't startle Cerdo beyond a slight quickening of his stride, a twitch of his ears. But at least he didn't try to dump his rider again.

A girl on a fine-boned bay Arabian horse arrived from the direction of the cross-country course, both looking hard-ridden. The girl swung down in the yard, where another of Raleigh's girl groom groupies rushed to take her reins. As the rider removed her crash helmet, I recognised Orlando's delicate features. She handed over care of her horse without eye contact or a backward glance, and climbed the steps to the café balcony.

There were grass stains on her knee, elbow and shoulder, I saw as she approached. Looked like Dina wasn't the only one who'd hit the dirt today.

When she saw me sitting with Torquil at the end table, her stride faltered momentarily.

"Hey, Tor," she greeted him stiffly as he finished his call, nodding to me in a vague way that suggested she'd completely forgotten my name. "What are you doing here?"

"Came to see what all the fuss was about," Torquil said airily. "After all, Dad has a couple of horse farms out in Kentucky, so maybe I should give this stuff a try."

110

Orlando almost smiled. "Your father has thoroughbreds, for racing," she chided. "They're not the kinda animals you could learn to horseback-ride on."

"I'm a quick study. And how hard can it be?" Torquil grinned, draining the last of his coffee and getting to his feet, leaving the empty cup on the table. For a moment I harboured the vain hope that he might be leaving, but he merely wandered over to the serving window for another coffee. "Get you ladies anything?"

"Coffee," we both said together.

That seemed, if not to break the ice, then certainly to start a thaw. Orlando considered me out of the corner of her eye for a moment, then leant in closer, keeping her voice conspiratorially low. "He gives me the creeps."

I glanced over my shoulder to where Torquil was still at the serving window. I didn't like to tell her he was growing on me. "At least you know they're the best creeps money can buy."

She giggled suddenly, hiding her mouth behind her hand like a kid. The gesture seemed to emphasise the anxiety in her eyes. They were an incredible shade of emerald green, I noticed, but then I saw the faint outline around her iris and realised she probably wore tinted contact lenses.

"What is it?" I asked gently. "What's scaring you?"

She let her hand drop away, the laughter falling with it. "He did this before," she said, speaking fast. "Tor. He'd just turn up, out of the blue, wherever I went. Like he was following me —"

Over her shoulder, Torquil had finished paying for the coffees, amazing me with the fact he bothered to carry loose change, and was carefully working out how to pick up and carry three cups at once. Judging by the hash he was making of such a simple task, it was a new experience for him. I knew I didn't have much time.

"Did this before *what*, Orlando?"

She looked at me, and now I saw a roiling mix of fear and guilt and shame. "Before I was kidnapped."

CHAPTER
FIFTEEN

Before I'd time to fully process that information, or even ask Orlando for more, the riding club's runabout, a GMC pickup, pulled up in the yard and Hunt got out. He appeared up the steps to the balcony, hands casually in the pockets of his chinos. Orlando's boyfriend was wearing a lightweight tweed jacket over a blue Oxford shirt, and his air of cool polish made Torquil's pseudo-rapper outfit seem like a child's fancy dress.

Hunt greeted me with cautious reserve, frowning at Orlando as though he immediately sensed her unease and suspected I might be the cause of it. She gave him a wan smile and he stopped behind her chair to put a reassuring hand on her shoulder.

"Charlie," he said with a fraction more warmth. "How goes it?"

"Fine," I said. "Are you into horses, Hunt?"

He gave a self-deprecatory shrug. "I dabble. My family kept quite a string before the anti-hunting lobby had their way and riding to hounds was banned. Damn shame."

I didn't point out that it wasn't following the hounds that people objected to, so much as setting the dogs on errant foxes as the object of the exercise. Still, I was in no position to be squeamish.

Hunt and Torquil were eyeing each other with tolerance rather than friendship, until Hunt asked if that was Torquil's new Bentley Continental Supersports in the parking lot, and then the two of them segued into a conversation about cars from which Orlando and I were pointedly excluded.

I rapidly tuned out Torquil boasting languidly about his latest toy — a birthday gift from his father. He incorrectly described the Continental's six-litre engine as a V12 when I knew for a fact Bentley used a W12 configuration. I'd always been more of a motorcycle nut than a car nut, but it was hard not to pick up the specs of high-performance luxury cars in this job.

In the arena, Dina and Raleigh were now ambling in our direction, the lesson over. I made my excuses and headed down the wooden steps into the yard, just as Raleigh opened the gate and Cerdo's hooves rang on the concrete.

Dina flashed me a wide smile as they halted. She patted the horse's damp neck with gusto, and I guessed that my advice to settle him down before she tried again might just have improved relations between us.

Raleigh took the horse's bridle as she dismounted, but as soon as Dina's feet hit the ground, her right knee buckled under her and, if the burly instructor hadn't been right alongside her with a steadying arm, she might have fallen.

"Dina! You OK?" He handed off Cerdo onto the girl groom who had been walking Geronimo round. By the

114

time he turned back, I was already putting my arm around Dina.

"Lean on me," I told her. "We'll find you a chair."

"Out of the way, Pom," Raleigh said with a wink, brushing me aside. "This is man's work." And with that he swung Dina into his arms and carried her lightly up the steps to the café balcony, leaving me biting my tongue as I trailed on his heels. Torquil, Orlando and Hunt immediately crowded round us.

Raleigh deposited his pupil onto the nearest chair and crouched in front of her, noting the smudge of dirt on the knee of her jodhpurs. "Must have clobbered it on something when you came off," he said. There was a hint of strain to his reassuring smile, as if he were worried about being sued if she was injured on his watch.

I flipped out my cellphone. As a matter of routine, I had already input the numbers for the Willners' personal doctor and dentist, as well as all the major local hospitals and trauma centres. Dina put up a staying hand before I could hit speed dial for any of them.

"I'm fine, really," she said. "Please don't fuss. It's not like this is the first time I've fallen off of a horse. My knee's been aching some, but I just wasn't expecting it to give out on me like that."

"You need to rest up," Raleigh told her, his hand still on her leg. "Why don't you leave the horses here tonight, see how you go? You can always run over tomorrow and pick them up."

Dina shook her head. "I'll be fine," she reiterated doggedly. "I'd rather take them home. Charlie and I can manage, if you'll help us load them into the trailer?"

Raleigh bounded to his feet. "Of course," he said. "I'll have the girls untack them and give you a shout when they're ready to go."

"So, your horse threw you?" Torquil asked, and I realised that incident must have taken place before his arrival. "You gonna get rid of it?"

"Of course not," Dina said, and it was a toss-up which of them looked the more astonished.

"Orlando took a tumble, too," Hunt pointed out. "All part of the game, eh?"

"What did you do every time you fell on your backside when you were out snowboarding, Tor?" Orlando asked in a wry voice. "Sack the mountain?"

"Only if I'd bought it first." He gave a sigh. "I guess that dinner in Miami will just have to wait," he grumbled, returning to his original seat and slumping into it. Anyone would have thought that Dina had damaged her leg with the sole intention of spoiling his plans. Not that he'd actually asked her out — or that she'd accepted — but he seemed to have taken it as read.

The girl groom who'd been walking Orlando's little Arabian horse round, meanwhile, called up that she seemed to have gone lame in her off foreleg.

"Aw, crap," Orlando said. She glanced at Hunt. "I told you she dropped a leg coming out of the water."

"Hmm, I may need to pop over and do some minor repairs to a few of the cross-country fences for you at some point," Hunt said, smiling apologetically at Raleigh. "For such a little thing, that pony of Orlando's does tend to go through them as much as she goes over them."

"The ground staff will be laying new sod around some of the fences where the ground's gotten a little churned up, so the course will be out of action for a couple of days next week," Raleigh said, frowning. "There's no need for you to get your hands dirty, though. They'll fix anything that's busted."

"I'd feel better about it," Hunt insisted with a disarming smile. "Like replacing your divots on a golf course."

Raleigh made a "no sweat" kind of a gesture and Hunt nodded to him before following Orlando to see to her horse.

Dina put her foot up onto a chair and the café provided a bag of ice wrapped in a cloth to deal with any swelling in her knee. Raleigh hovered, giving her a running list of advice for recovery. There was some horse-related event coming up that he was trying to persuade her to enter with Cerdo, I gathered. "You gotta be fighting fit for that," he warned. "But it's still a few weeks away. You'll be OK."

Dina did not look reassured on any level. "Look, Raleigh, I'm still not sure we're ready for this —"

"Rubbish, Dina! You could do it in your sleep. Just look at how well he went today. That horse could be a champion."

"Yeah," she muttered, "*after* he'd thrown me in the dirt."

A look of frustration crossed Raleigh's features, but he seemed to realise that arguing further right now would just make her more stubborn. He got easily to his feet. "Well, think about it, OK?" he said, more neutral, and glanced down as one of the girls waved to him from the yard. "I think we're all set."

I wondered about Raleigh's attitude, just a tad. What did he hope to gain by forcing Dina to enter a competition she didn't feel ready for — other than possibly more fees for intensive tuition on the run-up?

And I wondered about the possible connections, too. The kidnap victims might have been taken by someone who knew them. But Manda Dempsey had shown no interest in ponies when I'd been working for the family, and Benedict Benelli seemed more likely to bet on a horse than climb onto its back. I shrugged. Maybe I was just getting paranoid.

Dina refused to be carried back down the steps and insisted that she would lead her horse out to where the trailer was parked. Raleigh walked slowly alongside her, eyes on her face as if ready to sweep her off her feet the moment he saw she was in pain. I followed with Geronimo, who obviously realised we were going home and strode out briskly by my shoulder, barging me when I tried to slow him down.

I spotted Torquil's huge gold-coloured Bentley sitting in splendid isolation off to one side of the riding club's parking lot. Through the heavily tinted glass I could just

118

make out the figure of one of his bodyguards in the passenger seat.

Dina's trailer was parked, still hitched to the tow bar of the Navigator, in the middle of the lot, in a line of similar vehicles. I saw nothing amiss as we approached, stopping about four metres away.

"You sure you're OK?" Raleigh asked Dina. "I'll lower the ramp and walk Cerdo up for you."

"Thanks, Raleigh," she said with a sideways glance towards me as I brought Geronimo up alongside her. "Nice to have two guardian angels today."

"I do my best." As he reached up to unfasten the top catch on the far side of the ramp, he looked back over his shoulder towards me. "You wanna put your horse in first, Pom? Then you can give Dina a hand."

I didn't have time to agree, because at that moment a masked figure stepped out from behind the trailer. He had an aluminium baseball bat gripped in both hands and he swung it with all his might at Raleigh's unprotected head.

CHAPTER
SIXTEEN

"Look out!"

Even as I shouted the warning, Raleigh must have seen the shock in both our faces, sensed the rush of movement behind him. He hunched his neck down instinctively, but neglected to snatch his arm down from full stretch. The bat whistled past his head, skimming his hair, and landed across his extended forearm with a solid crunch. Some corner of my mind registered the sound of bones breaking. The shock of the sudden injury put him down, and the pain of it kept him there.

Geronimo had a sudden change of heart about being eager to get home. He spun on his haunches with a grunt of effort, jerking his lead rope through my hands. I'd taken off my riding gloves, so I let go rather than waste time trying to control him. He hightailed it back towards the safety of the horse barns.

At that moment, a second figure emerged from behind another parked trailer, over to our right this time, and closed in on us from the other side.

Like the first man, he was wearing dull nondescript clothing and a ski mask, dark glasses covering his eyes.

But this one was unarmed apart from what looked like PlastiCuff restraints.

His focus was completely on Dina, hardly even glancing in my direction until I moved to intercept. Then he tried to shoulder me aside with blatant disregard. To protect my hands, I hit him hard with an upswept elbow under his jaw. He dropped.

Cerdo had started to panic as soon as the attack began, skittering in a circle around Dina. Hampered by her injured leg, she could do little to stop him, although something made her refuse to jettison him as I had with Geronimo. With more courage than sense, she clung to his lead rope with both hands even when he reared up to wave steel-shod front feet in her face.

It was a toss-up, at that moment, whether the greater threat to my principal came from our attackers or from her own horse.

The man who'd clouted Raleigh, meanwhile, was standing over his writhing quarry with the bat still at the ready, as if he'd expected the downed instructor to put up more of a fight. It was only when Cerdo began his antics that he looked across and saw his partner on the ground. He twisted in my direction and stood there a moment, frozen, then hurdled Raleigh's legs and came for us with the bat upraised.

For a split second, time seemed to slow almost to a standstill, so I had time to analyse our situation with my options spread before me. All I had to do was choose. None of them looked good.

The parking area was out of direct sight of the yard itself. I could only hope that Geronimo's sudden flight would bring people running, but how much use they'd be when they got here was another matter.

In my peripheral vision, I could see the nose of Torquil's gold Bentley, one of his bodyguards still in the passenger seat. The man had jacked upright to get a better view — might even have drawn his weapon — but he was too well drilled to get out of the car and come to Dina's rescue. As far as he was concerned, I was on my own.

I gave momentary thought to reaching for my own SIG, but dismissed the idea before it had formed. If I drew against a charging batsman at such close quarters, I'd have to fire to stop him. And not just shoot, but keep shooting until the threat was neutralised.

Instead, I chose the biggest and best weapon I had to hand.

Cerdo.

The horse's flailing had spun him so that he was facing away from the trailer. As the man approached, I shoved Dina around onto the opposite side of the horse's neck, keeping her behind me and the horse between both of us and our attacker. Cerdo reared again, stabbing out furiously with his hooves like a giant boxer. Even armed with a baseball bat, the man faltered in the face of this towering aggression.

As the horse's front feet touched down again, I made a grab for his headcollar and, ignoring Dina's protests, yanked his head around towards me, reaching back to prod him sharply in the ribs with the stiffened fingers of an open hand at the same time.

Horses, like people, have a collection of nerve endings in their side which makes them sensitive to signals from the rider's leg. Cerdo, being a dressage horse, was more sensitive than most. The effect of a strike in that spot was calculated to produce maximum effect. I wasn't disappointed.

The white horse reacted immediately. I heard the furious clack of his teeth as he leapt away from the blow, ears laid flat, swinging his hindquarters in a rapid arc and cannoning into the man with the baseball bat. Three-quarters of a ton of fast-moving Andalusian, scared and pissed off in equal measure. It was not an even contest.

Cerdo's primeval fight-or-flight reflexes were well and truly awoken now. They told him to run from the danger. And if he couldn't run, to lash out at the thing behind him, before it had a chance to jump onto his back and sink teeth and claws into his neck. He humped his back and let rip with both hind legs.

If the man with the bat had been directly behind those flying hooves, he would have been in serious trouble. Fortunately for him, Cerdo's initial impact had knocked him to the side and he caught a relatively glancing blow to his upper arm. It was enough.

He dropped the bat and scrambled away, obviously terrified of what the animal might do next. People not familiar with horses are often frightened by the sheer size and unpredictability of them close up. Such animals may no longer be asked to go charging towards the enemy on a battlefield, but the basic fear they instil is why police forces around the world still use them for

123

crowd control. A mounted officer is deemed six times more effective than one on the ground.

I reckoned I'd get no arguments from our assailants on that score. The man with the restraints — the one I'd hit — had come round enough to reach his hands and knees, groaning. For a moment I watched his partner debate on leaving him to his fate, then he realised the drawbacks of such a move. He grabbed the fallen man with his uninjured left hand and dragged him to his feet. Together they stumbled through the line of trailers and were lost to view.

I was tempted to give chase, but Cerdo's nerves were in tatters and Dina was struggling to hold onto him with only one good leg to balance on. With a last regretful glance in the direction of our attackers, I managed to get a hand through the horse's headcollar and tried to calm him. He took some convincing that it was all over.

Out of sight, an engine cranked and fired. I caught a glimpse of a medium-sized van, possibly a Chevy Astro, go fishtailing over the gravel towards the driveway and freedom. It was moving fast and there was enough dirt liberally spread across the licence plate to make identification impossible.

Dina hobbled over to Raleigh and helped him sit up. He had turned a disconcerting shade of pale green and was clutching his arm. Dina wasn't looking much better.

"Be careful he doesn't throw up on you," I told her. She flashed me a look of distaste and said nothing. Cerdo had finally stopped trying to rip himself free of my grasp and was standing with his head low, blowing hard through flared nostrils, his muscles quivering.

Running feet nearly set him off again and I saw Hunt and Orlando hurrying across the gravel. I made a "slow down" gesture with my hand behind me and they finished their approach at a more cautious pace.

"What *happened*?" Orlando demanded, eyes huge as she took in Cerdo's distress and Raleigh's obvious signs of injury. "Did the horses get into a fight?"

Dina's face snapped in my direction and I saw the sudden pleading in her expression.

"Something like that," I agreed, rubbing Cerdo's damp ears. It was true, after all — to a point. I just didn't say who or what he'd been fighting.

Hunt helped get Raleigh to his feet, swaying. He stared at me through a hazy filter of pain and shock. "What the bloody hell —?"

"Don't talk," I said quickly, a warning wrapped up as solicitude. I glanced at Hunt. "Perhaps you could take him back to the yard and get some sugar down him."

Hunt nodded. Orlando began insisting that Raleigh go to the nearest ER and that distracted him from questions into making half-hearted protests about not leaving the yard unattended.

"We can stay —" Dina began, but I silenced her with a cutting stare.

"We're leaving," I said firmly. "Your leg needs ice and elevation, and both horses need a night in their own stable to calm down from all of this."

And I want you somewhere secure.

Dina might have thought about arguing, but not for long. She nodded meekly and limped back to take the lead rope from me. "Where's Geronimo?"

"He shot through the yard like his tail was on fire," Hunt said. "One of the girls caught him, I think, I'll check."

I nodded my thanks and he and Orlando walked back towards the horse barns with Raleigh stumbling dazedly between them. I leant down and picked up the baseball bat our attacker had dropped, handling it carefully even though I knew there was little chance of useable prints.

Movement caught my eye and I glanced across towards the yard, only to see two figures standing by the edge of one of the buildings, staring at us. It wasn't hard, at that distance, to recognise Torquil and his bulky bodyguard, the one he'd dismissed while he watched Dina finish her lesson. Now, the man was glued to his shoulder, tense, head constantly moving to survey the scene with his hand never far from the weapon hidden beneath his open jacket.

But it was Torquil himself who really caught my eye. He stood with both hands clenched at his sides, shoulders hunched and his neck rigid. I had no idea how long he had been there, or how much he'd seen, but where I expected to see shock, or maybe even a tinge of excitement at what he'd just witnessed, instead it looked for all the world like someone had just broken his newest best toy.

CHAPTER
SEVENTEEN

"I don't know who those two were," I said, "but they were amateurs."

"Tell that to poor Raleigh — they bust his *arm*," Dina said tartly. "And if they were *so* amateur, how come *you* didn't catch them?"

I heard the slightly shrill note in her voice and resisted the urge to snap at her, taking a quiet inhalation before I spoke. We were back safe in the living area of the Willners' house. Caroline Willner was in her customary seat with its back to the windows. Opposite was Parker Armstrong, while Dina and I were on another sofa to the side.

Parker had not come alone, arriving with Erik Landers in tow. Landers was a big guy from Colorado, solidly built, ex-US Marine Corps and proud of his service. He still carried himself with that fierce pride, took everything a little too seriously, never let standards slip. He was utterly dependable in a firefight, but was still adjusting to the very different world of executive close protection. Parker had struggled to persuade him to let his hair grow longer than the regulation millimetre of fuzz.

Landers currently stood behind Dina and me like a sentinel. Dina had changed into a pair of denim hot pants — which looked "distressed" via an expensive designer label rather than prolonged wear and tear — and a silk T-shirt. She had her foot up on a stool with an ice pack draped over her knee. I, too, had taken the trouble to change when I'd finished unloading the horses and now presented my client and my boss with as tidy and unruffled a facade as I could conjure.

I'd called Parker from the riding club and he'd surprised me by coming out right away, arriving back at the house before we did. I hoped that the only reason he'd arrived so fast — and brought Landers with him — was in case I needed more permanent backup, rather than to demonstrate a lack of trust in my ability to handle the situation on my own.

"Why didn't I catch them?" I repeated, keeping my tone even and pleasant. "Because that's not my job, Dina. My job is prevention, not cure."

"Which you appear to have done quite well," Caroline Willner said, her voice dispassionate. "Nevertheless, it is . . . unfortunate that these people escaped when the opportunity might perhaps have presented itself to apprehend them."

Before I could defend my actions, Parker spoke for me. "Charlie couldn't have gone after them without leaving your daughter unacceptably exposed," he pointed out. "It has been known for the initial attack to be just a diversionary tactic to try and draw off the close-protection team." He met my eyes, just the hint of a smile lurking in his. "And while it may be somewhat

128

unorthodox to throw a horse at an inbound threat, there's no doubt what she did was effective."

But despite the praise, I heard vague disappointment in his voice.

"Next time," I promised gravely, "I'll throw it harder."

His cheek twitched in an otherwise stony face. "Unfortunately, I think it's likely that there *will be* a next time," he said. "They've tried once and been unsuccessful. They may feel they now have your measure and try again — with more . . . determination next time." He pinned me with a gaze that willed me not to make an issue of this. "That's why I've brought Erik out to join you, purely as a little extra insurance. So, if they do make another run at Dina, you might just be able to grab one of them without putting her in harm's way."

"No!" Dina said, more sharp than firm. "I don't *want* anyone else." She twisted to offer the man behind us an appealing smile. "No offence to you, Mr Landers, but I want Charlie."

"Dina, be reasonable," her mother said stiffly. "We're merely trying to keep you safe."

"I am safe," she said. "You asked me to accept a bodyguard, and I've done that. Now you want me to have two. Where does it end — with me barricaded into my room, afraid to leave the house?"

Mother and daughter locked gazes, duelling silently. It was Dina who gave way first, but her weary yet dignified tone was more effective than any shouted argument. "Leave things as they are, Mother — please. I'll be fine."

"You're taking risks," Caroline Willner said quietly. "I . . . don't like it."

"I'll be fine," Dina repeated. Her body was tense. More was at stake here than just the question of an additional bodyguard. I wondered again at the power plays between them, about Dina's refusal to go to Europe, and who was winning their long-running, tortuous game.

After a moment longer, Caroline Willner sighed. "All right, darling," she said, glancing down as if distracted by an imaginary speck on her dress. "In that case, Mr Armstrong, I'm afraid I must decline your offer of extra protection, and trust to Ms Fox to do her best."

"She always does," Parker murmured. He rose, inclined his head to them both, his manner almost courtly in his capitulation. "Charlie. See me out, would you?"

"Of course."

I led both men down to the entrance hall and through the massive front doors into the gentle warmth of the late afternoon. Landers stepped to the edge and stood looking outward, head moving slowly as he checked the perimeter, the neighbouring houses, and the view of the road. The Navigator that had brought Parker and Landers out to Long Island sat off to one side of the driveway under the shade of the trees. It looked small in a space that would have swallowed a dozen limousines.

I could see by the tilt of his head that Landers was waiting for what Parker would say to me with avid concentration, but I suppose I couldn't really blame him for that.

Parker had leant back against the low wall that bordered the front of the house. "You carrying?"

Wordlessly, I reached under my open jacket and slipped the SIG from its holster. I thumbed the release to drop the magazine, worked the action to send the chambered round tumbling out onto the paving at his feet. I showed him the open breech to prove the gun was safe as I dumped it into his hands. Then I stooped to retrieve the fallen round, wiped it with my fingers and thumbed it back into the magazine, handing that over, too.

Parker gave the SIG no more than a cursory inspection, weighed the magazine in his palm to judge the load before slotting it back into the pistol grip without a fumble, even though his eyes never left my face. He could have done it all just the same in the dark.

He returned the weapon without comment. I pinched back the slide to feed in the first round again, the action working with a slick metallic double click, well oiled and well cycled. The SIG had no conventional safety catch, only a slide lock to hold the action back. Carried with the first round already chambered, it was instantly ready for use.

"So why didn't you use it?" Parker asked, as if reading my thoughts.

I tucked the gun away under the hem of my jacket, smoothed the cloth down again over the top. "Are you honestly telling me you'd rather be up to your neck in policemen at this very moment?" I asked. "Because if I'd drawn on the guy, the only way I could have stopped him was to shoot him. I wasn't prepared to use deadly force against a man armed with a piece of sports equipment. I don't suppose you're likely to get anything from the bat he left behind, incidentally?"

"You said they were wearing gloves, so I doubt it, and it's a cheap make, available from just about any sporting goods outlet," Parker said, brushing aside my attempt to divert him. "And you didn't know for sure he wasn't carrying."

"I didn't know he was, either," I countered. "And if he *was* armed, why did he bother clobbering the riding instructor? Why take the risk of losing control of the situation by physically engaging with Raleigh when he could have simply stood back and threatened all of us into submission at the outset?"

Parker's eyes narrowed a fraction. "Did you work all this out at the time, or after?"

I smiled. "If the first guy had shot Raleigh instead of smashing his arm, Parker, I would have put two through his mouth in a heartbeat, of that you need have no doubts."

Parker's answering smile was rueful. "Yeah, I guess you would," he said. He leant back against the wall again and folded his arms, reminding me painfully of Sean. "I just needed to make sure you didn't hesitate for the wrong reasons."

132

My chin came up. "Because of California, you mean?"

"Yes."

I'd come under attack while covering a principal out there and had fired on three men I'd been convinced were aiming to kill us. It turned out that I was mistaken — about part of it at least. I had escaped an attempted murder charge by the skin of my teeth, and had no wish for a repeat performance.

"There was also the additional factor that I seriously doubted Dina's horse had ever been in close proximity to a discharging handgun before," I added. "If I'd fired on our attackers and he'd gone crazy, who knows what kind of damage he might have done to the girl."

Parker's head tilted slightly, considering. "Now that one you *definitely* came up with after the fact."

I shrugged. "OK," I agreed meekly, "but the logic still holds. You didn't see the way Cerdo was acting up, or how determined Dina was not to let go of him. And he was panicking enough as it was — adding gunfire into the equation would have been a recipe for disaster."

"So instead you used the horse as an offensive weapon."

"It was the only thing I could do that allowed me to keep some kind of control over the situation. Besides, like I said — they were amateurs."

"Excuse me, ma'am," Landers broke in, his voice almost diffident, "but just 'cause they was not carrying sidearms does not make them amateurs — nor does failing to overwhelm a professional close-protection officer, if you'll pardon me for saying so. You underestimate yourself, ma'am."

"Thanks, Erik, but for God's sake call me Charlie, not ma'am. I was an ordinary grunt, not a Rupert," I said, grinning at him. No way had I been considered officer material back in the army. "And my assessment has very little to do with how they were armed."

Parker caught my eye and nodded his agreement. "If they'd been pros they would have taken you out as their primary objective, even though you were not the most obvious target," he said softly, "because they would have gathered enough intel to know exactly who and what you were."

"But they didn't," I said. "They were sloppy and slow to react and too fixed on Dina to see danger coming from another direction, so either their intel was bad, or they were working without any. Either way, *that* makes them amateurs."

Parker frowned. "But the other victims described well-planned and well-executed ambushes or snatches."

"Hmm," I said. "So either we have two different groups at work, or the connection between these kidnappings is not the social circle in which the victims move."

"Because anyone who was at the party on the yacht would have known you were Dina's bodyguard," Parker finished. He paused. "Doesn't narrow it down much."

"Yeah, but it may put Dina's mind at rest if we're looking for complete strangers rather than among her friends," I said. "Although . . ."

134

He waited a beat, eyebrow raised. "The Eisenberg kid," he supplied. "Orlando told you he was hanging around her before she was taken, and now he shows up at the riding club out of the blue, on the day an attempt is made on Dina. Coincidence?"

"I sort of doubt it," I said. "And you didn't see him after it was all over, standing there watching. If I didn't know better, I'd say he looked thoroughly pissed off that the attack failed."

"And his close-protection guys didn't intervene when this thing went down," Landers said, a soldier's disgust tightening his voice.

"I wouldn't have expected them to — they had their job to do and I had mine." Landers still looked dubious, but didn't outright contradict me.

"You tread very carefully around Torquil Eisenberg, Charlie," Parker warned. "His father has all kinds of influence you do not want to tangle with."

"If an opportunity arises to ask him a few questions," I said, stubborn, "I'll take it."

And if it doesn't, I might just have to make that opportunity happen . . .

Parker sighed. He moved forwards to rest his hands gently on my upper arms. Out of the corner of my eye, I saw Landers catch the gesture and snap his head away so fast he nearly ricked his neck in his efforts to see nothing untoward going on between us.

"I trust your judgement, Charlie," Parker said at last. "Whatever decisions you make in the field, I'll back them if I have to — you know that, don't you?"

I was reminded sharply of another time, when Parker's confidence in my judgement had been sadly lacking, to the point where he'd allowed me to undergo hostile interrogation at the hands of the security services. What had changed? And why?

Horribly aware of Landers' presence, I forced myself to step back, forced a cool note of distance into my voice. "What a shame you didn't always have such faith, Parker."

CHAPTER
EIGHTEEN

Dina didn't want to talk about what happened at the riding club in the period that followed. Instead, she wanted to talk about me.

Or rather, my relationship with my boss. Not an easy topic, because I had no idea about my feelings for Parker at that point.

It was two days since the ambush. Dina's knee had recovered, thanks to three sessions with a remedial masseur who'd come out to the house and applied ultrasound and various other treatments at some ridiculous cost. All this for a minor injury that probably would have sorted itself, given rest and ice, within a couple of days anyway. What it was to be so pampered.

Dina had an ulterior motive for wanting to be fit, however, which was an upcoming charity auction and gala dinner. It seemed to be the focus of just about anybody who *was* anybody on Long Island.

The biggest surprise, as far as Dina was concerned, was the fact that Torquil Eisenberg had texted to see if she wanted to accompany him. After agonising over the brief wording, she sent a message of assent by the same means, and all the logistics of the exercise were sorted without the pair exchanging a spoken word. Dina seemed to think this was entirely normal. I felt very old.

So, this morning she decided she was feeling sufficiently recovered to hit the boutiques of Fifth Avenue. Caroline Willner graciously lent her personal driver to save the hassle of parking garages, but I relegated him to the passenger seat for the drive into Manhattan — a considerable blow to his ego, if his sniffy silence for the entire journey was anything to go by.

We crossed onto Manhattan Island via the Queens-Midtown Tunnel and I surrendered car keys to our mute chauffeur. After that, Dina and I trailed round countless stores while she added to her already bulging wardrobe.

When it came to clothing, she had variable taste, ranging from some items I thought looked great on her, to others that just didn't work at all. I baulked at the point she started suggesting outfits for me, especially when I took a sneaky look at the price tags. You could have shifted the decimal points a place to the left and most of them would still have been too rich for my blood.

Eventually, we stopped for a late lunch at Brasserie Les Halles on Park Avenue South, and there she began her interrogation over casual Parisian food.

"So, what is it with you and Parker Armstrong, huh?"

I put down my glass of sparkling water very precisely. "There's nothing going on between us, Dina. Parker is strictly my boss."

"Oh, come on," she said, eyes dancing. "There's got to be more to it than that. I saw the way he watches you when you're not looking."

How did I tell her that Parker was probably checking for signs I was cracking up? That he knew, better than anyone, what I'd been through — was still going through, every day — with Sean.

"We're friends. Good friends. No more than that."

She was still smiling in a way that was a sudden irritation, but I knew if I let that show she'd assume she was right. I kept my expression neutral as the waiter deposited my French onion soup and Dina's green salad in front of us. I'd chosen a table inside rather than on the street, quietly insisting on a corner where I could watch the exits. I'd already recced our escape route, should we need one.

"Is he married? Is that it?"

Give it a rest!

I suppressed a sigh. "He was. He's a widower."

"Oh." She digested that for a moment. "What was she like, his wife? I mean . . . what happened to her?"

"I don't know," I said, not wanting to admit that until a few months ago I hadn't known that Parker had ever been married in the first place. A very private man, self-contained. "It was before my time."

"So, what's stopping you?" she pressed, not taking the hint. Her tone turned teasing. "I mean, he's kinda good-looking — for an old guy."

"He's only just turned forty," I said. "That hardly puts him in his dotage."

"And that makes him how much older than you?"

139

"Twelve years," I said. Not much in the great scheme of things. Sean was thirty-four, sitting halfway between us — and not just in age. I picked up my knife and fork. "Maybe Parker's not my type. Or maybe I'm not his."

"Hey, you're lovely. And if you'd let me take you in hand for a day, you could be stunning," Dina countered with a smile. "Don't sell yourself short!"

I remembered Landers telling me not to underestimate myself, too, but his assessment was all to do with how much I might scare a potential opponent, rather than lure them. Was it normal, I wondered, to value his opinion more highly?

"I'm not a doll you can dress up, Dina," I warned.

"I wouldn't dare — I have a feeling I'd lose my fingers," she said, laughing out loud now, but after a moment she sobered. "He's interested, though, I can tell."

I applied myself to my soup bowl, cutting through the cheese crust to the rich liquid and onion beneath, chewing, swallowing. When I glanced up, though, Dina was still watching me, her own cutlery poised. "Maybe I'm spoken for."

"Really?" she said, letting her hands drop. "You have a boyfriend? No way."

"And there you were only a few moments ago, telling me how pretty I was," I said, lightly mocking. "I'm wounded."

She had the grace to flush. "That wasn't what I meant." She took a breath. "What I *meant* was, it must be some special guy who understands what it is you do, and . . . lets you do it."

140

I debated briefly on telling Dina that it was Sean who'd recruited me into the business in the first place. That he'd recognised both a need within me and the means to fulfil it. It was only when I put down my soup spoon, very neatly in the centre of my empty bowl, that I answered.

"He understands."

She tipped her head on one side, considering. "Is he a bodyguard too?" she asked then, saw from my face the accuracy of that sudden flash of intuition. "He *is*! Oh, how romantic! Travelling all over the world to dangerous and exotic locations together. It's like something out of a movie." Her voice was positively wistful. "Tell me, have the two of you ever been in one of those life-or-death situations?"

I closed my eyes briefly, saw again the snap of Sean's head, back and right, as the fateful round hit, and felt my throat threaten to close up entirely. "Yes."

"So, spill — what's he like?" She was leaning forwards in her chair and her sparkling gaze had turned voracious.

Now there's a question. Saying nothing would only make her dig harder. Saying anything light-hearted would half kill me. I spread my hands in a helpless shrug and hoped the truth would shock her into silence.

"Sean is . . . the other half of me."

It made her regroup rather than retreat, a temporary respite that lasted until after the waiter had cleared away our plates and brought large tall glasses of iced coffee in place of dessert.

"Don't you miss him — this Sean? Doesn't he mind you being away from home all this time?"

I didn't point out it had been less than a fortnight. "Yes, I do miss him," I said honestly. "But he's in no position to argue."

"I guess not," she said slowly, forming her own conclusions. Then her face cleared. "Hey, why don't you and Sean double-date with me and Tor for the charity auction? That would be so cool!"

"Dina —"

"And it will look *much* less suspicious than you tagging along with us all on your own," she pointed out fast. It was an entirely logical suggestion, spoilt only by her eager but slightly self-satisfied expression. "What d'you say?"

I let my breath out hard, as much because I disliked being backed into a corner as because of the insurmountable difficulties.

"He can't," I said, flatly enough to stop any protests she might have been about to make. "Even if he could . . . Well, he just can't. Don't push me on this, Dina. It's not going to happen."

Dina took in my set face and was uncharacteristically silent for a moment. Then she said carefully, "OK, but . . . can I meet him?"

The denial was on my lips. I expected it. If Dina's disappointed air was anything to go by, she expected it, too.

"Sure," I said. *You asked for this.* "Why not?"

142

CHAPTER
NINETEEN

When we reached his hospital room, Sean was lying on his back with his head tilted towards the door as if awaiting our arrival.

We paused in the doorway. Dina because this was the last thing she had expected, and I was mean enough — or pissed off enough — not to have warned her what to expect. And me because I had a sudden recall of Parker's report on Sean's last CT scan.

"... *his physical therapist has been growing kinda concerned about some of his responses ... His brain activity ... they think it may be slowing down ...* "

Dina had asked plenty of questions on the ride over, but I'd been non-committal, thoroughly regretting the impulse which had made me suggest this meeting in the first place. After all, what the hell did I hope to achieve? My stubborn silence had only served to intrigue her further.

Now, I took a breath and stepped into the room. "Sean, Dina. Dina — this is Sean," I said over my shoulder. We'd stopped briefly to pick up coffee on the way in and now I flipped off the lid and put the cup down on the cabinet near to his head. There was no reaction.

When I turned back I found Dina had remained frozen, startled, in the open doorway.

"Maybe — if he's sleeping — we, um, shouldn't disturb him?" she whispered, too awkward to know where to put her hands.

"If you can do anything to wake him, Dina, be my guest," I said. I smoothed back the hair from his face, exposing the livid scar, and knew she still hadn't moved. "It's not contagious," I added roughly, aware I was being cruel to the girl and unable to stop myself. "He's been in a coma for three months."

She advanced a few steps, eyes huge and everywhere at once, and asked in a small voice, "What happened?"

I could have dressed it up for her, but I didn't. "He was shot in the head."

She flinched. "Did he . . . was it, um, while he was protecting someone?"

I nodded.

She swallowed. "And were they OK?" She saw my face, went scarlet and then pale in waves. "I mean, did he succeed? Or was it . . .?" She stumbled to a halt, but I could finish that one for her.

Was it all for nothing?

"Yes, Sean succeeded."

She flicked me a quick nervous glance from under her lashes. "You sound like you resent that."

"No," I said, giving it thought before I answered. "It was part of the job. Sean was unlucky, that's all. You can't be a soldier and ignore the part luck plays. Half an inch one way and the bullet would have killed him

144

stone dead. Half an inch the other and it would have missed him altogether." I shrugged. "Luck of the draw."

Something trembled around the corner of her mouth. "You still sound like you resent it."

"I resent the circumstances that led up to it," I admitted, my eyes on Sean's face. "They call us bullet catchers, but that is close protection in its crudest form. You get to the stage of having to put your own body between a principal and a bullet, it's a last-ditch, desperate effort." I skimmed over her whitened features. "We spend our lives avoiding that moment."

"But you're prepared to do it anyway," she said. "For a stranger. For someone you've only known a few hours, or a few days. Even though you've seen what might happen."

I heard the strain splitting the edges of her voice. "Yes."

She shook her head, bit her lower lip as if to keep from crying. "Why?"

It was a good question. I'd asked myself the same thing and never come up with an answer that didn't sound trite. I glanced at Sean again. He hadn't moved a muscle since we'd walked in, our voices rolling over him without eliciting any of the involuntary responses I'd come to hope for.

Would he rather have burnt hot and bright and fierce, and been snuffed out quick like a wet flame? Would he consider it good luck or bad, I wondered, the half an inch of life that he'd been left with? Survival was a long way from living.

I turned away, leaving the coffee on the bedside cabinet, putting up gentle sensory smoke signals into that sterile room. As I drew level with Dina she still hadn't taken her eyes off Sean, hadn't moved any closer.

"Why don't you want go to Europe to stay with your father?" I asked in return. "Why be so stubborn? Why increase the risk?"

For both of us . . .

"Because . . ." she began, and her voice trailed away. She swallowed. "Because Mother wants me to go and hide until all this trouble is over, but how long will that take? Why should I put my life on hold and give up riding my horses every day, for something that might never happen?"

There was bravado in her words, but I caught the flare of fear in her voice, her face. Whatever she might say or do to prove otherwise, Dina was scared. She must have guessed that I'd seen it, because her chin lifted, defiant. "I guess running away just feels like cowardice."

I nodded. "Then you understand how I feel."

It wasn't much of an answer, but I reckoned I'd bared my soul enough for one day.

CHAPTER
TWENTY

The charity auction, I soon discovered, was one of the highlights of the Long Island social calendar, and was being held at a sumptuous country club on the North Shore. There were so many VIP guests attending that the club had assigned a frighteningly efficient elderly woman called Harling, whose sole job was to liaise with the numerous close-protection personnel. Or, as she saw it, to stop us gorillas from tripping over our own bootlaces and stealing the silver.

I went up there and met her the day before. She was wearing a long narrow skirt and white blouse with a high ruffled collar, the overall effect vaguely Edwardian. I, in contrast, had come on the Buell to cut down the time I was away from Dina, and had on a bike jacket over a T-shirt and Kevlar-reinforced jeans. Until I stated my business at the reception desk, I think they were planning on showing me the door with all haste.

As it was, the indomitable Ms Harling quick-marched me around the place, firing facts and specs back over her shoulder in time with the machine-gun rat-a-tat of her sensible heels. From having a paramedic team on standby, to knowing off the top of her head the local police response times, to having already cleared an emergency exfil route from the grand ballroom through the kitchens to the rear parking area, she seemed to have everything pretty well mapped out. When I told her as much, she unbent enough to bestow a fractional smile.

"We certainly do our best," she said. Her tour had brought us neatly back to the front entrance and she glanced at her PDA — not quite as pointed as checking her watch. "Now, unless you have any questions . . .?"

"Just one," I said. "If anything goes down, what means do the various close-protection teams have of ID'ing each other? I'd hate to be in a situation where I draw my weapon, only to be mistaken for one of the bad guys." I thought it best not to mention the words "friendly fire".

Her plucked and carefully redrawn eyebrows rose slightly. "I will point out in the briefing packs that there are female protection personnel present," she said at last. "Although we have never encountered any problems in the past."

"Really?" I murmured.

Her mouth relaxed a little more as her eyes drifted over my appearance, and this time I thought I detected the merest hint of a twinkle. "No," she said. "Most of the time, my dear, bodyguards look like . . . bodyguards."

It took Dina all afternoon to prepare for the big night, from a facial and massage to a visit to her hairdresser and nail salon. She changed her mind at least three times about her outfit, despite having bought a selection specially for the occasion.

Eventually, I managed to talk her out of something I felt was trying much too hard and into a bold but simple bronze sheath of a dress that showed off her figure and hair to best effect. She teamed it with the pearl drop earrings she'd worn that first day I'd met her, out riding Cerdo on the beach. They had been her grandmother's, she told me.

When I finally left her hovering indecisively in front of the mirror, I had barely half an hour to grab a quick shower and scramble into my own posh frock.

I had been planning to drag out my all-purpose stretchy dress for a return match, but Dina had flatly refused to be seen out with me in the same thing twice, and insisted on treating me to something new. I tried to say no, but she would not be deflected. In the end it was easier not to put up a fight.

I found what I was looking for in a designer outlet store, much to her dismay, on the marked-down rack. It was another black dress, although the silky material flipped almost to silver according to the light, like pearl lacquer on paint. It was a little crumpled, but nothing a night under my mattress hadn't cured.

The dress was almost floor length, but had a split up the left thigh to give me mobility, and a bolero jacket that was sufficient to conceal the SIG.

The other advantage of the jacket was it had a high collar that largely hid the scar around the base of my neck. There were days now when I looked in the mirror and it wasn't immediately obvious to me that someone

149

had once tried to cut my throat. I'd learnt to cover it, partly with make-up and partly by how I dressed, and tonight a string of graduated pearls — fake, of course — did the rest.

I stashed some essentials into a small evening bag and headed out, only to find that I'd still beaten Dina to the living area where Caroline Willner waited in flattering dowager pale blue, glittering with diamonds. Alongside her, looking very suave in a well-fitting tuxedo, was Parker. He automatically got to his feet when I walked in, gave me a slow appraisal.

"Charlie. You look . . . wonderful."

"Thank you. I do scrub up on occasion," I returned with a wry grin. "You look none too shabby yourself, Parker," but he didn't smile back. I saw Caroline Willner flick us a shrewd glance and realised belatedly that I'd probably been a touch too flippant towards my boss in front of a woman who was not only a client, but one who also used to be a countess.

Fortunately, I was saved from having to stumble through an apology, or awkward silence, by Dina's dramatic entrance. Parker made gallant and appreciative noises, which Dina coyly accepted. Almost on cue, the arrival of the limo was announced, and we trooped out into the blood-warm night.

As Parker passed me he murmured a quick, "Sorry", which only served to confuse me. *Sorry for what?*

Outside, Torquil stood by the open rear door of a stretch Cadillac CTS, waiting impatiently for us to emerge. His usual pair of bodyguards were ranged behind him. Both wore boxy evening dress that had

150

been chosen more for ease of movement than for flattery of fit, like a conscript's uniform. Ms Harling of the country club, I considered, definitely had a point.

Caroline Willner sailed down the stairs first, with Dina behind her. Torquil managed to play the gentleman enough to greet his date's mother with civility and hand her into the limo, although his manner didn't alter noticeably with Dina. I wondered if she was disappointed that all the effort over her appearance seemed to have gone unnoticed.

As he ducked into the car, Parker nodded to the troops, who stiffened as if suddenly realising they were raw recruits in the presence of a veteran. One hopped in smartly behind us, the other took the front seat next to the driver.

Inside, the Cadillac was cavernous in a slightly tacky way, with inset LED lighting everywhere, mirrors on the ceiling, flat screen TVs, and champagne on ice. It could seat ten in squishy cream-leather comfort, three abreast at the front and rear of the huge rear cabin, and along one side on a four-seater sofa that would have been too big to fit most British living rooms.

When the door clunked shut behind us, I saw there were two other passengers already in occupation. One was a statuesque red-haired woman in a charcoal silk tuxedo, who was clearly security. The other, lounging at the far end with his back to the raised privacy screen behind the driver, was a thin man in his sixties. He cut a striking figure, with a shock of white hair and Colonel Sanders-style moustache and narrow strip of a beard. So, this was Eisenberg Senior, Torquil's gazillionaire father. Physically, they were not much alike, but in manner they mirrored one another. Of Torquil's mother, there was no sign.

Parker and I took the rear seats, with the security man who'd climbed in last alongside us. It was the same guy I'd seen shadowing Torquil at the riding club, rather than the lurker who'd stayed in the car. He glanced at me once, without a flicker of reaction in his face, then muttered an instruction into his radio that we were ready to roll out.

I guessed from the snatches of radio traffic I caught that two generations of Eisenberg men travelling together warranted at least two chase cars. They were not difficult to spot.

Torquil's cellphone rang twice before we'd made it half a mile. The first time was some kind of message that he glanced at briefly, but when the *Mission: Impossible* theme began its second run, his father gave him a hard stare that made him pointedly turn off the device — or at least put it on silent.

Meanwhile, Eisenberg Senior greeted Caroline Willner with a distant familiarity. Where Torquil came across as precocious and occasionally arrogant, Brandon Eisenberg had perfected this manner into a certain straight-talking charm, backed by obvious savvy. And he'd done his homework.

As he leant forwards to shake Dina's hand, he said smoothly, "I understand you're turning into quite the talented equestrienne, young lady. I have a few horses myself, so I appreciate the skills involved to handle them well."

152

Dina flushed at the praise, and self-consciously congratulated him on his recent winner in the Kentucky Derby.

"Well, we sure were lucky this time out," Eisenberg said modestly. Duty done, he turned his attention to those of us in the rear of the bus as we began to pick up speed. "Mr Armstrong, I understand. Your reputation precedes you."

"As does yours, sir," Parker returned in that entirely neutral voice he used to such effect.

Eisenberg nodded in acknowledgement, and his gaze slid sideways onto me. "And you must be Miss Fox," he said. "According to my boy, you put up quite a show the other day."

"I told you — those guys were total dumb-asses, Dad," Torquil put in sharply. "If they'd taken a swing at her first, instead of the riding club guy, who knows *how* it would have gone down."

Beside me, the bodyguard didn't quite heave a sigh, but his chest definitely gave a quick rise and fall outside its normal rhythm. I didn't need to suppose whose expert opinions Torquil had hijacked as his own.

Dina, sitting next to Torquil on the sofa, gave him a nudge in the ribs that was only half playful. "Hey, that's my personal bodyguard you're talking about," she protested, flashing me a smile. "Charlie was just great. A real action heroine!"

But Eisenberg was silent for a moment, as if giving his son's words due consideration. Or maybe he was simply wondering — as I was — why Torquil sounded

153

so annoyed about the inept performance by Dina's potential kidnappers.

It bothered me — Torquil's response to the incident. Dina had told me he was a risk-taker and a thrill-seeker in the extreme sports in which he regularly engaged. Did that mean he now fancied himself in the role of bodyguard, with all the inherent dangers that fantasy entailed? If so, he could well cause me some major headaches. Not to mention exposing Dina to possible harm.

I thought back to Orlando's comments at the riding club, just before the attack. She'd told me that Torquil had been hanging around *her* shortly before she was taken. Was his interest purely academic, or did he have some other, more sinister, involvement?

I glanced sideways at Parker, caught his brief frown and knew his thought processes had travelled a similar path to my own. Either way, Torquil needed to have his wings clipped before he got any of us into a situation where his proverbial wax melted.

CHAPTER
TWENTY-ONE

As we all climbed out of the limo outside the grand front entrance of the country club, Brandon Eisenberg turned, buttoning his immaculate dinner jacket, and said casually, "I have a table reserved. You'll be my guests, of course."

Caroline Willner smiled at him with every appearance of pleasure and said we would all be delighted. I dredged up one of the facts and figures that the ultra-efficient Ms Harling had flung my way the day before, and recalled that reserving an entire table, which seated twelve, could be had for an outrageous price running into thousands of dollars.

There were few limits, it seemed, to what you could get away with in the name of charity.

Before the dinner and auction took place in the Grand Ballroom, there was a cocktail reception in one of the smaller function rooms. Always a difficult occasion to manage from a security standpoint, because of the general crowding and the liquid nature of people's movements.

It was fortunate that Dina seemed keen to have me alongside her, otherwise I would have struggled to keep her fully covered once the place really began to heat up.

Maybe she just wanted the company. Torquil appeared more interested in making inroads into the complimentary champagne than taking care of his date. There was playing it cool, I decided, and then there was being positively chilly.

As we circulated I ran into plenty of other minders, and was on nodding terms with some of them from previous jobs. There were enough actors and celebrities attending to make casual lunatics alone a possibility, never mind specific targeted threats. The close-protection guys all looked tense as a result.

It was a relief to finally be rallied through to the ballroom to take our seats for the gala dinner. Brandon Eisenberg's table was one of the best, front and centre. Not where I would have chosen to stash my principal if I'd had a choice.

We were directly in front of the stage where the compère would later attempt to whip up his audience into a frenzy of generous bidding. Eisenberg was first to take his seat, at right angles to the stage, where he could keep an eye on the room as well, without craning his neck. His own bodyguard, the red-headed woman, claimed the chair to his right. I'd learnt from Parker that she was ex-Secret Service, called Gleason.

Gleason had not returned my smile of greeting, but turned on the charm as far as Parker was concerned, and was now attempting to impress him with her professional attention to duty. I assumed she was after a job. In this business, having the name Armstrong-Meyer on your CV looked good to anyone.

156

Caroline Willner sat next to Brandon Eisenberg and, practised in the social graces, immediately engaged him in quiet and earnest conversation. The rest of us sat down and spread out. Even with Torquil's own bodyguard, we were still only eight instead of twelve, which gave everybody a bit more elbow room.

I had Dina on one side of me and the security man from the back seat of the limo on the other. He had not developed his conversational skills during the ride in, and I'd privately nicknamed him Lurch as a result, but I was happy to people-watch and keep an eye on the flow through the ballroom as the late arrivals made their entrance. Dina was chatting stiltedly with Torquil. The elaborate table displays made it difficult to hold a conversation with the person sitting opposite.

From our vantage point, I spotted Benedict Benelli looking moody in all black, with his damaged right hand thrust into his pocket as usual. Manda Dempsey was on his arm in a white dress that showed the extent of her all-over tan and was causing many a double take from the male guests. Possibly they were all wondering how she managed to keep anything so skimpy to stay the right side of decent. I reckoned double-sided sticky tape had a lot to do with it.

It wasn't long before Orlando and Hunt also turned up, in a party that also consisted of several security guys and an older couple who looked to be Orlando's parents. None of them looked particularly happy to be there. The three former kidnap victims did not, I noticed, make any efforts to sit together, despite their apparent pally behaviour at the birthday party.

Dinner was served and cleared with inconspicuous efficiency and the auction began as soon as the coffee and mints were on the tables, leaving the staff to scurry about between the guests, trying not to be mistaken for bidders.

I was staggered at the lots on offer and the prices they fetched, from trips to the British Virgin Islands on the Eisenberg yacht, to a kiss for a rich man's daughter from the latest teen sensation heart-throb actor.

The auction took about an hour, after which the dancing started, more ballroom than disco, which at least meant the noise stayed at a comfortable level. The country club had employed live musicians to provide the accompaniment, including a Korean girl in a long red dress who, if I was any judge, played classical guitar to a far higher standard than the gig should have demanded.

Those who didn't dance took the opportunity to circulate and network, or simply to chat. Manda floated across and exchanged air kisses with Dina.

"Honey, I heard about what happened at the riding club," she said, hand still on Dina's arm. "That must have been horrible. How *are* you?"

"She's fine," Torquil said, leaning back in his chair to talk around Dina before she had a chance to speak. "After all, it wasn't much of an attempt."

Dina threw him a sharp look. "Well *I* was terrified, but Charlie was terrific," she said, sliding me another of those little sideways glances. "And I don't know how you can say that, Tor. Poor Raleigh's arm was bust up really bad."

Manda looked confused. "Raleigh?"

"My horse-riding instructor," Dina said. "He was walking us to the trailer when these guys appeared out of nowhere and just whaled in on the poor guy."

Torquil drowned a "humph" into his glass as he took a swig of his drink. Some people just like being argumentative for the sake of it.

Manda frowned at him. "Poor guy," she repeated. "Well, at least you're OK, honey. That's something." And with a vague smile, she drifted on.

I watched her go, noting that her return to the Benelli table seemed to spark a quiet disagreement between her and Benedict, who was in a worse temper than Torquil and was being stiffly ignored by the rest of his party.

Why, I wondered, amid all this luxury and excess, were all of them so determined not to have a good time tonight?

I turned back and met Caroline Willner's eye. She gave me a fractional smile as if she'd read my thoughts with accuracy.

"I should very much like to dance," she announced firmly, causing Torquil to bury his nose in his drink again, just in case she had him in mind as a partner.

His father had a more mature way of declining, patting what had seemed to be a perfectly healthy knee and shrugging apologetically. "I made it a policy a long time ago to dance in public only with my wife," he said with a smile, carefully not looking at his red-headed bodyguard as he spoke. "Causes less scandal that way."

"In that case," Parker said, rising politely and offering his hand. "May I?"

Caroline Willner inclined her head, her expression announcing, in a subtle kind of way, that this was the outcome for which she'd been aiming. "You may."

They moved out onto the floor. Dina fidgeted in her chair and stared pointedly at Torquil until he gave an ungracious sigh and pushed his chair back. What was eating him, I wondered?

"You wanna dance?"

Dina nodded and got to her feet quickly, in case he changed his mind. I glanced across at Parker, saw him pick up Dina's movement and give me a slight nod, knew he'd have her covered while she and Torquil were out on the floor. Torquil's bodyguard, Lurch, had been busy folding the silver foil from the coffee mints into mini origami shapes that looked far too delicate for his oversize fingers. Although he didn't seem to be paying attention, it was deceptive. He was on his feet before Torquil, and was heading for the dance floor.

"Do me a favour and help him to blend a little, would you?" Brandon Eisenberg said. For a moment I thought he was speaking to me, but when I looked up, Eisenberg's eyes were on his own bodyguard, Gleason. When she hesitated, he said, "I'm sure Miss Fox will keep me company until you return."

Gleason didn't like that at all, but there wasn't much she could do. She gave a curt nod and stepped onto the floor, holding herself rigidly away from her partner by way of protest, her eyes fixed on Torquil and Dina.

Eisenberg patted Caroline Willner's empty chair alongside him and, having no good reason to refuse, I moved round, keeping my own eyes on the dance floor as I took my seat.

Parker, I saw, had casually manoeuvred himself close to Dina and Torquil, without it being obvious to anyone, least of all the couple concerned. He was an excellent, fluid dancer. Caroline Willner looked like she was having a good time in his arms.

"That bother you?" Eisenberg asked. "Mrs Willner dancing with your boss?"

I looked at him in surprise, found him watching me with disconcerting pale-blue eyes.

"Excuse me?" I bit out, and remembered belatedly Parker's warning that Eisenberg was not someone to get on the wrong side of. I swallowed my temper and said in measured tones, "Mr Armstrong is my boss. Why does everybody assume there's more to our relationship than that?"

Eisenberg chuckled. In a flash I knew that Gleason's duties towards guarding his body went a little further than they should. I stood up again.

"Sit down, Miss Fox, I'm not done talking with you," Eisenberg said, his voice still pleasant even if his eyes had turned cold. "I'd heard you were . . . otherwise attached, shall we say, to Armstrong's partner, but he got himself shot a few months back and word is his condition may be permanent. That reaction just told me my information is correct, and you haven't transferred your affections."

161

I felt my facial muscles lock in an effort not to scream, or cry, or punch his nasal bone straight up through his frontal lobe. So, he'd had us checked out long before we'd climbed into his limo earlier tonight. No surprises there.

I kept my voice lethally calm. "And why would my relationships — imagined or otherwise — be of the slightest interest to you?"

He sat back looking vaguely satisfied, as if he took my trying to find a reason not to deck him as some kind of piqued interest.

"Because I want to offer you a job."

162

CHAPTER
TWENTY-TWO

I stared at Eisenberg for a moment with nothing in my eyes. After ten seconds, even someone with his monstrously thick skin began to realise he might have made a mistake. A flicker of unease appeared in his face.

I stood up again, remembering my manners, though it grieved me to waste them on someone without any of his own. "Thanks for the charmingly worded offer, but — no thanks."

Eisenberg sighed loud enough to be heard over the music, as if I were being deliberately difficult. "Don't you even want to hear what the job is?"

I twisted, gripping the back of a chair to give my hands something to choke. "Considering you apparently assume the only way I acquired my present job was by sleeping with Sean, and the only way I've kept it since is by sleeping with Parker," I said with icy precision, "I think I'd rather remain blissfully ignorant of the details, thanks."

"Clearly you're a woman of loyalty and principle, Miss Fox," he said. "I find those qualities admirable. Foolish, but admirable." He smiled, revealing a lot of expensive dental work that I had a sudden urge to ruin.

"I'm not a man who apologises often, but I see I've offended you and for that I do most humbly apologise."

I doubted his sincerity, but it would have been churlish to call him on it. "I'm in a job that demands absolute loyalty to principals of a different kind," I said instead. "Without it, I'd be no use to anyone."

He raised his glass slightly, conceding the point. "I like to find out what makes people tick," he said, eyes roaming the dance floor briefly before returning to me. "In your case, I believe it's loyalty to Mr Meyer. The medical facility where he's presently undergoing treatment is one of the finest in the country, as I understand, but not the finest in the world." He paused. "I could arrange his transfer to the one that is."

I let my eyebrow rise. "For someone you've heard may not recover anyway?" I said coolly. "Why?"

"Because I'm prepared to offer certain of my employees benefits tailored to their . . . specific needs, shall we say."

Despite myself, and blunt in my reluctance, a question forced its way out. "What's the job?"

He smiled more fully then, just for a moment before his face grew serious. He looked towards the dance floor again.

"My son," he said. "I want you to take over guarding my son."

Later, Caroline Willner moved to take her daughter's vacant chair while Dina danced with Parker, looking very self-conscious about it. Torquil had persuaded Manda onto the floor with him, while Benedict still sat

164

in sulky silence at his family's table. Orlando and Hunt danced together nearby. Orlando seemed to be doing her best to climb into her boyfriend's lap, even though he wasn't sitting down.

"So," Caroline Willner said, settling herself next to me and leaning close enough not to be overheard, "I assume the ever charming Mr Eisenberg took the opportunity to offer you some kind of employment earlier."

I glanced at her. "And why would you assume that?"

"Because, in coming to Dina's rescue, you reacted with instinct and initiative. That's sure to have been reported to him. From what I know of his business dealings, he has a knack for spotting talent and snapping it up," she said with candour. "Although I gather from your reaction that he misjudged your response."

"You could say that," I agreed. "I told him no."

"Well, I'm glad, my dear," she said, patting my hand. "He's a louse and a lecher. Never an appealing combination."

"I thought he danced only with his wife," I said, smiling.

"In public, yes. What they get up to in private is quite another matter. Mrs Eisenberg is currently cruising the Bahamas on the family yacht, surrounded by an attractive, young, all-male crew, I believe."

I managed to swallow my laughter along with a mouthful of sparkling water. "I'm beginning to think the boy Torquil actually turned out remarkably well balanced, considering his home life."

"He records his parents' infidelities," Caroline Willner said, as if reporting on a mildly inferior play. "Dreadful habit. One can't be seen to disapprove of him, of course, but it might be wise if you were to warn Dina that if she really must sleep with the boy, then to do it at a place of her choosing, otherwise she might find herself somewhat exposed on YouTube."

I nearly choked at that and had to put my glass down quickly, reaching for a napkin to blot my mouth. When I could speak again, I grinned at her, wondering if my mother had ever remotely considered handing out such practical and down-to-earth advice. "You wouldn't care to adopt me, by any chance?"

She gave me a slight smile. "You're very good for Dina," she said. "You've given her focus, confidence, shown her what's important."

My eyebrows went up again. "I've known her a matter of days."

"Nevertheless. You took her to see your young man — Sean, is it?"

"Ah, yes," I admitted. "Yes I did." Parker had not approved, citing a variety of reasons from scaring my principal to involving her in my private life, neither of which he recommended. These people, he'd reminded me, were not my friends. I should not take them into my confidence and expect them to care. "I'm sorry if you disapprove —"

"Quite the contrary," she said briskly. "It demonstrated beyond all doubt that the matter of her personal safety is not a game, and should not be treated as such, however lightly her friends seem to take their own experiences."

"I would have thought that Benedict's missing finger would be a permanent reminder," I said.

Over to my left, the Korean guitarist was engrossed in the piece she was playing, head down and eyes closed as her fingers caressed the strings of her instrument. I wondered if she was the cause of Benedict's enduring bad mood this evening. Or part of it, at least.

Caroline Willner followed my gaze and passed me a shrewd look. "Benedict Benelli was never as keen on becoming a classical musician as his family were on pushing him in that direction," she said. "And he could still pursue that path, if he so chose."

"With a missing finger?" I queried. "Wouldn't that be a little difficult?"

"He lost the little finger of his right hand," Caroline Willner said, dismissive. "Unless he was planning to take up flamenco, that's the one finger a classical guitarist does not use." She gestured towards the stage. "If you watch the girl's hands carefully, you'll see for yourself."

For a few moments I did, and although it was sometimes hard to tell, with the angle the Korean girl held her wrist, and the incredible dexterity of her fingers, I realised that Caroline Willner was entirely correct. I'd watched classical guitarists play before and it had always seemed like they had about ten extra fingers on each hand, never mind failing to utilise all the ones they had. It was the kind of snippet Sean would find interesting. I suppressed the instant twinge of associated thoughts and simply made a mental note to tell him about it, the next time I visited.

Out on the dance floor, Hunt had managed to disentangle himself from Orlando and cut in on Parker, although with great courtesy. If Dina showed a faint flicker of disappointment to have her dance with my boss cut short, Hunt soon proved adequate compensation. Parker headed back to the table and gave me a slight bow.

"I've been rejected," he said gravely. "Can I rely on you to bolster my flagging ego, Charlie?"

I knew he was only asking in order for us to be nearer to Dina, but it was a nice way of asking. I glanced at Caroline, feeling rude to abandon her in mid conversation, but she waved me up. As we walked back towards the other dancers, though, I could feel her watching the pair of us with that astute gaze.

I had learnt the basics of not treading on my partner's toes to music while I was still at school, at the urging of my mother. I think she had more or less despaired of me turning into a young lady by then, but that didn't mean I had to entirely lack the social graces.

Ironically, I'd brushed up my rusty skills more since going into close protection than I ever had before. Nothing allows you to stick close to a principal at a formal party than being able to dance right next to them, I'd found. Particularly if you can do it without looking like an elephant in evening dress. I caught sight of Torquil's bodyguard blundering around the floor

168

with a long-suffering Gleason in tow, and was suddenly thankful for my mother's stubborn insistence.

Parker caught the direction of my gaze and smiled. "Yeah, it's not hard to see why Eisenberg offered you a job."

I stared. There hadn't yet been an opportunity to give my boss the gist of that conversation when I hadn't been able to feel Brandon Eisenberg's eyes boring into the back of my neck. "Did he hire a skywriter?" I demanded sourly. "How the hell did you know that?"

"Because when I came back to the table after that dance with Mrs Willner, you looked like you wanted to rip off his head and spit down his neck," Parker said wryly. "And it's what I would have done."

And I thought I'd hidden it so well. "What — ripped his head off?"

Another smile, one that crinkled his eyes. "No, offered you a job."

"You wouldn't have been quite so crass about it."

"Thank you — I guess," he said. He paused. "Mrs Willner thinks you're a positive influence on her daughter, by the way."

"I'm doing my best," I said. "According to Dina, her mother's the one trying to hustle her over to Europe."

Parker nodded. "Uh-huh, and did she say why she's refusing?"

"Pig-headedness, mainly. Disguised as not wanting to give in and run away from danger."

He sighed. "It's never the cowards who get us killed," he said, then seemed to realise the implications of that. I felt his back stiffen under my resting hand.

169

"Don't say it," I said lightly. "You'll lose concentration and trample on me."

His muscles eased a fraction. "Just be careful. In a lot of ways, Dina's younger than she looks. Don't let her put you on a pedestal."

"Don't worry, I keep putting my foot in it too frequently for that."

"I don't know — you seem pretty light on your feet to me." He smiled again. "You dance well. Another of your talents."

"Thank you," I said, and recalled his earlier compliment, and my reaction to it. "Look, Parker, back at the Willners' place, you said —"

"That I was sorry?" he said. "I . . . embarrassed you, in front of a client. That was out of line."

"Embarrassed me?" I shrugged, eyes over his shoulder to keep a watch on Dina, but her body language was perfectly relaxed. "All you did was tell me I looked nice."

"No, I said you looked wonderful. There's a difference."

My gaze snapped back to his. "Yes, you did," I murmured, feeling my skin heat, my mouth dry. Almost with shock, I recognised the signs of my own arousal. "Parker, I'm —"

"I know," he said softly. "I know. Just dance, Charlie."

CHAPTER
TWENTY-THREE

It was a while before either of us spoke after that. Why Parker kept his own counsel, I can only guess. Me, because I couldn't think of a damn thing to say that wouldn't make things ten times worse — for both of us.

Parker was my boss, Sean's partner, our friend. He'd been a shoulder to lean on. More than that, he'd been a rock in a storm-lashed sea, and I'd clung to the support he'd offered since Sean's injury. But I'd never expected for a moment that I'd start to fall for him, with all the emotional turmoil that entailed.

The music eventually segued into another number and Hunt, with gallant reluctance, led Dina back to her table. Parker and I followed suit. Torquil, laughing, declined to release Manda and swept her into another dance. He'd lost his miserable air, but I think that had more to do with making Gleason stay on the floor with Lurch. Torquil's bodyguard had long since exhausted his repertoire of dance steps and the pair of them were looking increasingly uncomfortable.

If Torquil wasn't careful, I thought, his own team would knock him off just to be rid of him.

He only tortured them for a few minutes longer, however, then handed Manda back to Benedict and swaggered off towards the restrooms. I saw Lurch move to follow him, leaving Gleason to finally hurry back to our table and plonk herself down next to Eisenberg like she was determined not to get up again.

Torquil, however, had no intention of being followed everywhere by his bodyguard. I saw him whirl and plant a determined finger in the guy's chest. He was close enough for me to hear the exchange, which basically ran along the lines that Torquil felt he was old enough to take a leak unaided.

Lurch glanced over at Torquil's father for guidance, which only served to infuriate the son even more. He gave the bodyguard's face a light slap to bring it back to face him. I sucked in an involuntary breath, but Lurch had heroic self-control and didn't punch the little brat's lights out.

"Don't you look to him for orders!" Torquil growled. "You work for *me*, OK?"

Surreptitiously, I leant closer to Parker and, with minimal movement of my lips, murmured, "When you said Eisenberg had all kinds of influence I did not want to tangle with, did you mean he was connected to the Mob?"

Parker's lips quirked. "We don't think so. Why?"

"I just wondered why Torquil's behaving like something out of a bad junior version of *The Godfather*," I said, still keeping my voice low. "Perhaps this might be a good chance to find out?"

"Just be careful," he warned, almost into my hair. "After all, the Willners have horses — you do not want to wake up in bed with part of one of them."

172

I pulled a face and got to my feet as casually as I could manage, collecting my evening bag to add a touch of authenticity to the exercise. And just when Torquil's bodyguard might have overridden his principal's wishes, I heard Parker's voice behind me ask him some seemingly loaded question about his experience in the business.

I glanced behind me long enough to see Lurch torn between a possible job opportunity and disobeying a direct order. I think Gleason's scowl finally swayed him, like she thought he'd been chosen over her. Lurch hesitated a moment, then turned back and took the seat I'd just vacated next to my boss. I could have told him that — by doing so — he'd just lost any chance he might have had of being offered employment with Armstrong-Meyer.

Beyond Torquil's obvious charms, what was it about working for the Eisenbergs, I wondered as I headed for the restrooms, that made people so desperate to get away from them? But Brandon Eisenberg had offered to find a place for Sean in the best neurological rehab centre in the world. Despite the obvious drawbacks, was that temptation enough?

No, I decided. It wasn't. Because if Sean came out of his coma and discovered what I'd done, there would be hell to pay.

Not "if", dammit — "when"!

I excuse-me'd my way out of the ballroom, through a set of double doors and down a plushly carpeted hallway, punctuated by spotlit marble busts of what I think were supposed to be Greek gods, although one

173

bore an uncanny resemblance to Brad Pitt in laurel wreath and artfully draped toga.

I paused by the door to the men's room, undecided. The music was more muted here, so that the piercing notes of the *Mission: Impossible* theme ringtone was easily recognisable from within. It hadn't taken Torquil long, I realised, to reboot his phone once he was out of his father's earshot.

I hesitated a moment longer. Parker had told me to tread carefully around Torquil, so I pushed open the outer door to the men's room with great care. Like the ladies', it had a little vestibule which I assumed was supposed to operate as a kind of airlock as well as a modesty screen.

Not that it smelt in there. The country club did not permit that kind of thing. When I cracked the inner door a fraction and peered through the gap, the overwhelming odour was of expensive perfumed hand soap. It could have been a lot worse.

Inside was an extravagance of marble tiles and subdued lighting, which made the usual row of urinals seem more out of place than usual. Torquil was the only occupant, something he had evidently been told to verify, judging by the way he was nudging each of the cubicle doors open with his foot, the phone tucked against his shoulder as he did so.

"Yeah, yeah, so there's no one here," he said into it then, his voice impatient. "Why the cloak-and-dagger stuff? Why couldn't you just . . .? Oh, OK, I get it . . ." Then his voice rose, almost jubilant. "Cool, man!" And then he seemed to realise how gauche he sounded and made an attempt to play it down. "Hey, listen. Just make sure they make a better job of it this time, OK? I'm not fooling around —"

Suddenly, the outer door behind me swung open and I was faced with a startled man in a tuxedo.

Unable to think of any reasonable explanation, I beamed stupidly at him and lurched against the nearest wall, putting as much slur into my voice as I could manage. "Hey, buddy, I guess one of ush ish inda wrong placesh, huh?"

"Yeah, lady, and I think maybe it's you." He gave a nervous laugh and steered me towards the outer door, edging around me. "Try down the hall."

"Oh, OK," I said with false brightness. "'Cause I need to pee-pee *real* bad."

Any thoughts he might have had of lecturing me to be more careful where I headed in future died instantly. He shoved me back out into the corridor and disappeared towards the inner sanctum.

I quickly nipped behind Brad Pitt's marble effigy. The startled man reappeared shortly afterwards and headed back for the ballroom without checking the rest of the corridor. So, at least I knew he wasn't security of any kind. I debated briefly on whether he'd had time to do what he needed to *and* wash his hands. On balance, probably not.

Torquil emerged a minute or so later, still looking at the display on his phone. He looked up with a jerk as I fell into step alongside him.

"Hey, Tor, who's on the phone?"

175

"That's for me to know and you . . . not to know," he said, but his voice didn't have its usual brusque edge. However the call had finished, it had done so to his liking.

"If it concerns Dina's safety," I said quietly, "it *is* my business."

He just stared at me oddly for a moment. "Why? So's you can look good by 'rescuing' her again, that it?" he demanded, drawing little quote marks in the air with his fingers.

"What is that supposed to mean?" I put a hand on his arm when he would have brushed past me. He glanced down and I stepped in, speaking more urgently. "Talk to me. Please. You saw what happens when people get in the way — Raleigh's going to need surgery to use that arm again."

It was a slight exaggeration, but it seemed appropriate under the circumstances. Encouraged by his silence, I tried again. "If someone gets killed next time, even your father's money and power won't be able to save you from the consequences."

But I'd overreached, and if the stubborn expression that stiffened his face was anything to go by, he knew it. His self-doubt collapsed and he yanked himself out of my grasp.

One of the doors to the ballroom swung open and Lurch loomed in the gap.

"You got trouble there, boss?"

"No," Torquil said, stowing his cellphone into his pocket and putting all his superiority into a single dismissive glance. "No trouble at all."

CHAPTER
TWENTY-FOUR

And, for three days after the charity auction, *no trouble* was exactly what we got.

Despite her lack of actual employment, no one could accuse Dina of being inactive. Between her tennis lessons, and her lunches, and her personal shopper, and her personal trainer, there was barely a minute when her time wasn't organised with something or other. And if I had my doubts about whether it was all worthwhile, I kept those opinions firmly to myself.

But despite the trappings of wealth, the only time Dina seemed to be completely relaxed and happy was when she was out with her horse. Cerdo was possibly the only one who didn't make any allowances for how rich or influential his owner might be. He still tanked off with her along the beach if he was that way inclined, but equally he could behave like a gracious prince. I think his variable moods provided an area of rare uncertainty in Dina's life that she genuinely looked forward to.

Other areas of uncertainty were my concern. As soon as I'd got back to our table that night at the country club, I'd reported the content of Torquil's eavesdropped phone call in the restroom to Parker.

"But there was no concrete threat," he pointed out at last, keeping his voice low. "Not specific enough to warrant pulling her out of here."

"Still . . ."

He sat back. "You're the one in the hot seat, so it's your call, Charlie, you know that." He paused. "But if Torquil *is* involved, do you think he'd be dumb enough to do anything here? Look around you — the close-protection teams outnumber the guests, and however many corners Brandon Eisenberg may have cut in order to make his money, these days he keeps his hands pristine."

"Whereas," I said slowly, "if I call in alternative transport and whisk Dina home separately — not in the limo with him — who knows what might happen en route."

Parker simply smiled.

We stayed.

But on the ride back to the Willners' place in the stretch Cadillac, Torquil's attitude towards Dina had definitely changed — and I didn't think that was solely down to the amount of alcohol he'd consumed during the evening. He swayed in his seat as the limo rolled along, smirking like he was in on the world's best private joke, and it was all on us.

If I hadn't known for a fact that Dina had never been alone with him anywhere private, I might even have suspected he'd got his leg over. He still might've, I conceded — just not with Dina.

When we'd pulled up in the driveway, Torquil's father politely declined Caroline Willner's offer of a nightcap. Perhaps it was as clear to him as to me that she had not wanted him to accept. But they nodded to each other, honour satisfied.

Torquil cocked an eyebrow towards Dina. "What about you?" he said. "Wanna go find a nightclub or something?"

Dina, in the process of shifting forwards in her seat to rise, hesitated, glancing at me as if for advice. I kept my face professionally blank, even though I was willing her to make the right response.

"I . . . um, I guess I'm pretty tired, so —"

"No problem-o," Torquil said with insulting speed. He was still sprawled in his seat, making no moves to help her out. "I'll call you," he added with a carelessness that meant the opposite.

Dina flushed, eyes rigidly focused on him so she wouldn't have to meet anyone's embarrassed stares. He might show flashes of charm, but underneath Torquil was still a spoilt brat, I decided.

"Fine," Dina snapped, and faced his father with some small measure of bravado. "Goodnight, Mr Eisenberg. Thanks so much for the ride."

Torquil coloured up himself at that, opened his mouth and shut it again just as fast, scowling. I ducked out of the limo and slammed the door after Dina before I allowed the smile to form on my face.

"Nicely done," I murmured as we climbed the front steps behind her mother and Parker.

"I don't know what you mean," she said stiffly.

I let it go, but it was interesting that she had accurately pinpointed one of Torquil's Achilles' heels —

that he was beholden to his father for everything, even down to transport for the evening.

Needless to say, Torquil had not called the following day, nor the day after that, and Dina's reaction was a difficult one to fathom out. At first, I thought it was her pride that had been hurt, but there seemed to be more to it. I couldn't believe she'd fallen for him, but being dropped had clearly sent her into the doldrums more than I would have expected.

And now, walking the horses side by side along the damp sand, there was still a trace of mournfulness about her.

"He's not worth it, Dina," I said quietly.

For a moment I thought she hadn't heard me. Her eyes were fixed on a squadron of brown pelicans cruising the incoming wave crests in single file, ungainly birds on the ground who achieved an unexpected agile beauty as soon as they took to the air.

"I know."

"O . . . K," I said slowly, twitching the reins as Geronimo ducked his head to snort at a wading bird who'd almost nipped between his front feet. "So, why have you spent the last couple of days looking like you've lost a million quid and found tuppence?"

She twisted in her saddle. "Excuse me?"

I sighed. "Why the long face?"

She shrugged, turning away again, and when she spoke her voice had a brittle quality. "And how, exactly, is that relevant to your job?"

That sent my eyebrows rising silently. It was the first time she'd played the "lowly employee" card with me, although it tended to come with the territory on this kind of job. Back during the brief spell when I'd been assigned to the Dempsey family, I remembered suddenly, the young Amanda had reminded me on a regular basis that she considered me barely at a level with the gardeners. Still, at least she'd been consistent about it.

"Look, Dina —"

"Let it go, Charlie," she snapped, her tension making Cerdo break into an uneasy sidle. "For God's sake! Do I have to fire you?"

It would do me no good, I reasoned, to point out that it was actually her mother who had that privilege. Instead, I waited until she'd got the white horse to settle, and pushed Geronimo into a longer stride to catch up.

"We think Torquil Eisenberg is in on the kidnaps," I said then, conversational.

Cerdo bounced again, snatching at the bridle as he reacted to the slight contraction of her hands. It was as though Dina was sitting on a giant lie detector. Perhaps she realised that, because the abrupt way she grabbed at his mouth made him try to spring forward in response, and gave her an excuse to fuss for maybe half a minute persuading him to calm down to a walk again. Then she looked back at me.

"How do you know?"

It took me a moment to work out what was wrong about that — not just the question, but the way she asked it.

For a start, where was the instant denial? Where was the protestation that surely nobody she knew could possibly have been responsible for any of it, and especially not chopping off a victim's finger — albeit a largely redundant one? Where was the instinctive laughter, scorn even?

And, more than that, the emphasis was wrong. If she'd stressed the "you" part, it would have seemed more dismissive, but she didn't. If anything, the taut little sentence was weighted towards the "how". So instead of expressing doubt at my deductive powers, it became somehow almost an admission of her own guilt.

If she'd been thinking coolly, logically, she would have asked a rake of questions I had no answers to. We had no proof other than an overheard phone call, a suspicion, a gut instinct.

Instead, more than anything she sounded scared. As scared as she had done the day I'd taken her to see Sean and she'd refused to run away from danger. What did she have to prove?

"Dina —"

"Hey, there!"

The voice came from up in the dunes to our right. I wheeled Geronimo round to put him between Dina's horse and the shout, grateful for his quick responses.

Dina leant past me for a better view, shading her eyes with her hand. She stared at the figure who was now approaching in long sliding steps through the ankle-deep sand, and her agitation communicated itself clearly to Cerdo who began to stamp and fidget.

"*Tor?*" Dina's own voice was incredulous. "But . . . what are you doing here?"

Torquil made a show of cupping a hand behind his ear until he was less than five metres away. Then he spread his hands wide and grinned at us both.

"What?" he demanded. "C'mon, you're acting like you're surprised to see me, babe."

I assumed that question was aimed at Dina. She flushed as if he'd made an accusation.

"I am," she said blankly. "What *are* you doing here, Tor?"

"You asked me to come," he said, the big smile diminishing just a notch as the first trace of annoyance began to creep in. He checked both our faces, as if this was a practical joke at his expense that was being carried on just a little too far. But still he clung to the hope that, sooner or later, one of us would be unable to hold back the laughter and confess. All he saw was confusion. "You sent me an email . . . didn't you?"

"No, of course I didn't!"

I checked up and down the beach quickly in both directions. There were the usual joggers and power-walkers carving a path along the harder packed sand just above the waterline, a couple of quad bikers in the distance, the sound of more in the dunes, but it wasn't the kind of beach where you got crowds. It all looked quiet, normal.

Nevertheless, something at the back of my scalp began to prickle.

"What did it say, this supposed email?" I asked.

Torquil glanced at me with a knowing smile just flicking at the corner of his mouth.

"Oh, OK, I get it," he said. He sighed, as if being forced to go through the details when it was obvious that we all knew them. "The message said to meet Dina — here, this morning," he said, adding with a leer, "That she'd come alone and so should I."

"Why?"

"Whaddya mean, why?" He gave a splutter of full laughter that died when he realised that he was the only one laughing. His face twitched. "*She* knows what it said."

I glanced at Dina, found her white-faced. She met my eyes, mutely pleading.

I don't! I didn't!

I believed her. And from over the dunes I heard the sound of another engine approaching. Bigger than the higher-pitched quads that had masked it to this point, the note rising and falling as it ploughed across the soft ground.

"Torquil," I said, aware that my own anxiety was making even the placid Geronimo start to skitter a little underneath me, "where are your guys?"

"My what?"

I wanted to shake him. "Your bodyguards," I said, louder now. "Where are they?"

He didn't like my tone. It made him stubborn about replying, which wasted valuable time. "I told them to stay with the car," he said at last, grudging, jerking his head back the way he'd come.

"Call them in."

184

"Why?"

It was a good question, one I didn't have the time nor the inclination to answer. Every instinct told me this set-up stank, and, in that case, I wanted witnesses. If Torquil's bodyguards were in on whatever games he was playing, he wouldn't have needed to ditch them before that phone call at the country club, and he wouldn't have come alone now. They worked for his father, I recalled. Did that make a difference?

"Charlie, what's going on?" If Dina was sounding worried before, it had stepped up a level.

"We need to get out of here," I said, eyes on the dunes, straining to get a bearing on direction. The acoustics of the sand made it hard to judge exactly where the vehicle was going to pop out. "Just be ready."

"But, why?" she demanded, the timbre of her voice high and cracked. "Charlie, talk to me! What's happening?"

But at that moment an old Jeep Wrangler, its red body streaked with dust, came bowling over the top of the nearest dune and hurtled down the beach towards the three of us, kicking up a plume of sand and spray.

I yanked Geronimo in a tight circle, crowding Dina and Cerdo into the same urgent manoeuvre. I don't know what made me flick my eyes towards Torquil as I did so. And I don't know what I was expecting to see there in return. Reproach, regret, resentment — who knows? Maybe anger, like last time, or even some sense of growing alarm.

But what I wasn't expecting was a gleeful, wanton excitement.

CHAPTER
TWENTY-FIVE

"Go! GO!" I yelled at Dina, but Cerdo was way ahead of her. The white horse catapulted forwards with such violence that she was left scrabbling to stay with him. The two animals stretched into a full gallop, their eager rivalry compounded by the fact we were heading for home.

I kept Geronimo as close alongside as I could, holding back slightly into the line of fire as the red Jeep swerved down onto the flat sand behind us.

And in my head, the calculations swirled and formed like ice. A fit horse can gallop flat out at twenty-five to thirty miles an hour for maybe a mile before it's blown — two miles at the most. It was a shame Cerdo wasn't a Quarter Horse, too, because that particular breed has been clocked at closer to fifty-five over its namesake distance.

An off-road vehicle, on the other hand, can keep going until it runs out of fuel in the tank. The beach was firm, the ridged sand even enough to make fifty or sixty miles an hour feasible if the occupants didn't mind losing a few fillings in the process.

There was no escaping the fact we were not going to be able to run from this one. I was wearing the SIG on my right hip. This time, regardless of whether the horses were gun-shy or not, I knew I might have to use it.

As I urged Geronimo on, I checked back over my shoulder, fully expecting to see the Jeep gaining on us with every stride. To my intense surprise, it did not even seem to be giving chase. I yelled to Dina and sat up abruptly, managing to slow Geronimo's headlong flight. Fortunately, the initial burst of speed had taken enough out of him for the old Quarter Horse to be glad of the excuse to drop back to a shambling trot, head low. Dina went for the easy way of stopping, which was simply to steer Cerdo into the sea and let the water act as a drogue chute.

And without the jostling vibration, I could see the Jeep had never come after us at all. It had bounced down onto the sand and carved a sweeping turn around Torquil. Just for a moment, I thought it must be some friend of his, and that would explain his reaction when the Jeep had first appeared.

But the Jeep continued to circle, tightening in until it was literally kicking sand into the boy's face. Still he stood his ground, hand up to shield his eyes, not realising that the Jeep had neatly cut off his escape route back towards the car where his bodyguards waited, out of sight and earshot, oblivious.

"Run," I muttered under my breath. "Run, dammit."

But Torquil didn't run, didn't move at all until the Jeep swerved towards him suddenly, as though intending to mow him down. Only then did he take a couple of fast steps back, stumbled and went sprawling. The Jeep slewed to a halt just ahead of him.

As I pulled up, I saw a dark-clad figure jump out, pointing something at Torquil with his arm outstretched. I saw the boy paddle backwards, panic in every line of him now as he tried to scrabble away on all fours. The man — the outline was definitely male — stood his ground easily. He maybe even took a moment so the full import of what was about to happen to his victim really hit home.

Then the weapon in his hand jerked and Torquil lurched backwards into the sand, his body convulsing.

"Oh my God!" Dina cried, urging Cerdo back out of the surf, fighting for control. "They shot him! Torquil's shot."

I barged Geronimo in front of her when she would have gone barrelling back towards the Jeep, blocking her path.

"It's a Taser," I said, earning a furious look. I'd been hit with them enough to know.

"So what?" She pulled at her reins, trying to disentangle the two horses, and only succeeded in flustering the pair of them. I grabbed Cerdo's bridle and held on for grim death.

A hundred metres away, the driver of the Jeep had jumped out and helped his passenger load a largely insensible Torquil into the back of the vehicle. They took an end each and more or less threw him in, the way you'd toss a long heavy bag over the edge of a cliff. I heard the thump of his body landing, even from there. The two men jumped back into the front.

"Charlie, for God's sake, let go," Dina wailed, close to tears now. "*Do* something!"

"Leave it, Dina!" I snapped and, more quietly as the Jeep picked up speed and revved out of sight into the dunes, "Don't you understand? There's nothing I *can* do."

But there was one thing — the only thing. I checked my watch out of habit. It was 09.23. I grabbed my cellphone out of my pocket, started to punch in the emergency number.

"Don't!" If anything, Dina's voice was more stricken than before.

"What? Dina, I have to call this in, right now."

"No," she said, pale, her lips bloodless as a corpse, eyes huge. "Please. If it's the same people . . . *you're* the one who doesn't understand. You *can't* go to the police."

I eyed her for a moment in exasperation, then remembered the conversation I'd had with Manda at Torquil's birthday party. How she'd told me they'd threatened to kill her, slowly and painfully, if the authorities were called in. And Benedict, too. Despite the threats to their son, Benedict's parents had hesitated, and they'd mutilated him. I snapped my phone shut and shoved it back in my jacket.

"Let's go find his protection team," I said shortly. "After that, it's up to them who they call."

I didn't wait for her to answer, just nudged Geronimo forwards, heading for the spot where Torquil had been abducted. The horse seemed reluctant to approach, acting spooked as if he could sense that

189

something bad had happened. Or maybe he just didn't like the whiff of exhaust smoke that still hung in the air.

"What's that?" Dina asked suddenly from behind me, pointing into the churned-up sand. I followed her arm and spotted something gleaming darkly. Jumping down, I discovered Torquil's expensive PDA. It must have dropped out of his pocket when he fell. So much for the thought that Torquil might be able to call for help.

I picked it up automatically, shoved it in my pocket, and climbed back into the saddle.

The two of us rode up into the dunes until we spotted Torquil's big gold Bentley, with his two bodyguards sitting inside. They got out as soon as they saw us, alerted by something that all was not well with their absent principal. I saw a familiar dread in the way they carried themselves.

The shit, I reasoned, was just about to hit the fan in a very big way.

CHAPTER
TWENTY-SIX

"As soon as I'd informed Eisenberg's team of the situation, I got Dina out of there," I said.

Parker nodded. "Good work, Charlie." He paused. "How's she taking it?"

"Badly," I said flatly. "I think she blames me for not stepping in and saving him."

He put his hand on my arm, gave it a quick squeeze. "You did your job and protected your principal without distraction," he said. "Nobody can argue with that."

"I know." I shrugged, gave him a weary smile. "It's not much compensation somehow."

We were back at the Willners' house, which was more or less on a security lockdown. Dina had held it together until we'd got the horses back into the stable yard below the house, then had just about collapsed, weeping. The cynical part of me wondered if her fit of the vapours was a convenient way of avoiding the questions she must have known I was about to ask.

She was currently lying down in her room with the blinds drawn, being tended by her mother and their family doctor, with another of Parker's guys, Joe McGregor, on guard outside her door.

Parker and I stood in the living area, staring out at the relentless ocean, muted by the glass. I was still in my riding clothes and smelt distinctly of sweaty horse. Parker contrasted sharply in a dark business suit and sober tie. It was half past noon. Almost exactly three hours since Torquil's abduction.

"What the hell is going on with this kid, Charlie?" he murmured, eyes narrowed.

"I wish I knew," I said. "The other night, at the country club, I would have sworn Torquil was in on the attempt made to grab Dina, but in that case, today's developments don't make any sense. If he's involved, why have *himself* kidnapped?"

"Professional assessment — did it look real or fake to you?"

I considered for a moment, eyes focused back in memory, replaying the whole scene, from the moment the Jeep had leapt into view over the top of the dunes, to Torquil being unceremoniously tossed into the back of it.

"I suppose I would have to say . . . real," I said slowly. "Nobody willingly agrees to have himself hit with a Taser — not when he could just have been threatened with it."

"He might not have been expecting them to go to quite that level of authenticity," Parker pointed out. "And if it's the same people who took the others, they did chop off Benedict Benelli's finger, don't forget."

"Still, there was something about it . . . I don't know." I frowned. "When the Jeep first appeared, he looked surprised but happy to see it — excited, even.

192

And only when it came after him instead of Dina did he seem to panic, as if he'd been expecting to watch, not actively take part."

"Maybe he realised from what you said to him at the country club the other night that you were onto him, and he wanted to make it look good," Parker said. "Hence claiming he'd gotten an email from Dina asking for the meet."

"Ah, and there we might have a slight problem. He *did* get an email."

Parker stilled at the implications. "So . . . Dina set this up?"

"Not exactly, and that's the problem," I said. "I found this on the beach."

I handed Parker Torquil's PDA. He'd seen the boy using it in the limo on the way to the charity auction, so he didn't waste time asking whose it was. Instead, he scrolled through the menu and opened up the inbox, just as I had done as soon as I'd got back to the house.

And there was the message, clearly identifying Dina — or her email address — as the sender.

"*Meet me on the beach near the dunes in an HOUR. It's VITAL we talk about what's been going on before the truth comes out! Come ALONE and so will I. Tell NO ONE!!*"

"Looks kinda clear to me," Parker said. He glanced at me with a cool assessing gaze. "But you have doubts."

"I was with Dina all morning. She never had a chance to send an email, either from her laptop or her cellphone."

"You sure? It doesn't take more than a half minute."

I remembered again her shock when Torquil first appeared. If she'd been expecting him — expecting anyone — she was a far better actress than I'd given her credit for. Even if she'd been able to conceal her genuine reaction from me, Cerdo would have known.

"I'm sure," I said. "But I can appreciate this raises questions. Like, if she didn't send it, who did?" I watched him hesitate. "My job is to protect her, Parker. Just how far am I supposed to go in order to do that?"

Parker was silent for a moment, eyes on the rolling breakers although I was pretty sure he didn't see anything of the view outside the windows.

"My laptop's down in the Navigator," he said at last. He nodded to the PDA. "I can download the contents and we'll see if we can trace exactly where that email came from." He checked his watch, added grimly, "And, with any luck, I'll be able to do it before they get here."

"Who?" I demanded. "I told you what they said about calling in the cops —"

"No, Eisenberg's people," he cut in, already heading for the door, where he paused just long enough to send me a wry smile. "You think they haven't been tracking that thing since the moment the kid was taken?"

I didn't move from the window while he was gone. Without knowing about the supposed email that had lured Torquil into the ambush, I hadn't shown the fallen PDA to his bodyguards, hadn't mentioned it in fact. Not that they'd stopped to ask a lot of unnecessary questions. Or one or two I would have said were pretty bloody vital.

Still, it should have occurred to me that the first thing they'd do was attempt to track him via the GPS chip. In fact, I was amazed they hadn't bust the door down already.

Parker was back a minute or so later, without actually appearing to hurry. There was an economy of movement to him that inspired confidence. He was already opening up a case containing a slim laptop and setting it up on a side table that was probably not intended to hold more than an elaborate arrangement of flowers. He plugged in a USB lead, tapped a few keys, and coerced the PDA into opening up a dialogue with its temporary host. In moments, it was spilling its secrets.

In the midst of this operation, Caroline Willner came into the living area and sank into a chair. Her posture was still very upright, but she moved slowly, as though it physically hurt her to do so. For the first time, she looked like an old lady rather than a matriarch.

I would have asked her if she was OK, but something told me she would hate that weakness being so obvious, more than she hated the weakness itself. Instead, I rang for a pot of tea, and when one of the maids, Silvana, smilingly answered my summons, I politely asked if she could dig out something sweet to go with it, just as an excuse to bring some sugar into the equation.

When Silvana left, Caroline Willner flashed me a brief glance that told me she understood what I was doing, and was not ungrateful for it.

"How's Dina?" I asked. Safer ground.

"Still very shocked," Caroline Willner said. "They've given her a light sedative. She'll sleep for a while."

Parker met my eye briefly. "Probably for the best," he said much more soothingly than I would have managed. The PDA finished disgorging its content and he carefully unplugged it, coiling up the short lead and slipping it into his pocket, out of sight, before he began scanning through the captured files with the laptop's screen canted away from us.

But I knew he'd found something by his sudden immobility, the hardening around his mouth. He glanced up, caught me watching him.

"You better see this."

I moved round to stand alongside him, leaning over the laptop so I could see the screen too. It was a video clip of an interior scene, a bedroom. There were three occupants, engaged in activity that was as athletic as it was inventive.

Two thirds of the trio were uniformly muscular young men, one blond, one dark, tanned and tattooed. The woman was older, paler, but she had the well-preserved look that comes with surgery and stringent maintenance. Her haircut — and what was left of her lingerie after the young studs had removed much of it with their teeth — was expensive in cut and colour.

I raised my eyebrows at Parker. "Torquil wouldn't be the first immature male to download porn off the Internet."

"I don't think this is a straightforward download," Parker murmured, calling up file names and root

196

directories and a whole load of other stuff I had no clue about. "This was a direct feed from someplace."

I looked again. The picture was surprisingly high quality, all things considered, but the camera position never altered, even when the players' antics took them half out of the range of the lens. Never once did they seem aware of being filmed. There were no coy little smiles or knowing glances.

"Hidden camera?" I said.

Parker nodded. "That would be my guess."

I blanked the cavorting on the bed and focused beyond them, out into the room itself. Where had I seen that decor, those furnishings, that giant plasma screen TV hanging dark on the far wall, the oval detail in the ceiling . . .?

"Oh my God," I said faintly. "That's Eisenberg's yacht. One of the main staterooms."

And not just any of the staterooms, but the same one where Dina had gone for her private chat with Orlando and Benedict on the night of Torquil's party. I flicked my eyes to Parker's. "Is there sound with this?"

By way of answer, he dragged the cursor across a small sound bar in the bottom right-hand corner of the screen. The laptop's small internal speakers struggled to accurately reproduce the grunts and groans and squeals of the audio track for a few moments, before he quickly lowered the volume again, looking ever so slightly embarrassed.

The maid, Silvana, returned with a teapot and cups and various highly calorific snacks on a large tray. She put the tray down on the low table in front of Caroline

Willner, and obeyed her instruction that we would pour.

It was only when she'd left us again that Caroline Willner rose and said calmly to Parker, "I think you'd better let me see."

It was the first time I think I've ever seen Parker look flustered. "Ma'am, it's not the kinda thing you ought to —"

"For pleasure, no," she agreed gravely. "But it's entirely obvious what the boy was looking at, and I may be able to identify the, ah . . . participants, shall we say?"

"Ah," Parker said, still with a touch of pink across his cheekbones. He turned the laptop towards her and tried to studiously ignore the way she peered closer at the screen, reaching for her reading glasses, which hung on an ornate chain around her neck.

"My, my," she murmured after a few moments. "Well one has to admire their limber qualities, if nothing else . . ."

I grinned at her and she wrinkled her nose in brief response, before straightening.

"Anyone you know?" I asked.

"The young men, I haven't had the pleasure of making their acquaintance, and I'm quite sure I would remember. But the woman is undoubtedly Nicola Eisenberg — Torquil's mother." She frowned thoughtfully. "I shall view her power yoga classes in a whole new light."

Parker, old-fashioned in some ways more than others, looked in serious danger of spontaneously combusting with associated shame. He busied himself with the laptop again while Caroline Willner calmly went back to the table and, without a flicker, dealt with the tea.

"It looks like this video stream came in a few days ago, right about the time we were headed to the charity auction," he said.

"Torquil received a couple of incoming messages while we were in the limo," I recalled, "and he looked pretty smug about them at the time."

"Hardly surprising," Caroline Willner put in. "Brandon Eisenberg makes such an unseemly fuss about being faithful to his wife, when just about everyone knows he's sleeping with that red-headed bodyguard of his."

"So, how big a scandal would it cause if it came out that Eisenberg's wife was sleeping with half the crew on his yacht?" I asked, and out of the corner of my eye saw Parker wince slightly.

"Oh, I don't suppose it would ever have come out," Caroline Willner said, sounding surprised that I didn't know how this game was played. "I'm sure Brandon would have found a suitable financial incentive to prevent his son ever showing that video to anyone." She took a sip of her tea. "After all, he always has done in the past."

Now when I glanced at Parker, his gaze had lost any trace of self-consciousness and turned calculating.

"Maybe this time he got tired of paying," he said, reaching into his jacket for his cellphone. "How about I call him and find out?"

CHAPTER
TWENTY-SEVEN

"Hey, um, Charlie? There's folks here to see Miss Willner."

Joe McGregor's face appeared round the cracked edge of the bedroom door after a perfunctory knock, looking discomfited. I should have guessed why.

"Who is it?" I asked.

I was fully expecting a contingent from Eisenberg's security personnel, come to interrogate the pair of us about what we'd witnessed on the beach the previous morning. Instead, it was Manda Dempsey who insinuated herself through the gap and hurried forwards into the room with a dramatic cry of, "Oh, honey, we heard the news! How are you taking it? Are you all right?"

Directly behind her was Orlando, and through the open doorway I caught a glimpse of a guy in a suit who'd taken up station on the other side of the corridor with his back to the wall. He had the build of a rugby player, complete with broken nose. I didn't need to check the bulge under his arm to know he was security.

I glanced at Dina, sitting propped up against a heap of pillows, clutching the bedclothes tightly around her body as if suffering from a chill. She'd slept for most of the previous afternoon, after Parker's departure, and all through the night. It was now the following morning, and she'd turned away three or four trays of elaborate delicacies before being coaxed into eating half a bowl of fresh fruit for breakfast.

She'd asked for me when she'd woken, and I'd been sitting with her for around half an hour when Manda and Orlando arrived. I'd managed, by approaching the subject as you would a potential suicide on a high ledge, to find out that she denied categorically sending an email to Torquil the morning before.

I'd also got the distinct impression she might just be working her way up to telling me something important — something that scared her — and hadn't tried to hurry things. Now — with this interruption — I began to wish I'd pressed harder.

It was just after 10a.m. Torquil Eisenberg had been missing a little over twenty four hours with no ransom demand being made.

So far, we'd drawn one big blank when it came to answers. Parker had not managed to talk directly to Torquil's father the previous day. A man like that is not freely available at the end of a phone to anyone but his closest friends.

Parker had argued and cajoled his way up the food chain as far as one of Eisenberg's personal assistants before he met his match. By the sound of their one-sided conversation, she couldn't have blocked him any more effectively if she'd been in goal at an ice hockey match.

Ever discreet, my boss would only say that we had picked up Torquil's PDA, which he must have *mislaid* on the beach. I entirely understood Parker's reasons for being so circumspect but, put like that, it hardly shrieked of urgency, and was dismissed accordingly.

Eventually, he ended the call and shrugged. "I've done what I can at this point," he said, and only because I knew him well did I see the frustrated weariness beneath his controlled tone. "My instinct is to call in the FBI, but I can't do that without the family's say-so. It could be putting the kid at serious risk."

He left Joe McGregor on station as backup, which was no hardship. I'd worked with McGregor numerous times. A young black Canadian, his cheerful attitude belied solid combat experience and very good instincts.

Parker promised to keep us updated as soon as he had news, but we heard nothing for the rest of the afternoon and into the next day.

Now, the two girls came rushing in to offer Dina comfort, amid much fluttering and high voices. Orlando perched on the edge of Dina's bed, taking the girl's hands in hers and giving them a quick squeeze. I nodded to McGregor, who took one look at Dina's face and realised there was likely to be an outpouring of excessive female emotion. He flashed me a look that said, "All yours!" and went gratefully back to guard duty.

I stayed back and watched the three of the girls together for a moment, but it was difficult to read any new tension in Dina. She was already quivering like the wires of a suspension bridge in high wind. I wondered why. She hadn't responded this badly when the attempt on her at the riding club had failed. Why the dramatic reaction now? Unless she *had* been a party to the deception that had lured Torquil to his fate?

Manda was fussing round Dina, straightening the covers, talking nineteen to the dozen without giving Dina much of a chance to say anything in return. Manda looked as well groomed as I'd come to expect, but there was something about the butter-soft suede jacket she slipped out of and held carelessly in my direction — like she'd chosen it in a bit more of a hurry than usual. But I suppose that, for them, ten in the morning counted as being up at the crack of dawn.

I took the jacket without comment and dumped it across the back of an armchair. If she was expecting valet service, she was out of luck.

"I saw them coming and I . . . I thought they were coming for me," Dina said, her gaze unfocused, voice slightly reedy. "And I was frightened, after what happened to Raleigh, I —"

"Hush now," Orlando said, soothing. "You've had a shock. Try not to think about it. It's all gonna be OK. Tor's father and his people will do everything they can to get him back safe, you hear me?"

Dina moved her head in her direction, almost as though she was working on sound alone. "It could have been me," she whispered.

"Not with Charlie here to look after you, honey," Manda said, giving me a meaningful look to back her up on this one.

203

"I don't want to be taken," Dina said.

"You won't be," I told her.

"I —"

"Hush now, honey," Manda said firmly, leaning forwards and making sure Dina established and sustained eye contact. "You'll be quite safe. Nothing bad will happen to you, I promise."

Dina hesitated, then nodded, a fractional movement of her head. Orlando leant forwards and gently tucked a stray strand of hair out of Dina's eyes, smiling almost shyly.

Feeling like an intruder, I shifted my gaze to the window and the stunning view beyond it. The room was at the back of the house, overlooking the beach, but Dina rarely had the blinds pulled back to appreciate the view. I wondered if living with something beautiful all the time made you weary of it more quickly.

I'd been unable to offer this kind of sisterly comfort to Dina, and I doubted it was what she wanted of me. My instinct had been to tell her to pull herself together. She hadn't been physically injured, wasn't sick, so why hide herself away like an invalid?

But I hadn't voiced such thoughts. I could still remember a time when all I'd wanted to do was burrow long and deep. And hope, when I finally surfaced, the world as I knew it had simply gone away. It hadn't worked.

Behind me, Orlando was saying how they didn't want to tire her, that they'd just stopped by to see how Dina was doing. She gave her hands another quick squeeze and stood up.

"Get some rest, honey," Manda said, picking up her jacket. They kissed her cheek, headed for the door. I followed them out, collecting the silent bodyguard, and led the little party through the lower levels of the house. Manda and Orlando talked critically about how shaky Dina had looked, as if it never occurred to them that I might repeat their comments to her.

We emerged through the garages to the driveway where a big silver BMW sat at a rakish angle on the gravel, the driver still behind the wheel. He hopped out when he saw us approaching and opened the rear doors. The engine was already running to maintain the climate control — either for his passengers' benefit or his own.

"How did you hear about Torquil?" I asked before they could climb inside.

Orlando froze in the middle of digging in her handbag for her sunglasses, glanced at Manda. "His father called, asked if I knew where he was. He called all of us, I think," she said carelessly, and Manda nodded in agreement.

I tilted my head to take in the pair of them. "Is Torquil playing some kind of game with his father?"

"What do you mean by that?" Orlando demanded, flipping the designer shades in place. They were huge and very dark, with such ornate side arms it must have been like walking around in blinkers.

"It's not a difficult question," I said coolly, moving sideways so she'd have to step round me to get into the car. Out of the corner of my eye, I saw the bodyguard shift his position, caught the way Manda gave a tiny shake of her head to prevent him intervening, then asked with reluctance, as if she didn't really want to know the answer, "What kinda game?"

"The kind that might get taken too far."

"You don't think —?" Manda began, stopped and tried again. "You think he had something to do with his own kidnapping? That's crazy."

"Maybe it is." I shrugged. "But that doesn't mean it wasn't someone close to him."

"But . . . why?"

There was something just a little off about her responses, but I couldn't entirely put my finger on what exactly. Maybe it was just down to the fact that we'd never had the kind of relationship that involved exchanged views or confidences, and it was proving an awkward fit now.

Orlando gave a heavy sigh, tipping the glasses up onto the top of her head so she could confront me with a naked gaze.

"Look, Charlie, Tor's a weird kid. Life is just one big game to him," she snapped. "Who knows?"

"But you *do* know, of course," I said carefully, "that he likes to record what goes on aboard his father's yacht?"

That got a reaction I wasn't quite expecting. Orlando turned white then flushed scarlet. Her eyes darted sideways, as if looking for a viable escape route, or maybe just hoping for intervention from her friend. It wasn't forthcoming.

Orlando didn't quite scramble her way into the Bee-Em's rear seat, but it was as close as you could get without entirely abandoning her composure. Heedless of the danger to her manicured and painted nails, she grabbed at the interior door handle and yanked the door shut. If I'd been any nearer, I would have lost fingers.

The bodyguard with the broken nose didn't say anything, but made it clear that opening the door to speak to her further was not an option. I glanced at Manda. She shrugged and calmly walked around to the other side. The bodyguard waited a moment longer, just to make sure I got the hands-off message, then took the front passenger seat.

I stepped back as the car pulled away faster than it needed to, leaving little divots in the gravel. I watched the brake lights flare briefly before it turned out onto the street, then it was gone.

"Oh yeah," I murmured. "You know about that all right, don't you, Orlando?"

"Hey, Charlie!"

I turned. McGregor was standing in the open garage doorway, one hand on the frame and his cellphone open in his hand. "It's the boss," he said. "He wants you back at the office, a-sap."

I started to walk back towards the house. "Fine. What's the rush?"

"Apparently Mr Eisenberg's en route to the office. He wants to talk to you and Mr Armstrong," McGregor said, handing me the phone. "The kidnappers made contact."

It was nearly 10.30a.m. The kidnapping was almost exactly twenty-five hours old.

CHAPTER
TWENTY-EIGHT

Brandon Eisenberg swept into Parker's office three-quarters of an hour after his appointed time, with an entourage in double figures.

This included an icy blond woman in a lace-edged cream designer suit that seemed to emphasise all her hard edges rather than soften them. I had to look twice to recognise her as Nicola Eisenberg from the video clip Parker had siphoned off Torquil's PDA. It was tempting to mention the fact she looked different with her clothes on, just to see if the barb would penetrate that cool facade. Somehow, I doubted it.

Of the others, I noted the red-haired Gleason, still standing protectively close to her principal, but wearing a slightly less possessive face than she had done the night of the charity auction, when Eisenberg's wife was not in attendance.

Nicola Eisenberg had come with her own personal bodyguard, too. A solid-looking older guy who, I guessed, Eisenberg had selected as much for his middle-age and bland looks as for his experience.

The remainder of the party were assistants, and assistants to the assistants, and extremely high-priced legal people in handmade shoes. The latter were easy to spot by the way they mentally priced up the fittings through narrowed eyes as soon as they came in.

Leaving McGregor on guard with Dina, I'd travelled into Manhattan from Long Island by the fastest means possible after Parker's summons. That meant I'd used the Buell. Fortunately, it was a house rule to keep a spare business suit at the office, so while I couldn't remotely compete with the power couture on show as they all trooped in, I was at least no longer in my bug-splattered bike leathers.

Parker rose to greet them, urbane and radiating competent composure. Brief, forgettable introductions were made and he gestured the Eisenbergs to the low client chairs, clustered around a coffee table in the centre of the room.

There was seating for six in comfort, and hierarchy was quickly established by who got a seat and who was forced to stand. Eisenberg seemed slightly bored by the jockeying for position, as if people behaved like this around him all the time and he'd learnt simply to let them get on with it.

Nicola Eisenberg pretended not to notice. I understood she'd just flown in from Nassau, no doubt utilising the Lear 85 Torquil had mentioned so artlessly that day at the riding club. Maybe she was just suffering from executive-jet lag.

"So," Parker said once the dust had settled. "You wanna read us in?"

To my surprise, it was Eisenberg himself who took a long inward breath. He glanced momentarily towards the most senior-looking of the lawyers, sitting bald-headed and gaunt-featured to his left. The man stared back, inscrutable, which didn't seem to afford much by way of sound legal advice.

"I trust I can speak frankly and in complete confidence, Mr Armstrong?" Eisenberg said then.

Parker's eyebrow twitched at the implied slur to his reputation, that the man opposite had felt the need to ask. "Of course," was all he said, voice neutral.

"As you are no doubt aware, it seems that our son, Torquil, was kidnapped yesterday morning from a beach on Long Island."

"'It seems'?" Parker repeated. "An interesting choice of words, sir, considering one of my people witnessed the abduction."

The lawyers frowned collectively. Eisenberg ducked his head a little. "Relax, Mr Armstrong. I was not doubting that Miss Fox saw what she says she did, nor was I insinuating that the kidnap did not take place."

His gaze swept over me, standing behind Parker's desk where the light from the nearest window fell over my shoulder into the room. "I'm sure Miss Fox is aware of how highly I . . . value her skills," he added, and there was a tinge of regret and reproof in his tone, as if all this could have been avoided if only I'd accepted his job offer.

"You think he arranged his own abduction as some kind of prank," I said, just to watch the lawyers squirm. They didn't disappoint me. Nicola Eisenberg continued to look detached from the whole experience.

Eisenberg pursed his lips. "I can't say it didn't cross my mind at first."

As much to see if I could get a reaction out of his wife as anything else, I said, "What possible reason could he have for doing that?"

"I get my thrills from corporate finance, Miss Fox. Torquil? He's hooked on thrills, period. Like I say, at first I thought this might be his idea of another one."

Well, that explained their lack of urgency or action so far. "What's happened to make you change your mind now?"

"We received a package earlier today," he said, reaching into an inside pocket of his jacket and bringing out a clear case containing a recordable CD or DVD. He held it up over his shoulder and there was an unseemly scuffle behind him as two of the assistants hurried forwards to whisk it from his outstretched hand. The most senior — or the one with the sharpest elbows — took possession and carried the prize round the desk to Parker.

My boss eyed the unbagged evidence with concern, making no immediate moves to touch it. "How many people have handled this?"

"My security people have already checked it out thoroughly for prints, trace elements, biological or digital viruses — just about every damn thing you could think of, and a few more besides," Eisenberg said gravely, flicking his gaze briefly to Gleason. "They tell me it's clean. An ordinary DVD-R, the kind you can get at any office supply store across the state."

Parker nodded, and didn't ask the obvious question. If we wanted to know what was on the disk, clearly we were going to have to see for ourselves. He moved back around his desk and slotted the DVD into his laptop, his movements economical and precise.

It took a moment to load, then went straight into a video clip like the one from Torquil's PDA I'd watched the day before, but this was no sexual adventure. Not unless you were catering for a very specific and twisted audience.

I only recognised Torquil because that's who I was expecting to see. He was sitting on a steel-framed chair, ankles tightly bound to the front legs with wire. By the awkward hunch of his shoulders, his arms were secured behind him. He was wearing the same clothes he'd been taken in, now as torn and bloodied as their owner.

Someone with a professional interest in the job had worked him over very thoroughly indeed, I saw, falling back on detached clinical judgement to avoid a connection with the victim I could not afford to feel.

It took me back too easily to a time when I'd been the one taking punishment and, although they hadn't tied me down, in the end they hadn't needed to.

I swallowed, kept my face dispassionate, glanced across at Parker and found he was doing the same.

They'd paid particular attention to Torquil's face, probably knowing that would prove the most effective emotional lever against his parents. His nose had been broken and possibly a cheekbone, but it was hard to tell under all the discoloured swelling. One eye was puffed shut, the other open a mere slit. His hair was matted with blood. From the rigid way he held himself, the rapid shallow breaths, I guessed at busted ribs, too.

212

I looked up abruptly, found Eisenberg watching me as if in condemnation. Because I hadn't taken on the job of protecting his son, or hadn't stepped in yesterday, regardless of formal contract? It was hard to tell.

After maybe thirty seconds of silence, Torquil's head lifted slightly at some off-camera prompt. He swallowed with effort, running his tongue carefully over split lips before he spoke. Even with the volume cranked up, it was hard to catch his mumbled words clearly.

"Mom . . . Dad, I'm sorry," he said. "I'm . . . real sorry. For everything, I guess. I —" He broke off, cowered as if subjected to a sudden additional threat.

I glanced at the clock high on the far wall. It was now reading a few minutes after 12.30. Torquil was twenty-seven hours gone. For this recording to have been made and delivered by this morning, they'd worked on him hard and fast. It was a measure of what had been done that *wasn't* visible, that they'd broken him so utterly in so short a space of time. It must have been relentless.

On screen, Torquil hung his head, unable to continue for a moment. I strained to see past his battered figure into the room itself, but they'd spotlit the chair brightly. Beyond him were only dark shadows. Maybe Bill Rendelson, who'd become Parker's electronic surveillance expert, could finesse more detail from the background . . .

And that led to a rapid cascade of other thoughts and realisations, not least of which was why we were being shown this footage in the first place. My gaze flicked to

213

Parker again, filled with questions I didn't need to ask aloud. He shifted the cursor to pause the clip, straightened.

"Mr Eisenberg —?" he began, but Eisenberg was ready for him.

"Just watch the damn tape," he said quietly. "Watch it and then you'll know."

CHAPTER
TWENTY-NINE

Parker didn't immediately respond to that, just stared at Eisenberg across the expanse of desk and office. It was an interesting silent confrontation.

Here were two men, both with power and minutely aware of its extent, but Eisenberg's authority seemed wholly exterior by comparison to my boss. Parker was a natural leader, an intangible quality that came from something inside himself. Eisenberg, on the other hand, seemed to need the constant presence of his retinue as reassurance of his potency. I scanned their bland expressions and wondered if he knew how quickly they would desert him, should his fortunes ever wane.

We would have followed Parker anywhere without hesitation, but Eisenberg had to buy such loyalty. I hoped he kept the receipts.

At last, Parker lowered his gaze and clicked the mouse to resume the playback. Torquil's desperate gasps and murmurs filled the room again, eclipsing all other considerations.

"They say . . . you go to the cops . . . they kill me. You call in the FBI . . . they kill me. You delay . . . or try to double-cross them . . . or don't do *exactly* as they say

. . . they kill me, and you won't never find my b-body. Please — Mom . . . Dad — I'm sorry. I . . . just do what they want, OK?"

For the first time, I thought I saw Nicola Eisenberg close her eyes briefly.

The picture faded out to black, and the sound of Torquil's laboured breathing died away, replaced by an electronically synthesised voice.

"Listen very carefully, Mr Eisenberg. The price for returning your son intact is that fancy string of beads your wife flashes in public every chance she gets, to be delivered to a location of our choosing. You have until six-thirty tomorrow morning to make the arrangements. If you fail to comply, or involve the cops, you will start receiving body parts in the mail. There will be no negotiation and no second chances." There was a pause, then the cold mechanical voice added with a distinct sneer, "Oh, and one more thing — tell the Willners' little bitch of a bodyguard she makes the ransom drop. Nobody else. We'll be in touch."

I let out a long breath, slowly enough for it not to be audible. Nevertheless, Parker shot me a fast glance.

No!

What other options are there?

The clip had ended with the usual invitation from the software for a replay. We would replay it, I knew, over and over, looking for anything to suggest identity or location, but I didn't think any of us were ready for that quite yet.

"OK." I shrugged. "I'll make the drop."

Eisenberg's chief lawyer brightened at the prospect of a third party to shed some blame onto. Parker held up a hand that cut him off more successfully than any high court judge.

"Mr Eisenberg, just so's we're clear on this, what exactly is it you expect from us?"

Eisenberg made a gesture of tempered impatience. It was, no doubt, a question he himself would have asked, if the positions had been reversed. "It's simple — all we want is for Miss Fox to deliver the ransom." He gave us both a bleak stare. "I'll pay her what I have to, naturally."

"Let's not get ahead of ourselves here," Parker said quickly, before I could chuck that one back in Eisenberg's face. "How do you intend to handle this demand? Do you mean to negotiate?"

That got our first reaction from Nicola Eisenberg. She gave an explosive snort and threw up her hands, glaring at the entourage as if they'd forcibly gagged her up to that point.

"Negotiate?" she demanded. "You saw what was on that disk! You heard! You tell me, Mr Armstrong, if it was *your* son, how exactly would you plan to *negotiate*?"

Parker paused, as if making sure she was finished. "You rush into this, ma'am, and you'll surely regret it," he said. "But, you let them control things from the get-go, and you'll regret that all the more. In this kind of situation, paying up too fast can be as dangerous for the hostage as dragging your feet. How much is the Eisenberg Rainbow worth?"

"As a piece, it's priceless," Eisenberg said without modesty. "And too renowned to sell as a whole. But, if they broke it down into the individual stones they'd probably realise about five million on the black market."

I watched the slight wince as he spoke about the necklace being stripped for its parts. Interesting that the kidnappers had asked for something more than money, I thought. They'd picked something it would hurt him to give up, and that could not easily be replaced — like the boy himself.

"You think we give a damn about the money? Five million?" Nicola Eisenberg flicked her fingers as if at a troublesome mosquito. "That's just noise in the accounts for people like us."

That was about the time I decided I really didn't care for Mrs Eisenberg.

"But not for the kidnappers," Parker said quietly, his voice pleasant even though I could tell he shared my instant impression. "For them, it's a starting point. An amount so far out of reach they don't think they've a chance in hell of getting anywhere near it. You agree to pay without hesitation, without negotiation, and before long they start to wonder if they should have asked for more — a lot more. And that makes them angry. Who do you think they'll take that anger out on, ma'am?"

When she paled but didn't reply, I said, "If these are the same people who took the others, they accepted half their initial demand in the first two cases and the hostages were released unharmed. The problem came when the Benelli family dug their heels in too far, and

218

the kidnappers cut off Benedict's finger as a means of persuasion. Handling this successfully is a very delicate game, and Parker is an expert."

Had they made Benedict choose which one? Was that why he'd lost the finger that mattered least to his musical career, or was it purely down to luck?

I didn't mention the fact that although Manda reported rough treatment during her own captivity, the beating had not gone anywhere near as far as the one delivered to Torquil. The level of violence seemed to be increasing as the perpetrators went on, perhaps as they grew bolder with each successful kidnap. Or had Torquil done something special that the others hadn't? Despite his unlikely physique, he was into extreme sports, I recalled, and no coward. Had he tried to escape?

The experts reckoned that the best time to get away from potential kidnap was in the first few moments. At that point, you are an object of high value to your captors. They may ultimately kill you if the risk, or the fear of exposure, becomes too great, or they realise they aren't going to get their money. But at the point of contact they need you demonstrably alive.

After the initial window of opportunity has passed, the recommendation is that you should remain calm and compliant. Resistance is likely to earn punishment, just to keep you manageable. I could not imagine Torquil had taken easily to the concept of absolute obedience.

For most victims, their ultimate survival depends on the skill of the negotiator. Parker was patient and implacable, and had a growing reputation as one of the best. He had even, on occasion, managed to arrange the return of those kidnapped without any money changing hands. According to the statistics, only eleven per cent of hostages are released under those circumstances, and in the last year Armstrong-Meyer had been responsible for more than their share.

If their people had done their homework, the Eisenbergs would be well aware of those figures.

"Advise us," she said at last, shaping it as a command rather than a plea. Her eyes slid to her husband's stony face and when he offered no immediate objections, she added, "Hypothetically speaking, naturally. How would you *handle* this situation?"

Parker's expression clearly said he knew there was nothing hypothetical about it, but he answered anyway in an even tone. "When they next contact you, it will be by phone —"

"What makes you so sure?" butted in the chief lawyer, as if justifying his existence.

Parker nailed him with a studied glance. "Experience," he said, succinct. "They need to gauge your attitude, how far they can push, and they can't do that any other way. When they make contact," he went on, leaving a pointed gap in case the lawyer felt the need to jump in again, "you need to tell them you can't get your hands on the piece in time. You send it to London to be cleaned, I understand?" There were surprised nods. "Don't be afraid to sound stressed, worried. It's what they want. You need to make them feel you're doing everything you can to resolve this, but events are beyond your control. They need to be assured that they have you worried enough to comply in the end, even if they don't get everything they initially ask for."

Eisenberg pursed his lips, considering. "I have to admit, I hate the idea of giving in to these kind of threats," he allowed.

His wife snorted again. I was reminded of Dina's arrogant white horse, with half the elegance and none of the charm. "If it was some damned company takeover, you'd sure as hell manage to pay up with a smile on your face," she said in a bitter growl.

"Offer them a lesser piece from Mrs Eisenberg's extensive jewellery collection. Something with a value of say, one million, max," Parker said, doing his best to ignore the bickering. "Tell them it's a good offer for a couple of days' work. They know that the longer they have him, the greater the risk they take."

To an outsider, it must have sounded like Parker was being cheap for the sake of it, but there was a lot more to it than that, even if Nicola Eisenberg's reaction was one of outrage.

"You're suggesting we *bargain* for my son's life?" she said, her tone rising like etched glass.

Parker sighed. "Mrs Eisenberg, suppose you were . . . buying a property? You go in with a crazy low offer, expecting the owners to throw it right back at you. Instead, they fall over themselves to sign the contract. First reaction?"

Nicola Eisenberg frowned for a moment, but I could hear her brain whirring from across the room. "That there must be a catch," she admitted at length.

221

"That maybe there was something wrong with the place that we'd missed."

"And if there's nothing wrong with it?"

"I guess I'd assume the vendors were in a hole financially, and we could have gotten a better deal," she said, sliding a sideways look at the lawyers. "I'd stall, look for legal loopholes that would allow us to revise our offer, then nail their balls to the wall."

The lawyers, all male, shifted uncomfortably in their seats.

Parker waited, his expression bland, for the penny to finally drop, saw the second that it did. "Yeah," he said. "I'm not suggesting a bargain just for the sake of it, or because I have any intention of saving you money. I've had a lot of experience. I know how these people think and react. And, trust me, paying up their full initial demand, without a flicker, will not be a wise decision for your son's safety."

Eisenberg, however, merely glared at his wife. "You think I can't handle this?" he demanded. "I handle multimillion-dollar deals every day of the week. All we need is for the damn girl to make the drop."

"Oh, I know *precisely* what you handle —"

"Mr Eisenberg!" Parker cleared his throat. "You're an acknowledged expert in your field," he went on. "If I was looking to buy out one of my competitors, I'd want you on my team, but this, sir, is a whole different ball game . . ."

He didn't need to finish.

Eisenberg looked like he was still going to argue, but his wife put a hand on his arm, suddenly, squeezing the

222

cloth of his six-thousand-dollar suit with impossibly long fingernails painted blood-red. He glanced at her, the taut lines of her face, and a short silent battle of wills ensued. When it was over, his shoulders seemed more rounded than before. Nicola Eisenberg frowned, as if she'd rather fight with him in public than see him slouch.

"OK, OK," he said hollowly. "In that case, Mr Armstrong, I'd like to retain your professional services." He made a kind of general see-to-it gesture to the lawyers, who ducked their heads. He spread his hands in a gesture of submission, or maybe he was just trying to shake off his wife. "What do we do now?"

"We'll see what information can be gleaned from the DVD," Parker said. "See if we can get any leads as to where your son is being held and formulate a recovery plan, just in case."

"I will *not* sanction any action that might endanger him," Nicola Eisenberg said.

"It would be a last resort only," Parker agreed. "I assume you've considered calling in the FBI?"

That gained him a firm head shake. "You heard what they said. How could we be certain there'd be no leaks, in an organisation that size?"

Parker ignored the slur to the Bureau's integrity, asking instead, "Have you interviewed your son's security personnel?"

Eisenberg grunted. "Only to fire their asses," he said sharply. "Why — you think they might have had a hand in all this?"

"If they did, then keeping them on the payroll, where you can keep an eye on them — apply a certain amount of pressure if it came to that — might have been useful." Parker gave a grim smile. "And, if they turn out to be innocent, you could be assured of one thing — they would never let anything happen to the boy again."

CHAPTER
THIRTY

Parker's office seemed very empty after Eisenberg's hordes had departed. I watched the door close behind the last of the assistants' assistants and noted the way Parker's own shoulders dropped a little.

"They're the kind of high-profile clients we want to attract," he said ruefully, then shook his head. "But I don't mind admitting there's a lot about this job makes my spine itch."

Me, too.

"Hey, look on the bright side," I said, aiming for a light tone. "At least they're not likely to haggle over the fees."

Parker rubbed the side of his temple and gave me a weary smile. "You'd be amazed. These people didn't get to be rich by letting go of their money too easy."

I waited a beat, then asked, "Why didn't you give them Torquil's PDA?"

He let his arm drop. "I guess it's partly because I don't entirely trust them," he murmured, "and partly because I have a vested interest in making sure they don't try and screw us around on this one." And there was something abruptly intense and intent in his eyes. "Sean's relying on me to look out for you."

But I remembered that last dance, the night of the charity auction, and swallowed, suddenly uncomfortable, gauche, and unable to find anything remotely useful to do with my hands. I busied them collecting up some of the discarded coffee cups from the centre table, putting them on a tray next to the coffee pot. And either because my heart or my hands were clattering, I didn't hear Parker cross the room until he was very close behind me.

"Have you been to see him?" he asked.

I turned round too fast, found him too close. "I was going to slip over now, before I go back and take over from McGregor," I said. "Why — have you?"

"Yesterday." He hesitated. "Charlie, I've been talking to the hospital, and we may have some tough decisions to make, real soon, concerning Sean —"

I held up my hands, tried to keep the desperation out of my voice. "Parker, I know. I do. But . . . does it have to be now — while we're in the middle of all this?"

His lips twisted but there was no humour in them. "I seem to remember having a conversation very like this with you, one time before."

"I remember," I said softly. "And the same answer fits then and now — when this is over."

Gallantly, he didn't remind me how badly that decision had turned out. Instead, he nodded, stepped back, and I wasn't sure whether to be relieved or not when he let the subject go — for the moment, anyway.

"I don't like the fact the kidnappers asked for you specifically," he said. His tone was businesslike again, but he was frowning. "It smacks of vendetta."

"If it's the same crew who tried for Dina at the riding club, maybe I pissed them off more than I realised by getting in their way," I suggested.

"But you said yourself they were amateurs," Parker argued. "Everything about this one — the timing, the fake email — speaks of professional involvement."

"The guy with the Taser did not look as though this was his first time out, that's for sure."

"It's unfortunate Eisenberg got rid of Torquil's close-protection guys so fast," Parker said. "Whoever took the kid must have been watching him for days, maybe weeks beforehand. One of the team might have remembered a face, a vehicle, that didn't seem to be an overt threat at the time, but in retrospect . . .?"

"I would have sworn Dina wasn't being watched, either, but somebody still made a play for her, even if they did make a mess of it."

"Seems they've gotten better with practice."

"Yeah," I muttered. I moved away, restless, gathered up the last of the cups. Parker lifted them out of my hands with an impatient sigh.

"C'mon, Charlie, there is no way you are to blame for any of this," he said, his voice quiet but sharp, like the snapping of a twig in dry air. "Eisenberg's guys let the kid go down onto the beach unprotected. You did your job, but they sure as hell didn't do theirs. You could not have prevented Torquil being taken without leaving Dina vulnerable. For all you knew at the time, that's exactly what the kidnappers were hoping for."

I stepped round him and sank into one of the client chairs. "I know," I said, staring down at my hands. "But still . . ."

My train of thought trailed off as I caught sight of something pale cream stuffed down the side of the leather seat cushion. I pulled it out, found a gossamer-fine scarf that matched Nicola Eisenberg's suit, and realised this was where she'd been sitting.

Parker raised an eyebrow, and almost on cue came a knock on the door. He called for the visitor to come in, and the door was opened by Nicola Eisenberg's bland bodyguard. His principal walked through and gave him a meaningful nod. He stepped back outside the door and shut it again behind him.

"Ah," she said, seeing the scarf dangling from my hand. "I see you found it."

"What can we do for you, Mrs Eisenberg?" Parker asked, with no loading in his voice, but at the same time making it clear that he knew she'd engineered this excuse to return.

She had the grace to look momentarily disconcerted, but it was quickly replaced by her more familiar imperious manner.

"I want you to keep me informed of the negotiations — separately from my husband," she said, taking the proffered scarf without looking at me directly, and tucking it into her handbag.

Parker gave her a calm stare. She stared back.

"That is a somewhat unusual request," he said at last. "May I ask the reason for it?"

Her chin lifted, still haughty. "No, you may not."

"In that case, ma'am, I regret that as it's your husband who has engaged the services of this agency, he is officially our client. I report to him. I'm sure —"

She scowled, unused to being thwarted. "I'm concerned he may not have my son's best interests at heart," she cut in.

Parker's eyes flicked to mine. With every appearance of innocence, I asked, "This wouldn't have anything to do with Torquil's skills as a budding . . . cinematographer, would it?"

"What?" Her response held frustrated confusion rather than outrage. "What are you talking about?"

Parker walked back to his desk, slid open the central drawer, and took out Torquil's PDA. He powered it up, went through the menu, hit "Play" and put the PDA down on the desktop, swivelling it round so Nicola Eisenberg had no doubts about the content of the video clip. I was relieved that he'd turned off the sound.

Watching her face, I saw recognition of the device, and from the way she leant over, squinting at the small screen, that she was too vain to admit to a need for reading glasses. Perhaps that was why it took her a moment longer than it should have done to identify the who, what, where, but if I was expecting shame, I was disappointed.

Instead, she looked rather self-satisfied, as if we were seeing her at her athletic best. I got the feeling she would have found it far more embarrassing to have been snapped without make-up, in old workout sweats, than indulging in an energetic threesome in such luxurious surroundings.

"Well, it's nice to see all that damned exercise pays off," she said, reminding me all of a sudden of Caroline Willner.

"It would seem that your son made this recording while you were on your recent vacation in the Bahamas," Parker said. "It was sent to his PDA by remote feed, on the night of the charity auction at the country club."

"Ah . . . yes," Nicola Eisenberg said, as if, had he not narrowed down the precise date, she would have struggled to remember the experience among many others. Her gaze sharpened. "How did you get this?"

"Torquil dropped it — yesterday morning on the beach," I said, and explained about the messages Parker had left in his attempts to return it. "Your husband didn't ask for it, so it . . . slipped our mind," I said mildly, receiving a surreptitious wink from my boss by way of response.

"We understand that Torquil may also have been recording your husband's . . . activities on board the yacht," Parker said. "How would he react if Torquil threatened to go public with the footage?"

She laughed, a high brittle note. "Oh, my dear Mr Armstrong, it would never have come to that. Brandon would most likely have patted him on the head, praised his ingenuity, and given him a raise in his allowance."

"Really?" Parker said. "And yet Mr Eisenberg seems to set such store by his . . . reputation."

"We have an understanding, my husband and I," she said, letting her eyes trail up and down Parker's lean suited figure with insolent appraisal. "He doesn't

230

interfere in my life and I don't interfere in his." She moved round the desk towards him, ran a predatory finger under his lapel and murmured throatily, "Perhaps that's something we could discuss — say, over dinner."

"Mrs Eisenberg," Parker said easily, standing his ground, "right now it would seem *you* are the one who does not have your son's best interests at heart."

When she looked startled, I leant over and said helpfully, "What he means is, if you keep that up he'll tell both you and your husband to get stuffed — you can deliver the ransom yourself."

She threw me a vicious glare, face tightening unattractively, but snatched her hand back and whirled away.

Parker's face remained neutral, but I saw the flat-out amusement in his eyes. He let her take three or four huffy strides towards the door.

"When you said your husband would reward your son's blackmail attempts, is that because he's always done so in the past?" he asked, coolly objective. "Is that why he took this kidnapping so lightly at first?"

The questions stopped her dead. She turned slowly. "Yes," she said. "Torquil has a generous allowance, but you know how kids are these days. He always wanted more."

I thought of the elaborate and extravagant birthday party, the Bentley, the use of the family yacht and the executive jet, and wondered what "more" was out there to be had.

"So, you let him blackmail you," I said slowly. "And when his security reported that he'd been kidnapped, you assumed this was a variation on that theme."

"I know this looks bad." For the first time, she hesitated slightly. "We can't afford for the media to get a hold of the story," she added, flattening any hopes I might have had that this was a sign of surfacing maternal instinct.

"We are not in the habit of revealing details of our clients' private lives," Parker said stiffly, more insulted by that, I think, than by the pass she'd made at him. "Unless they're engaged in illegal activities, we'll protect them any way we can."

She paused at that, shifted her stance. "May I be totally honest with you, Mr Armstrong?"

I doubt she knows how. I didn't say the words out loud, but from the look on Parker's face, I didn't have to.

He inclined his head politely. "Of course."

She took a breath, flicked her hair back, then said baldly, "I am not convinced that my husband will go the extra mile to ensure my son's safe return. I want to be kept appraised of the situation so I can . . . step in, if I see the need. Whether you believe me or not, I *do* have my son's best interests at heart. Like I said, I'm not convinced Brandon feels the same way."

"He said he hates giving in to threats — is that all there is to it?" Parker asked, hitching his hip onto the corner of his desk and folding his arms. "Or does he have financial problems?"

232

She laughed at that. "Oh, no, Mr Armstrong. His only *problem* is that he really doesn't want to give it away to a bunch of crooks. Not for —"

She broke off suddenly. Honesty, it seemed, only went so far. The lines around her mouth deepened as she frowned.

"Not for what?" Parker asked. He sighed. "Mrs Eisenberg, you're asking my operative to risk her life making this ransom drop for you. I'm willing to let her do that, but only if you level with us," he said, his voice gentle, persuasive. "If you know something that affects how far your husband — or you — are prepared to go to ensure your son's safety, we need to know, and we need to know right now."

She brought her chin up, arrogant, defiant. "Torquil is not my husband's son," she said. "He wanted an heir but couldn't give me a child, so I made . . . alternative arrangements." She waited, furious, for our condemnation. When we stayed silent, she went on, clear and bitter, "And knowing it would not be his genes that carried on, he had that damned necklace commissioned in a bid for immortality — the Eisenberg Rainbow." Her lips twisted, derisive over the name. "Let's just say, given a straight choice between that and Torquil, Brandon wouldn't be heartbroken if he ended up with the jewels."

CHAPTER
THIRTY-ONE

Two hours later, just as I was leaving the rehab centre, my cellphone buzzed in the inside pocket of my leather jacket. As I pulled it out, I checked the display and saw the number for Parker's office line.

"Boss," I said, hanging my bike helmet on the mirror of the Buell while I dug for my keys. "Any news?"

"Our new clients are fools of the highest order," he said, and even filtered through layers of traffic in the background and the deficiencies of the phone's tiny speaker, I heard the anger tightly compressed into his voice.

I stilled, a cold pool forming at the base of my skull. "What have they done?"

"The . . . vendors just called them about the sale," Parker said, knowing I would catch exactly what he meant and highly sensitive to electronic eavesdropping on an open line. We could have been talking about anything from property to shares in a racehorse. "They agreed to pay the asking price."

"Shit," I muttered. "In full? Just like that?"

"Apparently, things got a little heated during the negotiations, and there was some screaming and shouting down the phone," Parker said in a

234

matter-of-fact tone that made all the hairs riffle along my arms. I could guess exactly what kind of screaming he was talking about. "They reckoned they couldn't afford to lose the sale, so . . . they caved."

"That's . . . unfortunate," I said, struggling to stick to the same neutral language. Completely on autopilot, I stuck the Buell's key in the ignition, turned it far enough to release the steering lock. "Where does it leave us?"

He sighed. "They went directly against my advice, Charlie, and put the whole deal in mortal jeopardy. I had no choice but to withdraw the agency's services." I heard the forced lightness in his voice. "Can't win 'em all, I guess."

"Oh," I murmured. *Mortal jeopardy*. Not words chosen lightly, I knew, and I could feel his anger and anguish at the risks they were taking with Torquil's life.

"My gut tells me this whole thing is gonna fall apart real fast," he said. "And when it does we can't afford to be anywhere near it if they're not prepared to work with us."

"I do understand — completely," I said. "All they want you to do is stick around to take the blame for their cock-ups. I suppose I would have made the same decision, for what it's worth."

"Thanks, Charlie, I appreciate that."

"What about . . . taking this further?" I asked carefully, knowing Parker would realise I meant the authorities, the police and FBI.

I could almost hear his head shake. "Considering the direction things are moving, nothing would make me happier, but you know as well as I do that we can't betray confidentiality like that." He paused. "I do need you to stop by the office on your way back, though," he said, apparently casual, but there was something off in his voice that caught at my senses.

"Of course. Problem?" Even as I spoke I knew, with a rising sense of dread, what he was going to say.

Oh, you have to be kidding me . . .

"They still want for you to handle the . . . exchange of contracts," he said, "but it's been arranged for tomorrow morning. I have explained to them you may not be available at that notice —"

"No, I'll do it."

Another sigh, a long pause, anguish. "They don't deserve such loyalty, Charlie. Like you just said, all they want is a scapegoat."

"Yeah, I know," I agreed. "But I'm not doing it for them."

As I snapped the phone shut, I checked my watch. It was two-thirty in the afternoon. Torquil had been at his kidnappers' tender mercies for twenty-nine hours.

CHAPTER
THIRTY-TWO

By 6.00a.m. the following morning, after a restless and largely sleepless night, I was beginning to question the wisdom of my decision.

Parker and I were sitting in the large office suite in the basement of Brandon Eisenberg's gothic mansion just outside Southampton, up towards the eastern end of Long Island, drinking coffee with Gleason, who turned out not simply to be Eisenberg's bodyguard, but also his head of security.

Gleason's attitude did not seem to have softened towards me since the night of the charity auction. I don't think she'd forgiven her boss for offering me a job, or Parker for failing to extend the same courtesy towards her. But, she was professional and polite, dressed in a mannish dark-blue suit with wide lapels. To me, the outfit screamed authority and insecurity in equal measure.

Now, Gleason ran us through the detailed instructions the kidnappers had left, including playing the recording made of their last telephone conversation with Eisenberg.

She played the whole thing in full, including the part where they brought Torquil to the phone and persuaded him to speak. As I listened to the boy's gargled screams, I felt Gleason's cool gaze soaking up my reaction. I was careful to show her nothing more than a frown of concentration. It took effort to hold it in place. Parker's expression, I noticed, was a mirror of my own.

"We'll call again at six-thirty tomorrow morning," said the mechanised voice. "Have the girl ready to answer. She'll be given precise instructions on where to go first. She comes alone and I hope she's in shape, because if she misses one single rendezvous by more than half a minute, the kid's dead." Then, with a click of finality, the line followed suit.

Gleason sat back in her executive swivel chair, rocking slightly, and regarded me over the steam rising from her insulated coffee mug. "So, Charlie, you in good shape?"

"I manage," I returned equably. "And besides, there's the Buell."

The only bit of personal information the security chief had shared with us was that she was from East Troy, Wisconsin, where Erik Buell had his motorcycle factory and, in Gleason's voiced opinion, it was a damned shame they didn't make them anymore.

At that moment my Buell Firebolt sat in one of the garages that lined the motor court to one side of the house, rubbing shoulders with two Lamborghinis, three Aston Martins, a Ferrari, a classic Morgan, and a Bugatti Veyron. I could see the lowly little Buell among them on one of the many monitors Gleason's people were watching down here.

238

Parker wasn't happy about me using the bike, but there were a lot of arguments in favour, not least of which was the time restriction the kidnappers had stressed. Logically, it was the only way to guarantee cutting through traffic to make what promised to be the first of many rendezvous points. Keeping me constantly on the defensive and operating at full stretch was standard procedure for these people.

The Buell's engine was warmed through and it had a full tank of fuel. Sean's Glock 21 was taped securely behind the front fairing, just as a backup.

I'd hesitated, when I'd gone to the gun safe in the apartment, about taking Sean's gun. Apart from cleaning it, unloading it, and putting it away, the last time I'd handled it in anger was three months ago, when I'd taken it from his hand and come within a hair's breadth of using it to kill the man who'd shot him. When I'd lifted the Glock out of its case yesterday evening, an echo of that time and place had shivered through me.

Forsaking my usual line of sober suits when coming into contact with clients, this morning I'd put on my leather bike jacket and Kevlar-reinforced jeans, which would be easier to move in than full leathers if I had to run. Under the jacket, in place of its winter lining, I wore the latest covert body armour, complete with thin polycarbonate sheets for an extra layer of protection. For the sake of mobility and stealth, I had rejected the optional ceramic trauma plates front and back. If we were up against weaponry of a calibre heavy enough to warrant them, I was probably fucked anyway.

For weaponry of my own, I had my usual SIG 9mm in the small of my back, and a KA-BAR combat utility knife taped, hilt downwards, to the outside of my boot. The kidnappers had not specified that I should go unarmed, and I intended to make full use of that oversight.

Gleason had already explained to me how their comms system worked, but I'd taken in no more than I needed to in order to operate it on the fly. The dual in-ear earpieces fitted neatly underneath my helmet, small and comfortable, and she produced a tactical throat mic to go with them. This had the advantage that I could use it hands-free on the bike, and it would stay with me if I was forced to go walkabout.

The throat mics I'd used in the past had all sat high and tight under my jaw, but we checked this one would pick up acceptably when it was placed down nearer my collarbone instead. At first glance it would be hidden there by the tube scarf I usually wore on the bike to prevent both wind and wildlife from disappearing down the neck of my jacket.

It was high-grade 'ware and they reckoned the range was plenty good enough to reach back to the situation room here, unless the kidnappers were planning on taking me practically out of state. Gleason had assigned four mobile teams. This would allow them to track me while hanging back far enough not to make themselves too obvious.

Gleason fitted my gear herself, under Parker's watchful eye. I saw the security chief's eyes flick over the last remnants of the scar around the base of my throat as she was adjusting the mic, but if she recognised the old knife wound for what it was, she wisely passed no comment.

"OK, you're all set," she said when she was done.

I checked the clock again. "So, where's the glitter?"

"Here."

I turned, found Brandon Eisenberg standing in the doorway. The billionaire looked a lot less urbane than he had done on the night of the charity auction, but I couldn't hold that against him under the circumstances. He did seem genuinely scared for the boy who bore his name, if nothing else. Gripped tightly in his fist was an expensive-looking rucksack, as though he couldn't bear even to deliver a ransom in some cheap tourist luggage.

"It's in there," he said, his voice an unhappy mix of defiance and strain.

From the way Gleason stared at her boss, I assumed there had been words between them about the wisdom of paying what they asked for, and that she hadn't approved this tactic. I suppose that Eisenberg had succeeded for so long by throwing money at a problem until it went away, that he now couldn't conceive of any other course of action.

For a moment, I thought he was going to say something profound to all of us, but in the end he just handed over the rucksack, turned on his heel, and departed.

Gleason unzipped the bag and checked inside. The Eisenberg Rainbow was in a flat padded box, lined with black velvet that separated the individual strands and set off the stones to their most alluring sparkle. It still looked like paste to me. It seemed a very small box to be worth so much money.

The sudden buzz of the designated phone on the nearest desk made me start, even though we'd been expecting it. I waited a couple of rings, took a deep breath, and picked it up.

"Hello?"

"You the English bitch?"

You better believe it, sunshine. "Oh, hell yes."

The laugh sounded like two rough metal plates grinding together. I winced. He mentioned somewhere called Turtle Cove at Montauk Point. "Just south of the lighthouse. You know how to get there?"

I glanced at Gleason. She nodded. "I'll find it."

That unnatural laugh again. "You better. You've got thirty minutes."

Click.

As I put the phone down and hit the stopwatch on my wrist, I was already on my feet, reaching for my helmet. Parker was by my elbow all the way. He didn't speak, but he didn't have to. It was, I realised, enough to have him there. Gleason was on the other side, giving me immediate instructions and telling me they'd guide me to my location.

I glanced at her. "GPS tracker in with the necklace?"

She nodded. "And another in your comms gear, just in case the two of you become . . . separated."

"I thought that was the whole idea?"

"The teams will keep station in a rolling diamond formation around you," she said, ignoring the question.

242

"They'll stay at least a half mile from your position at all times."

I shrugged. "Just make sure they don't scare this guy off."

"They won't."

Parker helped me into the rucksack and tightened the shoulder straps in place. I checked I could still access the SIG beneath it.

"Good luck, Charlie," he said softly.

I grinned at him, threw my leg over the bike, twisted the key and hit the starter. "Just be ready to intervene if some bloody traffic copper decides to pull me over for speeding," I said, and toed the Buell into gear.

I rolled out through the open garage door and down the driveway, taking a moment to settle myself, then hit the street and caned it.

Torquil had been taken forty-five hours, just short of two full days. With any luck, we'd have him back before that milestone was reached.

Through the earpieces, I could hear the tense comms traffic, the brief relayed instructions to the chase teams, who had started out wide and were now converging on the location we'd been given as the first rendezvous point. Gleason's directions were calm, clear and concise, to keep straight or turn, as one set of traffic lights or another flashed past. The four teams had to hustle to keep pace and maintain the gap around me. Well, that was their problem. I wasn't going to miss a deadline waiting for them to play catch-up.

I was moving through the middle of Southampton village, the leafy streets lined with upmarket boutiques and bistro cafés. I even passed a sign warning all persons they were required to wear proper attire on the streets. I had two guns, a knife, body armour and a bike helmet. That sounded like proper attire to me.

Ahead of me, a set of traffic lights at an intersection hopped up to amber, then red. The street was still quiet at this hour, but I eased off anyway.

"We have you slowing down, Charlie," Gleason's voice said in my ear. "Problem?"

"Just traffic lights, just traffic lights," I said, making sure the voice-activated mic caught my words. "If you want me to jump them, you're going to have to pay my tickets."

"No need to attract any unwanted attention if you don't need to," Gleason said. "You're looking good on time. Just —"

A voice I didn't recognise cut straight across whatever she'd been about to say, louder in my earpieces. "All teams, hang back. Repeat, hang back!"

"Who gave that order?" Gleason snapped. "Identify yourself!"

I heard an engine turning lazily along the street behind me, glanced over my left shoulder and saw a big four-door family Dodge roll up slowly towards the lights, which were still on stop.

I turned back facing front, toed the Buell into first gear with the clutch in, ready to make a clean getaway as soon as red dropped to green.

Come on, come on! What's taking so long?

And then all hell broke loose in the form of high-frequency white noise flooding the comms

244

network. I let go of the clutch and the bike lurched and stalled under me, but that was the least of my worries. I was too busy scrabbling for my helmet strap, my only thought to get the pain out of my head.

Even above the horrendous volume in my earpieces, though, I heard the rising howl of the Dodge's engine, felt the rumble through the road surface. I opened my eyes and jerked my head round, just in time to see the car pick up speed and swerve straight for me.

"Ambush, ambush!" I yelled into my useless radio. Then all I could do was hope to survive.

CHAPTER
THIRTY-THREE

A moment before impact, I yanked my left leg upwards. The front end of the Dodge hit the side of the bike's frame just about where my knee would have been, and kept on coming.

The Buell was whipped viciously sideways by the force of the collision. Weighing less than one of the car's axles, it never stood a chance. As I hiked my leg up over the tank, the bike started to disintegrate under me, scattering aluminium and plastic like shrapnel. And all the time, the dreadful screeching noise drilled into my brain.

I never had a second's suspicion that this was a simple traffic accident. I didn't need to flick my eyes to the two occupants and see the ski masks covering their faces, but I did it anyway, just to be sure.

Then I was hitting the ground hard enough to jolt the air out of my lungs, the bike partially on top of my right leg as we skated across the asphalt. The Dodge's horns were locked into the tangled machine that had once been my pride and joy and it wasn't letting go.

Bastards, bastards, bastards!

There was nothing I could do to stop being ploughed across the deserted intersection, so I kept my arms and head tucked in as much as I could to avoid injury and waited until they deemed I'd gone far enough. There wasn't a whole hell of a lot else I could do.

Fortunately, the jacket and jeans and boots I was wearing had been designed with just this kind of road contact in mind. They kept skin and bone intact, so when we finally slid to a stop almost at the far kerb, the only damage was to my nerves and my temper.

My right foot was still pinned by the bike, which itself was half underneath one of the vehicle's front wheels. I kicked at it with my left leg, but I was totally trapped. Heart pounding, hands suddenly cold as fear squirted adrenaline into my system and primed my body to run, the only course left to me was to fight. I scrabbled for the SIG, but I was lying awkwardly, sprawled on my back, and the way the rucksack had been dragged underneath me as I'd been scraped along the asphalt meant I couldn't quite get my fingers to the gun. I reached for the KA-BAR instead, ripping it free of the tape that held it in place to my boot.

The car doors slammed and two figures converged from either side, looming over me. The driver raised his arms, hands clasped. I had a flash image of Torquil's paralysed fall on the beach, and instinctively knew what was coming.

Oh shit — not again . . .

The last time I'd suffered direct contact with a Taser I had not enjoyed the experience. It was only as the driver's hands tightened that I realised he had something altogether more permanent in mind.

And then he shot me.

Even with body armour, taking a round to the chest at close range hurts like a bitch. I dropped the knife and doubled around the point of impact, gasping. The second man stepped over the ruined tail of the bike, kicking the KA-BAR away as he did so, and slashed through the straps of the rucksack, dragging it off my shoulders roughly. They backed away.

Ironically, removing the rucksack freed up my access to the SIG. Still panting, I snaked a hand behind me and freed the weapon, but the two men were already out of eyeline beyond the car's bonnet, climbing back inside. I couldn't even see the windscreen from down there, so I went for the softest available target, putting four rounds straight through the front grille.

The engine was hot, the coolant system under pressure. The rounds punctured the radiator and sweet yellow-green antifreeze sprayed out like blood. As the Dodge reversed rapidly, bumping down off the mangled remains of the Buell, at least I had the satisfaction of knowing the wounds I'd just inflicted on the car in return were mortal.

I tracked its retreat with the SIG, firing into the glass as soon as it became visible. The vehicle lurched into a messy J-turn and gained speed. I kept firing until the slide locked back on an empty mag, then snatched up the Glock from behind the broken front fairing, but stayed my hand.

The Dodge was too far for legitimate damage, and even though the street had been deserted when the ambush began, the sound of gunfire had brought people to windows and doorways. The chance of hitting bystanders was too great.

I let the muzzle of the Glock drop, dumped it into my lap and finally wrenched off my helmet and dragged the screaming earpieces out. The whining buzz continued, but at least my ears weren't actually bleeding. Neither was my chest, although it felt like they'd hit me with a damn truck. I took a deep breath and satisfied myself that, whatever the undoubted bruises, the armour had absorbed the impact without cracking any bones in the process.

The bike didn't want to release me. My boot was staked by some part of the frame underneath, and from that angle I couldn't lift it off me single-handed. I stretched across to turn off the ignition and patted the tank, regretful. Like a faithful warhorse who'd seen its last battle, it lay tangled on top and around me, bleeding fuel and lubricant in a slimy trail into the gutter as it died. Now I thought about it, I was bloody lucky I hadn't ignited any of it.

I was still lying like that ninety seconds later, when the first of Gleason's chase teams reached me.

CHAPTER
THIRTY-FOUR

Long before the cops arrived, Gleason's men scooped me — and what was left of the Buell — off the road, but that didn't mean they had my best interests at heart. In fact, once I was back in the situation room at Eisenberg's place, the whole thing turned into more of another hostile interrogation. I supposed, with something worth a minimum of five million in play, they had every right, but I was glad of Parker's presence more than ever.

As if in response to my quip about his lack of faith, made that day at the Willners' place, he stayed close while Eisenberg's in-house medic checked me over and pronounced me remarkably fit, under the circumstances. When they peeled me out of the body armour, I collected the stopped round from the lining. It was a .380 with a light load behind it, if the relatively minor dent in the inner polycarbonate sheet was anything to go by. Anything heavier calibre, or higher grain, and I would have cracked a rib at the very least.

Of course, to begin with this seemed to Gleason's suspicious mind less like a lucky escape and more like complicity with the kidnappers on my part. I went over every second of what happened for her, again and

250

again, from the moment the traffic lights at the intersection turned against me, to the Dodge's slightly limping departure.

It was hard to keep my temper while all this was going on. There was a large digital clock on the wall above the bank of monitors, and I watched the minutes flip over, one after another, while Gleason and I went round in combative circles.

Meanwhile, Torquil's period of captivity stretched past forty-eight hours and into its third day. Still they were refusing to call in the authorities, despite my and Parker's urging. I don't know if Gleason was truly protecting her employers' privacy and interests, or if she was hoping she could present the FBI with a fait accompli — one which included me in the bag.

And then the CCTV footage came in.

I've no idea how Gleason managed to get hold of it ahead of the police, but could only guess it was a measure of how far Eisenberg's influence stretched. Even Parker allowed himself to raise an impressed eyebrow.

The footage was not high quality, but considering the whole of Eisenberg's supposedly secure comms system had been effectively jammed from the instant the white noise kicked in, it was the only proof I'd got that things had gone down the way I'd claimed.

The camera had been mounted high, looking into the mouth of the intersection with both sets of traffic lights clearly visible, so anyone who jumped the lights could be shown irrefutable proof of their guilt. It couldn't have been better placed to capture everything that happened.

Gleason's techs had already isolated the relevant segment. It began just as the lights flicked to amber and then red ahead of me, and the Buell came into view a few seconds later. I watched myself cruise to a halt in the bottom right-hand corner of the screen and put my feet down. I was obviously tense, head ducking to check my mirrors as I heard the vehicle behind me. I saw me put the bike into gear, ready, just as the nose of the Dodge came into view at the extreme edge of the picture.

"Stop it there, please," Parker said suddenly. He stood, moved closer to the screen and turned back. "What's wrong with this picture?"

Gleason shrugged. "You tell me."

"The lights," Parker said. "They've gone to red for Charlie, but they haven't changed at the cross-street. See — still on red. Whoever did this had control of the lights."

Gleason's eyes narrowed, but then she nodded slowly, reluctantly. She pressed the remote and I could spot the instant the jammer kicked in, even without the sudden spike to the video that must have coincided with it.

On the screen, my body jerked and went rigid. I let go of the bars and barely kept the bike upright as it stalled, wrestling unsuccessfully with my helmet as if it had suddenly melted red-hot to my head. The Dodge's bonnet soared as the driver floored the throttle to ramming speed, and ran it full tilt into the side of me.

From up there, it looked impossible that I'd got my leg out of the way in time. The bike was hurled sideways, skittering halfway across the intersection with me first tumbling off backwards and then underneath it. I heard a quiet intake of breath from Parker as the Dodge seemed to be doing its best to climb on top of both of us.

The way the car drove me down was nasty for being so obviously deliberate. They must have kept going until I'd disappeared from view under the front end. The only thing that stopped them then was probably the fear they might not be able to separate me from the jewels.

On screen, I was struggling for the SIG, then reached for the KA-BAR knife as the men leapt out. And I saw the totally calm way the driver shot me as the passenger scuttled round to retrieve the rucksack.

Parker waved again and Gleason stopped the tape without needing to be asked. "This was a very well-timed operation," Parker said, face taut. "They must have had the jammer with them in the car to have reacted so fast. They were moving almost *before* the interference began." He picked up the remote himself, ran the footage back a little to watch my shooting again, his gaze hard and coolly objective.

"The driver is the one in charge. He showed no doubts, no hesitation. He can't have known Charlie was wearing a vest, and yet he went for a body-mass shot without hesitation." His eyes slid to me. "I think, if you'd managed to get your helmet off before they hit you, he probably would have gone for a head shot instead. He didn't want to miss."

"But the passenger flinches when the gun fires," Gleason said, not to be outdone. "And everything about his body language says he's afraid of the guy with the gun. Like, if he gets out of line, he'll get a bullet, too."

Parker nodded and pressed the remote again.

I was mildly gratified to see that I had my own weapon out before the men had managed to get back into the Dodge, that I was pouring shots into the front end of the car as it reversed off the wreckage of the Buell, the action of the SIG cycling rapidly, gases spurting the dead brass out alongside me. I saw the spreading dark pool from the Buell's ruptured fuel system, and realised again how lucky I'd been not to catch fire.

The car swerved round to roar away into one of the cross-streets. The passenger side was closest and, cynically, I wondered if the cold and calculating driver had deliberately put himself furthest away from the gunfire.

"You got him, Charlie," Parker said with grim satisfaction as the car disappeared. "If we run it back a few seconds you'll see that jerk — *there*. Just as the side glass disintegrates. I think that was a hit."

"Can we zoom in on the car a second?" Gleason said over her shoulder to one of the techs.

The picture froze, rewound again, and jumped to close-up, focusing on the passenger side window as the glass blew in from the first shot. In slow motion, I saw the passenger flinch back twice. Once from the shock of the flying glass, lifting his arms to protect his masked head, and the second time with the distinct involuntary snap as a round caught him.

I had another rapid full-colour flashback. The way Sean had jerked as the bullet struck the side of his head. That same dancing twitch.

"Oh yeah, she got him," Gleason murmured with a satisfaction that sickened me. She paused, eyes flicking me up and down. "Good job."

"No, it wasn't," I said tiredly, getting to my feet and discovering I ached from my ears downwards. "If we'd got the kid back, kept hold of the Eisenberg Rainbow, and caught the bastards, *that* would have been a good job. This was just a bloody disaster."

CHAPTER
THIRTY-FIVE

By the time I climbed stiffly into the front passenger seat of one of the agency Navigators alongside Parker, I was feeling thoroughly beaten up.

It was five-thirty in the evening. Torquil had been missing fifty-six hours and counting.

When we left the house, there had still been no word from the kidnappers with the boy's location. Nicola Eisenberg had thrown a fit of hysterics and had to be sedated. Her husband didn't look in much better shape.

The GPS tracker had led the chase teams to the still-burning wreck of the Dodge, two miles from the scene of the ambush. It was highly unlikely that the men responsible had gone to all that trouble to grab the necklace, only to set it alight shortly afterwards. We had to assume they'd found the tracker and abandoned it with the car.

"They're not going to release him, are they?" I said as Parker steered us out onto the main road.

He glanced over at me quickly, as if to judge how badly I was likely to take it.

"No," he said, voice flat. "I don't think so."

I absorbed that one in bitter silence for a moment, then asked, "Who knew about the ransom arrangements?"

Parker shrugged. "Gleason, her staff, the Eisenbergs, possibly their household staff, too. Hell, apparently Mrs Eisenberg kept her appointment with the pro at the tennis club yesterday afternoon, just so's no one suspected there was anything out of the ordinary going on. For all we know, she could have let it slip to half the membership." He put out a gush of breath, frustrated to be involved in such a peripheral role, with no influence over major decisions. "Just about everyone at the meeting yesterday knew you'd agreed to be the courier. Doesn't take much to work out you'd be leaving the house with a priceless object."

"They went to a lot of trouble — so why didn't they disable the traffic cameras?"

"Pride, would be my guess," Parker said. "They thought they could get away with it, quick and slick, and they didn't care who knew about it after the fact. They both had masks on, the car was stolen and on fake plates. I reckon they planned on torching it when they were done anyhow, even before you shot out the coolant system."

"For all the good it did," I murmured with a sigh. "I think you're right, but I get the feeling it goes deeper than that. It's not quite that they didn't care who saw it. I think they actually *wanted* Eisenberg to watch them walking away with his money, easy as pie. There was something . . . I don't know . . . almost *gloating* about the whole thing."

His eyes slid away from the road ahead for a moment. "Didn't count on you running interference, though, did they?"

I gave a hollow laugh. "I rather think that you calling my going down under their front wheels 'interference' is on a level with trying to bruise someone's knuckles in a fight by repeatedly thumping them with soft parts of your body," I said dryly.

"These people were pros." Parker shook his head. "Which doesn't square with the guys who tried for Dina at the riding club. You said yourself they were amateurs. Not the kinda guys who would know how to manipulate the lights at an intersection, or jam Gleason's comms network."

"So, maybe they've called in reinforcements. The guy with the gun definitely wasn't one of the two at the riding club." I rubbed my eyes. "And if they're such pros, why haven't they released the boy?" I demanded wearily. "I can't help believing they never really intended to let him go, just like they never intended to run me ragged all over Long Island this morning. I think they were always planning to hit me hard and fast, the first opportunity they got, and it worked like a charm."

"Don't second-guess it," Parker cut across me, savage in his softness. "If you'd put up more of a fight, you'd have more holes in you now, and some of them might even have gone right through."

"I can't help but wonder what would have happened if I'd avoided the ambush, and the chase teams had closed on my last-known position, and I'd made it to

Montauk Point inside the time. I mean, had they even bothered to lay in another rendezvous point from there, or was it all a con from the start? What was so special about the place, by the way?"

Parker opened his mouth to respond, then shut it again, frowning. Before I could go on, he'd thrown the Navigator into an abrupt U-turn. I held onto the door pull and waited until the unwieldy vehicle had wallowed back onto an even course before I risked a question.

"Jesus, Parker! What the hell are you doing?"

But my boss had his foot hard down on the accelerator, weaving through the sparse traffic like he was on the last lap of a Grand Prix. "You asked what would have happened if you'd got to Montauk Point," he said, jaw tight with a mix of concentration and anger. "But the answer is we don't know, because after you were hit, Gleason didn't bother sending anyone there to find out."

That cold feeling of fear came over me again. "Please tell me you're kidding."

Parker shook his head, and after that I didn't ask any more stupid questions, just left him to drive.

Getting to Montauk Point proved easier said than done. Most of the road out there was single-lane in each direction, crowded with trees, and undulating enough to make overtaking almost impossible.

"There's no way I could have made it out here in thirty minutes, even on a bike," I said, remembering the kidnappers' deadline. "They must have known that."

Parker nodded. "In a perverse kinda way, that should make you feel a little better," he said. "Knowing this was a set-up from the start."

It didn't.

Eventually, we hit the dead-end loop at Montauk, marked by an old-fashioned white lighthouse with a strange brown band round the middle of it. Parker jerked the Navigator to a stop at the base of the shallow incline that led up to the lighthouse itself, ignoring the half-empty parking lot on the other side of the road.

"What's here?" I demanded, aware of an elevated heart rate, a dry mouth. "What was I supposed to do when I got here?"

"Maybe there was no *afterward*," Parker said, his voice grim. "Maybe this is where you were supposed to find Torquil."

I snapped him a fierce glance. "Was that before or after I disentangled myself from what was left of my bike?"

He didn't respond to that, just reached for the door. "There are two beaches on either side of the point," he said. "You want north or south?"

I shrugged, still unconvinced. "South."

We parted company. I jogged back along the edge of the road to a path that led through a wooded area, where a sign promised I would find Turtle Cove. It sounded a lot more picturesque than it was, turning out to be a small crescent-shaped beach with a stony shoreline below golden sand.

I stood for a moment, shading my eyes with a hand. The breeze was brisk, crashing the ocean onto the rocks

260

that surrounded the base of the lighthouse. There were a few hardy souls fishing from them, casting out into the surf like they were trying to whip back the sea. Apart from that, I had the beach to myself.

I tried to jog along the beach, but the sand was soft and heavy. I justified my lack of energy with the excuse that I'd crashed and been shot already today.

I only found the bucket because I was looking at the shoreline and I damn near tripped over it. A child's red plastic bucket, like they use for sandcastles, upturned high above the tideline. It rattled against something when I kicked it, and when I bent and lifted it up, I found a length of grey pipe sticking out of the sand beneath.

"Oh shit," I whispered, fumbling for my cellphone. Parker answered almost before it had time to ring out, and when I spoke, my lips seemed numb. "Parker, get over here. I think I've found something . . ."

I snapped the phone shut again without waiting for his reply, grabbed a piece of nearby driftwood, and began to dig.

It was just after six-fifteen, the evening warm but with a sharpening wind. Almost fifty-seven hours after Torquil had been kidnapped.

Dig, twist, throw . . .

CHAPTER
THIRTY-SIX

"Torquil's dead," I said.

The words sounded curiously flat and emotionless, even to my own ears. I had just walked into the living area at the Willners' house, soiled and ragged from hours spent with numerous cops and medics and crime scene techs. If the Eisenbergs had tried to avoid the authorities before, they were neck-deep in them now.

The local and state police had been quickly followed by men in aggressive suits with aggressive haircuts and equally aggressive personalities, who were probably FBI agents or something similar. They'd told me, no doubt, but after a while the IDs they waved under my nose all began to blur together.

Not for the first time, I was glad of Parker's calm presence. When it came to dealing with people like that, he had played the game for a long time.

I needed a very long, very hot shower, and to crawl straight from there into bed, but by the looks of it I was a long way from either.

Now, a small collective intake of breath greeted my news, but by then they must have been expecting the worst. By the time I reached the Willners' place, with every outside light blazing, it was dark — way on the wrong side of midnight and almost back round into morning again.

I confess I'd harboured a vain hope that the household would be safe asleep by the time I got in, and I could put off the whole wretched business of explanations until the morning. I was so tired my vision had started to shimmer around the edges, and it was easier to list the parts of my body that didn't hurt, rather than those that did. I should have known I was onto a losing streak.

Parker had tried to convince me to go back to Manhattan with him for what remained of the night, make the return trip out to Long Island when I'd had a few hours' sleep — maybe even take a day to myself. Reading between the lines, I knew he was trying to save me from having to be the one who broke it to Dina, and though I appreciated the gesture, I couldn't shirk that responsibility.

As it was, I ended up with everyone else's share of it, too.

Dina wasn't alone in the living room. She was sitting in the chair her mother favoured with its back to the view. After today, I might be joining her in not wanting to face that expanse of sandy beach.

Opposite Dina, on the leather sofa Parker and I had shared during our first visit, was Manda Dempsey, with Benedict sprawled alongside her. Hunt and Orlando were together on another sofa, which had been arranged at right-angles to make chatting easier. They didn't look like they'd been doing much of that.

So, the gang's all here.

263

As soon as I came in, everybody got to their feet and watched me approach with varying degrees of apprehension. Perhaps there was a little disgust thrown in there, too. I was filthy and I stank, and I recognised that I was not likely to be at my tactful best. Hence my opening statement, and their reaction to it.

Maybe I should have taken Parker's advice after all.

Nevertheless, I skimmed their faces out of habit, seeing expressions of shock and surprise, but there was something just a little off about them. Maybe, if I hadn't been so bloody tired, I might have worked out what that was.

The security personnel who habitually accompanied the various members of this group had positioned themselves in the outer reaches of the room, maintaining a perimeter. They eyed me, coldly assessing, judging my abilities purely on the results I had obviously failed to achieve.

Over in the far corner by the edge of the windows, Joe McGregor stood quietly, inconspicuous and self-contained. He appeared to be taking absolutely no notice of whatever stilted conversation had been going on in that room before I turned up, but I knew I'd get the full rundown from him later. He made eye contact and gave me a fractional nod — of condolence or support, I wasn't sure which.

Right now, I'd take whatever I could get.

"Did he —?" Dina began, and swallowed, hands to her face. "I mean . . . what did they do to him, Charlie?"

I glanced down at my sweat-stained, dirty clothing. "They buried him."

Dina's face spiked in horror. "*Alive?*"

I hesitated. From what I'd been able to glean by the line of questioning I'd faced, there was some doubt about the time and manner of Torquil's death. That could just have been me projecting my own fears onto it.

If Torquil was alive when he went into that box, then if I'd been quicker, or we'd put it together faster, he might still be alive. But the moment Parker and I had wrenched that lid loose, had seen the boy's arms slack by his sides and no sign that he'd tried to scrape his way out through the timber that encased him, I hadn't needed to wait for a pathologist's report.

He might have been drugged, I supposed, but in my heart I knew that he'd been dead when they put him into the ground. The plastic pipe — the one I'd mistakenly thought was to provide an air supply — turned out to be little more than a marker post, unconnected to the inside of the box. With a bitter anger, I remembered the care I'd taken digging round it.

But the bottom line was that the sole purpose of this morning's exercise had been to ambush me for the Eisenberg Rainbow, at a point where the chase teams would be able to do damn all about it. It had taken timing that was military in both conception and execution, and although none of these rich kids had seen service, they were surrounded by people who had.

So, why had it been such a pair of amateurs who'd tried to ambush Dina at the riding club? I recalled again, from the CCTV footage Gleason had shown us, the way the passenger from the Dodge — the one who'd grabbed the rucksack — had flinched when the driver shot me. Had they realised their past mistakes and recruited a real pro in time to snatch Torquil?

And if he was such a professional, why had he killed his victim instead of returning him in exchange for the necklace?

I glanced at the faces again, realised I didn't trust any of them with these speculations, but wasn't sure why. I shrugged, said dully, "Who knows if he was alive or dead when he went into the ground?"

Dina sank back into her chair as if her legs had suddenly ceased to support her weight. Manda threw me a dark look and moved across to perch on the arm to put a comforting arm across Dina's shoulders.

"You might show a little compassion, Charlie," she said, eyes filled with reproach. "You must know how claustrophobic Dina is."

There was no right way to answer that, especially to admit I hadn't known. She'd never mentioned it, and the subject of phobias had not come up. When I thought back, I realised that she'd always taken the stairs or escalator in the department stores we'd visited, if there was a choice, but I'd assumed that was more about personal fitness than fear.

"Oh, poor Tor," Orlando murmured, turning her face into Hunt's shoulder. He put his arms around her and favoured me a mildly reproving look, also.

So, suddenly he's your best friend . . .?

It was left to Benedict to voice my cynical thoughts out loud. He made a gesture of bored annoyance and flung himself back onto the sofa.

"Oh, come on, Orlando, don't go soft on us now," he said, almost jeering. "It's not as if you ever *liked* the guy." But there was a little too much studied bravado in his tone. I wondered who he was trying to convince.

Orlando yanked herself out of Hunt's embrace and whirled on Benedict, tilted forwards, arms rigid and her tiny hands clenched into fists.

"*How could you?*" she shouted. "He might not have been our *friend*, but he's still *dead*, isn't he? Doesn't that mean *anything* to you?"

Benedict looked momentarily shocked at her outburst, but he recovered his sullen poise quickly enough. "No," he said with an arrogant stare. "It doesn't. People die every day. That's life."

I thought Orlando was going to fly at him, all claws and fury, and was glad it wasn't my job to intervene. Fortunately, it was Hunt who gently took hold of her arms, turned her so he was between the two of them with his back to Benedict, as if preventing them seeing each other would dispel the anger. If the way Orlando wilted in his grasp was anything to go by, he was right.

He spent a moment simply holding her. When he seemed to be sure she wasn't going to let rip again, he put her away from him and nudged her chin up with his curled forefinger, smiling into her eyes.

"This isn't just 'people', is it, Benedict?" Hunt said quietly then, over his shoulder. "Torquil may not have been someone you liked, but he was someone you knew, and he's died going through an experience that *you've* been through personally. That alone should have given you both some kind of connection, so show a little humanity for once. There but for the grace of God, eh?"

I silently applauded, keeping my face neutral. I knew if I'd said half that, Manda would have jumped straight down my throat, but she just looked grateful — if not a little admiring — that Hunt had headed off a possible slanging match.

Fed up with the lot of them, I started to turn away. "Look, it's been a hell of a day. I'm tired and dirty and I'm going to bed. If you want to ask anything else, you'll have to come back in the morning." I paused, turned back. "Speaking of which, how come you're all here in the first place?"

They glanced at each other, not quite furtive but not far off it.

Eventually, it was Manda who admitted, "Ben-Ben ran into Mrs Eisenberg at the tennis club and asked if there was any news." She shrugged. "Sorry, but she kinda mentioned you were . . . helping them, so we thought Dina might know something."

So much for security.

Dina gave me a defiant stare, but I was too weary to get into it with her right now. "Fine," I said. "She doesn't. Go home."

It was only ten minutes later, standing with my hands braced against the tiles in the shower, letting the

268

spray pound onto my back, that I realised all the things I should have asked.

Like why had Benedict bothered to ask Nicola Eisenberg for news of her kidnapped son, when he claimed to hold Torquil in such contempt? And, for that matter, why had Manda bothered to explain his actions, when she'd never given a damn in the past what I might think of her, let alone apologised to me?

I shook the water out of my eyes and, with marked reluctance, shut off the water, grabbing a towel off the rack as I stepped out of the cubicle. If there was one upside to looking after wealthy people, at least they always had nice bathrooms with constant hot water and plenty of fluffy towels.

I quickly blotted the water away from my body, wrapped one towel around me and was roughly drying my hair with another as I moved through into the bedroom that had been allocated to me.

Dina was sitting on the corner of the queen-sized double bed, facing the bathroom door and waiting for me to emerge. She was nervously plaiting her fingers in her lap. My heart sank.

"Where are the others?"

A minor shrug. "They've gone home, like you said."

"And McGregor?"

She nodded to the doorway leading out into the corridor. "I'm sorry, Charlie, I know you just want to go to bed and I promise I won't stay long, but I just won't be able to sleep unless I know what really happened to Tor," she said all in a rush, eyes suddenly jittery with a fear she had almost managed to hide while she was upstairs. "Please. I . . . really need to know."

I leant against the door-frame, aware that being wrapped in a bath towel that only covers you from armpit to mid thigh is not the best way to retain any authority over a situation. Ah well, at least I wasn't naked.

"Why?" I demanded.

She blinked at the staccato question, looking small and lost as she fumbled her way into speech.

"Because, it's all my fault," she said mournfully, tears gathering in her eyes.

Give me strength!

I sighed, dragged a hand across my gritty eyes and tried for a gentler tone. "How is any of this your fault, Dina?"

It seemed that sympathy was her undoing. The tears fell freely then. "Because I know who arranged for Tor to be kidnapped."

That woke me up better than a pint of espresso. I moved forward and crouched in front of her, trying not to lose the towel in the process.

"Dina, listen to me. If you know who these people are, you've got to tell the police. You can't let them get away with murder."

"I kn-know," she sobbed. "Don't you think I don't *know* that?"

"Then what's stopping you —?"

"It was us!" The words burst out of her, a wailing cry full of rage and pain and utter remorse. "Don't you understand? *We* did it!"

270

CHAPTER
THIRTY-SEVEN

"You better start at the beginning, Dina," I said heavily. "Tell me everything, and don't skimp on the details."

I was dressed again, and we were sitting in the silent kitchen, drinking coffee. It was very much a staff environment rather than a family room. The kitchen was set on the side of the house that didn't get any direct sun, and was clean and uncluttered rather than stylish, its appliances picked for utility and not just because they bore the right badge.

Dina hadn't really seemed to know where to find the ingredients for coffee, and had dithered a little over putting them together in the right order. Considering the state she was in, I suppose I couldn't hold that against her.

"You must think I'm a really horrible person," she said now, flicking her eyes sideways at me, as if hoping for an instant knee-jerk denial. As if hoping for my approval even.

I had just been hit by a car, shot in the chest, had my bike trashed, dug up a corpse, and come as close to having my fingernails pulled out under interrogation as the Feds thought they could get away with. I had nothing approving to say to her.

As if realising that fact, Dina flushed, cradling her coffee mug with both hands and staring miserably into the creamy liquid. After a moment, she lifted her head briefly to mutter the age-old excuse so often trotted out by those who find themselves sucked into violence and suddenly way out of their depth.

"Nobody was supposed to get hurt!"

I managed to suppress a snort of outright disbelief at her naivety, and shook my head wearily instead. Not hard under the circumstances.

We sat in a pool of subdued light from the fitting that hung low over the kitchen table. The rest of the room was in shadow. I thought it might encourage Dina to spill her secrets if the atmosphere was less bright and harsh, and I had positioned myself across the corner of the table from her rather than directly opposite, keeping it less adversarial. All friendly — for now.

"Dina, even before what happened to Torquil today, Benedict lost a finger. Was that part of the plan?" I asked, trying for coaxing rather than exasperated. "And what about Raleigh? Your poor old riding instructor will be left with an arm he can use to predict changes in the weather. *If* it knits well enough for him ever to work again to full capacity. Did he sign on for that?"

I'd once had my arm broken in a similar way, I reflected, and could now use it as my own personal barometer.

"Of *course* not," she said, her voice genuinely wretched. "It's just that I never —"

"— thought anyone would get hurt. Yeah. You said."

272

She glanced at me, dropped her eyes again. "They told me it was like . . . a game," she said eventually, choosing her words with care now. "That's all. Just a game."

"Yeah," I said again. "So is Russian roulette."

If Dina's head hung any further, she was going to have her nose actually resting in her drink.

I sighed. "Tell me."

She looked straight at me then, her face fierce and focused. "You have to promise me, Charlie, that you won't say anything to anyone about this. Promise me!"

"Torquil's dead," I said quietly. "This is not a game anymore, if it ever really was. You know I can't make that promise. *But*," I added quickly, seeing her suddenly stricken expression, "if I can help you, I will. You'll just have to trust me to make that decision. Take it or leave it."

If she noticed the word "help" rather than "protect", she didn't comment on the distinction.

I rubbed a tired hand across my face and said, "When you said it was 'us' who was behind the kidnappings, who were you talking about, exactly?" just to try and get her started before I fell asleep in my chair.

I saw her face twitch, identified a brief flicker of shame and guilt.

"We are," she muttered, almost too low to hear.

" 'We' being . . .?"

She bit her lip, stubborn. "The group of us," she insisted.

"O . . . K." I let that one pass for the moment. "Why?"

"What do you mean?"

I raised an eyebrow. "Why did you decide to do it? I mean, were you just all sitting around one day, bored, and someone came up with . . ." My voice trailed off. "Oh, no. *Please* don't tell me I've got that bit right."

"The way they all talked, it was glamorous and exciting," she cried. "Being snatched and held to ransom. It was like something out of a movie. None of it was real." She realised what she'd said, dropped her gaze again. "None of it was *supposed* to be real."

"So, the pair who tried for you at the riding club, they were actors or something?" I demanded. "Because they certainly weren't professional crooks."

"I don't know who they were. I don't! I don't know how they knew where to find me, even. That's how the whole thing was explained — that I would never know the details."

"Wait a minute. If you were arranging to have yourself kidnapped, why go to the trouble of hiring a bodyguard? Was I just window dressing?"

"Of course not, it's just —" She broke off suddenly, swallowed. "You were great that day at the riding club. Honestly, Charlie. Just terrific."

"I hear a 'but' . . ."

"You were *too* good. That was what they told me. They said they didn't think they could get past you easily. Too many risks."

"They were amateurs," I murmured, remembering all too easily. "And who told you that?"

She flushed again, one shoulder lifting. "The others," she said, evasive again. There was something else there, too. It took me a moment to put my finger on it.

"You're angry," I realised. "What did you expect me to do, Dina? You can't get a guard dog and then be upset when it bites people."

"I know, but getting a guard dog, as you put it, wasn't exactly my idea."

That made sense, at least. "Ah — your mother." I paused. "You didn't have to accept me. But when we met, that first day on the beach, you seemed . . . pleased."

"You were a girl." She had the grace to blush. "I didn't think —"

If I'd had more energy, I would have laughed. I shook my head sadly instead. "So, you *did* think I was window dressing."

"Sort of." Another flush, embarrassment and shame. "But then when we went to Tor's party on the yacht, and Manda recognised you, she told me you were . . . good."

I did laugh then, short and bitter. "Yeah, I'll bet that's how she put it."

"'One scary, hard-faced bitch' I believe were her exact words," Dina admitted.

So, Manda Dempsey was involved. No surprises there.

"But not scary enough to put them off having a go?"

"You don't understand, Charlie. They were talking about maybe a million! I . . . talked them into going through with it."

275

"A million?" I repeated flatly. "That's probably a fraction of what this house is worth. So, it's all about squeezing cash out of your mother, is that it?"

Dina was silent for a long time after that, playing with her empty mug, turning it round and round so the unglazed rim of the base grated against the tabletop.

"You must think I'm so lucky, living someplace like this," she said at last, jerking her head to indicate the house, the town, or maybe Long Island itself.

"And you think you're not?"

"Oh, I *know* I'm lucky, but once you've had it, it makes losing it all so much harder to bear."

That surprised me. Parker would have checked out Caroline Willner very carefully, as he did with all potential clients. If he'd found anything untoward in her finances, he hadn't mentioned it.

"And you believe you might be in danger of losing it?"

She shrugged, an unhappy bunch of one shoulder. "Mother came from money, and she's forged a successful career, but my father spends it as fast as she can make it."

"I thought they divorced years ago." I took a sip of my coffee. It was weak and tepid. Dina needed practice at the domestic arts if she was facing a life without staff. "The financial side of it should have been settled then."

"It was," Dina said. Her lips twisted. "But that doesn't mean he hasn't talked her into investing in a half-dozen crazy schemes. His family have some kind of castle, I guess you'd call it. A few years ago he wanted

276

to renovate the place and open it as an upmarket health spa. Like *that* was ever going to work. Then he wanted to buy into some stupid old vineyard. And just because he had fancy ideas about seeing his precious family crest on some stupid bottle of wine, Mother had to foot the bill." She flushed again. "It's like her business sense goes straight out the window every time he comes begging."

"Is that why you didn't want to go to stay with him?"

Dina nodded. "Mother was desperate to get me away from Long Island, and I guess she thought I might be able to talk him out of some of his more hare-brained schemes . . ." Her voice faded away as she saw my expression freeze. "What? What did I say?"

"*Mother was desperate to get me away from Long Island . . .*"

"She knows, doesn't she?" I said. "What you've been up to, I mean."

"No! Of course not. I —"

"Of course I know," said Caroline Willner from the gloomy doorway. "A mother always knows."

CHAPTER
THIRTY-EIGHT

Caroline Willner took the high-backed chair at the head of the kitchen table. She was in her nightgown with a matching robe over the top, belted tightly at the waist. Her face, devoid of its usual subtle make-up, looked almost as tired as I felt. She settled herself with the air of a presiding judge about to pass sentence. If the pale horror on her daughter's face was anything to go by, she probably was.

Dina seemed frozen with shock, so I was the one who made a pot of Earl Grey while the two of them faced each other in silence.

The staff were used to their employer's liking for real tea, served hot rather than over ice. There was an electric kettle on the wiped-down worktop — something of a rarity in an American kitchen.

Caroline Willner inclined her head slightly in thanks as I put cup and saucer down near her right hand. I resumed my seat on the table's long side, where I could referee if it became necessary.

"So, Dina, I expect the courtesy of an explanation."

Not quite the cajoling start I might have hoped for, but I recognised that Caroline Willner, despite appearances, was as hurt and bewildered as any parent

278

would be under similar circumstances. She just hid it well behind a haughty mask and icily precise diction.

Dina flushed immediately. "How can I hope to expect you might understand what it's like?" she demanded. "Watching him bleeding you? You've been divorced for *years*, and still he comes crawling back —"

"Dina, this is not going to get you anywhere," I broke in quietly, before she could get into full flow. "If anything, you should be happy that your mother still has some kind of fondness for your father. You were a product of that marriage, after all. Would you prefer there only to be bitter memories?"

Both of them looked taken aback at that, even a little insulted that I should presume to comment. Dina resumed a slightly sulky air, gaze firmly fixed on the tabletop.

"I think you better just tell me," Caroline Willner said then, but her tone was more conciliatory this time. "What were you afraid of?"

Dina's head came up. "Losing Cerdo," she blurted out. "I don't care about the rest of it, but I couldn't bear to lose my horses."

I stared at her, frowning. "And how the hell does stinging your mother for a ransom help?"

"Ah," Caroline Willner said, before Dina could answer — even if she'd a mind to. "I have an insurance policy against kidnap. It was taken out some years ago, but it's still perfectly valid. I was visiting South America, and I was told it was prudent to take such precautions." Her gaze skimmed over her daughter, strangely dispassionate. "It covers immediate family members, so the money would not have come from me directly."

Funny how no one minds swindling insurance companies, from an ageing camera "dropped" on holiday, to an overinflated estimate for storm damage repairs. And we all end up paying for it in the end, via rocketing premiums which only perpetuate the cycle.

I didn't ask if Dina knew about the insurance. It was common enough in her social circle, and one look at her guilty face was enough to prove her mother had scored a direct hit.

"You think an insurance company would just pay up that kind of money without making strenuous efforts to recover it?" I demanded, not hiding my own incredulity. "And if it was all for your mother's benefit, how the hell were you planning on giving it to her — claim you found it stuffed down the back of a sofa?"

Dina's skin pinked all the way up to her hairline, and she gripped her coffee mug like a lifeline. "*I* don't know," she muttered. "I hadn't thought that far ahead."

"Well, I cannot begin to tell you how extremely disappointed I am at this level of dishonesty," Caroline Willner said, nothing in her voice. "It will be a long time before I feel I can trust you again, Dina."

"I was trying to *help*!"

"By stealing?" Her mother's response came back like a whip. "And let us not forget that a boy is dead because of you and your friends."

"That was an accident," Dina said, heard her own desperation and swallowed it down. "It must have been. They would never *hurt* anyone. Not like that . . ."

280

There was an edge of panic in her voice, her eyes, and I remembered Manda's assertion that Dina suffered from claustrophobia. The prospect of being buried alive held particular terrors for her. Caroline Willner's face showed no sympathy for her daughter's fears.

"And what about the Benelli boy?" she asked. "Was he behind his own . . . mutilation?" She took a sip of her tea. Dina simply stared.

"Benedict was a classical guitarist," she said, almost a whisper. "I don't know what happened. They wouldn't tell me. Maybe that was another accident. Why would he agree to anything so horrible?"

"As a way of avoiding his parents' ambitions for him in that direction, which were always far more . . . aggressive than his own," Caroline Willner said coldly. "While also serving as a constant reminder of their own vacillation when it came to paying the ransom."

"I —"

"Tell me," she continued, raising a pale unpencilled eyebrow, "what means of persuasion did you have in mind to convince me to pay promptly? Have them tell me you'd also been buried alive?"

Dina swayed in her seat, put a steadying hand on the table.

"OK, that's enough," I said quietly. "I think you've made your point, Mrs Willner."

She glanced at me, mild surprise in her face. "But, you see, that's just the problem, Ms Fox, I don't believe I have." Her eyes shifted to Dina's face, scanned over it briefly. "What kind of child have I raised, that she thinks it's remotely acceptable to commit such crimes?" Her voice was a murmur, as if speaking rhetorically.

Dina, who'd seemed on the verge of fainting when her mother mentioned premature burial, now just looked sick.

"I think you underestimate the influence Dina's friends exert," I said, feeling compelled to take the girl's side even though I thoroughly agreed with her mother. "I used to work for Amanda Dempsey's family. That girl could persuade any saint to turn sinner."

Caroline Willner allowed a small smile to flutter her lips. "I was a child of the Sixties," she said. "I took part in the big anti-Vietnam protest marches in Washington in sixty-nine, much to my father's disgust. Yet he very much admired my grandmother's participation in the women's suffrage movement, although that's beside the point." Another flicker of a smile. "My friends at the time were talking about involving themselves with more violent forms of protest. Some of them were people I very much admired, but I did not agree with their philosophy, so I did not take part." She paused, the reminiscence fading. "You were brought up to know better."

Dina hunched in frustration. "You were never there! I was raised by a succession of nannies. All I wanted was for you to *notice* me."

Caroline Willner's jaw tightened. "Well, you've certainly gotten my attention now, Dina," she said. "And I'm sure there will be plenty of notice taken if this comes to trial."

282

"You'd turn me in?" Dina gasped, then shook her head. "No, you wouldn't. But only because they'd drag your name through the mud alongside mine, Mother, and you couldn't stand that, could you?" She waited a beat, but there was no reply. I doubt she'd expected one. "Yes, I've been stupid, but what happened to Tor was nothing to do with me. And it was an accident!"

"If you want us to believe that," I said, "you're going to have to shop them." *Because they'll shop you in a heartbeat, if the tables are turned.*

"No." Dina shook her head again. "They're my friends."

"Dina —" Caroline Willner began heavily.

"Friends who broke Raleigh's arm just because he happened to get in the way," I cut in. "Friends who murdered Torquil Eisenberg, and had a pretty good go at killing me."

She wouldn't look at me, wouldn't answer. Guilt was a good sign, I told myself.

"You are to sever all contact with these people," Caroline Willner commanded, as if that alone was going to be enough to end the matter.

"I already told them I changed my mind," Dina said. "I told them tonight, even before we knew about Tor. There won't be another attempt on me."

Caroline Willner nodded and rose gracefully to her feet. "Well, that's a start," she said. "First thing tomorrow you will call the police and arrange an appointment to see the officer in charge. You will cooperate fully with the authorities," she added in a voice that allowed for no arguments. "And then you will call your horse-riding instructor."

"Raleigh? Why?" Dina asked, confused. "I already apologised to him. You can't mean I should *tell* him about —?"

"An apology is not enough, Dina," her mother cut in. "You will call him and arrange to have your horses delivered to him immediately. It seems a fitting manner of compensation for your crimes."

"*What?*" Dina leapt to her feet, her chair screeching back on the polished tile. Interesting that the prospect of telling all to the authorities had not raised the same kind of reaction as the prospect of losing her precious horses.

"Actions have consequences, my dear," Caroline Willner said, absolute finality in her tone. "It's high time you realised that fact."

CHAPTER
THIRTY-NINE

I called Parker as soon as I got back to my room. It had been a hell of a long day for both of us, but he still answered his phone on the second ring. With Joe McGregor hovering over by the window, pretending not to listen in, I ran through the gist of Dina's confession and Caroline Willner's reaction to it.

McGregor had not been present in the kitchen, so it was news to him, although judging by the look on his face, it didn't exactly come as a big surprise.

"What happens now?" he asked when I snapped the phone shut.

"We both get some sleep before one of us speaks her mind to these bloody people and does something she might regret."

He grinned at me. "Not you, Charlie. You might speak your mind, but you'd never regret it."

"At the moment, I could cheerfully strangle the lot of them," I muttered, shaking my head. "I should have known Manda Dempsey was trouble from the moment I laid eyes on her again."

"When they were all in the living room, before you'd gotten back, it didn't seem like she was the one in charge," McGregor said slowly. "If anything, I woulda said the other girl, Orlando, was making all the noise, with that Brit boyfriend of hers backing her up."

"Hunt does seem the protective type," I agreed. I opened my mouth, about to ask him what else he'd noticed while I'd been otherwise engaged, but shook my head. "Look, I can't think about this anymore tonight. Parker wants me to go into the office tomorrow. You OK to stay on out here?"

"Sure. For how long, you reckon?"

I shrugged. "Until Mrs Willner stops writing the cheques, I expect. But I'll be back by mid afternoon and you can fill me in then." I paused, diffident. "Actually, while I'm over there, I wouldn't mind going to see Sean — if you can stand another few hours of Dina's company?"

His face softened slightly. "No sweat, Charlie. Take as long as you need. I don't have any plans."

Five hours' sleep was all I needed to feel reasonably human again. Plus a long hot shower and an equally long hot coffee — in that order.

As I left the house, I found Raleigh was already loading Dina's horses into a trailer hitched to the back of the riding club pickup. His arm was in a scuffed cast, and he had brought along one of the ubiquitous girl grooms to help him with his cargo.

When he spotted me, he gave me a brief wave, but didn't stop to chat. I guessed he was anxious to be out of there with his remarkable piece of good fortune, before anyone came to their senses about exactly what it was they were giving away. Geronimo might be getting on a bit, but he was a willing ride, and Cerdo had the potential to develop into a top-flight dressage horse. More than worth having an arm broken.

I didn't see Dina before I left the house. She was, according to Silvana, locked in her bedroom, weeping. I wondered if Caroline Willner knew that her daughter would probably never forgive her for this. It was a sad reflection, I thought, that Dina was more upset by being forced to give away her horses than she had been about Torquil's murder.

With the Buell consigned to the nearest breaker's yard, I was in the agency Navigator. For once, I can't say I was sorry to have more than three tons of steel around me as I went hand-to-hand with the morning traffic. Not to mention the visibility afforded by the vehicle's extra height.

That, and the fact that the Navigator lived up to its name by having the latest satnav fitted — as did all Parker's vehicles — the system linked to the traffic reports. It suddenly began warning of heavy congestion ahead on the 495, and advised me to get off the freeway, fast.

Without that, I might not have spotted the tail.

He wasn't very good, which was the first reason I caught onto him. The second was because of a cluster of slow-moving trucks that meant I had to accelerate hard and then change lanes late to make my exit.

I heard a cacophony of horns blast behind me, and checked my mirrors just to make doubly sure I wasn't the cause, even though I knew I'd left the other vehicles plenty of room and completed the manoeuvre smoothly.

One advantage of this job was the opportunity to take plenty of offensive and defensive driving courses.

In my rear-view mirror, I saw an old tan-coloured Honda Accord pop out of the line of trucks onto the slip road behind me, like a cork squeezed from a bottle. I saw the front end of one of the Peterbilts dip as it braked hard enough to fishtail the trailer behind the massive chrome-laden cab.

I sucked in a breath, but the truck driver corrected the wriggle before it got anywhere near out of hand. His fist was still wedged on the horn as his rig disappeared from view, giving a nice working demonstration of the Doppler effect.

The lights at the top of the slip road were against me, which was maybe another reason I was feeling twitchier than normal. I wondered how long it would be before I'd be able to view a red light as anything other than the prelude to disaster.

With my foot on the brake, I watched the Accord roll up slowly behind me, just to get a look at the driver's face. I suppose I was part suspicious, and part curious about a man who enjoyed the thrill of almost becoming the puréed filling in a truck sandwich on his morning commute. I half expected to catch him yacking on his cellphone, oblivious.

Instead, his reflected image showed someone who was intensely uncomfortable. It was a dull day, leaning towards overcast with a chance of rain, but he was wearing dark glasses and a baseball cap with the brim pulled well down. I could just make out the intertwined NY logo on the front. He was a young guy, from what I

288

could see of the rest of his features, dark hair sticking out at the sides, pale skin, wearing a T-shirt. He rang no bells.

One hand gripped the top of the steering wheel so hard he was going to leave dents for each finger. He didn't seem to know quite what to do with the other, and currently had his elbow resting on the door top, fingers rubbing at his temple in a self-conscious gesture that only drew attention to how hard he was trying to mask his face.

I'd already glanced down at the front of the Accord before it was hidden behind the Navigator's tail, but there was no plate. Nothing overtly suspicious about that. Nineteen US states did not require a front licence plate, and neighbouring Pennsylvania was one of them, even if New York was not.

Still, it was . . . convenient, if nothing else.

I drove on, sticking to the speed limits, making no sudden moves and giving no indication that I'd spotted my tail, if that's what he was. Coincidentally, he happened to be heading from Long Island towards Manhattan, but so were thousands of other people at that time of day.

My cellphone was slotted into the hands-free kit on the dash, and I had Parker's number on speed dial. As usual, it hardly seemed to ring out before he answered.

"Hi, boss," I said. "I think I may have a problem."

"Tell me."

So I did, short and sweet, adding, "Could be nothing, but after yesterday I'm sure you'll forgive me for being a little jumpy in traffic."

"You did right, Charlie. How d'you want to play this?"

"I'm tempted to simply call the cops and get them to pick him up. After Torquil's death, I would have said they'll play ball with that."

"Yeah," Parker agreed, and I heard the marked reluctance in his voice. "But that may well cause big trouble for our client."

"Nothing she doesn't deserve."

I heard him sigh. "Yeah, well, not everybody gets what they deserve. While we're still in Mrs Willner's employ, we have to protect her interests as far as we can — and yours. Drive straight to the office. The parking garage has a security entry system. He can't follow you there."

"So, we just let him get away?"

Another set of overhead lights loomed in front of me. I must have just hit the timing wrong, because all of them seemed to be turning against me. Maybe I'd offended the small god of traffic lights and he was showing his wrath in the only way he knew. I eased off the throttle. My tail was still following, again unhappy about being forced to close up.

"We're not law enforcement, Charlie," Parker said, a hint of pleading behind the firm words. "In theory it's not our job to catch the bad guys."

"It's our job to stop them." I glanced in the mirror again. "What's the difference?"

"Charlie, I —"

But suddenly I wasn't listening to what Parker was saying, because in that moment's slice of view, I realised the identity of the guy in the tan Accord, and now this wasn't about theoretical boundaries anymore.

This had become very personal.

CHAPTER
FORTY

"He's injured!" I said, cutting across whatever Parker was saying. "He's wearing a T-shirt and he's just lifted his right arm, but stiff, awkward. I see a bandage."

I remembered the close-up CCTV image of the guy in the passenger seat of the Dodge, throwing his arms up as the side glass rained around him. Maybe even throwing an arm into the path of my next round. The arm nearest the window. His right arm.

Parker went silent for a moment, all arguments about law enforcement intervention put on hold.

"Can you engage with minimum risk?" he asked then.

Risk. An all-purpose word with a raft of meanings. Risk of success. Risk of discovery. Risk of imprisonment. Risk of injury or death.

"Yes."

"OK," he said, his voice shortened and tense. "If you can, lead him somewhere . . . quieter. What's your current location?"

"On Atlantic Avenue — don't ask, it was the satnav's choice. I was going to take the Williamsburg Bridge in but there must have been some sort of traffic snarl-up."

"Stay on Atlantic and head for Bushwick. Plenty of places there to have a nice long . . . *discussion*, without being disturbed."

Places where the residents aren't likely to call the cops, more like.

I said dryly, "The last time I went to Bushwick, I was arrested in a brothel."

"Yeah, try not to do that again, huh?" He paused, as if hating to ask, but doing so anyway. "You need backup?"

"No time. I'll call you."

"You better, or I'll be sending search parties." Another pause, and this time I heard the smile in his voice. "And when you talk to this guy, Charlie, be polite."

No lasting damage.

"I'll do my best," I said, and hung up.

I got off Atlantic at the next lights, started threading deeper into run-down side streets lined with decrepit apartment buildings that looked barely able to support the weight of their own roof. The factories were huge old red-brick affairs, closed mostly to the point of dereliction. Someone had told me that Bushwick had the cheapest rents in the whole of New York City, but you got exactly what you paid for. I saw nothing to disprove it.

As I'd reminded Parker, the last time I'd been here — the last time I'd done more than drive through the place with the windows up and the door locks buttoned — it had ended badly. I'd been arrested in a police raid on a brothel, in the company of Sean, my father, and an underage hooker. Not one of our finer moments.

My tail, meanwhile, stuck within a couple of cars' lengths all the way. He was too anxious about getting cut off at lights and losing me to ask himself where the hell I might be leading him. He might as well have had a flashing neon sign on the roof.

Eventually, after several abrupt turns, I found myself back in the same kind of area as that seedy brothel. The scenery was overwhelmed by gang-tag graffiti and litter. Not so much quiet as cowed, with no inquisitive faces likely to appear at windows. Hardly any windows, for a start, and most of those had part-rotted plywood instead of glass.

It was not a side of the city mentioned on the tourist tours, but perfect for what I had in mind.

I slowed, ducking in my seat and making a big show of looking at the buildings on either side of me, as if searching for an address. The guy in the Accord naturally hung back, so he was caught flat-footed when I hit the accelerator and the Navigator's massive V8 attempted its best impression of a fighter jet leaving an aircraft-carrier catapult along the empty street.

The Accord driver floored the throttle in an attempt to close the gap. Immediately I was up to speed, I stamped on the brake pedal and stuck the gear lever into "Reverse". The transmission thunked in protest, but Lincoln build 'em tough and I had actually managed to pick up some rearward velocity when I connected with the nose of the Accord.

The laws of physics took over at this point. The Navigator's large ground clearance and twenty-plus inches of departure angle meant its fat rear tyres were already attacking the Accord's front bumper before the overhanging body fouled on the low-slung bonnet.

The tyres gripped and lifted, carried up and on by buckets of torque and a driver who was not about to let her foot off just yet. The Navigator mounted the front end of the Accord and sat on it, crushing the engine bay. I can only imagine what it must have looked like from inside the car.

I rammed the gear lever back into "Drive" and, with less difficulty than I'd imagined, bounced back down onto the road surface. I'd always been taught to ram a solid object with the back of a vehicle rather than the front, if that were possible. Fewer vital moving parts to damage, for a start. As it was, the Navigator still felt perfectly driveable. The airbags hadn't even deployed. Glancing in the mirrors, I was pretty sure the Accord was a write-off.

Well, good!

By the time I was out from behind the Navigator's wheel and level with the wreck, leading with my left shoulder, I had the SIG out in a double-handed grip and pointed firmly at the driver's fear-frozen head. It took him about half a second to jerk both hands up in surrender, palms facing.

The speed with which he got his right hand in the air, in particular, gave me a moment's horrible creeping doubt. Bullet wounds, in my experience, severely restricted all movement, regardless of the situation. In the back of my mind, I began to wonder if I might have to go for a variation on the "I'm just a girlie and my foot slipped off the brake" excuse.

Ah, well, too late to worry about that now . . .

"Out!" I barked, firm but not shouting. The driver's window was down, so I didn't have to. "Keep your hands where I can see them. Put them out of the window, right now! Come on, both hands!"

I moved round towards the A pillar, staying forward of the door hinge and keeping my knees soft in case he tried anything.

He didn't.

In fact, the Accord driver fumbled in his haste to comply, fingers scrabbling awkwardly for the exterior door handle. He climbed out, shaky, his bandaged right arm beginning to droop. As he shuffled forwards he was leaning to that side, as if to compensate or maybe hoping to disguise the injury.

I transferred the SIG to my right hand only and edged closer, flicking the sunglasses and baseball hat off with my left and chucking them back into his car. He flinched as I uncovered his face, almost cringing.

My pursuer was maybe in his early twenties, late teens at a push, neither fat nor thin, with dark blondish hair, casually cut so its natural curl was taking over. His T-shirt and jeans were tight enough that I could tell he wasn't carrying without having to frisk him. I frisked him anyway, just to be sure.

In the back pocket of his jeans I discovered a battered canvas wallet. Inside, along with a credit card and loose change was a driver's licence that could well have been genuine.

I checked the picture, compared it to the face in front of me. Ross Martino, with an address in Elizabeth, across in New Jersey, right under the final approach for Newark International. I memorised it, threw the wallet back to him. And then, more in fear of a random police patrol than anything else, I tucked the SIG back under my jacket.

Ross Martino relaxed visibly as the gun disappeared from view. Or maybe not *relaxed*, but certainly became so much less tense that the effect was the same. And as his fear released its grip on his senses, his peripheral vision opened up again. Maybe that was why he suddenly realised the state of the flattened Accord.

"My car! Aw, man, you wrecked my car." His accent wandered under stress, I noted, veering from an artificial neutrality down towards more working-class origins.

"You wrecked my bike," I fired back. "This just makes us even."

"I didn't!" He went almost squeaky with outrage. "Shit, man, are you crazy? Just *look* what you did . . ."

"Crazy? No. Livid? Well, *now* you're talking."

"Hey, I —"

I didn't have time for this. So far, nothing had stirred in the buildings on either flank, but how long that state of affairs would continue was anyone's guess. I lunged forwards and grabbed the biceps of his right arm, just about in the centre of the bandaged area, and dug in hard.

The effect was immediate and severe. His speech chopped off, eyes ballooning as the spike of pain locked him up solid. He staggered back against the door-frame, almost fell. I pushed up close.

"Yeah, getting shot's a bitch, isn't it?"

"*Shot*? What the shit are you talking about? I ain't been shot!"

Under the pain I registered surprise — shock, even — but no desperate invention. No outright lies.

"Prove it — whatever's under there," I said, and when he wavered, I sighed and reached towards the SIG again. "Or I will give you something to compare it with. Lose the bandage."

I didn't even need to clear the holster. As soon as my hand flipped under my jacket, he was already tugging at the dressing, letting it unravel down his arm like a loosely dressed mummy, paddling it on its way.

Beneath the bandage was a simple rectangle of gauze and a mass of intertwining bruises with a definite shape at their epicentre. I gestured and, with obvious reluctance, he peeled back the gauze. Only then did I recognise the central pattern on his discoloured flesh.

It was a near-perfect partial imprint of a horse's hind shoe.

Horses' hind feet are a very different shape to the front, more oval, less rounded, so their hoofprints are distinctive. And I realised at the same time that I'd been coming at this from completely the wrong direction.

When Cerdo had let rip with both back legs at Dina's would-be abductor, that day at the riding club,

298

he'd landed a direct hit on the man's upper arm. That much I knew.

The thin curve of metal with its central fullered groove — designed to give more grip in soft ground — had caused a small but nasty gash, even through the guy's clothing. It should have been professionally stitched, but I could understand why he'd kept away from the hospitals.

The sheer horsepower behind the blow had also caused a welter of bruises. After several days, they were dispersing in multicoloured array in all directions along his arm. It looked like he'd probably torn up the muscles at the same time.

But no way was it a gunshot wound.

"Don't you think it's ironic," I said after a moment's inspection, "that you clobbered Dina's riding instructor with that baseball bat, and it was her horse who laid into you?"

Ross scowled, carefully sticking the gauze back in place and gathering up the streamers of bandage. He didn't want to even look at me.

I shrugged. "OK, you don't want to talk here, that's fine — talk to the police instead." I hooked my cellphone out of my pocket, started to dial. "But *you* were the one following *me*, don't forget."

He hadn't forgotten, not for long. He barely let me key in the first digit.

"OK, OK! Jesus, why d'you think I've been on the run, man? I daren't go home, in case the cops are there already. We thought the big guy at the riding club was the bodyguard, all right?" he admitted through his teeth. "All we knew was she had a bodyguard called Charlie, and it sounded like she called him that. How the *hell* were we supposed to know you'd be a chick, huh? I mean, c'mon — shit, I thought your name was Pam or something."

It might almost have been funny, if it wasn't so bloody tragic instead. "What were you going to do if you'd managed to grab her?" I asked. "Bury her alive? Or beat her to death first, like Torquil?"

"*No!* No way! Listen, that wasn't anything to do with us. You gotta believe me." His tone had turned wheedling. I wondered if he knew it did nothing for his cause.

I squared up to him, glanced at the phone still in my hand, as if in warning. "Who's 'us', exactly?"

The emotions that crossed his face might have been comical in other circumstances. On the one hand, he wanted desperately to confess to the crimes he saw as his own, but he must have known he was hopelessly compromised if he did.

"I'm not the police," I added, hoping he wouldn't pick up on the fact I hadn't promised not to call them regardless.

"Me and Lennon," he said at last, unwillingly convinced.

"So, does that make you McCartney?"

The Beatles reference was lost on him. He gave me a puzzled frown.

I sighed. "OK, Ross, so you admit you and your pal were behind the attempt on Dina at the riding club —"

"No!" he said again. "We just carried it out, OK? But the brains behind the whole thing? No way."

"Now, why doesn't *that* surprise me?" I murmured. "Who was giving you your orders?"

He flushed at that, but gave me a shrug that seemed as frustrated as it was reflexive.

"Lennon was the one who dealt with them, man. He just used to get text messages. Instructions, directions. That's how we knew where to find Dina and that she had a bodyguard. Lennon showed me the texts, but I never knew who sent them. He just asked me to help him out, so I did, y'know? We're buds."

I remembered the old saying about a friend is someone who will help you move, but a real friend will help you move a body. Looked like Ross was a real friend . . .

"Helping out your 'bud' probably just earned you life with no possibility of parole," I said coldly, going for the phone again.

"Wait!" he cried, the desperation sending his voice climbing. "Look, I'll tell you everything, but you've gotta help me. Lennon asked me to give him a hand to take the other three, sure, and we had a go for the kid you were with — at the riding stables. But it was all, like, play-acting, not for real! Jesus, what d'you take me for?"

"From where I'm standing? A kidnapper and murderer."

"*Murder?*" he demanded, almost a squawk. "Hey, I tell you, someone's trying to frame us for killing the Eisenberg kid." He shook his head vigorously, shivered in the mild air. "That was nothing to do with me. I never signed on for that."

"So, where do I find your buddy Lennon?" I asked, grim. "Sounds like he and I really need to talk."

"That's just it, man, I don't know," he muttered, sour and defiant in equal measure. "You not been listening? Why d'you think I'm here? He's gone. All I know is he got a message a couple days ago. He went out, saying he'd be back real soon, and how they'd promised him something big, and I ain't seen him since!"

CHAPTER
FORTY-ONE

"Lennon got me into this whole thing," Ross said dully. "We were on the same basketball team in college."

"College kids?" I murmured. It didn't quite have the ring of the ghetto about it. "So, what went wrong?"

"My dad lost his job, and his medical benefits, so when my mom got sick . . ." He gave an expressive twitch of his shoulders. "I was bussing tables, parking cars, anything to earn a dime. Only trouble was, I had no time to study. I flunked out. This was like a gift, y'know? Man, I *needed* that money."

"Spare me," I said shortly. "Not everyone who's having a hard time of it turns to kidnapping to make ends meet."

His gaze flashed out, sharp and angry. "Yeah? Look around you!"

We were sitting in a grubby little bar about a mile away from the site of our collision. I'd called the breakdown recovery service Armstrong-Meyer used, given them directions, and told them to collect the wrecked Accord and wait for further instructions.

Ross left the keys tucked above the sun visor — not that they would do anyone much good. What was left of the car's engine was proving quietly incontinent on the cracked asphalt, and both front wheels currently sat at odd angles where the whole of the suspension had collapsed.

Nevertheless, the Navigator had made light work of dragging the carcass to the side of the road. A sturdy tow rope was standard equipment for all Parker's company vehicles.

I persuaded Ross into the passenger seat of the Navigator with the promise that, if we talked and I liked what he had to say, I'd lobby Parker — and through him, Brandon Eisenberg — for a good defence attorney and new set of wheels. Preferably something of considerably later vintage than his elderly Honda. Eisenberg would no doubt be willing to pay a substantial reward for information leading to an arrest, not to mention retrieval of the missing Rainbow.

Ross was desperate enough to grab the lifeline I offered him, so I didn't have to resort to Plan B, which was to PlastiCuff him and throw him in the back of the SUV.

Now, we perched on a pair of cracked vinyl stools near the doorway in a small bar on one of the main drags. It had obviously been converted from some kind of store, with big front windows and a long darkening slot leading to the smokers' haven outside at the back. The bar ran almost the full length of the room and was studded with similar stools. The varnish on the planked floor had been long since scuffed away by the stumble of many beer-clad feet.

I sat with my back to the wall, where I could watch the doorway and the street, with Ross hunched alongside me. I'd been able to park the Navigator right outside. From this angle, I could admire the damage to the rear bumper and contemplate Bill Rendelson's ire when he had to submit the insurance claim forms.

Every cloud . . .

The barman had managed to deliver two beers and take the money I offered without uttering a single word. The beer was cold, at least, but it seemed that glasses were not an option. Neither was change. I thought briefly of asking for a receipt for my expenses, but he was already disappearing into a ramshackle storeroom at the back, leaving us with the place to ourselves.

"It didn't seem like breaking the law — not at first," Ross said now, his face intent. "It was never supposed to be anything really, y'know, *criminal*. Lennon said how he'd met these rich kids at a couple of parties. They wanted some kinda big thrill, and being held to ransom was it. Some kinda role-playing thing, I guess. Easy money, he said, for letting them act out their dumb fantasy."

"Just a game," I murmured, recalling Dina making much the same protest.

"First couple of times — those two girls — it was." He took a rapid sip of his beer, pulling a face at the taste or the temperature, I wasn't sure which. I tried mine and probably gave off much the same expression. It wasn't the most sophisticated brew, but it was effective at stripping the fur off your tongue.

"So," I said mildly, "what kind of role play was it when you cut off Benedict Benelli's finger?"

Ross paled and put his beer down slowly, picking at the edge of the label.

"He did it himself," he said at last, shocked and low. "You should have seen him — when Lennon told him his folks wouldn't pay. That they'd laughed at the idea. He went ape-shit, man, screaming and swearing, saying how he was gonna make 'em real sorry for what they done." He swallowed. "Then he grabbed a knife and just . . . did it."

"Just like that?" I sat for a moment, eyeing him. Was it as totally unbelievable as it seemed? I remembered Benedict's permanent scowl, Caroline Willner's statement that his classical music career was more his parents' choice, and his defiance towards everything, from his friends to his life. It might have started out as a game, but he'd taken it onwards in a big way. "What kind of a knife?"

"Kitchen. One of those big mothers with about a nine-or ten-inch blade."

"How the hell did he just so happen to stumble across a kitchen knife?"

Ross heard the acidic tilt to my voice. He checked out the dark gloss ceiling, the dirt under his fingernails, the ingredients' list on the back of the beer bottle. Anywhere but my face.

"We was in the kitchen," he mumbled. "We'd been keeping him tied up in the basement, like always. Keeping it real, y'know? Like they wanted." He blushed. "But after the Benellis said nothing doing, there didn't seem much point in keeping him down there any longer, huh?"

"What happened?" I asked, still not entirely willing to take his story at face value.

"I threw up," he admitted, looking thoroughly ashamed. Hardened criminal, he was not. "It wasn't the blood. Man, it was the *noise*. Like cutting through chicken bones. Right across the knuckle." He gave a shudder and reached for his beer again. "Still makes me wanna puke, thinking about it."

I had once witnessed someone lose both legs in a marine hydraulic door. Even now, the soggy dull crunch of splintering bone stayed with me, rising up at odd moments. Still, I'd seen worse.

I'd done worse, for that matter.

I took a pull of my beer and didn't wince this time. Either it was mellowing, or I was getting used to it. "So, you sent the finger to Benedict's parents."

"Lennon did." Ross nodded miserably. "I never thought anything like that would happen."

I recalled a comment Manda Dempsey had made, the night of Torquil's birthday party — his *last* birthday party — about her supposed ordeal. About how they'd beaten her and photographed the bruises. "Not averse to getting physical with your hostages, though, are you, Ross?"

"Manda, you mean?" he said bitterly, not needing to be prompted. He shifted uncomfortably on his bar stool. "That is one crazy bitch. Lennon said that was all part of it — the fantasy. Some chicks get off on that kinda thing, y'know? And she had a safe-word, for if'n we went too far, but she never used it. I swear!"

"Did Torquil have a safe-word he never used as well? Is that what happened?"

"Look, man, how many more times? I didn't have nothing to do with the Eisenberg kid! I swear on my mom's grave, OK?"

But I heard the doubt and the fear in his voice. He genuinely might not have been involved, I realised, but I was willing to bet that his old school pal was in it up to his ears, and Ross must have known that, too.

"Dina told me she'd changed her mind," I said. "That true?"

He nodded. "We got that she'd called the whole thing off. I was kinda glad, to be honest." His shoulders slumped, and he asked in a small voice, "What . . . um, what happens now?"

I put my beer down again. It was a good question. By rights, I should have dialled the cops as soon as I recognised Ross for who he was, and let them handle the whole thing from there. But if Lennon had gone into hiding, hauling in his co-conspirator would do little to make him break cover. If anything, it would push him deeper underground.

Ross was denying that he and Lennon were involved with Torquil Eisenberg's abduction, but it seemed too much of a coincidence that there should be two gangs of kidnappers preying on the same group of kids. Lennon had recruited Ross, but he'd discovered at the riding club that they'd taken on more than they could handle.

So, it was entirely possible that Lennon had gone out and recruited somebody else in Ross's place. Somebody like the man who'd Taser'd Torquil on the beach, and beaten him into delivering his own ransom demand to camera.

Somebody like the driver of the Dodge, the one who'd coolly and calmly shot me in the chest as I lay helpless under his front wheels. A professional. *That* was who I wanted, so badly I could taste it.

"What happens next depends entirely on you, Ross. It sounds to me like you've been somewhat dragged into this against your better judgement by your mate, Lennon." I kept my tone casual, conciliatory, but that still earned me a quick hard glare. He was bright enough to know where this was heading, and didn't like it. But he didn't stop me going any further even so.

"Torquil Eisenberg was beaten to death," I said bluntly. We hadn't had any official reports yet, but Ross didn't know that. "Ever since the Lindbergh baby, kidnappers have been reviled in this country, you should know that. Like I said, somebody's going down for this, and they're going down for keeps." I paused. His face, in profile, chin sunken, was tormented. "With your boyish charms, you're going to be popular as hell in prison." That jerked him out of his stupor a little. "You still got all your own teeth?"

"What? Of course I have, man!"

I shook my head again. "Not for long, you won't," I told him cheerfully. "First thing they do is break the new guy's teeth so he can't bite down on anything that's put in his mouth —"

"OK, OK! Jesus Christ, man. What do I have to do? Tell me!"

"Give us Lennon," I said, and saw him waver. "You think — if the positions were reversed — he'd hesitate?"

He picked up his beer, but the bottle was empty. He cast a mournful glance towards the storeroom, but the shopkeeper did not appear, by magic or anything else.

"No," Ross said at last, so low I almost missed it. "I guess not."

CHAPTER
FORTY-TWO

"If you really weren't in on Torquil Eisenberg's murder," I said, "the only way you're going to prove it is to help lead us to the people who were."

"Jesus, man, I only followed you today because I wanted you to know I didn't kill the Eisenberg kid, but what you're asking . . ."

Ross sat for a long time with his head down, staring at a puddle of condensation that had formed around the edge of the bottle, drawing his finger through it so it spread and dried to his design.

Eventually, he turned and looked right at me, defeat in his eyes. "OK, yeah," he said. "I'll do it." And shook his head afterwards like he couldn't believe the scope of his own treachery.

I nodded carefully, not wanting to spook him into changing his mind. I closed my mind to the fact I was probably committing all kinds of offences to do with not handing him straight over to the Feds. He might have acted dumb, but he wasn't stupid, and if he'd any sense he'd lawyer up so fast they'd get nothing useful out of him for weeks. By which time, who knew where Lennon and his new playmate might be?

"Where's the place you were using to hold the others?" It seemed best to start with something easy.

"Over in Elizabeth," he mumbled, and I realised he'd been foolish enough — or Lennon had been cunning enough — to use Ross's own house for this. Maybe Lennon had him pegged as a scapegoat from the outset. Even so, Ross still clung to the thought of his mate's comparative innocence. "Lennon can't have had the Eisenberg kid, though, man. Not there, anyways, 'cause I hardly left the place myself the last few days, y'know?"

Damn! Still, worth a try . . .

"When you last saw Lennon — just before he went out — who called him?" I asked. "You ever see the guy?"

He shook his head. "No, man. I picked up the phone, that's all. He asked for Lennon and I don't ask no questions."

"What did he sound like?"

He shrugged. "Just . . . ordinary, y'know?"

This was heading nowhere. I tried a different tack. "And you haven't heard from Lennon since?" I asked, and saw the quick but honest denial in his face. "How does he normally get in touch?"

Ross shrugged. "He calls me, but he changes his cell, like, every week. The last number I have for him is dead. I have to wait for him to call me."

I paused, considering. For what it was worth, I believed him, and I'd become pretty good at spotting when people's body language was not aligned with what came out of their mouths. My instincts told me Ross was scared enough to grasp at the possible way

312

out I was offering, but not so scared he'd promise anything, just to get rid of me.

That part, if necessary, would come later.

The hard part now was that, to make best use of him, I was going to have to turn him loose. That rankled. For all his apparent innocence when it came to Torquil's death, he'd still attacked Dina at the riding club. He'd been the one who'd swung the bat that had broken Raleigh's arm. And if it had connected with the man's head, as had clearly been intended, it could easily have broken his skull.

My fingers itched to dial 911 and have done with it. I remembered the carcass of the Buell being dragged onto a breaker's yard truck. I remembered opening the makeshift coffin and finding Torquil already dead inside.

"Give me your cellphone."

He frowned, as if I wasn't intending to give it back. The phone he handed over was old and scratched to the point where it didn't look worth stealing. All I did was punch in my own cell number and dial just long enough for the number to register on my device. An easier, and safer, way to make sure he could get in touch with me and — more importantly — I could get in touch with him.

"OK," I said as I handed it back. "I think we can help you, if you help us. When Lennon next gets in touch, you need to stay calm, arrange a meet, and call me, yeah?"

I saw the compulsive swallow as he nodded. "OK, man," he said, almost eager. "I can do that."

"You better." I slid off my bar stool, leaving half my beer untouched on the sticky counter, and straightened my jacket over the SIG, making sure Ross knew the gesture for what it was. His eyes, a blue-grey with pale lashes, were wary, but I read no deceit in them. I leant in, saw his gaze flick to my mouth, as if I were about to kiss him.

"I know who you are, and where you live, Ross," I promised in a husky murmur. "You try to screw me, and it won't just be your car that gets crushed. I will find you, and I will hurt you in ways you cannot imagine. Just remember that I keep my promises, good and bad. Yeah?"

"Yeah, sure," he gabbled. "I hear you, man."

"One last thing, Ross," I said. "Don't call me 'man', OK?"

I walked out of the bar, across the dirty sidewalk, and popped the locks on the Navigator. Before I pulled out into traffic, I glanced back, expecting to see Ross still sitting on his stool. The window of the little bar was empty.

I checked the street, but it looked like Ross had taken the back way out. A bar like that, in an area like this, it must have been a pretty well-worn route. I was aware of another twinge of guilt that I'd let him go, and hoped to hell that his rapid disappearance now was not an indicator of things to come.

My cellphone started to buzz in my pocket. I fished it out, half expecting it might be Ross, but Parker's number came up.

"Hi, boss," I said. "That's good timing. I've just had a long chat with one of the guys who tried for Dina, and I —"

"Charlie." Parker's voice cut raw through my explanation.

"What?" I demanded, drenched with a sudden cold fear. "What's happened? Is it Sean?"

"No," Parker said. I heard him take a breath. "It's Dina. She's been snatched."

"We got that she'd called the whole thing off . . ."

Lying bastard!

"No . . . no," I muttered. "I left McGregor looking after her. He should . . . What the fuck *happened*?"

"He did his best, Charlie. They shot him."

CHAPTER
FORTY-THREE

When Parker walked into Caroline Willner's private sitting room at 1900 hours that evening, Dina had been gone nine hours with no word from the kidnappers. I took one look at his face and feared the worst.

"How's Joe?" I demanded, not waiting for the social niceties. There were too many echoes of Sean with this one, too many shards. Inside, I bled deep from every one of them.

"Out of surgery," Parker said, passing me a tired smile. "If he's lucky, he'll make it." His eyes flicked to Caroline Willner's white face, wary of saying anything that might touch a nerve. "They obviously learnt from the attack on you, Charlie," he added quietly. "They fired low enough to go under a vest, even if he'd been wearing one. Pelvis."

Nothing else, short of a head shot, would put a man down faster. So many vital organs were cradled in the pelvis that a gunshot injury there was bound to do critical, immobilising damage. And, unlike the head, the pelvis was often the most static part of an otherwise fast-moving target. I couldn't see McGregor, a veteran of the Iraqi conflict, making things easy for them.

But he was alive — for the moment. That was something at least.

I closed my eyes briefly, unwilling to show more relief than that. Parker nodded, understanding, and moved across to greet Caroline Willner. She had not reacted to his arrival, and remained sitting rigidly upright in her chair, eyes fixed on a point in the distance as if willing herself to hold together. Now, she seemed to notice him for the first time and allowed him limply to take her hand.

"Mrs Willner, I'm very sorry," he said gravely. "We will get your daughter back for you."

"I believe you will try your hardest, Mr Armstrong," she said stiffly. It was not exactly a glowing declaration of confidence, and by the way Parker's face turned instantly neutral, he recognised that fact.

"Do we know how this happened?"

He glanced across, not so much at me, but at Erik Landers, hovering discreetly across the far side of the room. Landers lived in north Brooklyn and had been first on scene after Dina's abduction. He'd stayed at Caroline Willner's side ever since. When I arrived, shortly afterwards, I'd been the one who'd talked to the staff and watched the CCTV footage, and pieced together what had taken place.

I'd been through it over and over, looking for the exact point when the day turned from clear to dark. And each time, I fought a sick dread that sat high under my ribcage.

What struck me most was the same sense of ruthless purpose that had characterised the ambush on me. I'd watched Dina sneak out onto the driveway, looking behind her as she came, furtive, eager. I'd seen the van pull up with its licence plate just beyond the reach of the cameras. Dina's stride had faltered as she'd neared it and realised the unexpected danger. She'd begun to retreat — faster when two masked figures leapt from the van and came for her. One grabbed her immediately. The other stayed back, more warily. From the way he carried himself, I would guess he had to be the guy from the passenger seat of the Dodge.

The one I'd winged. The one I now suspected might be Lennon.

There was no audio on the house CCTV, but even without it I heard Dina start to scream. McGregor appeared so quickly from the direction of the house that I believed he'd already noticed her attempt at stealthy departure. He'd barely entered the picture when the man holding Dina yanked out a silvered semi-automatic and fired, three shots, as fast as the action would cycle.

McGregor went down on the second. It hit low in his body and his instinct was to clamp both hands to the wound. He'd managed to draw his own weapon, but had no clear shot. It dropped unfired onto the gravel as he collapsed, writhing.

With every repeat viewing, I willed him to move just that little bit faster, or the bad guy a little bit slower. The outcome was always the same.

But it had been good to have a purpose, because it stopped me thinking too hard about the fact that while Ross might not have taken part in this, I'd still had one of Dina's erstwhile kidnappers in my hands, and had let him go. Now, I prayed it would not turn out to be one of the worst mistakes I'd ever made.

"How did they lure her out of the house?" Parker asked.

"She got a text, apparently from Orlando, saying she was at the riding club when Raleigh arrived back with the horses," I said. "According to the message, Cerdo slipped coming out of the trailer and was injured, and she should come at once," I said. Nothing would be more guaranteed to make Dina throw caution to the winds.

"You've checked, of course." It was a comment rather than a question.

I nodded anyway. "Raleigh says he hasn't seen Orlando since the last time I was there with Dina, and the horses are fine."

"So, either Orlando's complicit," Parker murmured, "or this was definitely a pro job."

"We know that whoever this guy Lennon's hooked up with, he's an expert when it comes to hacking technology — Dina's email, the traffic light system, and Gleason's comms network. I shouldn't imagine Orlando's cellphone would cause him much trouble."

Parker raised his eyebrow, just a fraction. I'd already briefed him fully over the phone on my conversation with Ross, and the agreement we'd reached. He agreed, even with the benefit of hindsight, that handing the college kid over to the authorities would probably have got us nowhere — certainly not as far as recovering Dina was concerned. For better or worse, we had to trust him to deliver his end of the deal and lead us to his former friend. It was a calculated risk. I just hoped my calculations weren't way off.

"What will happen now?" It was Caroline Willner who spoke, her voice hoarse with strain.

Parker turned back to her. "We wait, ma'am," he said. "No doubt they will be in contact with their demands. Until then, we just have to wait."

She cleared her throat. "I would very much like for you to negotiate for my daughter's release," she said, eyes sliding away from his. "I regret that, if they ask for a substantial amount, I . . . may not have the money to pay."

"You mentioned yesterday that you had kidnap insurance," I said. "What about that?"

Her face had hardened into a brittle mask, refusing to allow her fear and pain to break surface. "If I make a claim, and then it comes out — as it is bound to — that my daughter and her . . . friends were in any way responsible for their own predicament, I would likely face prosecution for fraud," she said, selecting her words with care. "Besides, Brandon Eisenberg was prepared to pay in full for his son's life, and much good it did him."

I heard the bitter thread, felt compelled to point out gently, "I know Dina told them she had changed her mind. Whatever's happened to her now, it's not of her choosing."

Caroline Willner nodded, very slightly, grateful. "I know," she said. "And I pray that we both get the chance to ask forgiveness."

★　★　★

We waited for the ransom demand most of the night.

Parker had connected a recorder to the house phone. As soon as the line rang out, caller ID was displayed on the screen of his laptop, allowing Caroline Willner to take the call if she recognised the number, or let Parker handle it.

There were a lot of rubberneckers, of one form or another. People who thought they might have heard a rumour and wanted to check it out. Caroline Willner rebuffed them all equally, telling them Dina had caught a chill and was resting in her room. They obviously came from a stratum of society where such a minor ailment was a viable excuse for bed rest. Either way, it seemed to satisfy them. If I hadn't been able to see the sorrow in her face as she spoke, I would have believed her, too.

And when Manda called, just before midnight, pushing to speak with Dina, Caroline Willner dismissed the girl's apparent concerns and told her, in a slightly obstreperous tone, that Dina was simply not available to come to the phone.

The kidnappers finally called a little after 6.00a.m., no doubt aware of our sleepless night. Dina was twenty hours gone. Even though it wore the same mechanical disguise, I knew the voice belonged to the same man I'd spoken to, yesterday morning at the Eisenberg's house.

And I knew, without a single shred of physical evidence to back it up, that this was also the same man who'd shot me.

Parker saw the unrecognised number and took the call. Caroline Willner had gone to lie down and rest in her own room, so he put it on speaker. The kidnapper did not seem surprised to find him on the other end of the line.

"You want Dina back alive," the voice said flatly, "this time it's going to cost you ten million dollars."

"Ten million?" Parker allowed his incredulity to come through. He would have shown surprise regardless of the amount asked for, as a stalling technique. But this time there was little acting required. He paused, then pointed out calmly, "That's double what you asked for Torquil Eisenberg."

"Yeah, and if his old man hadn't tried to screw us over, maybe we wouldn't be having this conversation right now, but he did. Get over it."

Parker's eyes narrowed and his voice turned soft and deadly. "How, exactly, did Eisenberg screw you over?"

"That worthless pile of coloured glass. How long did you think it would take us to spot you'd given us a replica of the Rainbow instead of the real thing?"

I sucked in a quiet breath, remembered Nicola Eisenberg's certainty that her husband might not have her son's best interests at heart. She had collapsed after the failed ransom drop, I recalled. Did she know what he'd tried to pull?

"That's a huge amount of money. The kind that can't be raised overnight," Parker said. "Mrs Willner is not rich. She doesn't have the same sway with banks —"

"Not rich?" the voice cut in, distortion or disgust making it screech. "She lives in that fucking great palace on the beach, with servants and horses and all the rest of that privileged shit, and you try to tell me she's not *rich*?"

"Having assets is not the same thing as having available cash," Parker said, and his tone stayed easy even as his eyes burnt cold. "Not the kind of available cash you're talking about."

"Dina was going out with Eisenberg's kid, so tap up his father. He's rich enough and he owes us, big time. Either way, you got a day and a half to put it all together. We'll call you 4.00p.m. the day after tomorrow with when and where to make the drop. No bargaining. No second chances. After that, the old lady starts getting her daughter back a piece at a time, you hear me? Dina's a good-looking girl. Would be a shame if anything happened to that pretty face, wouldn't it?"

"How do we know you'll keep your word?" *This time.*

"You don't." Another short, rough laugh. "Guess we'll just have to trust to luck that nobody's going to be stupid enough to try screwing anybody else this time."

The connection severed and the line went dead. An electrified silence remained for several seconds afterwards. Parker reached out and killed the speaker slowly, as if his limbs suddenly weighed very heavy.

"I don't trust him as far as I could spit him, never mind throw him," I said bluntly. "Even if it's true about the necklace being a fake, we know Torquil was dead long before they could have discovered that fact."

"We could play along and set a counter-ambush," Landers suggested. "Grab him before he gets to the ransom drop — like they pulled with Charlie last time."

"What then?" Parker asked. "Subject him to extraordinary rendition until he talks? If he puts Dina in the ground someplace before he arranges to collect the ransom, he'll know time will not be on our side. She could easily die before we get her location from him."

"And she's claustrophobic," I said, suddenly recalling her admission. "She freaked out when she found out what had been done to Torquil."

Parker paused, frowning. "Do the kidnappers know that?"

"I don't see why not — they seem to know everything else." I stood, suddenly restless. "Look, I can't just sit here and wait for this guy to torment us. I'm going to go and pay a visit on the previous 'victims' — see what I can shake loose."

"You rattle the wrong cages, and you may provoke the kidnappers into acting prematurely," Parker pointed out.

But I was already shrugging into my jacket. "Whereas they've behaved so impeccably up 'til now." I favoured him with a cynical smile. "If I can find out which of them hired Lennon, it may give us another line on finding her before he buries her."

I snatched up the keys to the Navigator and headed for the hallway, only to find Parker on my heels. He touched my arm just before I reached the front door.

"Charlie, wait. I'll come with you." There was something close to anguish in his voice that was enough to stop me, turn me back towards him.

324

"You're needed here, Parker," I said, almost gently. "What if they call again?"

He sighed. "Take Landers then. Don't go alone."

"No offence, but Erik looks too threatening. I'm trying to coax them into talking rather than scare them." Not true, but it sounded halfway convincing at least. "I really think I'll get more out of them if I'm on my own." That much *was* true. "And you need him here to look after Mrs Willner."

"I know," he said, and I realised he was only too aware that it was Landers' sense of fair play I was trying to avoid, for what I might need to do. "Sean once told me your courage was the thing that terrified him most — that you never flinch, never hesitate," he said then, with a smile as twisted as my own. "Now I think I see what he meant."

CHAPTER
FORTY-FOUR

"I'm sorry, Miss . . . *Fox*, did you say your name was?" Orlando's father said with the offhand snub perfected by the ultra-rich towards people who are clearly not their social equal. "But as our housekeeper, Jasna, explained to you, I'm afraid our daughter is not here at present. And as for your . . . suggestion that you will go to the police, I've already spoken to their chief today — he's a friend of the family — regarding the Eisenbergs' tragic loss. So, you see, I really can't help you."

For "can't", I read "won't". In big letters.

Orlando's family didn't so much have a house as an estate. A sprawling place with manicured lawns and clumps of trees that were too artistically grouped to possibly be natural.

The house was weathered red-brick, with gothic pointed arches, turrets, and an intricate series of what looked like blocked-up windows decorating the front facade. I dredged my distant education and recalled it was called something like "blind arcading". The whole place was traditional and imposing, and must have cost more in window cleaning and gardening bills than I earned in a year.

I got my first glimpse of all this from the wrought iron gateway at the end of a long drive when I arrived. I pressed the intercom and waited, staring up into the lens of the CCTV camera, which was supposed to be hidden in the beak of a stone griffin.

It was just after eight in the morning. Two hours since the kidnappers' call. Twenty-two since Dina had been taken.

When the intercom buzzed, I explained I was a friend of Dina's, here to see Orlando. There was a long pause, then a woman's voice said, "She not here. She go away."

"In that case, I'd like to speak to her parents."

"They busy. You go now." The accent was eastern European of some description, although it was difficult to be more accurate through the distortion of the tinny speaker. I was suddenly reminded of the kidnapper's mechanical voice.

"No, I not go now," I said with pleasant precision. "Tell them Dina has been kidnapped, and I need to speak with them before I go to the police, OK? Police, cops, FBI — they'll all be down here, asking questions. You understand me?"

There was a long pause. So long, in fact, that I feared the woman had simply gone away herself and left me to stew with my veiled threats. But a minute or so later the gates began to swing open and I nosed the Navigator through.

There was a motor court around the side of the house, where there was undoubtedly also a tradesman's entrance. I parked at a jaunty angle on the stone setts outside the front door, just for badness.

Now, sitting in one of the coldly unwelcoming drawing rooms, I assumed I was supposed to be so overcome at the orchestrated grandeur on display I would Know My Place.

I offered Orlando's father a lazy smile. "As I mentioned to Jasna when she let me in, I'm just trying to ensure Dina's safe return — that's my only concern. Anything else is a matter for the police. You said you'd already spoken to them, but I can assure you they'll be back. And the FBI. Kidnapping is a federal crime, after all." I waited a beat for that to sink in, then said, "I need to know if anyone had access to Orlando's cellphone yesterday."

"Of course not," he said, brusque.

I crossed my legs, draped an arm along the back of the brocade sofa they'd steered me towards. "You seem very certain, considering your daughter is apparently not staying here with you at the moment?"

He bridled at that, a tall tanned figure I recalled from the charity auction, who had allowed his hair to grey a little around the temples, but drew the line at actually looking his age. He was wearing an open-necked shirt with a pale-pink sweater draped around his shoulders, and loafers with no socks. His face showed distinct signs of regular Botox injections, which made his micro-expressions difficult to read. Nevertheless, gentle provocation always seems to get people to reveal themselves.

328

"Look, Miss Fox, I fail to see what business this is of yours, but Orlando left here only yesterday morning for one of our other properties, and she accidentally left her cell behind. It's on the desk in my study. What can that possibly —"

"Orlando's cell number was used to lure Dina away from her close-protection officer, and into a successful kidnap," I said, piling over his bluster, shutting him down completely. "Her bodyguard was shot trying to prevent her abduction. He's still critical. You know what happened to Torquil Eisenberg, only a few days ago. If your daughter knows anything that might save Dina's life, we need to know."

"Of course she doesn't know anything!" he snapped, and though his face betrayed nothing, his voice told another story. Stress, guilt, and just an underlying trace of anger. But *not*, interestingly enough, directed at me. Not all of it, anyway.

As if realising how much he'd inadvertently given away, he sighed, aimed for a more reasonable tone. "Look, Miss Fox, I can appreciate your concern, but Orlando's cellphone hasn't been outside this house, and my daughter is not available. She's in shock about the death of the Eisenberg boy, of course she is. Orlando's a sensitive girl. I will not have her disturbed."

There was going to be no moving him. Even the prospect of FBI involvement had not shifted him. But he was rattled, and it showed.

My turn to sigh, but quietly, under my breath. Always best to leave of your own volition before you were thrown out. I got to my feet, dug in my jacket pocket for a business card.

"If you won't put me in touch with your daughter direct, then at least please tell her I'd like to talk to her — urgently," I said, handing him the card. He took it by the edges, as if it were dirty. "The office number is on there. It's manned twenty-four hours a day."

"Of course," he said, his relief plain. He put the card down on the side table and rose to shake my hand, going for the elbow clasp with his left, to show what a sincere kind of guy he was. "I hope Dina is returned safely, I really do."

He showed me out into the tiled hallway, where Jasna reappeared instantly to shepherd me to the door. I wondered how much stick she was going to take for letting me through it in the first place.

The business card I'd given him remained on the side table, and I would have taken bets that's where it would stay until the cleaning staff swept it away.

I still wasn't quite sure who'd come out of the encounter ahead as I reached the end of the long straight driveway, and the gates drew slowly open. It was only as I reached them and pulled through that I found another car waiting, pulled up on the other side of the road.

I stopped to catch the number on the front plate, and as I did so the driver climbed out and waved in greeting. I dropped the Navigator's window and watched him stride across the road towards me.

"Hey, Charlie," he called when he was halfway there. "You're looking good."

330

"Hi, Hunt. If you're here to see Orlando, you're out of luck. According to her folks, she's gone away."

To my disappointment, Hunt did not fall into my cunning plan and reveal Orlando's present whereabouts. Instead, he pulled a wry face.

"I've been getting the runaround from her folks, too," he said. "I was hoping that by hanging around here I might spot her coming back." He looked a little shamefaced as he said it, like he was embarrassed to be caught mooning over a girl. "I don't suppose they told you where she is?"

I shook my head.

Hunt was in jeans and a sports jacket, and looked a lot younger, dressed like that, than Orlando's father had managed. "I'm worried about her," he admitted. "She took Tor's death rather hard. I'm not surprised her parents are trying to protect her from the press and stuff like that."

I looked at him, then said dryly. "Yeah, I suppose they might have a bit of a field day when they find out she fixed her own kidnapping."

Hunt stared at me for a moment, then gave a crooked grin. "Ah, so you know about that, do you?" he said. "I thought you'd figure it out eventually."

CHAPTER
FORTY-FIVE

"I didn't meet Orlando until after her kidnap," Hunt admitted. "I was at some party last autumn and she arrived. I found out later it was the first time she'd been out since it happened, and everyone was making a big fuss of her." He gave a small rueful smile. "I thought she'd been ill or something."

We were sitting in a pair of matched leather armchairs in the bar of the tennis club, which happened to be a short hop down the road from Orlando's home. Hunt was a regular, it seemed, and was greeted with deferential respect by the staff, which they temporarily extended to me.

Hunt had ordered a pot of Queen Anne blend tea rather than the usual coffee, explaining that they brought it in from Fortnum & Mason in London, and the kitchen here actually knew what to do with it once it arrived. The tea was presented on a silver tray, in translucent china and a strainer provided, just to show it was none of your bagged rubbish.

The atmosphere was calm and exclusive, and the only similarity with the grubby little bar in Bushwick, where I'd had my chat with Ross, was that — apart from the two of us — the place was deserted.

I kept my face and hands steady, even though I was only too aware that time was ticking on. It was now 9.40 a.m. and Dina had been missing for just shy of twenty-four hours.

"How did you find out?" I asked, as Hunt sat forwards in his chair and poured milk into the cups before giving the teapot a gentle swirl. "That it wasn't a genuine kidnap, I mean."

"She told me — eventually," he said. "I was pretty dumbstruck, to be honest." His voice hushed, even though the staff were too far away to overhear. "I mean, who arranges to have themselves kidnapped, for God's sake?"

"Bored rich kids," I said, accepting the cup he offered. "How else can they get their kicks?" I took a sip and discovered he was right about the tea-making abilities here, raised my cup to him in salute.

He nodded in a distracted way, still frowning. "She said she was going to confess everything to her parents. I'm afraid I tried to talk her out of it on the basis that what was done was done. No point in making trouble for yourself if you don't have to, eh? But I'd guess she went ahead anyway, and that's why they've whisked her away somewhere out of reach, until all this dies down."

"Torquil Eisenberg is dead," I said. "I don't think it will simply die down. The Feds will catch up with her eventually."

His handsome face stayed grave, hands fiddling with his teacup. Eventually, he looked up. "And now Dina's been kidnapped . . . I mean, for real, do you think?"

"They shot her bodyguard," I said. "I'd say that makes it pretty bloody real."

"I thought you were her bodyguard?"

My turn to drop my gaze. "Yeah, so did I."

He was silent for a moment. "I suppose . . . Mrs Willner will have to pay them, won't she? I mean, what choice does she have — after what happened to Tor?"

I took a breath, put down my cup and rubbed a tired hand across my eyes. "It may be a case of willing but not able," I said. "Her ex-husband's been bleeding her dry over the past few years."

"So, what are you saying?" He gave a half-hearted smile. "That she's all fur coat and no knickers?"

"There's a phrase you don't hear much on this side of the Atlantic. But yeah, that's the gist of it."

"Dina must *know* what her mother's situation is. What on earth made her want to get involved in . . . all this?"

"Mrs Willner had kidnap insurance, but Dina's activities make it void. She realises she can't claim on it." I checked my watch, but only a few minutes seemed to have inched by. "Look, I'm sorry but I need to go —"

"Of course," he said, signalling for the bill. One of the hovering staff hurried over to comply. When the waiter had gone, Hunt said, "Hell, Charlie, I'm sorry for the kid. But, if anyone can get her back, I'm sure you can."

Grateful for his apparent confidence, I closed my mind to any other possibilities. "We'll do our best."

334

"Yeah, you don't give up easily, do you? Even after they wrecked your bike and shot you, you're still determined."

I stood. "Well, maybe I just hate to lose."

We shook hands. He had a firm dry grip without the fake sincerity antics of Orlando's father.

"If you find Orlando, tell her I'm thinking of her," he said, giving me a lopsided smile. "Tell her I miss her like hell."

After the reaction of Orlando's father, I wasn't expecting much in the way of cooperation from the other families, but Benedict Benelli's parents had no such qualms about keeping me away from their son.

I gathered shortly after being shown into the art-cluttered living room of the family's palatial home that the cops had already spent most of the morning interviewing Benedict, and if his parents didn't know about the kidnapping scam beforehand, they certainly did now.

The two of them sat one on either side of their son on an oversize sofa, as though to prevent him making a break for it. If the sulkier-than-usual look on Benedict's face was anything to go by, that was a distinct possibility.

He sprawled between them with his arms folded and his fists tightly clenched, staring resolutely at a huge art deco tome on the coffee table in front of him, as if he'd developed a sudden fascination in the work of Clarice Cliff.

Even without their surname, Mr and Mrs Benelli were clearly Italian, from their Mediterranean skin tone and stature, to their clothing style and temperament. Mrs Benelli, in particular, could have been listed as the simple dictionary definition of *voluble*.

"Tell her!" she snapped now, and when that didn't produce instant results, she leant across and cuffed him across the back of the head with her open palm. Serious injury would have resulted if she'd used the back of her hand instead. She wore gold rings on every finger, like some kind of ornamental gemstone knuckledusters.

Benedict flinched away from the blow with more annoyance than pain. His mother was barely five feet tall, even in her stout heels, and probably almost the same in circumference.

"Tell her that you cut off your own finger, that you *disfigured* yourself! And for what?" She appealed to me, talking with her hands as much as her voice. "So he wouldn't have to work hard, that's what!" She shook her head, dabbed at her eyes with a lace handkerchief. "Your father and I, we came here and we started from nothing. *Nothing!* We worked our hands to the bone, and for what? To give our family the chance of a better life. And this is how you repay us? You bring the police to our door!"

"Mama, I never meant —"

That was as much of a protest as Benedict managed before his mother was off again, jewellery vibrating like a seismic recorder in an earthquake zone.

"To what?" she shrieked. "To *cheat* money out of us? Is that how we brought you up? To *lie* to your own flesh and blood? To *steal* from us? Already today we have *lied* to the police for you. We told them you had an accident with your hand, that it was nothing to do with these *kidnappings*." She slapped her hand down on the arm of the sofa, punctuating her words. "No. More. Lies! The girl is missing. She is in danger. You tell her what she wants to know, *Benedetto*."

Mr Benelli, meanwhile, sat in glowering silence at the other end of the sofa. His dark eyes flicked occasionally to his son and reminded me of a Rottweiler — capable of intense emotion and also of showing no humanity at all.

I waited a beat to see if Benedict's mother was going to launch another broadside, or his father was going to bite somebody, before I turned my gaze onto the boy himself.

"Was it you who originally made contact with Lennon?" I asked. I'd chosen the question carefully, intending to drip onto him how much I appeared to know, without giving away how little that really was. It didn't quite get the reaction I'd been hoping for.

"Who?" Benedict demanded, with enough genuine confusion and anger to ring true.

"Answer her!" Mrs Benelli yelled, fetching him another stinging blow round the back of the head.

"Mrs Benelli, please," I protested, torn between letting her beat some sense *into* him, and managing to get some sense *out* of him before brain damage set in.

"I don't know any names," Benedict muttered, trying to rub his sore scalp and make it look like he was smoothing his hair down instead. "Manda knows. She got me into this." As he spoke, he flicked his eyes towards his mother. Her lips thinned expressively at the name and she folded her hands under her ample bosom. I found myself mentally wanting to do the same thing.

Manda Dempsey. No surprises there. I might have known that new leaf was just a version of the old one.

"How long have you known her?"

"I guess she was around, but I never noticed her 'til after she was kidnapped. She was . . . different afterward." He shrugged. "I don't know — kinda empowered. We got to be friends."

Mrs Benelli restricted herself to a powerful harrumph.

"So, she talked you into it." I tried that one on him to see how it fit. He grabbed the metaphorical lifebelt with both hands.

"Yes! She kept on about how easy it was — to gain independence. Not to have to go crawling to anybody for money."

"Like normal people have to," I said dryly. "Who crawl to their bosses, or their customers, every working day of their lives."

"Benedict will be working from now on, and he will be working hard," his mother said fiercely. "He will start right at the bottom, like his father, in the factory. And he will work his way up. Any money he gets from now on, he will earn!"

I suppressed a sigh as Benedict's face closed up again. Reminding him of what he'd lost — and what he had to lose — was not going to get him to talk more

338

openly. The Benellis were, I reflected, as protective and obstructive in their own way as Orlando's father had been.

"So, did Manda also recruit Dina and Torquil, or was it your turn?"

Colour lit along his cheekbones. "I knew Dina wanted to get involved," he admitted. "That's why we went to that stupid party — to meet with her and talk about it. And that was our big mistake."

I wondered briefly how he managed to narrow down one error among so many others. "In what way?"

"That's where Tor found out what we'd been doing. How were we to know he had that goddamn stateroom wired?"

His mother made another protest, but a more automatic one this time, more at the language than the meaning.

I remembered Orlando's flustered reaction, the day she and Manda had come to see Dina after Torquil had been snatched, when I'd told her he liked to record what went on aboard the family yacht. I'd thought that, like Nicola Eisenberg before her, Orlando might have been caught in some kind of compromising position of her own. But it was clear Torquil had captured more than just sexual indiscretions.

"So he knew about the fake kidnaps and he tried to blackmail you, is that it?"

There was a flash in Benedict's eyes. "He wanted in, but of course he wanted his to be bigger and better than all the others," he said, bitter. "But we knew we couldn't trust him not to shoot his mouth off.

Especially after the fiasco at the riding club. He was gonna blow the whole —"

He broke off suddenly, realising that what he'd been about to say sounded very much like motive for wanting Torquil out of the way. Permanently. Mr Benelli's eyes flickered in his direction, and I swear I heard an almost subliminal growl start up somewhere deep in the man's chest, although it might simply have been the air con cycling.

I asked quietly, "So, what did you decide to do about that? Kidnap him to keep him quiet, and then shut him up for good?"

"No!" The fear in Benedict's face was stark and uncompromising, but I didn't necessarily take it as a sign that he was innocent. "I had nothing to do with that." It seemed to be a company line.

"So, who arranged the 'fiasco' at the riding club? How did you get in touch with the guys who made the attempt?"

He shrugged. "I didn't. Manda and Orlando handled it. They told the guys where and when, gave them the details. I didn't know any of it."

Didn't want to know. Hmm, maybe Benedict wasn't an entirely lost cause. His mother's plan for hard labour might either break or make him.

"And Torquil?"

"I don't know!" His voice was almost a shout, eyes darting towards his mother as if expecting to dodge another blow. She kept her hands clasped in her lap with an obvious effort of will. "I swear! I. Don't. Know."

340

I stared at him for a long time, but his gaze remained defiant and unblinking. I wondered, if he'd been alone, how long it would have taken me to get any more out of him. Too bad I wouldn't find that out.

"OK, Benedict," I said wearily. "Just remember, though, that the cops will be back, and they really don't like being lied to. Try it with the Feds and you'll find yourself on the first plane to Cuba. And people like the Eisenbergs will not let things like this go unpunished." I rose, gave him a last hard stare. "There are worse places to spend the next twenty-five years than the factory floor."

It was just before noon. Dina had been missing almost twenty-six hours. I was willing to bet that, wherever she was right now, it had to be worse than anywhere Benedict's parents could devise.

CHAPTER
FORTY-SIX

"I wondered how long it would take you to get around to me," Manda Dempsey said when she opened the door to her penthouse apartment.

She'd had a little time to prepare for my arrival on her doorstep. The glossy Manhattan apartment building had uniformed security who took their role more seriously than simply being a human doorstop with gold braid. They'd valet-parked the Navigator and called up to see if Miss Dempsey "might be willing to receive me", seeming almost disappointed when she said yes.

Now, Manda led the way into the split-level living area. The room occupied a corner of the building, and faced partly north up Fifth Avenue, and east to catch the light. It was dominated by glass, as with Caroline Willner's house in Long Island, but here the view was of the Empire State and the Chrysler Building, their outlines hazy in the afternoon sun.

"Quite a place you have here," I murmured.

She paused by a low sofa, following my gaze as if the view was something she looked at so rarely she'd forgotten it was there.

"I like it," she said, and sat down. There was a bottle of wine open on the table by her elbow and she picked up her half-drunk glass, but didn't offer one to me. "Any news of Dina?"

Only that she's now been gone twenty-nine hours . . .

"They've asked for ten million," I said, noting the way her eyebrows climbed a little as she drank. She held the gesture a fraction too long for it to be entirely genuine. "But you knew that, didn't you, Amanda?"

"No," she said evenly. "I was just thinking that they're getting kinda ambitious. They only asked one million for me."

"Ah, well, now they have experience on their side," I said, sitting down without an invite, as it didn't look like she was going to extend one.

I debated on telling her about the kidnappers' claims over the authenticity of the Eisenberg Rainbow, decided against. Parker was still trying to verify that information, and Brandon Eisenberg was proving evasive to say the least. "Lennon and his pal got away clean with those jewels last time. Maybe it's double or quits."

"Ah," she said, giving me a smile that made her cheeks dimple, "so you know his name. Very good." She paused. "Or were you hoping that alone might shock me into a full confession?"

"Everyone should have a dream," I said dryly. "You don't deny you know him, then?"

"Not much point in that." She snorted into her wine, put the deep-bowled glass down on the side table. "You already know Lennon and Ross were doing the kidnappings for us — the *fake* kidnappings, that is." The smile grew broader. "And I was the one who gave them Dina's schedule, told them when she'd be at the riding club. I even told them she had a bodyguard called Charlie who was a tough customer. I completely overlooked the fact they'd automatically assume you were a guy. I mean, what a laugh!"

"Oh yeah, hilarious . . ." I muttered, remembering again the crunch Raleigh's arm gave out as his bones splintered. "So, you recruited Lennon at a party? How did *that* come up in conversation?"

She shook her head, wagged a finger. "Uh-uh, not guilty. Maybe I should warn you, Charlie, I've had some very dour detectives here all afternoon, and they didn't succeed in beating a confession out of me, either. Can't get what isn't there, honey."

"You sound disappointed. But then, you paid to have Lennon and his mate rough you up, didn't you, Amanda?"

She shrugged. "Why not?" she asked. "It's a free country, and I kinda like it." She leant forwards, checking my face for signs of shock, and reached for her glass again. "Maybe you should loosen up and give it a try. Pleasure and pain are very closely related, after all. All those endorphins rushing around your system! Until you've had the experience, how do you know you won't like it?"

I fought to hold down a sudden memory that threatened to burst loose. A dark bitter night, four distinct male shapes, the rancid fear, and the huff of expelled breath from the effort they were putting into working me over. It was a long time ago but it might have been only last night for all its vivid flavour. "Been there, done that, thanks all the same," I said calmly. "Didn't think much of it."

Another sideways little smile. "Maybe they simply weren't very good."

"Trust me, they were experts."

Her smile faded to a frown, but she refused to give me the satisfaction of asking more. Which, in turn, saved me the trouble of telling her to mind her own bloody business. I reckoned that made us even.

"Is that what happened to Torquil?" I asked. "You were trying to broaden his horizons as far as the enjoyment of pain went, and it all got a bit out of hand?"

"Nice try, Charlie, but for once you're way off base. Torquil wasn't in the game plan. Personally, I didn't want anything to do with him. Can't blame us if he looked elsewhere and wasn't careful enough about who he talked to."

"So you're saying he bypassed your exclusive little club and did a deal direct with Lennon, is that it?"

"Lennon?" Her eyes were positively sparking. "Lennon and his friend couldn't plan their way out of a paper bag, honey. Why do you think we had to spoon-feed them every scrap of information?"

"But since then Lennon's found himself another partner, hasn't he? And this guy is playing for real. You aren't calling the shots anymore, Manda."

345

"Who says I ever was? I told you that you were off base, Charlie, but *I* wasn't the first one kidnapped, now was I?" She toed off her shoes and tucked her feet up on the sofa underneath her, for all the world relaxed. Only the tightness of her fingers around the stem of her wine glass gave her away. "If you want answers about Lennon and who he might have gone to, you're going to have to speak to the person who knows him — the one who first recruited *me*, in fact."

"And that is?"

"Oh come on — Orlando, of course." She smiled again. "But I reckon you're gonna have your work cut out getting to her. Good luck with that."

"Yeah," I agreed, "she hasn't even told Hunt where she is."

"Well, then." She raised her glass in mock salute. "From what I've seen of that pair, they're besotted. If she hasn't told *him* where to find her, you've no chance."

I left soon after that. There wasn't much more I was going to get out of Manda, and the urge to smack her around was beginning to get the better of me.

As I waited for the valet to retrieve the Navigator from wherever they'd stashed it nearby, my cellphone began to buzz in my pocket. When I pulled it out and saw Parker's number on the display, my heart gave a sudden lurch in my chest.

"Hi," I said sharply. "What's happened?"

"I think I should . . . tell you when I see you."

Oh, shit! Please, not another body . . . ?

346

I checked my watch for the hundredth time. It was after four in the afternoon. Dina had now been held over thirty hours. A lifetime, but surely too soon for Lennon and his new partner to have killed their hostage?

"Is she —?"

"No, we think she's still alive." I heard the cautious note, and the strain, and could have screamed at his refusal to speak plainly over an open line.

"You *think*? Parker! What the fuck does that mean?"

The valet pulled up smartly at the kerb and hopped down out of the Navigator's driving seat, a cheery comment dying on his lips as he caught sight of my face. He stuffed the valet ticket into my numb fingers and scurried away without waiting for a tip.

"Look, just . . . you better get back here, Charlie," he said, and I heard his shaky sigh. *Whatever it is, it's bad.* "Fast as you can."

CHAPTER
FORTY-SEVEN

Trying to get from the middle of Manhattan out to Long Island, by four-wheel transport, towards the close of the afternoon, will not put you in the running for any official land-speed records. I did my best, but as I sat and cursed in traffic, I mourned the demise of the Buell all over again.

Meanwhile, the clock ticked round to 7p.m.

Thirty-three hours.

Finally, I reached the Willners' driveway. And as I braked hard and swung the Navigator through the entrance, I nearly sent the four security people stationed there into group cardiac arrest. As one, right hands dived inside jackets. I made sure I kept both mine well in view as I came to a more moderate halt on the gravel.

It was only then that I recognised a couple of the guys as Gleason's men. Or rather — Eisenberg's.

What the . . .?

I got out slowly, making no overtly threatening moves. They recognised me soon enough not to slot me, which would have put the capping piece on a thoroughly shitty day.

348

I nodded to them as they relaxed back into hyped alertness, and jogged up the steps, aware that things were probably not about to get any better.

Parker was waiting in the open-plan living area, with both Brandon and Nicola Eisenberg occupying one sofa, and Caroline Willner in her usual high-backed chair. Nicola Eisenberg's own personal bodyguard was hovering discreetly nearby with Gleason. Landers was in the far corner, out of direct line of the windows, watching all the exits. Not that we were expecting a direct attack, but it was the kind of ingrained behaviour Parker paid him for.

Through the glass, clouds were gathering darkened over the ocean, and the sun had begun a spectacular dying fall in the western sky, leaving a trail of streaks and sorrow.

Nobody was watching the sunset.

Parker was standing alongside Caroline Willner's chair, as if providing support on a proximity basis alone. His lean face was tired, but there was more to it than that, and with a jolt I recognised it as defeat. He had the look of a field commander fresh from a bloody skirmish, who had never expected to lose the troops under him.

"What's happened?" I demanded.

Parker hesitated a moment and glanced at Caroline Willner. She caught the gesture.

"Go on, Mr Armstrong." She gave a slightly mechanical nod. "Please, say what needs to be said." She was deathly pale, but holding.

349

Parker stepped over to a side table. On it was an untidy cardboard package, sliced open. He pulled a latex glove out of his pocket and used that, folded over, to hold the box out to me. I checked the set faces, staring with varying degrees of horror and sympathy. Then Nicola Eisenberg averted her head, trying to make it look as if she were merely leaning her chin on her fist, resting on the arm of the sofa, rather than covering her mouth. Gleason had me under observation on a near-molecular level.

I leant forwards, and looked in the box.

Nestling inside was not the finger I'd been half expecting. Instead, it was a small bluish-white rubbery triangle, two edges smoothly rounded, and the last ragged and stained with dark flecks. It would have been hard to identify as part of a human body, were it not for the piercing through the lobe of what had once clearly been the lower half of a left ear.

One of the pearl drop earrings that Dina had inherited from her grandmother was still studded through it.

I swallowed, forced myself to be objective, rational, and channelled all the revulsion into a bright flame of rage. When I looked up, my gaze was as cold and empty as I could contrive.

"When did this arrive?" I asked. "And who delivered it?"

"It came not long before I called you," Parker said tightly. "We already checked. Local courier company, pickup from the lobby of an apparently random apartment block, delivery instructions left with the package, cash in an envelope."

A dead end, in other words. Still, discovering that much in the time it had taken me to battle with traffic was fast work.

I looked at Parker and saw he was waiting for me to ask the next question — the obvious question — the way you wait for someone to flinch.

"So, was it cut off when she was still alive?" I lifted my chin. "Or after she was dead?"

Over to my left, I heard Nicola Eisenberg suck in a harsh breath. "My God," she murmured, "you're one hard-faced bitch . . ."

Well, it takes one to know one.

I might have voiced that opinion out loud, but Parker silenced her with a single, lethal stare. "There's a forensic pathologist on his way now," he said, checking his watch. "I called in a favour. He should be able to tell us how long it's been . . . severed, and under what circumstances."

He put it so much more diplomatically than I had, which is why he was the boss.

"We need to know quickly — before we go any further negotiating their demands." *My God, they've had her less than two days and already they're hacking bits off.*

I didn't need to see the anguish in Parker's eyes to know the same thought had passed through his mind.

Brandon Eisenberg cleared his throat. "I have suggested to Mrs Willner that I be permitted to make a substantial contribution to Dina's ransom." His wife shot him a poisonous glare, gave his arm an unsubtle jab. "Pay it, is basically what I'm saying," he added flatly.

Well, that answered the question of whether Nicola Eisenberg knew about his attempt to cheat her son's kidnappers with the Rainbow replica. I remembered again that she'd collapsed shortly after the ransom drop had gone so badly awry. Was that when she found out?

Caroline Willner, meanwhile, had come stiffly upright in her chair, no mean feat when she already looked racked tight enough to crack her bones. She made to speak, but Nicola Eisenberg flashed a palm in warning.

"No. We *will* do this," she said ominously. "For Torquil, as much as for Dina."

She looked about to expand on that theme, but Eisenberg diverted her. "We can argue about the details later," he said, brusque when Caroline Willner herself would have baulked further. "For now, let's just concentrate on getting your daughter home safe and sound, hmm?"

He had the air of a man who was approached by people constantly for handouts and found all these polite "oh, no, I couldn't possibly" coy protestations rather irksome.

Caroline Willner must have sensed this. She paused a moment as if to collect herself, then said simply, "Thank you."

He nodded a couple of times, not making eye contact, but his linked hands flexed briefly in his lap.

Nicola Eisenberg gave a grim and bitter little half smile. Regardless of the fact that Torquil had almost undoubtedly been dead before we could have reached him, ransom paid or not, I realised she now had a stick to beat her husband with to the end of his days. I wondered if she would ever feel it was worth the price.

For the moment, however, the new-found power had its compensations. She rose, graceful in victory. Eisenberg automatically followed suit, as if either staying or going held no great appeal.

"What do the authorities say about all this?" I asked, looking around at them. Suddenly, nobody wanted to meet my eyes. I jerked a hand towards the box with its grisly contents. "How have you managed to keep *that* away from them?"

"We are not without considerable influence in government," Nicola Eisenberg said, as if that answered everything. "We'll take our leave." She bent to exchange distant air kisses on both cheeks with her hostess. She shook hands with Parker, covering both his with her own. "Do let us know as soon as you need the money." Her eyes slid sideways in the direction of her husband, half a pace behind. "It will be available immediately."

"Thank you," Parker said neutrally, disengaging himself. "I'm sure we'll speak soon."

I didn't merit a handshake, just a vague smile as the entourage headed for the door. Gleason gave me a cool nod in passing, though, which was the equivalent of a high five and a bear hug in this business.

When they'd gone, Caroline Willner got slowly to her feet, as if suddenly feeling her bones, and stood with one hand resting on the back of her chair.

"I believe Mr Armstrong has something important to tell you, Charlie," she said gravely.

A muscle jumped in the side of Parker's jaw. "It can wait."

"Really?" she said, her voice cool. "Your decision, of course, but I couldn't help overhearing the phone call you received, and it sounded rather urgent to me." She gave me a slight smile. "I shall be in my sitting room, if there's any news of my daughter." And with that she turned on her immaculate heel and walked out of the room, tall and composed by what could only have been a major act of self-control. Landers caught Parker's eye and followed her out. If I didn't know him better, I might have suspected he was relieved by the excuse to leave.

There was a long uncomfortable silence after they'd gone. I stuffed my hands into my pockets and waited for Parker to speak. He did not appear to be in any hurry to do so.

"Is it Sean?" I asked then, keeping my voice level with the same kind of effort that Caroline Willner must have employed.

"No," Parker said, suddenly realising what I must have thought. "Jesus, no. Don't you think I would have told you something like that right off the bat?"

I closed my eyes for a moment, relief flooding in. I'd missed seeing him the last couple of days, my mind so filled with life and death of another kind. For once, his condition had failed to fill my every waking minute. So, now — alongside the relief — guilt came crashing in over the top like a freak wave.

354

Am I leaving him behind? Is it starting already?

Unbidden, unwelcome, I felt the burn of tears behind my eyelids and my ears were filled with a roaring so fierce I didn't hear Parker cross the floor between us until he took hold of my arms.

"I'm sorry, Charlie," he said softly. "I didn't mean . . ."

"It's just, the last time we talked about . . . Sean, you said there were signs . . ." I paused, swallowed all that betraying, useless emotion back down again. "That he wasn't going to come back from this." I stopped, shrugged helplessly.

The action loosened Parker's grip. He let his hands glide up and down my arms, soothing.

"And you said you couldn't deal, Charlie, and I totally get that. I won't burden you with any decisions right now."

"Oh, great." I gave a shaky laugh that turned sharply downhill somewhere in my chest. "So, now I'm going to worry about you keeping bad news from me."

His hands tightened again, and he ducked his head, forcing me to make eye contact. "I won't lie to you, either," he said. "Nothing's changed since we last spoke, OK?"

Parker's concern and his integrity were two of the characteristics I valued most about him. But suddenly the image of dancing together at the charity auction seemed very fresh and clear in my mind. My heart rate accelerated, mouth drying. I looked into those cool grey eyes and saw I wasn't the only one assailed by the memory.

"*He's interested*," Dina had said. "*I can tell*." At the time, I'd dismissed it as her attempt to get a rise out of me.

But if it wasn't . . . what then?

"I'm sorry," Parker said again.

And then he stepped in close, cupped my face between gentle hands, and kissed me.

CHAPTER
FORTY-EIGHT

It was the tenderness that was almost my undoing. With Sean, the sexual fascination between us had always been so fierce, so intense, that at times it almost seemed like confrontation.

But Parker revealed himself completely in the brief longing of his touch. It lit along my nerves like ice and fire and drew responses I wasn't prepared for, including the urge to meet him more than halfway.

This wasn't just sex. This was love.

Confusion reigning, I broke the kiss, stepped back. But, glancing into his face I saw anguish in the realisation of what he might have given away of himself in that evanescent moment. Of what it might mean — for all of us. He took a breath.

And I realised with a flowering dismay that I could fall for him. If I let myself. They might share many traits, but he was not Sean. I would not open my eyes every morning and see an echo of what I had lost. This could be something else completely. If I let it.

I reached up, touched his cheek, murmured, "Don't."

He captured my hand with his own, held it while he turned his head and pressed his lips into my palm. "I'm sorry," he repeated. "I never meant for —"

"I know," I said. "Neither did I."

He gave a rueful smile that did nothing to quiet the chaos of his gaze, and let go of me. With distance, we could both regain some semblance of sanity.

In a voice that was still woefully inadequate, I said, "Wow, it must be bad news if you're prepared to go to those kind of lengths to distract me."

He knew what I was doing, of course he did, but he let it ride. Eventually, with great reluctance, he said, "I had a call from Epps."

"*Conrad* Epps?" It was a stupid question, but the connotations knocked me sideways into stupidity. Conrad Epps held some high-grade position within the US security services. I could only guess at the scope of his power, but when my father had found himself in serious trouble over here the previous winter, only someone with Epps's clout had been able to disentangle him.

The only trouble was, once you turned over the kind of rock men like Epps liked to lurk under, it could never quite be turned back again. He didn't do favours for nothing — he kept score. And because of that, we were sucked into his private war with the Fourth Day cult in California, during which . . . Well, let's just say that if Epps had left well alone, Sean would not be in his current condition.

I had very mixed feelings about Conrad Epps.

"What does he want now?" I demanded roughly. "And what's it going to cost us this time?"

Parker raised an eyebrow. He was regaining his poise, but there was still a tension about him that I mistakenly put down to our encounter, rather than the news he had to impart.

"He called with an apology — and a warning," he said. "Charlie . . . they lost him."

"Lost . . .?" It took me a moment to put the correct meaning on that word. *Lost* as in *misplaced*, as in *escaped*. As in *free and clear* . . .

And this time, I didn't need to ask who he was talking about.

I knew.

The man who had put Sean in his coma, who had lied and cheated, and murdered, for no more desperate reason than his own desire to possess something that didn't belong to him. For greed. For power.

Shit!

"I should have killed that fucker when I had the chance."

"Then we wouldn't be here," Parker said quietly.

"No," I agreed. I tried to raise a smile and only got halfway. "At best, I'd probably be on Death Row."

Parker shook his head with a hint of sadness. "Epps wouldn't have let you die, Charlie," he said. "How could he just let someone with your . . . talent go to waste? But he would have owned you to the grave."

I didn't respond to that. It's always hard to counter an argument you recognise to be bloody impregnable.

"How?" I said then. "How did he get away, I mean?" I couldn't even bring myself to say the man's name. It was easier to be coolly objective about the whole thing. To speak about him as an abstract concept, rather than an utterly worthless human being.

"Epps was not forthcoming with details," Parker said dryly.

"Yeah, no surprises there."

He sighed. "Look, I know how you feel. Trust me. I was there. I saw what that bastard did — and not just to Sean."

I swallowed down the sour taste in my mouth, recognised that Parker had been as hurt by what had happened almost as much as I had. We'd both lost Sean, however permanent or temporary that might turn out to be. Perhaps it was the solidarity of loss that had just brought us together — or so I tried to tell myself.

"I thought Epps would have used him up and spat out the empty husk by now," I said instead. "It's not like him to be merciful."

Parker leant his shoulder against the glass wall, his face bathed in soft reflected light from the last of the evening sun. "Well, I guess the guy could be pretty persuasive, you have to give him that." And if he sounded regretful, it was perhaps because we'd both been taken in, at one time or another. "In this case, all I know is he persuaded Epps he could give him a lead into various militia groups Fourth Day had ties to. Offered to go undercover."

I stared at him. "Jesus H Christ," I muttered. "Epps just bloody let him go and he did a runner."

Another twisted smile. "That would be my guess."

"When?"

"Six weeks ago."

"He's been on the run for *six weeks*?" I repeated. "And Epps is ringing you *now*?"

Parker's eyes flicked to mine. "Apparently, he believed he might still be able to retrieve him without making the fact public," he said solemnly. "The guy's dropped right off the grid."

"I'd lay odds I could find him."

Another flicker. "Maybe that was another reason he didn't tell us."

"Parker, I —"

He moved closer and all the spit dried on my tongue, but all he did was look down at me, eyes roving my face. I don't know what he was searching for, or if he found it.

"Revenge is a poor servant, but a worse master," he said. "Don't let it rule you, Charlie."

I won't. Not yet.

"In case it's escaped you," I said, forcing a lightness I was a long way from feeling, "we're up to our necks in a situation here. How can I think of going after anyone when we don't know if Dina is alive or dead?"

If Parker saw through the blatant evasion in my words, he didn't get a chance to call me on it. Footsteps in the hall had us both turning. Landers entered, gaze taking in our tension, if not — I hoped — the reasons behind it.

"Pathologist's here, boss," he said.

Parker nodded and turned away, pulling on a set of gloves to pick up the gruesome package. By the doorway he paused, glanced back.

"And when we know — one way or the other," he said, "what then?"

CHAPTER
FORTY-NINE

The buzz of my cellphone brought me paddling resentfully out of sleep. By the time I was alert enough to react, the noise had stopped, as is always the way. I sat up, muttering under my breath, and reached for the phone anyway, recognising as I did so that it was a text message rather than a missed call.

I was still fully clothed and lying on top of the bedclothes after Parker more or less ordered me to get some rest. It was only when I'd got to my room and crawled onto the bed that the aching tiredness caught up with me. All in all, I hadn't had much sleep over the past few days.

I glanced blearily at my watch, realising I'd been out like the dead for over four hours.

It was close to midnight. Dina's ordeal had so far lasted thirty-eight hours, and showed no signs of ending yet.

I didn't recognise the number on the display but opened the message anyway.

"MUST meet with you! Very urgent! I have vital info! Come alone! Tell no one! PLEASE!! Orlando."

The similarities with the message sent to lure Torquil into ambush were stark enough to kick-start my brain.

I sat for a moment, furiously processing. Orlando had left her usual cellphone at her parents' place. Or — more likely, I thought now — they'd made her leave it behind in the vain hope of breaking off her contact with her friends. But Orlando was clearly more resourceful than that.

Only thing was, how had she got hold of my number?

The Willners had it, of course. I'd made sure it was programmed into Dina's phone, but that had been switched off since her abduction, the GPS tracker disabled. And if Dina had given the number to Orlando *after* she'd been taken, that meant Orlando was party to the other girl's mutilation.

I could only hope not.

The only other person I'd given it to had been one of the original kidnappers, Ross, and I couldn't see why he would have gone to Orlando with that information.

I staggered into the bathroom and splashed cold water onto my face. It was only partially successful in waking me up. I was still stiff from being knocked off the Buell and this brief period of inactivity seemed to highlight every bruise and bang.

I cleaned my teeth, changed my shirt for something slightly less crumpled, and headed back upstairs to the living area.

Parker was sitting drinking coffee alone in the quiet room. Outside the glass, rain was falling at a steady slant in the moonlight, one of those freak weather events. I could see it pounding patches of water flat like wind across a field of corn.

Parker rose when I came in, and the smile he gave me contained an inner brightness that both warmed and chilled me.

"Hi," he said, his voice husky. "Feeling better?"

I said, awkward, "Too early to tell," which was the truth on many levels. "Any word on McGregor?"

"Stable. No change. They're hopeful, at least."

"Good." I held up my phone. "I've just received a text I think you ought to see."

I helped myself to coffee from the insulated cafetière on the table while he thumbed through the brief message, frowning.

"I don't like it," he said bluntly. "It's a trap and they don't care if we know it." He looked up, his eyes narrowed. "You want to do it, huh?"

I nodded. "They've cut off half Dina's ear, Parker. How can I not, if there's a chance she's still alive —?"

"She is," he said. "Or, she was when the ear was severed, according to the pathologist. Something to do with the amount of blood in the tissue." He paused. "He reckons they probably used a pair of shears. Must have hurt like hell."

I shut that one out. "I'm going to this meet."

"Charlie —"

"I've already sent a reply asking when and where."

His eyebrow went up. "Last time I checked, you still work for me," he said. "That makes me responsible for your safety."

"What safety? The bottom line in this job is to get ourselves killed before our client," I said, keeping my voice even. "Either this message really is from Orlando, in which case she might be able to give us something that gets us closer to Lennon or the guy he's working with, or it's a trap, as you say. In which case, I may have the opportunity to grab whoever's sent to grab me. I have to go, Parker," I added, when he would have cut in again. "It's as much part of the job as standing in front of them in a hostile crowd."

"Let me come with you —"

"You can't," I said gently. "What if they call again? We can't take the risk."

He was silent for a moment, then he nodded. "OK, but stay sharp. And keep me informed. Understood?"

"Yes, boss," I murmured.

My phone buzzed again and I checked the incoming message. "Ten minutes," I said, reading it. "The parking area just off the beach, near where Torquil was taken."

Parker's face was grave. "Let's just hope they're not planning on a repeat performance."

I reached the parking area Orlando had specified exactly seven minutes later and found it deserted. There was a single multidirectional lamppost in the centre, but only half the bulbs appeared to be working, casting lopsided shadows across the space. The rain was still gusting through the beams, clouds scudding past a high moon.

As I swung the Navigator round in a slow circle, the headlights played across wind-blown sandy asphalt and not a lot else.

I parked up in the centre, on the darker side of the lamppost, facing the entrance. There, it would be difficult for anyone to advance from the scrub without being seen. I cracked the window, and cut the engine and the lights.

The smells and sounds of the ocean drifted in through the slot above the glass. In the dark, the rush of breakers on the beach took on a monumental quality, even above the drum of rain on the SUV's roof. I was suddenly very aware of my own insignificance in the great scheme of things.

I touched a finger to my lips, as if I could still feel the imprint of Parker's mouth on mine. What had happened between us still felt a little unreal, so that I was almost afraid to mention it to him, just in case it really had all been a dream. But then I remembered his smile, when I'd walked back into the living area.

No, it hadn't been a dream.

But what the hell did I — did *we* — do about it?

The attraction to Parker had taken me by surprise. He'd been brilliant since the shooting, compassionate, a real friend. But I'd never had eyes for anyone other than Sean and I felt loathsomely unfaithful, regardless of the circumstances leading up to that kiss.

I rubbed a hand across my eyes. Combat stress could heighten emotions of all kinds, and maybe that was part of the reason for my confusion — little more than a dramatic release of tension. I told myself there would be a time to sort out my feelings. But later — much later.

"How long are you going to wait for Sean?" whispered an insistent little demon on my shoulder. *"And how long do you think Parker will wait for you?"*

366

It was a relief to see a set of headlights turn off the main road at that moment. I squinted in the glare as the lights panned across the Navigator's windscreen. They bounced a little as the vehicle behind them negotiated the rough shoulder leading to the car park.

It pulled alongside me, nose to tail, and I recognised the outline of a 7 series BMW. Probably the same one that had brought Orlando and Manda to visit Dina, the day after Torquil had been kidnapped.

A lot seemed to have happened since then.

The driver's door opened and a man got out. A big guy, built like a rugby player. As he turned, I caught him in profile and saw the broken nose that triggered my memory. So, she'd brought the same personal bodyguard with her as well.

I opened the Navigator's door and stepped down, keeping my arms relaxed. The rain instantly drenched my bare head and found its way straight down the back of my jacket collar, but the air was surprisingly warm.

The bodyguard muscled in and flicked his fingers towards my hands, indicating I should spread for a search. I stood my ground and stared right back.

"Either she wants to talk to me or she doesn't," I said tiredly. "But you lay a finger on me and I will rip off both your arms and beat you to death with the wet ends. Your choice."

He hesitated, his expression mulish. I shrugged and reached for the Navigator's door handle, like I really didn't care. It was a calculated risk.

"Wait!"

I stopped. The Bee-Em's darkened rear glass had dropped a few inches and Orlando's face appeared, paler than ever in the mix of sodium and moonlight, blinking as the rain splashed inside.

"Charlie, please," she said, sounding genuinely distraught. "Vincent, it's OK. Please, just let her get in the car."

The bodyguard, Vincent, didn't like it. I wouldn't have done, in his place, but he opened the rear door and jerked his head to signify I should get in. I took my time about it, taking a perverse satisfaction from the fact he was getting just as wet as I was.

Eventually, I shrugged and climbed in. Orlando slid over to the far side of the rear bench seat to give me room, and the bodyguard slammed the door after me with a certain amount of venom. He got back into the front, twisting round in his seat so he could keep an eye on me.

I don't know where Orlando had been hiding out, but she looked terrible, which for her probably meant she hadn't been near a hairdresser or a nail salon for the best part of a week.

"Is it true about Dina being taken?" she demanded by way of greeting.

I raised a dripping eyebrow. "How do you know anything's happened to Dina?"

As far as I was aware, it wasn't public that she had been kidnapped. Certainly we'd done our best to keep the information away from the authorities, at Caroline Willner's insistence. The only investigating they were doing related to Torquil Eisenberg's death.

Orlando's eyes slid towards Vincent and I nodded in understanding. The ex-military grapevine was better than any twenty-four-hour news channel. I glanced back at the girl on the back seat.

"It's true that your boys sliced off her ear, yes."

Her hands flew to her face, fingers rigid. "Oh, God," she choked. "They're not 'my boys'. How can you say that? You think I'd do something like that to one of my friends?"

I sat back into the corner, making it harder for Vincent to watch me. "Why not?" I said mildly. "Torquil was supposedly one of your friends, wasn't he? And you had him beaten to death."

"No! That wasn't . . . I didn't —"

"Didn't what, Orlando?" I let my voice harden. "Didn't authorise that? So who did? The same person who told you to feed me that crap about Torquil stalking you before your kidnap?"

"Nobody told me to *do* anything! Nobody 'authorised' anything!" She let her hands fall back into her lap, her head drop, looked about to weep. "They must have done it themselves."

"According to your friend, Manda, Lennon couldn't plan his way out of a wet paper bag. So, who's he working with?"

"I don't know," she muttered.

"Well, think harder," I said. "You created this monster. You're going to have to help me deal with it."

Her head shot up again. "But . . . that will mean everyone will know . . . about us. What we did."

"Yes," I said, not in the mood to let her down gently. That the prospect of exposure and disgrace seemed to horrify her more than murder, did little to arouse my sympathy. "How did you approach Lennon — who is he?"

She shrugged. "Just some guy I knew from college," she said. "We did drama classes together. He wanted to be an actor. And then I saw him again, at some party last spring. We got chatting. I asked him how he was doing, and he said the only decent piece of work he'd gotten was playing one of the bad guys in some TV cop show pilot that never took off. And the idea just . . . came to me."

"To have yourself kidnapped." I tried to stay neutral, but it came out flat instead. I sighed. "Why, Orlando? What possessed you to get yourself into this mess in the first place?"

That brought a little fire into her eyes, a little colour into her cheeks. "You have absolutely no clue what it's like," she said, voice low. "You think it's so fine, having money, horses, cars, clothes, but it's like being in gaol."

"I can think of a few prisoners who'd disagree with you."

She made a gesture of impatience, as if she hadn't expected someone like me to be able to comprehend something on the scale of her life. "You saw my father, right? My mother's in Europe someplace, touring art galleries, or museums, or something like that. I don't think he even knows which country she's in. If they pay that much attention to each other, how much do you think they ever paid to me?"

CHAPTER
FIFTY

"All my life, someone else has decided things for me," Orlando said, in a voice bitter-edged with sullen. "My father wanted a boy — had this name all picked out. When I turned out to be a girl, they couldn't be bothered to think of another." She paused, pleating the belt of her coat with nervous fingers. "I just wanted some control over my own destiny for a change."

I stared at her. "And how exactly do you achieve that by putting yourself completely at the mercy of a stranger?"

"You just don't get it," she snapped. "I was in control, deep down. I knew I was safe. Even when I was locked up, tied up, I knew they wouldn't do anything I didn't want them to."

"You put a hell of a lot of trust in someone you knew slightly from college."

Her turn to stare. "But I was paying him," she said blankly, like that was enough to ensure anyone's loyalty.

"How much?"

She shrugged, as if it were vulgar to discuss it. "Fifty grand," she said at last. She might as well have said fifty bucks, for all it meant to her. "I don't know how much of that he gave to the other guy, Ross."

I wondered if she had any concept of what that amount of money would mean to the average college kid, or what they'd be prepared to do in order to get it.

"How did you get in touch with Lennon if he's always changing his cellphone number?" I asked.

"Yeah, when he played a part, he really played it," she said frowning. "If the one I had for him was dead, I had to go sit in a coffee shop down near the boardwalk on Coney Island, around ten in the morning." She gave me the name of the place and I filed it away.

"And . . . what? He met you there?"

"No, but he must have been able to see me or something, because he'd take that as a signal to call my cell, and then I'd have his new number."

Lennon must work or live nearby, or have a trusted contact at the coffee shop itself. It wasn't much, but it was a lead.

"You know I'm going to have to pass this on to the FBI, don't you?" I asked, and saw something like relief flicker through her face. "Was that why you called me, Orlando — to do your dirty work for you, so you can keep your distance?"

"No!" The denial came too quick, too easily. Her eyes filled, but I wasn't completely convinced she couldn't do that at will. She had, after all, taken acting classes with Lennon. "Everything's gone so wrong! Supposing they come after me again — I mean, for real this time? I didn't know what else to do."

"Well, going to the cops as soon as Torquil turned up dead would have been a bloody good start," I muttered, and watched her head hang.

"It was supposed to be a game," she repeated stubbornly.

I sighed. How did you deal with someone who was so far removed from everyday real life, it was like they were from another planet? "So, did it live up to your expectations — being kidnapped?"

Another shrug. "I guess," she said, but I'd caught the quick smile, the satisfaction that came and went in her face, quickly masked. Maybe it had given her the control she craved. Or maybe it had simply got the attention of her parents — both of them — for the first time in her life. I wanted to shake her.

"So then Manda wanted out from under the family thumb, too, and you offered to do another deal with Lennon?"

"Yes," she admitted.

I glanced at the bodyguard, Vincent, sitting motionless in the front of the car. His slightly crooked face was professionally impassive, but there was something disdainful in his eyes.

"You knew, didn't you?" I said to him. "How could you not?"

"Of course," he said, almost a sneer. "You think a couple of punks like that could get away with snatching my principal from right under my nose otherwise? How incompetent d'you think we are?"

"So, it stands to reason, in that case," I added with slow realisation, "that her parents knew, also?"

I heard a disbelieving gasp from Orlando, but kept my eyes on Vincent. His gaze flickered across to her, then back to meet mine. "Yeah, course I told 'em," he said. "Why d'you think no cops?"

"But . . .?" Orlando's voice trailed off into misery. "They paid," she whispered. "Why did they pay the ransom, if they knew . . .?"

"Maybe they were indulging your little fantasy," I suggested. After all, in a twisted way it was only like going to a dude ranch and pretending to be a cowboy for the weekend. *And what's half a million dollars if there's plenty more where that came from?* I waited for her to absorb that one, then turned back to Vincent. "What about the others? Did they know, too?"

"Dempseys, yeah. We let their security know — professional courtesy, y'know? I think they were kinda relieved that kid was going after herself instead of her old man for a change. Benellis were told, and I think maybe they decided enough was enough and refused to go along with it. But after the kid lost a finger, well, I guess they convinced themselves it was for real after all."

I remembered the screeching of Benedict's mother, the quiet seething of his father, and realised there had been more to it than simple surprise. Neither of them liked being taken for fools, but they'd been prepared to ignore it, until that wasn't possible any longer. So, part of their anger was directed at themselves.

I shook my head, looked at Orlando's dejected figure slumped in the corner of the luxurious leather upholstery. Above us, the rain hammered on the roof and bounced up into an ankle-deep layer of mist across the ground outside.

I glanced at Vincent's indifferent face. "You didn't feel it was worth extending the same *professional courtesy* to me, then, when I started looking after Dina?"

The bodyguard shrugged. "It was on a need-to-know basis, and Mrs Willner isn't in the same league as the others," he said, dismissive. "The threat wasn't taken seriously."

And neither were you. He didn't need to say it, I saw it in his eyes, his face, and wondered if I was going to be butting my head against this same misogynist attitude for the rest of my career.

"Yeah, and look how well that turned out," I said, turning back to Orlando without waiting for his response. "First thing tomorrow morning," I told her, "you're going to go back to that bloody coffee shop, and you're going to sit there until Lennon calls you."

"What if he doesn't?"

"He may not," I agreed. He may have been working for her at the beginning, but clearly he was taking his orders elsewhere now, and *that* was who I wanted. "Torquil's dead because of things *you* set in motion, Orlando. Dina is missing, injured, and they're asking ten million dollars for her release. Right now, I'd make you parade up and down Union Square naked if I thought it might help."

A hopeful thought struck her. "But I don't have my cell. He won't be able to call me."

"So get it," I said bluntly. "I'm sure if you explain to your father what's at stake, he'll give it back, don't you?"

She nodded, gave a pathetic smile. "I never should have told my parents. Hunt told me not to, but after Tor . . . I felt so *guilty*. If I'd known they already *knew* . . ."

Confessing all, I realised, had simply meant they couldn't pretend ignorance any longer, nothing more. I ignored the plea for a sympathetic response, reached for the door handle. "You'll call me if and when you hear from Lennon?"

It was Vincent who nodded. "It's my cell," he said. "I'll call, don't sweat it."

He was the one who had obtained my cellphone number, I realised. Being in the industry, it wouldn't have been hard.

As I cracked the door and waited for a brief lull in the rain, I said over my shoulder to Orlando, "Hunt sends his love, by the way. Says he misses you."

"Huh," she scoffed. "Yeah, I bet."

But there was more than just ordinary sulkiness in her voice. I pulled the door to and looked back at her. "What does that mean?"

She flushed. "We've been going out together for ages, and we've never . . . well, you know. Made love," she said, wriggling with embarrassment in her seat.

Vincent, I saw, had quickly reverted to his stone-faced demeanour in the face of these girlie confidences. One of those macho guys who would happily discuss any amount of blood, unless it was menstrual.

"Perhaps he's just straight-laced," I suggested. "Doesn't believe in sex before marriage."

Yeah, and perhaps I'm in the running for Homecoming Queen . . .

She hunched a mournful shoulder. "At first I thought maybe he was, y'know, gay, and in denial or something," she said, with the assurance of someone who's been through therapy and picked up all the right words. "I thought he was maybe trying to hide it, but then when we were at the party on the yacht, Tor played me a tape — of Hunt and Manda, in the cabin together, and —" She broke off, choked back a sob. "He was all over her."

"Ah, I'm sorry, Orlando," I said, and meant it. "Sometimes it happens, when a group of you spend time together —"

"But it wasn't like that," she burst out, face crumpling. "He and Manda knew each other long before. She was the one who introduced us. Manda's my friend. So, why would they *do* that?"

CHAPTER
FIFTY-ONE

As soon as I got back into the Navigator, I called Parker, watching Orlando's chauffeured BMW roll out of the parking area and back onto the main road as I did so.

He listened to my explanation of Hunt's prior relationship with Manda without interruption. On its own, it meant little, but Manda had deliberately misled me when I'd seen her at the apartment. *Besotted* was how she'd described Orlando and Hunt's relationship. If she was supposed to be Orlando's friend, then surely she would know all was not well in paradise. So why had she lied? I couldn't ignore my gut instinct.

"I'll get straight onto Bill, get him to check this guy out more thoroughly," he said when I was done. No arguments, no doubts.

"He'll still be awake?" I glanced at my watch. It was 1.15a.m. Dina had entered her fortieth hour of captivity. Was she even still alive? I felt the tension in my shoulders, my hands, and tried to relax.

"Until we get Dina back, everyone's on call twenty-four/seven," Parker said grimly. "Get back here soon as you can, Charlie. And you were right to go — good work."

The return journey took only a minute longer than the outward one. There was almost no traffic on the rain-lashed streets, but it was no night to be out. The water had started to pile up in the gutters, sweeping debris down the enormous storm drains that characterise the sides of American roads. They buried coffins deep enough over here not to rise in a flood, I remembered, and couldn't suppress a shiver that had nothing to do with cold.

When I reached the house, I found Parker had roused both Landers and Caroline Willner. A sleepy-looking Silvana was handing round fresh hot drinks, and I accepted a steaming cup of coffee gratefully.

"I don't know anything about the young man," Caroline Willner was saying. "He's been here a couple of times, with Orlando, and he's always seemed polite, attentive. I got no — how would you say it? — bad vibes from him."

"Neither did I," I said. "He had an answer for everything. Although, when I mentioned that Trevanion was a Cornish name, he didn't seem to know." *Should I have known?* I shook my head in disgust. "He took me in completely. He seemed so plausible, so bloody *nice*, compared to the rest of them. I —"

I broke off suddenly, drenched with cold. Hunt had been so approachable, so friendly, so without an axe to grind, that I'd chatted openly to him about the current situation.

Parker had moved to my side to ask quietly, "What is it?"

I jerked my head towards the hallway and when we were alone I told him, in detail, about my apparently chance meeting with Hunt outside Orlando's family estate, and about our oh-so-civilised pot of Fortnum & Mason tea at the tennis club.

"I told him Caroline Willner doesn't have the money to pay," I finished in a horrified voice, eyes flying to Parker's. "He could already have decided this is a dead end."

In which case, he could have decided Dina is a dead end, too. And if she is, it's my fault . . .

"It's not over yet, Charlie," Parker said, tense. "Bill's looking into him right now. Someone using the name Hunter Trevanion is renting a house in Sag Harbor for the summer, but so far we can't find a previous address for him. He doesn't have a US driver's licence, but if he's a Brit, he might never have gotten around to it."

"He told me he'd been out here five years," I said, focusing inward to recall our earlier conversation at Torquil's party. "Said he'd been at Oxford and implied the university, but for all I know he could have been living rough in doorways. Oh, he also said his family were in the music business, if that helps?"

"I'll let Bill know."

I frowned. "Ross said Lennon's mystery pal was American."

"He could have used a go-between," Parker said.

I moved over to a small sofa that lined one wall of the hallway. It was uncomfortable, intended more for decoration than for use, but I sank onto it anyway. I was desperately tired but too buzzed to sleep. "Still nothing from the kidnappers?"

Parker shook his head. "We're taking no news as good news until we reach the deadline they set — we still have thirty hours," he said carefully. "Brandon Eisenberg called to say he's making progress securing the ransom. And the hospital called to say McGregor's conscious. His family flew in from Toronto this afternoon."

"Well, that's good, anyway," I murmured. I leant my head back and let my eyes close briefly as I took a sip of coffee. *One less thing to worry about.*

"How you feeling, Charlie?" Parker asked. I opened my eyes again and realised he was watching me closely. I made an effort to sit up.

"Fine," I lied. "Why?"

"You up to a quick trip back to Manhattan? I think we need to have another talk to Amanda Dempsey, see what she knows."

I put my half-drunk coffee down regretfully on the side table and pushed to my feet. "OK," I said, giving him a weary smile, "providing you don't mind driving? I think I'm likely to fall asleep at the wheel."

We didn't talk much on the way over, mainly because I reclined my seat slightly, bunched up my jacket between the Navigator's headrest and the side window, and catnapped for most of the way.

I jerked awake at the touch of a hand on my arm, reaching for it almost before I had a chance to counter the automatic reaction.

"Easy, Charlie," Parker said. "We're nearly there."

"What time is it?"

"A quarter of four," Parker said briefly, without needing to check.

Dina had been held for nearly forty-two hours.

By the time he'd braked to a halt outside Manda's apartment block, I was sitting up again and with it, if a little groggy. It was still raining, the streets of the city washed clean and glistening in the lights.

"You OK?" Parker asked again as we entered the lobby area.

"You don't need to keep asking," I told him gently. "If I'm not, I'll let you know."

It was a pleasure to watch my boss intimidate the night security guy into *not* calling up to warn Manda we were on our way. He did it with a soft lethality that reduced the man to fluster in less than a minute.

"Bully," I murmured as we rode up to Manda's floor.

Parker flashed me a quick smile in reply. "You ain't seen nothing yet . . ."

It took a lot of loud banging on Manda's front door, and leaning on the bell, before she answered, wearing a thin peach satin nightgown and matching wrap. As someone who slept in an old T-shirt — if I slept in anything at all — the cynical half of me wondered if the delay had been partly caused by her searching for something alluring to put on.

"Charlie!" she exclaimed, covering the frightened note in her voice with a gloss of annoyance. "Do you have *any* idea what time it is?"

382

"Yes," I said pleasantly. "May we come in? Or do you want to wait for the FBI?"

She hesitated, by which time I had moved forwards, smiling, and before she knew it we were inside with the door closed behind us. Manda realised she wasn't going to get rid of us easily and shrugged. She led us into the living area with its fabulous view of the skyline, which was lightening towards dawn but still dominated by the beautifully lit, iconic buildings.

Once there, she tugged the flimsy garment closer around her body and glared at us with a certain amount of scared truculence.

"What do you want?" Her eyes flicked to Parker as if she thought he might be easier to manipulate. He stared back, radiating menace because of the total lack of emotion he projected.

"You know what this is all about, Manda," I said quietly, snapping her attention back to me. "Tell us about Hunt."

"Hunt?" She made a show of surprise at the question, stalling furiously. "I hardly know —"

"You want us to dig out the tape Torquil made of the pair of you screwing on the yacht?" I demanded. "Orlando's already admitted that you introduced them. So — who is he, where did he come from, and why have you lied about him?"

She gave a mirthless laugh. "I might have known that little bitch would try and stir things. Why on earth should you believe anything she has to say?"

I sighed, half turned away, and whipped back to punch her in the mouth.

I led from my shoulders rather than my hips, so it was little more than a tap, but Manda let out a shriek and fell backwards across one of the armchairs in a tangle of arms and legs. Parker shot me a disapproving glance. I shrugged and waited until Manda had gathered herself, dabbing at her split lip with experimental fingers.

"You *bitch*," she muttered, in a dazed voice.

"I've been called worse — by you, as I recall," I said blandly. "And I don't have time to play nice, Manda. I tried that last time, and you sat there and smiled at me as you lied your arse off. Stop LYING to me!" I let my voice snap into loudness, watched her jerk of automated response. "Dina's got less than a day. They already sliced off her ear. These are the same people who beat Torquil to death. We believe Hunt's involved. Where do we find him?"

"How the hell would I know?" she demanded, pushing back to her feet, defiant. "And even if I did, you think I'd tell *you*?"

Parker sighed. He reached into the pocket of his immaculate overcoat and brought out a folding lock knife, which he opened up carefully. As it reached full extension it made a sharp click that made Manda flinch. I think it was the contrast between his totally urbane appearance and the threat implicit in the blade. He glanced at me, nothing in his face.

"Left ear, wasn't it?"

CHAPTER
FIFTY-TWO

Manda, I realised quickly, had no doubts that Parker might be bluffing.

The combination of that and the shock of a smack in the mouth brought the words tumbling out of her. I wasn't especially proud of what we'd just done, but it was certainly effective in the time we had available.

She told us how she'd met Hunt the previous spring and been both frustrated and intrigued by the fact that he seemed so unimpressed by her wealth.

Listening to her, it was painfully obvious that Hunt had played her like a cheap violin. He was a charmer, as all good conmen are, and he'd used Manda to carefully insinuate himself into the social circle in which she moved.

The fact that he'd specifically asked her to introduce him to Orlando, rather than presenting himself as being involved with Manda, had been a masterly touch. It allowed him to influence the other girl, while Manda got her claws into Benedict. And the hands-off approach had kept Manda well and truly hooked in a way he couldn't have done if they'd been having an open relationship.

"After Benedict's kidnapping didn't go according to plan — when his parents nearly refused to pay — Hunt said it would be better if he was the one who made contact with Lennon and Ross," she explained, her voice a mumble, staring at her clenched hands. "He said it would keep us one step removed from any of it."

"But?" I said, hearing the hesitation in her voice.

"He wanted to take things a lot further. Actively look for other people — people with money — who wanted to be kidnapped for the thrill of it, too. Make a business out of it, almost."

"And you went along with that?" Parker left me to ask the questions, while he hovered in the background, projecting just the right level of intimidation.

"He made it sound like . . . fun," she admitted. "Like a game, where everybody wins and nobody gets hurt."

"And where did Torquil fit into that theory?"

She coloured at that. It was nice to see even someone as amoral as Manda was not immune to shame.

"That was . . . different," she said, stumbling over the words. "Tor found out what we were doing and was threatening to expose us — all of us — unless we let him join in. But he wanted it all to be perfect, like a movie or something. He was so furious when the snatch on Dina went all wrong. He said it was pathetic, that he'd give us all away."

I remembered Torquil's expression as he'd watched the two men I now knew to be Lennon and Ross escaping from the botched attempt at the riding club. His anger and disappointment now seemed understandable. At the time I'd worried it was because he might be behind the kidnaps, not that he was waiting impatiently for his turn.

"So he was killed to keep him quiet."

"Yes. No!" Manda said, head hanging. "Look, they don't tell me the details. As far as I know, all that was supposed to happen was Tor was to be kidnapped and held for a couple days for a decent ransom — he talked about making his parents pay with something that would hurt them. I guess now he was talking about the Eisenberg Rainbow."

"So, where is it?"

She looked disbelieving. "Why the hell would you want it? It's a fake."

"Ah, so you haven't quite severed *all* ties with the kidnappers, have you, Manda?" I said. "How else could you know about that?"

She flushed. "Hunt told me," she said in a low voice. "He said that Lennon was furious, and who knew what he might do to get even."

"And you believed that?" I demanded. "Did Hunt also tell you that Torquil was dead before I ever left the Eisenbergs' place with the necklace? That they'd no intention of letting him go, regardless of whether the jewels were real or not?"

"No," she murmured, shaking her head. "No, that can't be right. Hunt said that if we went ahead and kidnapped Tor, like he wanted, he wouldn't be able to do anything against us, because then he'd be a part of it. But I never thought for a second that they'd kill him. You have to believe me . . ."

* * *

"Would you have done it?" I asked twenty minutes later, as Parker pulled the Navigator out from the kerb. His eyes switched from the rear-view mirror across to mine, with a flicker that could have signified just about anything.

"Would you?" he countered dryly.

I smiled. "It might have been a difficult one to explain away in court as justifiable force."

He nodded, as if that was his answer, also. "The trick is not what you're prepared to do, Charlie. It's what *they believe* you're prepared to do."

"I know."

But Sean would have done it, I realised, for real, without hesitation. Maybe that was the difference between them.

Stop making comparisons!

"The important thing is, did *you* believe *her*?" Parker asked now, as if reading my thoughts.

I twisted slightly in my seat, watching him drive through the lightening streets, heading east for the Queensboro Bridge.

There had always been an easy competence about Parker, but where previously he'd seemed relaxed and confident, now he showed an uncertainty around me that I didn't like. That kiss had changed things, not necessarily for the better, but there was no calling it back, I realised. Sooner or later, we'd have to deal with it and move on.

"Some of it," I replied. "I think the bit about her becoming a little obsessed with Hunt is true. It made her angry to be under his thrall like that. From what I know of Manda, she hates having to admit to any kind of weakness."

"Particularly to you," Parker judged. "You must have left quite a lasting impression on her."

"Well, I stopped her from killing her father," I said. "That would tend to stick in anyone's mind." I shook my head sadly. "They should have got some serious help for her back then. Who knows how differently she might have turned out?"

"Some people just don't want to be helped."

Parker's cellphone buzzed and he slotted his Bluetooth headset in place before he took the call. I realised he'd been waiting for it, hence taking the bridge rather than the Queens-Midtown Tunnel, where the signal would have been non-existent.

"Bill," he said shortly. "Go ahead."

He seemed to spend the next few miles listening more than talking, his face growing darker all the while. When he finally ended the call, he took the headset off and chucked it onto the dash in frustration.

I raised an eyebrow. "I'm assuming that wasn't good news."

"Bill can't find anything on Trevanion," he said. "And I mean *anything*. Fake name, fake addresses, fake references. No record of him with Immigration. Zip. Looks like he'd created a legend for himself that would stand up to initial scrutiny, but as soon as we dug down a layer, it all collapsed."

"Shit."

"Yeah, that's about the size of it," he agreed with a little sideways glance. "That's not all. This guy's good

— good enough to hack into a secure comms network and traffic light control programs. Bill said by digging around he's triggered some kind of alert in the system."

"*Shit.*" I said again, with a touch more feeling this time. "So he knows we're onto him."

He might kill Dina and run, just to cut his losses . . .

"There's ten million at stake," Parker said tightly. "He won't cut and run now. This is what he's been working toward."

I wished I shared his confidence.

We headed east out of the city, against the traffic and into a fresh sun rising weakly from the ocean as if waterlogged by last night's storm.

Dina had now been kidnapped for forty-four hours.

The deadline was ten hours away.

I cursed again the chance meeting that had caused me to open up to Hunt. "But how did he know where to find me?" I wondered aloud into the quiet interior of the vehicle, and caught the twitch of Parker's head in my direction. "The more I think about it, the more I can't believe it was coincidence, him just happening to turn up as I was leaving Orlando's parents'."

"You think he might have slipped a tracker on you?"

"It wouldn't be the first time," I said. "Mind you, he didn't have to bother doing that with Torquil's ransom, did he? Gleason had two trackers on me then — one on me and one on the money. If Hunt's so clever he can interfere with traffic lights, I'm sure he could have hacked into the GPS system and followed me that way."

Parker's face was grave. "All the company vehicles have on-board trackers in case of theft," he said. "If he's activated this one, he knows exactly where you've been over the past twenty-four hours, and who you've talked to."

"There's one person I didn't meet at a known location," I said. "One person Hunt couldn't know for certain I've been in contact with." Parker merely raised an eyebrow in my direction. "Ross. At least, I bloody well hope he doesn't know — for all our sakes."

CHAPTER
FIFTY-THREE

"He's not going to call, is he?" Caroline Willner said quietly.

We were gathered tensely in the living area at the Willners' house. Beyond the wall of glass was a dull grey sky, specked with seagulls squabbling over the heaped kelp and general detritus that marked the edges of the tideline.

It was ten minutes past four o'clock in the afternoon. Ten minutes past the deadline the kidnappers had set. Ten minutes past the time we should have received detailed instructions about the ransom drop.

"With this much cash at stake? He'll call," Brandon Eisenberg said, his voice more confident than his tightly clasped hands would suggest. His wife had stayed away this time, I noticed, although Gleason was in attendance, taking up her usual position just behind his chair.

I wondered if Eisenberg felt guilt or vindication that he'd tried to palm off a paste copy of the Rainbow onto his son's kidnappers. In the end, it hadn't made any difference to the outcome. The boy was still dead.

But if they'd got their prize, would they have taken Dina so soon afterwards, and asked so much by way of retribution?

392

Parker glanced at me and said nothing. He'd spent the day fending off the authorities. I didn't ask how Eisenberg himself had got them off his back. Made a few calls, probably. A guy like that always had a little black book of the right phone numbers.

When we'd got back to the house earlier this morning, we'd driven the Navigator straight into the garage and checked out the underside. Sure enough, we'd found a small magnetic GPS tracking device attached to the chassis where it was well hidden from our daily inspections. Nevertheless, I'd be beating myself up about missing it for some time to come.

I was beating myself up about so much at the moment that it could take a number.

If she dies, it's on your head, Fox . . .

Bill Rendelson was currently trying to backtrack the signal from the tracker, but it was configured to fire off high-speed bursts of information that were almost impossible to follow   unless you were set up for the task.

Hunt, it seemed, had been one step ahead of us all the way.

He'd now had Dina for fifty-four hours, and the clock was still ticking.

I closed my mind to the fact that by the time Torquil had been gone this long, we knew for certain he was already dead.

I admit I was so tense that I jumped when my cellphone rang. I rose with a murmured apology for the interruption, moved across to the window. I didn't recognise the number on the display, so I answered with a cautious, "Yeah?"

"Uh, hi there, ma'am," said a man's voice, careful and polite, a lifelong Brooklyn accent. "I'm tryin'a reach Charlie Fox. He there?"

"Sort of," I said. "I'm Fox. Who's this?"

"Ah . . . oh," the man's voice said, and I had the impression of his heart suddenly landing in his boots as whatever news he had to impart took on an added element of difficulty. "Well, ma'am, my name's Officer O'Leary, from the Sixtieth precinct. We just picked up a gunshot victim, a young kid, asking for you."

I said sharply, "A girl?" Aware that Parker's head had snapped round.

"Uh, no," O'Leary said, caution forming around his words like frost. "Guy by the name of . . . um . . ." I heard rustling as he leafed through his notebook, ". . . Ross Martino. You know him?"

"Yes," I said faintly. "I know him." I reached automatically for the Navigator's keys, which were still in my jacket pocket. "Which hospital? I can be there in —"

O'Leary gave a heavy sigh. "There's no need to rush, ma'am," he said, and I heard years of weary experience in his voice. "Look, I'm sorry to be the one to have to tell you this, but . . . the kid didn't make it. It was a real nasty one, and by the time the paramedics reached him . . ." I heard the shrug as he broke off. Wasn't the first time he'd had to make this kind of call and no doubt it wouldn't be the last.

"Oh," I said blankly, mind reeling. *Shit*. "I'm sorry, but I don't really know him all that well. Can I ask . . . why are you calling me?"

Without any background to our relationship, O'Leary seemed taken aback.

"Well, *he* seemed to think it was real important we contacted you," he said, with a note of censure. "Look, by the time we got there, he wasn't makin' much sense, y'know?" He paused, obviously reassured enough by my claims of distance from the victim to expand. "He'd taken one in the gut. It was kinda messy, if you know what I mean?"

"Yeah, I know," I murmured, remembering the shot the masked kidnapper — Hunt? — had aimed squarely into my own body. McGregor, Parker had told us, had lost his spleen and a part of his intestine as a result of his injuries. And I remembered, too, in a stark flash, Hunt's apparently casual greeting when he'd engineered that meeting outside Orlando's place.

"*You're looking good . . .*"

Yeah, not bad for someone he'd shot in the chest only a few days before.

I realised O'Leary was waiting for me to ask the obvious question, and hoping to avoid having to volunteer the information if I didn't. I wasn't about to let him off lightly.

"So, what did he say?"

"Well, it was kinda garbled," he admitted. "Like I said, he wasn't makin' much sense by then, and the medics, they was pumping him full of morphine. Something about lending somebody a horse?" The furrows in his brow were almost audible as he spoke. "Then he mentioned something about Florida, and a casket. Did somebody close to him die recently? Horseback riding accident, maybe?"

"Can you remember exactly what he said?" I asked urgently, ignoring his query. "The *exact* words?"

"Um, I guess," he said, so slowly I wanted to reach down the phone line and throttle him. "He definitely said about lending the horse, that I do recall. Or it mighta been horses."

I made frantic writing motions and Parker immediately dragged a notebook and pen from his inside jacket pocket. I smiled briefly in thanks and scribbled down "lending/Lennon?" and "horse/s?" Parker read the words over my shoulder and frowned.

"What else?"

"Well, I have to say I'm kinda hazy on the rest of it."

I reined in a scream. "But he said Florida, specifically?"

"Yeah, Orlando — and next fall. Maybe he was planning on a vacation he never got to take, huh?"

I ground my teeth for a moment, wrote down "Orlando" and "fall" below the other two words on the pad.

"And he mentioned a casket?" I persisted. That one got everyone's attention and didn't need much explanation, although I'd hardly dignify the rough-hewn box Torquil had been buried in by using such a term.

"Casket, coffin — something like that. Yeah, I think so," O'Leary said.

396

"Which was it?"

"Hell, lady, I —" He bit off whatever he was going to say, sighed again. "What's the difference?"

"Casket is American, coffin is English," I pointed out. *There might be a big difference.*

"Listen, what's going on here, ma'am?" His voice was terse now. "This sounds kinda like something we should be aware of right now."

"It's a federal case," I said, aware of sounding pompous. I softened it down by adding, "But you may just have given us a big break."

"For real?" he said, all suspicion gone in the face of pride. "You be sure to tell that to my captain, huh?"

"I will," I promised. "Oh, where was Martino found?"

"Under the boardwalk down on Coney Island," O'Leary said. "He'd been worked over some, too, finished with a slug in the gut. I'd guess a thirty-eight or a nine. Kid was a mess all round."

Poor bastard. "Well, thank you for letting me know."

"I'd say 'you're welcome', but I guess this is not the kinda news anyone wants to hear, huh?"

"No," I agreed, "but thank you anyway."

I thumbed the "End Call" button and sat staring at the brief notes I'd made for a second, until Eisenberg cleared his throat impatiently.

"What the hell was that all about?"

"Ross, the kidnapper I made contact with — the one who promised to help us catch whoever murdered your son," I said bleakly. "He's just been shot dead."

397

*So, you'll never get your new set of wheels now,
Ross. Sorry, kid . . .*

"Sounds like our boy is cleaning house," Parker said.
"Tidying up the loose ends."

"But, if he was one of the kidnappers . . .?" Caroline
Willner trailed off, her throat moving convulsively as
she fought to keep her voice calm. "What's going to
happen to Dina?"

"I don't know," I said. I added "casket/coffin" to the
list and read the apparently disconnected words,
backwards and forwards, trying to get the gist. "But I
think Ross was trying to tell us."

Why the hell couldn't you have been more coherent?
I cursed heartlessly, but I remembered all too clearly
what it was like to be shot. To experience such intense
pain that it totally consumes you, blanks out everything
around you until there's nothing in the world but you
and the agony, and even the prospect of dying seems
welcome, because then it will stop. I don't recall I said
much at the time that anyone could have understood
clearly.

But still, whatever internal sense of cruelty I might
possess was squashed by the image of what Dina might
be going through, right now. I thought of her terror at
confined spaces.

If he's buried her . . .

"Horses," Parker said, eyes on my face as if he knew
exactly what I was thinking. "Dina's horses?"

"What about the riding club?" Caroline Willner
asked abruptly. "Clearly he knows that Raleigh now has

398

Dina's horses, or he would not have been able to lure her away with that message."

"Surely the place is too busy," Parker argued. "Horses have to be looked after full-time, don't they? There would always be people around."

"But there's acres of space out on the cross-country course," I realised. I grabbed my phone again, dialled the riding club office. After our visits there, it was already programmed in, as were numbers for everywhere Dina had visited on a regular basis. I fervently hoped I wouldn't have cause to delete them all just yet.

The number rang out twice, then the answering machine picked up with Raleigh's cheery greeting that everyone was busy having a great time away from the phone right now, and anyone enquiring about livery or lessons should leave their name and number after the beep.

I rang off without doing so. "Answer machine."

"It's still worth checking out," Parker said.

He had that closed-down look, I noticed, as if all his muscles had bunched in on themselves. It was a look I'd seen in Sean many times, when we were about to go into action. An economy of movement, a sureness of purpose, focus. Intent.

"I'm coming with you."

I turned to find Caroline Willner had risen and was standing very still and straight by her chair.

"Mrs Willner, that's not —" Parker began.

"I know," she cut across him, imperious. "But nevertheless, I'm coming with you."

"You'll slow us down," I said, making it cold because it was the only way to make it hit home.

She flinched a little at that, but drew herself up to her full height and stared back at me. "The life of my daughter may be at grave risk because the man holding her believes I cannot pay the ransom," she said, hitting back on the point of a nerve with matchless precision. "I think you can trust me not to get in your way, but I *will* see this through. Now, we're wasting time."

Eisenberg cast her an admiring glance. "I'm going, too," he said, thrusting his chin out. Gleason's expression went from smug at our troublesome client, to consternation as the tables were turned on her.

"Sir, I really don't —"

"Stow it," he told her. He retrieved a set of keys from his trouser pocket and jingled them with a grim smile. "Lucky I decided to give the new Aston a run-out today, huh?" he said. He glanced at Gleason's furious face, at Caroline Willner's pale determination, and heaved a sigh.

"OK," he said at last, lips twisting in a rueful grimace. "I guess I didn't get where I am by sending the wrong guy out to do the job." He threw the keys across to Parker, who caught them one-handed, almost snatching them out of the air. "You driven paddle-shift before?"

"Yes, I have," Parker said, and tossed the keys over to me instead. "But Charlie will be faster."

CHAPTER
FIFTY-FOUR

If Brandon Eisenberg was a little twitchy at the thought of letting loose a six-litre V12, on damp roads, with a girl behind the wheel, he manfully constrained the bulk of his dismay. The car was a brand-spun four-door Aston Martin Rapide, with oodles of torque and a top speed in excess of 180mph. About the same as an average sports bike, but at roughly twenty times the cost.

Nevertheless, when I slid into the cream leather bucket seat and fired up that rasping great engine, I could entirely understand the appeal. The interior still had that fresh-off-the-cow, new-car smell.

Parker had ordered Erik Landers to stay behind and man the phones, just in case the kidnappers did decide to call. But at this moment Landers was eyeing the gleaming dark-green Aston and not exactly looking overjoyed at the prospect of being left behind.

"We'll be right behind you," Eisenberg said, nodding to Caroline Willner. He leant into the open doorway and added more quietly, "Let's go find this kid alive, huh?"

"We don't even know we're on the right track," Parker warned from the passenger seat. "This could all be a wild goose chase." He had argued against taking civilians along, as much as Gleason, but to no avail. The rich were too used to getting their own way.

Eisenberg shrugged. "It's better than waiting around here." He straightened, glanced across at his stony-faced bodyguard who was standing by the Navigator. "Quit whining and get your ass moving, Gleason."

I shut the heavy door on her furious scowl and snicked the gears into first. The transmission dropped in, firm and precise, and then we were rolling.

I waited until we were out onto the road before I booted it, catching Parker in mid sentence. He went abruptly silent as the big car squatted down and wriggled its hips, wrestling to put all that grunt down through the fat rear tyres, while a giant hand punched us back in our seats.

"I know I said you'd get us there fast, Charlie," Parker said when he could speak again, "but try to get us there alive, too."

I took my eyes off the road just long enough to flash him a small hard smile. "Just wanted to show you that all those driving courses you sent me on haven't gone to waste."

"OK! I'm convinced."

It took a couple of miles of three-figure speed and slingshot overtaking manoeuvres before he began to relax, I noticed. Parker had not driven much in Europe, whereas I'd experienced the German autobahns at full throttle. And the Aston had the kind of road-holding and handling characteristics — not to mention the sheer power delivery — that made driving gods out of men.

"Even if the riding club *is* the right place," he said then, "where do we start looking?"

"We take a ride round the cross-country course and look for disturbed earth," I said.

If he's buried her . . .

I clung to the thought that Dina was not yet dead, that we stood a chance of getting to her in time. But burying her alive, when she had a phobia of enclosed spaces, and was horrifyingly aware of what had happened to the last victim, might be enough to send her over the edge.

The guilt was a solid mass, pressing down on me, threatening to crush my chest until I couldn't breathe, couldn't think, for the weight of it on top of me.

I pressed my right foot down a little harder and was rewarded by another surge of speed. The chasing Navigator, with Gleason behind the wheel, was already nowhere to be seen. Parker had all the company vehicles chipped for additional power and torque, but against this kind of supercar engineering, she may as well have been pedalling it.

"So, what's with the mention of Orlando, and the fall?" Parker asked, unconsciously bracing himself against the centre transmission tunnel.

The half of my brain that wasn't occupied with controlling the Aston flipped back to the day of the abortive kidnap attempt on Dina at the riding club, when I'd used Cerdo to kick out at Ross. If I'd known then that the one with the PlastiCuffs — the one I'd put on the ground first — was Lennon, the ringleader, I would have made sure he stayed down. Permanently.

Hunt had been there, as had Orlando. She'd been out on the cross-country course with that fine-boned little Arab horse of hers. It didn't look robust enough to survive a round with fixed timber fences and, indeed, the horse had come back with a swollen knee from clattering against something solid . . .

"It could be that we're looking at this wrong," I said quickly. "It may not be *the* fall, but just *a* fall. Orlando had a fall, the last time she did the course. I wonder where?"

"You're reaching, Charlie," Parker said, doubtful.

"Ross gave us this practically with his last breath, and for all we know, finding it out was what got him killed," I said, blasting past a slow-moving RV and just managing to dart back into my lane through a disappearing gap between that and an oncoming Kenworth. "If you can suggest a better place to start looking, I'm all bloody ears."

The Navigator stood no chance of catching up with us now. *Well, good.* It was one less thing to worry about — two less things, if I counted Eisenberg as well as Caroline Willner.

"OK, OK," Parker said, and I realised he'd gone quiet again during the last manoeuvre. "But for the moment, please, just drive."

I totally ignored the signs welcoming careful drivers on the driveway leading to the riding club, spraying the verges with gravel on every turn. It certainly didn't make for a stealthy approach.

So much so, that when I pulled up close to the stable yard, the Aussie instructor, Raleigh, was waiting for us by the gate, arm in a black sling, looking highly pissed off.

"Hey, Pom!" he shouted as soon as we climbed out of the car. "What the bloody hell d'you think you're doing, driving up here like that, mate? You trying to scare half the horses to death or what?"

"Where's Hunt?" Parker demanded, and though he didn't raise his voice, he didn't need to. He had an innate air of natural command that had Raleigh's attention instantly diverted.

"W-what?" He jerked the thumb of his unbroken arm over his shoulder. "He's out on the cross-country course. Said as he knew the course was out of use for a few days while the new sod beds in, he'd come to fix up one of the fences that Orlando busted last time she went round. I told him he didn't need to, but he'd brought his mate over with a ute and all the gear."

I felt the jolt of it go through Parker. It must have done, because it hit me hard enough to make my nape prickle.

"How long ago?" My turn to fire off a question. I clearly didn't have Parker's touch, though, because Raleigh just gaped at me. I reached under my jacket and pulled out the SIG. That seemed to get his notice. I felt my voice rising. "How long ago did he go out on the course?"

"I dunno. About an hour, maybe. I've been busy in the yard," he gabbled. "Now look here, Pom, what the bloody hell's this all about?"

"Where?" I snapped instead. "Which fence?"

I saw his colour start to rise in temper, and was close to losing my own when Parker stepped between us.

"Dina's been kidnapped and we believe Hunt may have her," he said, the tone of his voice leaving no room for not taking this seriously. "We need to find him, and we need to find him *now*."

Raleigh's colour ebbed away. "Jeez, mate. I dunno. He said it was over on the far side somewhere. I wasn't really taking note. Look, there's a map in the tack room." He wheeled away. "Come have a look for yourself."

We hurried after him and found that, in keeping with the riding club's upscale facilities, the map was actually a large framed satellite image, with the track of the course plotted and the obstacles clearly identified at every point. I was impressed and dismayed in equal measure.

"Wow, I didn't realise it was this big."

"Yeah, I spent a couple of years in the UK, studying course design — Badminton, Burghley, Gatcombe," Raleigh said, justifiably proud. "If you take the difficult route, it's well up to international standard."

"My God," Parker murmured. "Where do we start?"

But one fence caught my eye. Leapt out at me in stark clarity. I stabbed a finger on the course map.

"That one!"

"You're reaching again, Charlie," Parker warned tightly.

"No, I'm not," I said, already starting to move. "Look at the name of it."

As soon as I'd seen it, Ross's cryptic dying warning made perfect sense.

The fence was called The Coffin.

CHAPTER
FIFTY-FIVE

The Aston Martin may have been an utterly brilliant car on the road, but it wouldn't have gone more than a few metres off it. Last night's rain had turned the ground slick. The grass was so soft in places that just to walk on it broke through to liquid mud underneath.

Raleigh insisted we take the club runabout — the GMC pickup he'd used as a tow vehicle to collect Dina's horses. It was sitting on the yard with half a dozen fence posts and a bale of straw stacked in the back. We drove out of the yard making a beeline for the far side of the course, and The Coffin. If the size of some of the other fences we passed on the way were anything to go by, it was going to be just as scary as its name suggested.

Back when I'd had horses of my own as a teenager in Cheshire, I'd never ridden beyond inter-county level, with the fences smaller and less well nailed together than these. But even so, coffins had never been my favourite.

They were a three-part obstacle with a straightforward rail in that tricked you into approaching too boldly, but the landing surface dropped away unexpectedly. At the bottom of the slope was the lined ditch that gave the fence its name, then usually a single stride back uphill to another rail.

Get the first element wrong and there was very little chance of recovery. It was a test of rhythm and control on the part of the rider, and bravery and fitness on the part of the horse.

The Coffin on the riding club course was possibly at the furthest point away from the stable yard and any chance of disturbance or discovery. Without Ross's garbled warning, we would never have had any reason to look for it.

The natural landscape had that slightly too-perfect look about it that made it certainly artificial. The whole place had been reshaped to provide changes in elevation, and planted with trees to make the approaches to obstacles sudden and surprising. When Raleigh had been let loose to design this course, it seemed they'd given him an open chequebook and he'd taken full advantage of the fact.

Now, we bumped over the rough ground, slithering despite the four-wheel drive, following a set of similar tracks to our own.

"Should be just past that next bunch of trees up on the left," Parker said, tense, reading from the pocket version of the map, which Raleigh had given us. "Stop here, Charlie, and we'll go in on foot. We don't want to spook him."

I pulled the pickup a little closer to the shelter of the trees and cut the engine. The sudden silence was broken as Parker pulled out the Glock he carried and racked a round into the chamber.

He glanced across, a question in his eyes, and I realised that this was the first time I'd been into a situation alone with him. On a rational level he completely understood that I was up to the job, but purely on an emotional level, that was another matter.

"You don't have to worry about me, Parker," I said tightly. "Just stay out of my line of fire."

He nodded, a flicker of a smile lingering around his eyes, and we both climbed out, dropping down lightly onto the grass. Parker reverted to hand signals immediately, indicating we split up round the trees to approach from different angles, then loped away, moving with a stealth and speed that did not fit with his suited attire.

I skirted the copse as fast and quiet as I could, keeping my own SIG out and ready. I could smell fresh earth and wet leaves, hear birds squabbling in the branches overhead, the drip of residual water from the leaves. Apart from that, it was quiet as the grave.

So, into that peaceful background rustle, the crack of a single gunshot somewhere ahead of me was loud and shocking.

CHAPTER
FIFTY-SIX

I abandoned any attempts at stealth and ran. As I knew from experience, the noise of an unsuppressed gunshot would cause a temporary hearing shift in those at close proximity. It should be more than enough to mask the sound of our approach.

I hoped Parker was taking advantage of that fact, too. And I realised, much as he had reservations about me, I was just as unsure of him. I'd been in so many tight spots with Sean that it was as though we worked by some kind of psychic link, knowing instinctively what the other was thinking, how they would react, what they would or would not do.

Parker, by the very nature of his position, no longer spent much time in the field. Hell, he didn't even carry his sidearm with a round ready in the chamber . . .

As I neared the far side of the trees, I slowed, moving at a sideways crouch and leading with the SIG, straining to hear above the pounding of my heart. I took a couple of deep breaths to steady my aim, and edged closer, forcing myself to trust that Parker was mirroring my advance.

And then, beyond the branches, I caught sight of colour and movement. A man, standing in the back of a pickup, shovelling earth through the open tailgate. He was working fast and furtive, head down with the effort of his labours, putting his back into it.

Hunt.

I stilled, eyes sliding around me. Raleigh had said he wasn't alone, so where was Lennon? And what about the gunshot we'd heard? Had Hunt decided to give Dina the mercy of a quick and relatively painless death rather than the long slow agony of suffocation?

I clamped down hard on that thought. If she was dead, then I had failed utterly.

Soft-footed now, cautious, I moved forward, right arm straight and left locked in to support it, keeping the SIG canted up so the centre of Hunt's body mass stayed firmly in my sights. He had stripped down to a plain white shirt and rolled back his sleeves. The shirt was glued to his back with sweat, and was thin enough that I could tell he wore no protective armour underneath it.

Mind you — this time, neither did I.

As I cleared cover, I saw that Hunt had backed the pickup down to one end of the ditch element of the obstacle, and was currently filling it in with frantic haste. He bent again, his back still towards me. I reached the first rail part of the fence. It came up to my waist, telegraph-pole thick and forbidding.

And as I looked over it, down the slope, I saw a piece of cloth sticking out of the new earth in the ditch. Not just cloth, but the leg of a pair of trousers. More than that, a half-bent knee. I froze.

Dina?

412

And as the thought formed, I dismissed it. The leg was the wrong size, the wrong shape. Male . . .

"Hello, Charlie!"

Disappointingly, Hunt's voice did not sound in the least surprised at my sudden appearance. What surprised me about *him*, however, was the fact that all trace of his British accent had disappeared.

He'd straightened while my attention had been momentarily distracted by the body, and instead of the long-handled shovel, he was now gripping a silvered semi-automatic, probably a Colt, with self-assurance and familiarity. I remembered the almost casual way he'd shot McGregor in the gut during Dina's abduction. Another good reason to kill him.

"So, absolutely nothing about you is for real, huh?" I said. "Not even your voice."

"Fooled you, though, didn't I, Charlie? You swallowed that bullshit tale about Oxford and fox-hunting without a flicker."

I remembered my doubts about his accent, the first time we'd met. I'd put it down to elocution lessons, or snobbery. My mistake.

I focused on him, avoided looking round too obviously. *Where the hell is Parker?*

"I don't suppose you believe for a moment that I've come alone," I said cheerfully, not lowering my own weapon.

He laughed. "Why not?" he asked. "You're certainly arrogant enough."

"You've room to talk."

"Yes, I suppose I have. Is this the point where I'm supposed to ask how you found me?"

"Ross," I said. "If you're going to shoot someone, you really should learn how to make it count."

He pulled a wry face and gestured towards the body half-covered in earth below him. "As you can see," he said, "I've been practising."

"Lennon, I assume. Not very loyal to your associates, are you . . .?" I paused. "What do I call you, anyway? I assume the name Hunter Trevanion is as fake as everything else about you?"

"It was OK for a while," he agreed. "I've already got something better lined up to step into. A whole new life. Not quite as comfortable as it should have been, but hey . . ." he shrugged, ". . . you win some, you lose some."

"Why cut and run so early?" I said. "What about the ten million you asked for Dina?"

"The ten million *you* told me Caroline Willner hadn't a hope in hell of raising, you mean?" he queried, derisive. "The secret of gambling is knowing when to fold a losing hand, Charlie, and although I say so myself, I'm a very good gambler."

"In that case, you should have held your nerve a little longer before you chucked in your cards, Hunt," I said, adding a scornful edge. "Mrs Willner might not have the cash, but you told her to tap up Brandon Eisenberg and she did just that. There we were at four o'clock, with the money sitting waiting for you, and you never bothered to call."

414

Emotions whipped across his handsome features, from disbelief through rage to a sudden twisted amusement. "No shit?" he murmured. He eyed me cynically. "So, are you telling me you still want to make a deal?"

"No," Parker's voice said from the exit rail of the fence, popping up out of nowhere at the far reaches of Hunt's peripheral vision. "I rather think the time for bargaining is over, don't you?"

Hunt's head snapped round, took in the shooter's stance, the cool gaze, and knew Parker for the professional he was. Then he smiled again, almost to himself. "Oh, I don't think that's the case at all," he said lazily. "After all, I still have what you want, and I'm sure you don't need me to tell you that you don't have much time."

"We've caught you standing over a half-filled grave, you little bastard," I said. "Do you honestly expect us to believe she isn't in there?"

She's alive. She has to be alive . . .

Hunt merely smiled at the betraying desperation in my voice. He was still pointing the Colt at me, but when he spoke, it was to Parker.

"I think I'd put the gun down if I were you, old cock, because not only can you *not* take the risk that Dina might be buried somewhere else, but you know I'll shoot the lady first."

"So?" I challenged, trying to keep his attention on me, to give Parker his chance. *What the hell are you waiting for, Parker? Can't you tell all that shit about Dina is a bluff — where the hell else would she be?*

415

Hunt laughed again, eyes still on me. "She doesn't see it, does she?" he asked. "It was pretty bloody obvious to everyone at the country club do who watched you two dance together that you're desperate to get into her knickers, but she's still pining for her vegetable lover and —"

The shot took Hunt in the side, just above his left hip, spun him round and knocked him back onto the pile of earth still in the back of the pickup. The gun went clattering from his fingers and clanged loudly against the metal side of the bed. A scatter of birds took to the air from the trees around us, shrieking their outrage.

We ran forwards. I ducked to retrieve the Colt while Parker kept his Glock firmly trained on Hunt. He had started to moan, hands clutching at the greasy wound.

"You took your bloody time about that one," I said sharply, clicking the safety on the Colt and shoving it into my pocket. Boss or no boss, the adrenaline was surging. "Where else would Dina be, for fuck's sake?"

Hunt, despite the pain, managed a gasping laugh. "What did I tell you? *Still* she doesn't see it. Tell her, Parker. Tell her that's not why you hesitated —"

"Shut up," Parker said through his teeth, "or I'll shoot you again."

I could have told them both that I knew exactly why Parker had hesitated, but I wouldn't give Hunt the satisfaction of being right. That Parker had been afraid of him getting off a shot at me if he did.

I put the SIG away, jumped up into the back of the pickup, and dragged Hunt closer to the edge of the

416

tailgate. I half expected Parker to lift him down from there, but he just grabbed hold of the injured man's ankle and yanked.

It was almost a metre to the ground, and Hunt landed with a solid, satisfying thump, but he refused to cry out.

Parker reached into his jacket and brought out a giant plastic tie-wrap. "They were in the truck we borrowed," he said when he saw my raised eyebrow. "I think they use them to hold the fences together. It should do the job."

He looped the substitute PlastiCuffs round Hunt's wrists and zipped them up tight, forcing his arms back behind him. The wound, I noticed, continued to bleed steadily, but I didn't really care much about that. Parker flicked Hunt's discarded jacket off the corner of the tailgate and packed that roughly under his belt to act as a dressing. An unnecessary kindness, in my view.

I picked up the discarded shovel and jumped down, reaching the half-filled ditch in a couple of strides. When I scraped the earth away from the body I'd seen, a young man was revealed, eyes still open and an expression of hurt surprise on his face. There was a small black hole just under his right eye, slightly deforming his features.

I didn't recognise him, but I realised I'd never seen Lennon unmasked. When I checked his right arm, I found it had been bandaged, somewhat amateurishly, and had no doubt I'd find a gunshot injury lurking beneath.

417

When I reached down to drag him clear, he was still warm to the touch.

Parker jumped into the ditch alongside me and helped. With the body shifted, there was only a shallow covering of earth on top of another rough wooden box.

"Dina!" I yelled, but there was no reply. I shot Hunt a poisonous glare, but he had drooped over onto his side and his eyes were closed.

Between the two of us, Parker and I scraped the lid clear enough to get to the fastenings. I glanced at him, suddenly fearful, with a bleak rising memory of having been here before, standing over Torquil's body that day on the beach.

"Oh my God, have you found her? Is it Dina?"

We straightened sharply to see Caroline Willner approaching at a run across the sodden grass, Gleason and Brandon Eisenberg not far behind her. The noise of Parker's gunshot, it seemed, had done a similar job of deadening our hearing.

Caroline Willner slithered to a stop at the top of the slope and gripped the rail as she stared down at us. There were splatters of mud on her skirt, and her shoes were ruined. Her face was death-mask white.

Eisenberg arrived, panting, while Gleason barely seemed out of breath. She took one look at the situation, and drew her own weapon to stand guard over Hunt. Maybe Parker would offer her a job, after all.

"Are there any tools in the truck?" I demanded. "We need a tyre iron or a crowbar — *right now*."

418

It was Eisenberg who obeyed without questions, skirting carefully round Hunt's body to open the cab door of the pickup. He pulled out a scuffed toolbox and yanked the handles apart. Inside, he quickly found a hammer, long flat-bladed screwdriver and a pry bar and jumped down into the trenches without a thought to his own thousand-dollar shoes.

The three of us attacked the lid of the coffin with a vengeance. It seemed to take for ever before the last of the screws tore loose, and we could finally rip the lid loose.

I took a deep shaky breath, and looked inside.

CHAPTER
FIFTY-SEVEN

Dina lay slightly on her side, her knees wedged hard against one side of the box, her back against the other. She was groggy, filthy, bleeding, in shock.

But alive.

Most definitely alive.

We lifted her out with great care. Her whole body was shaking and the tears streamed down her face, leaving tracks through the grime. There was a stained dressing covering the amputated part of her ear and, not to put too fine a point on it, she stank. Infection, I considered, was a very real possibility.

Caroline gathered her daughter in her arms and held on tight, rocking her like a child.

"I'm sorry, Mom," Dina kept repeating, an edge of barely contained hysteria slashing through her voice. "I'm so sorry. I —"

"Hush, darling. I know." Caroline Willner pressed her face into the girl's matted hair as if she'd never smelt anything so sweet. "It's all over now."

I skimmed over Hunt with a dark gaze. His eyes were open, watchful but calm. Rarely had I met a beaten player with such composure.

420

Parker had his phone out and was already calling in the cops, the FBI, and the paramedics. It would not take long before this whole place was crawling with officialdom.

"Gleason, I'd like you to go back to the stable yard and wait there for the cops," Eisenberg said. There was something in his tone that snatched my attention. It was too polite, too controlled. I turned and found him staring down at Hunt with smouldering intensity.

Gleason saw it, too. She opened her mouth to argue, then shut it again, and nodded. She gave me a narrow-eyed stare as she came past, as if searching for something in my face. I'm not sure if she found it, but she walked away up the slope leading from the ditch without looking back.

Parker moved closer, touched my arm. "You OK?"

I took a moment to reply. It was as though Hunt had opened a wound between us, and sooner or later we were going to have to swab out the grit or risk it starting to fester. But now was not the time. "Yeah, fine."

He nodded. "I'll go fetch the pickup. The ground's bad for getting an ambulance up here. We'll take Dina back to the stable yard."

I murmured assent and, after only the slightest hesitation, he followed Gleason's tracks. It was suddenly very quiet out there, with only Dina's muffled sobbing and the cries of the disturbed birds circling back into the trees.

Eisenberg continued to stare down at Hunt, hands clenched.

"You murdered my son," he said at last, his voice deep and rusty. "He was dead before you even tried for the ransom money. Why? Why did you do it?"

Hunt lifted his head up slightly. His face was pale now, bathed in sweat, and his breath came short and shallow. The bullet wound must have been pulsing like hell, but still he managed to talk.

"What do you care? You weren't going to give up those pretty stones anyway. Not your kid, was he?" he threw back. "How was I to know he had the whole of that boat wired for sound, that he'd catch me calling Lennon and realise I wasn't who I said I was. Little bastard was going to tell everyone. Couldn't trust him."

"So this was all about protecting your false identity," I said flatly, "and nothing to do with the kidnapping scam?"

He tried to smile, but it turned into a grimace. "That was a bonus. These kids were playing at it. There was big money to be made, if it was handled right. They were never going to take advantage of it. So I took advantage of them. Just needed that damn kid to keep his mouth shut. Fortunately, he wanted his moment in the spotlight. Got it, too."

"You were never going to let him live, were you?" Eisenberg said, sounding immeasurably tired. "From the moment you snatched him from the beach that day, he was as good as dead."

The gaze he turned on me was reproachful.

If you'd stepped in . . . If you'd stopped them . . .

I looked away. I had enough burden of regrets. "And was Dina supposed to die, too?"

422

Hunt gave a "who cares" shrug that ended in a gasp of pain. "I woulda played the game," he said, mouth twisting cruelly, "if you hadn't told me there was no chance of winning."

"And so you did *this* to my daughter," Caroline Willner said suddenly, her voice cold as steel. "You tortured her, and brought her here to bury her with no intention of telling us where to find her. She might never have been found." She took a breath. "In the name of God . . . why?"

Hunt's laugh sounded more like a weak giggle. He was losing it, voice starting to slur. "She wanted danger. Excitement. I gave it to her in spades. Enough to last a lifetime, hey Dina?"

Dina shrank back at the sound of her name on his lips. Caroline Willner wrapped her arms more tightly around her daughter and glared at him. "I hope you die soon, young man," she said. Her tone was perfectly even, her diction clear and precise. "And I hope when you do that you are raped by every demon in hell."

"You got *that* right," Eisenberg muttered bitterly.

Caroline Willner shifted her gaze to me, and in the same detached tone, asked, "Do you remember, Charlie, when we first met, I asked you if you were prepared to die to protect my daughter?"

"I remember," I said softly.

"Now, after everything Dina's been through, there is still the horror of the trial to come, and no doubt the appeals and legal arguments may drag on for years," she said. "So I would very much like you to save her from those further agonies . . . and kill this man."

423

"What?" Eisenberg whispered, as much in awe as disbelief.

I looked across at Hunt. The bleeding had slowed and he was still conscious, so Parker's shot must have missed anything vital. With medical attention on its way, he would most likely survive, and very probably recover.

He had shot me, I reminded myself. Coldly, deliberately, fully intending to kill. He had done the same to Joe McGregor. He had beaten Torquil to death, and murdered his two accomplices. He had sliced off Dina's ear and buried her alive.

He absolutely deserved to die.

"We'll act as witnesses, say he attacked you — that you had no choice," Eisenberg said urgently. "Just do it. I'll pay you — whatever you want. Name your price."

"Don't be so foolish, Brandon," Caroline Willner snapped. "Charlie will not do something like this for the money. She'll do it for justice. That's what I want for Dina — justice."

I hadn't taken my eyes away from Hunt's and saw, finally, the fear begin to seep in. I reached into my jacket pocket and brought out the Colt that Hunt had dropped when he'd fallen. Now I had a chance to study it, I saw it was a Government Model, a scaled-down .380 version of the .45 ACP. The same gun he'd used to shoot me, the day he'd trashed my Buell. I could see the irony of that was not lost on him.

The gun weighed about the same as my SIG but was more compact, with a shorter barrel and a smaller

424

magazine capacity of just seven rounds. With one gone to dispose of Lennon, there were six shots left.

More than enough.

I thumbed off the safety and held the gun loosely by my side. Hunt shifted uneasily, not wanting to beg, but realising he may be forced into it. It took me a few seconds to realise I didn't want him to.

I turned back to Eisenberg and Caroline Willner, flicked the safety back on and held the gun out towards them, grip first.

"You're both wrong," I said. "I won't kill for money, and I won't kill for justice, either. Die to protect? Yes. Even kill to protect if I have to. But you don't want a bodyguard here, you want an assassin." I shook my head. "If you really want this man dead, you're going to have to do it yourself. I won't stop you."

For a moment, nobody moved. Eisenberg shifted his feet, his expression a torment of frustration and grief. He didn't have it in him to take a life in cold blood, I saw, whatever the provocation. I dismissed him.

But Caroline Willner carefully disentangled herself from her daughter's clinging grasp, letting her hand stroke lightly across the girl's bowed head. Then she straightened, took a step towards me, and closed her manicured and bejewelled hand around the pistol grip.

I let go of the barrel slowly, letting her get the measure of the weight and the shape of it.

"Safety's to the left of the hammer," I said, conversational. "Up for safe, down for fire. Use both hands and keep the front sight up. Point and shoot."

425

Eisenberg turned away, almost staggering. He hadn't the stomach to watch, never mind take part.

Caroline Willner nodded absently, as if I'd been explaining how to operate a pocket camera. She squared her shoulders, and stepped determinedly towards her prey.

CHAPTER
FIFTY-EIGHT

"I really think she would have done it." I glanced across at Sean. "That lady has a lot of spine. I've a sneaking suspicion you'd like her."

Sean — lying on his back today with his head tilted slightly towards me on the hospital pillow — did not respond. He had lain without any movement at all throughout my report. I tried to tell myself that I had his full attention, the way he'd focused on me so absolutely in the past, but in truth I found his stillness unnerving. I leant across, stroked the back of his hand with a soft finger. Not a quiver.

The only reason Caroline Willner had not slotted Hunt Trevanion out there on the cross-country course was because of Dina. Bereft of the comforting embrace, the girl had lifted her head — just as her mother raised the gun and aimed it squarely at Hunt's chest.

"No!" she'd cried, her voice raw from the screaming she'd done, I later discovered, when she woke from a pill-induced slumber and found herself in the middle of her own worst nightmare, just as the first shovelfuls of earth splattered down onto the lid of her coffin. "*Please*, Mom, NO!"

Caroline Willner had paused, her hand already tightening around the grip and trigger, and glanced at her daughter.

"Why not?" she'd asked simply.

Dina had swallowed, her throat working convulsively. "Please . . . don't let him do this to you," she said at last, cracked and pleading. "I'll remember what's happened to me here for the rest of my life. Don't let him do the same to you."

Caroline Willner had stared at her for what seemed like a long time, her features very controlled. Then she'd swivelled her gaze towards Hunt, examining him minutely as though he was something she'd found stuck to the bottom of her shoe.

I don't know exactly what she saw there, but the fire went out of her. Her hand dropped slowly to her side, and I'd stepped in, taking the gun from her unresisting fingers, thumbing the safety back on.

She'd turned, studied me with eyes that were curious and just a little afraid. "How do you do it?" she'd demanded, a tinge of bitter wonder in her voice. "How do you make killing seem so . . . easy?"

"I told her it was all down to practice," I said now to Sean, a half smile twisting my lips. He would have appreciated the irony of it all, but he lay waxy quiet on the sheets, so pale beneath the dark fall of his hair that it was hard to tell where the linen ended and he began.

Caroline Willner, I recalled, had been much the same colour. Shortly after I'd retrieved Hunt's gun from her, Parker had arrived with the GMC. He'd scanned the taut faces arrayed in front of him, and seemed neither

428

dismayed nor relieved that the status quo remained unchanged. He'd loaded Dina and her mother into the pickup and driven them away, slow and careful, across the grass.

In the whirl of police and federal agents that followed, I hadn't seen my principal again for twenty-four hours. When I did, she was lying in a hospital bed in a private room not dissimilar to this one.

Dina had been propped up on pillows, though, alert, as well as clean and rested, with a neat antiseptic dressing enclosing her foreshortened ear lobe. She was almost as pale as Sean, but looking into her eyes, I'd seen she had attained at least a surface measure of calm.

"I'm so sorry, Charlie," she'd said, her voice a husky whisper. "I —"

"Forget it," I'd told her. "There's no need. Just . . . get over this. Don't let him beat you. Live large." I'd watched the way her hands knotted nervously with the sheets, and said teasingly, "I assume your mother will ask Raleigh for the return of your horses?"

That had got a response. Dina gave a lukewarm smile that could easily have turned into a sob, shaken her head slightly, not meeting my eyes. "He's already offered to give them back. And she's been . . . wonderful."

I'd sighed, pulled my chair a little closer to the bed and bent low enough that she was forced to look at me directly.

"I'm going to give you some advice, Dina," I'd said. "You don't have to take it, but you're at least going to listen, OK?"

A flush of colour had lit across her cheeks, a confused mash of shame and anger and sadness and self-pity, but she nodded, just once.

"Don't waste this experience," I'd told her. "Never forget that your mother was prepared to kill for you. That is one hell of a declaration of love on her part. And it would have been so easy for you to let her, and then you would have been blaming each other for that wretched haul of guilt for the rest of your lives." I held her startled gaze. "But you didn't force her to prove herself to you then. Don't make her do it later, over and over. Get past this. Move on."

She'd looked about to protest, but I'd seen something connect in her eyes. Maybe it was the realisation that here was an opportunity to go forwards into an adult-to-adult relationship with her mother, finally. As equals bound by courage in extreme circumstances, like soldiers.

Or maybe that was just wishful thinking on my part.

Whatever, she'd nodded a couple of times. There was a long pause that stretched into discomfort, so I'd asked, "How's the ear?"

"Sore." She'd managed a wavery smile. "Now's my opportunity to become a famous painter, huh?"

I'd smiled back. "I think it's been done, but you can always have cosmetic surgery."

She gave a small shake of her head. "I know. Mother's already suggested it, but . . ." she shrugged diffidently, ". . . I'm kinda tempted to leave it as it is. As a reminder. Does that sound stupid?"

"No," I said slowly. *There's hope for her yet.* "It doesn't."

"And I guess I can always wear my hair over it, or a clip-on earring, hide it that way." Another pause, more of a hesitation this time. "Like you hide your scar — round your neck."

"You'll find that hiding it matters less, as time goes on."

She'd nodded gravely, then a flash of guilt had crossed her face and she'd asked in a small voice, "How's Joe?"

"As I told her — McGregor's going to be off in rehab for about three months," I said to Sean. "So, we need you back. We're short staffed. Hell, I think Parker was even tempted to offer Gleason that job she was angling for. She's a redhead, by the way, so maybe that explains his interest . . ."

My voice trailed off and I sat in silence for a while, just watching his face with utter concentration, praying to see some rapid movement of his eyes beneath the almost translucent lids.

There was nothing.

How did I tell him what had happened between Parker and me? What I'd felt could still happen. Did I tell him at all?

He would know, I realised, as soon as he saw us together, he'd know by the way we tried to put distance between us. He always had been able to read me like an open book. And what then?

431

Caroline Willner had known. When I'd left Dina's hospital room that day, she'd been waiting for me in the corridor outside.

"Thank you, Charlie," she said to me. As much for what I'd said, I realised, as what I'd done.

I shrugged. "It would have been better to stop her being taken in the first place," I said. "Then there wouldn't have been the need to get her back."

"Not just for that, although I rather think I shall be in your debt for some time." She gave a slight smile. "And I think you'll find that I always pay my debts."

I had no ready answer to that one. People often sounded incredibly grateful in situations like these, but I'd learnt not to set too much store by it. The memory would fade.

She held out her hand. "Goodbye, Charlie," she said. She paused, as if working out whether it was her place to say what she had in mind, then plunged on anyway. "I realise the situation is awkward, with your young man in a coma, but I hope you and Mr Armstrong come to some kind of understanding between the two of you. I confess I thought you seemed remarkably well matched."

Would she have said the same if she'd met Sean? I'd told him he would like her. Would the same be true in reverse?

By Sean's head sat the open cup of coffee I always brought, its aroma gently wafting upwards and outwards, teasing his nostrils.

It made no impression on him.

432

"Epps let him go," I said out of nowhere, hoping for the shock effect of the sudden swerve. Aware, too, that Sean would know exactly who I meant. "The bastard offered to go undercover in a militia group and Epps fell for it — let him walk. He's been away on his toes for the last couple of months, more or less, and they still haven't found him." I paused again, head on one side. "Do you care?" I wondered aloud. "Does any of it really matter anymore?"

"It matters, Charlie," said a voice behind me. I swung round in my chair to see the nurse, Nancy, standing in the doorway. Her face was grave. "Don't you ever give up hoping."

I rose, gave a shrug. "I'm tired," I admitted. I glanced down at Sean. "Parker said the doctors are losing *their* hope. How can I keep hold of mine?" *Perhaps it's already lost*.

"Doctors!" Nancy sniffed, waving a dismissive hand as she bustled forwards, checked Sean's vital signs, straightened the covers. "What do they know? I seen people come out of sleep way longer and deeper than your boy here. He'll come back when he's good and ready." She stroked a hand over his hair, but he didn't stir for her, either. "Maybe he's waiting for something, ain't that right, Sean?"

She cast me a semi-reassuring smile and left.

"*Is* she right?" I murmured. "*Are* you waiting for something?"

I reached under my jacket and pulled out the SIG. I put the gun near his head, finger outside the guard, and pulled back the slide to feed the first round out of the

433

magazine, letting the action snap forwards with a sharp metallic sound that would have been as unmistakable as it was familiar — to both of us.

Sean never moved.

I leant in closer, battling to drive the tears out of my voice with anger instead. "Get up, soldier. Get up and fight it, damn you. Don't leave me here without you. What the *hell* are you waiting for?"

But I didn't wait for an answer. Instead, I slipped the SIG back into its holster, checked the lie of my jacket over it, and walked out without looking back.

Behind me, I left the coffee steaming delicately on the cabinet by his bed.

Outside, it was raining again. I turned up the collar of my jacket, hunched my shoulders to close the gap, and headed for the nearest subway station that would take me back downtown. Parker had offered me use of one of the Navigators after the death of my Buell, but parking was always a problem.

Sean's bike, a Buell Ulysses, was sitting under a dust cover, itself covered in dust, in the parking garage beneath our apartment building. I suppose I could have used that, but somehow I couldn't bring myself to do it.

Out of the corner of my eye, I saw the big Mercedes pull into the kerb just level with me. I even altered my pace a little, but still wasn't prepared for the sound of my own name.

"Hey, Charlie!"

I turned, saw Eisenberg's head of security, Gleason, climbing out of the passenger seat. Today she wore a high-necked cream blouse and black wool trousers, and looked as casual as I'd seen her. I stood my ground and waited for her to cross the sidewalk towards me in a couple of long strides.

She jerked her head towards the building I'd just left. "How is he?"

My instinct was fast anger, like she had no right to ask, but I swallowed it down far enough to be civil. "No change."

Gleason nodded at that, as if she hadn't expected any other reply. As if she'd only asked for form's sake. I felt my teeth clench with the effort of not telling her to go to hell by the shortest route possible, but she spoke before I could phrase the words.

She nodded to the car, still idling by the kerb. "Get in," she invited. "It's a lousy day to be walking outside."

"I like the rain."

"Well, I don't." She sighed. "You think I was sent all the way up here to stand around ruining a perfectly good pair of shoes and arguing with you?"

I altered my stance, noticed she'd done the same. Combative. Any moment now, we were going to be brawling. I made a conscious effort to ease off. Besides — sent?

"My mother told me never to get into cars with strange men — or women, come to that."

"Yeah? Well, mine told me never to date musicians. Looks like they're both disappointed." There was a trace of dark humour lurking in her eyes that faded as she glanced pointedly towards the building behind me again. Towards Sean. "Get in the goddamn car, Charlie," she said with quiet intensity. "Trust me, you'll want to hear this."

CHAPTER
FIFTY-NINE

"Where are we going?" I asked as I settled back into the leather upholstery of the Mercedes. The driver was another of Eisenberg's men. From the back seat, he seemed to have no neck, his ears going straight down into his collar with no discernible alteration in width.

"Nowhere in particular — yet," Gleason said as we pulled away and accelerated into traffic. "That's up to you." She settled herself. The Merc was a brand-new S600, with enough room in the back for her to cross her legs negligently. "As you know, my employer is a very wealthy man. He has contacts, connections, in the highest places, and the money and power to get just about whatever he wants."

A small smile slipped across the side of her mouth, and from it I deduced that she herself had been one of the things Brandon Eisenberg had coveted and then acquired.

"Fascinating. How does this relate to me?" *And to Sean?*

Gleason's face flickered. She'd got this little speech all worked out, and wasn't going to let me hurry her to the punchline.

"I'm coming to that. As you are probably aware, I am ex-Secret Service," she said, straightening the cuff of her shirt, and there was more than a hint of pride in her voice. "I was tasked with guarding the President."

"Let me guess," I drawled. "Bill Clinton?"

Her mouth tightened, but she ploughed on doggedly. "As such, I, too, have friends in . . . interesting places. Including Homeland Security."

My expression gave me away, I know it did. She saw my reaction and smiled.

"You know Epps?" I said. It hardly needed to be a question.

"I guess just about everybody knows Conrad Epps," she said, pulling a face. "Unfortunately."

Oh yeah, you know Epps all right . . .

"Word is that he's been attempting to track a certain fugitive for the past couple of months — without success. Until now, that is," she continued. "It would seem that the guy they're after has just popped up on the radar in Omaha, Nebraska, of all places."

I was aware of a burning sensation in my chest, which I recognised as both relief and resentment. So, they'd got him back again — maybe. But for how long? Looked at coldly, how could Epps actually charge him without having to admit his own mistakes? And if his guys slipped in and grabbed him again, quick and quiet, who's to say he'd ever be called to any kind of account anyway?

I sighed. "Look, this is all very interesting, Gleason," I said. "And I appreciate Mr Eisenberg feeling the need to keep me informed, but I don't see —"

438

"I have it on very good authority — the best, as a matter of fact — that nobody will be going to check out this lead until Monday," she cut in. "We've confirmed that one of Epps's guys is booked on a flight out of LaGuardia early Monday morning."

Today was Friday. That gave the whole of the weekend for something to spook the guy. For him to disappear, escape, evade. Again . . .

"So?"

Gleason studied her fingernails. "Mr Eisenberg believes you would like the personal satisfaction of being the one to bring this fugitive in yourself," she said. "Or . . . taking whatever alternative action you deem appropriate."

"Why?" I seemed to be reduced to speaking in monosyllables, but it was the best I could manage.

Gleason found a rough edge on her thumbnail and frowned over it, as she said casually, "Because you caught the man who killed his son."

"That was something of a team effort."

She shrugged. "He still reckons he owes you, for some reason," she said. "Take some advice — if a billionaire reckons he owes you, don't argue. I think Mrs Willner may have put a word in for you, too."

She reached into the seat pocket in front of her and pulled out a plain manila packet, handed it across. It weighed heavy in my hand.

"The intel reports are all in there — I'd burn the whole lot when you're done, if I were you," Gleason said, conspiratorial. "Mr Eisenberg's private jet is waiting on you. The pilot has a take-off slot booked in about an hour, and a flight plan to the West Coast has already been filed." She paused, her tone blandly conversational now. "By coincidence, that would take you right over Nebraska. I'm sure no one would object to an unscheduled stop."

I was silent, staring at the unopened packet in my hand. A real Pandora's box. What would be let loose if I opened it?

For what seemed like a long time, I sat there and thought about actions and consequences, about scars and grief, about justice and death.

Gleason was looking out of the car window, her head turned away as if to give me privacy. Her body was relaxed, belying the importance of this decision. The thick-necked driver continued to circle aimlessly through the busy streets. The rain continued to fall.

Eventually, I glanced across. Gleason must have caught the movement reflected in the glass, because she turned back to me, nothing but polite enquiry in her face.

"I've always wanted a ride in a new Lear 85," I said gravely.

Only then did she allow herself a smile, as if she'd won some small internal bet, but she didn't make the mistake of allowing satisfaction to creep into her voice. "Sure," she said. "It's a very nice airplane."

CHAPTER
SIXTY

Omaha was deceptively warm. I sat under the awning outside a small delicatessen in the historic Old Market district, drinking espresso and watching a lazy afternoon fade towards evening amid the old brick warehouse buildings and chic boutiques.

I'd been in Nebraska for two days and been pleasantly surprised by the place. It was an area of the States I'd never visited before, and seemed to be somewhere even Americans flew right over on their way from one coast to the other.

It was a good place to disappear.

As soon as I'd made my decision back in New York, Gleason had taken me to Eisenberg's private plane, with only a brief stop-off at the apartment so I could throw some clothes into an overnight bag. I'd hurried through packing, as though I knew I'd change my mind if given more time to think things through.

Before I left, I'd carefully locked my SIG away in the gun safe in the bedroom — a precaution against being tempted to use it. Almost as an afterthought, I'd placed my cellphone alongside it, but first I'd sent Parker a short text message, telling him I was taking a few days' personal time, that I'd be in touch, and not to worry about me. I shut the phone off and locked it away before he had chance to send a reply.

Leaving that behind was a harder decision than the gun. I was torn between not wanting to be out of touch in case anything drastic happened regarding Sean, and not wanting to be easily tracked. In the end, head won over heart.

When I'd landed in Omaha, there was a nondescript Ford Taurus waiting for me, rented by one of Eisenberg's myriad companies, and an open-ended room booked at the Embassy Suites on 10th and Jackson. The hotel had a convention of some description going on over the weekend and was crowded enough that I could move through the public areas with a comfortable degree of anonymity.

There were even ponds full of giant koi in the lobby to further distract people's attention. I restrained myself from snapping at a group of little brats who were taking great delight in dropping coins onto the fish, watched with apparent indulgence by their parents. With some regret, I decided that slapping their legs for them — adults as well as children — would not help me maintain my desired low profile.

I had performed countless counter-surveillance routines since my arrival, but as far as I could tell, nobody was following me or taking undue interest. I spent most of my time on foot. The Taurus had not moved from the hotel parking garage since I'd checked in.

This evening, I'd been out for early sushi at a place called Blue. I'd always been wary of eating raw fish so far from an ocean, but it was some of the best I'd tasted outside Tokyo. Afterwards, I'd queued for specialty ice cream at Ted & Wally's, a short walk away, and now I was finishing off with coffee at a third stop. It was a good way to keep a casual eye on the area while I watched and waited.

Gleason's intel packet had given me the approximate location where there had been sightings of my quarry. It was a relatively compact area of boutique stores and restaurants, and it wasn't hard to keep an eye on the main drag.

I sat with my back to the building, soaking up the last of the late sun, relaxed. A guy tried to join me, his smile ingratiating and hopeful as he indicated the empty chair opposite. I shook my head.

"Sorry," I said cheerfully, putting on an all-purpose American accent, "but I'm just waiting for my boyfriend to finish up teaching his karate class."

His smile froze a little and he edged away with a muttered apology. I watched him take an inside table in the back, far enough away that he could not be easily pointed out to my mythical boyfriend, when he finally turned up.

My thoughts turned logically to Sean, who'd never been the jealous type, at least not as far as other men were concerned. He had too much in-built self-assurance for that. But trust of all kinds had been a constant issue between us.

He'd felt the difference in our social backgrounds more keenly than I had, not helped by the fact that my parents had gone out of their way to make him aware of it. They had never approved of our relationship and at one point they'd tried actively to drive us apart. They had very nearly succeeded.

And now there was Parker to worry about. An added complication I could do without. When I'd checked my email on the computer in the business centre at the hotel before I'd come out, I found half a dozen messages from him, the subject line of each growing in anxiety. The last one was headed "CONTACT ME — URGENT!"

But knowing that Parker — or Bill Rendelson — would probably be able to trace my location if I opened it, I hadn't done so. I hadn't opened any of them. I would not lie to Parker about where I was or what I was doing, but that meant not contacting him or he would know, instinctively. It seemed, on some level or another, he knew already.

Unless, of course, he was trying to get in touch to tell me something had happened to Sean. Because, if I didn't know, maybe I could put off the awful truth for a little while longer.

A horse-drawn carriage rolled past, strangely silent on the brick street. When I looked, I found the horse was wearing clip-on rubber boots to muffle its tread. With the music and chatter going on around me, I wondered who had objected to the gentle clop of hooves.

A fragment of an old WH Auden poem slipped into my mind, something about silencing pianos and keeping the dog from barking with a juicy bone. About believing love would last for ever.

444

About being wrong.

I took a breath, lifted my chin and stared at the couple taking a ride in the carriage. They were leaning together, heads touching, hands entwined. I looked away sharply, watched the steady nodding motion of the horse instead.

I would miss Geronimo and my morning rides on the beach with Dina, I realised. Maybe she wouldn't mind if I joined her every once in a while — just until she went to Europe at the end of the summer.

She had finally decided to make her peace with her father, she'd told me. I wondered how Caroline Willner really felt about that. After all, the main reason she had been so keen to get her daughter away from Long Island was to prevent her becoming the fifth victim. Her fears had been both realised and neutralised. But Dina seemed determined to recover from her ordeal, and at least the sight of me did not provoke hysterics. There was a chance we might remain friends.

On the far side of the wide street, a guy ambled into view, weaving between the people and the colourful planters.

"There you are, Roy," I murmured under my breath. "Right on time."

According to Gleason's security services contacts, he was currently using the name Roy Neese, and he'd made it fit. His hair was short and ginger, which it had not been the last time I'd seen him. It was a clever choice, I considered. Men do not often choose to be redheads.

He had also affected a neatly trimmed beard and moustache, which gave him a surprisingly distinguished appearance. He was wearing chinos and loafers, and a lightweight dark-blue jacket over a polo shirt. A pair of designer sunglasses perched on top of his head, which meant either contact lenses or he'd had laser treatment for his eyes. He looked reasonably affluent and totally relaxed. Not at all like a wanted fugitive.

If he had any inkling that Epps's people were closing in, he hid it well.

And if he had any inkling that *I* was half a step behind him, he hid that better.

I'd tracked him down the first evening, had been trailing him ever since. Epps's guys were due to arrive early the following afternoon, and when they did I planned on having all the answers. So, I'd been following him on and off since I'd first identified him, more by his gait than his appearance. It seemed he had turned into a creature of habit.

I stood up, trapping a dollar bill under my empty cup. I'd paid for my coffee when it arrived, so I could make a quick getaway when I needed to. I left the receipt the waitress had provided, though. I didn't think I'd be putting in an expenses claim for this trip.

Casually, I crossed the uneven street, stepping down carefully from a kerb that seemed to be the best part of a foot high. The cars were all parked nose-in on a slant, and a number of the regulars had one corner of the bumper bashed in as testament to the unexpected steepness of the camber.

446

I waited for a custom Cadillac to rumble past, floating along on a blue neon glow that reminded me of Eisenberg's yacht. The windows were down and the stereo was thumping. It was Sunday evening in old Omaha — the perfect time to show up and show off.

It was also my last chance.

My quarry, meanwhile, had turned the corner at the end of the street and disappeared from view, but I didn't hurry. If yesterday and the day before were anything to go by, I knew exactly where he was heading.

The packet of intel Gleason had provided was brief but solid at the same time. There hadn't been much in it, but what there was turned out to be accurate, and that was worth pages of *ifs* and *maybes*.

By the time I reached the corner, I could see Neese a hundred metres ahead, walking briskly but showing no alarm in his stride. I crossed over at the lights with a group of conventioneers who were heading back to the Embassy Suites, lurking amid their chatter just in case he glanced back.

He did, just once, in what had clearly been a habit of survival at one point, now grown somewhat lax. I veered unnoticed away from the group when we reached the hotel entrance, dipped quickly through a park and jogged down a sloping side road, glad of my dark jeans and trainers. I was heading towards the Missouri River that wound along Omaha's eastern edge and partly separated it from neighbouring Iowa.

Getting into town from the prosaically named Eppley Airfield, I'd discovered to my amusement, had involved crossing briefly into the next state. The river's meandering course had changed and nobody had bothered to redraw the borders.

Away from the stores and restaurants, it was apparent how fast the light was dropping, stars beginning to pop above the slow relentless river. In the distance I could see the hulking flyover for Interstate 480, and beyond that the twin uprights of the swooping pedestrian bridge linking Nebraska to Iowa.

The footbridge was known locally as "Bob", for a reason I'd yet to discern. I'd walked across it the day I'd arrived, during my first recce, and found it bounced alarmingly under foot. I didn't know if the flyover had an official name, although the graffiti artists who'd clambered into its steel rafters with their cans of spray paint had made up plenty of their own.

A planked walkway led under the flyover, over the top of the railway line and past an old pumping station, before coming out alongside the river. During the day it was a popular spot for walkers and joggers and a few tourists. At night, even though it was lit, the whole area tended to be more secluded.

Secluded was good.

I reached the point under the flyover where the traffic made eerie howling noises on the concrete high above, eyes searching for my target. Yesterday, he had stuck to the roadways, which were better lit, before cutting across to the paved area beside the river. If I had my timing right, he should have appeared there just ahead of me. But when I reached the turn in the walkway, there was no sign of him.

Shit!

Had I moved too fast and got too far in front of him? Or had he taken a different route back to the river — maybe headed to Rick's Café Boatyard for a drink? I reminded myself that I was not an expert when it came to surveillance. My job was to blend into the scenery and to spot people who were themselves out of place, not track and trace.

I hesitated, and then some sixth sense made me turn abruptly, twisting to look over my shoulder.

The man who had become Roy Neese was standing on the walkway about four metres behind me. There was a gun clasped firmly in his right hand, pointing at my stomach. The muzzle didn't waver.

"Hiya, Charlie," he said. "Did ya miss me?"

CHAPTER
SIXTY-ONE

"OK, let's see the weapon," the man said, and even his voice seemed different, lower and more gravelly, although that could just have been the tension. "Take the piece out, nice and slow, and toss it over the railing."

I shook my head sadly. "I'm not carrying."

He was silent for a moment, then he flicked towards my torso with the barrel of the gun. It was another nine-mil Glock, I saw, like the one he'd used to shoot Sean. He was getting a taste for them.

"Show me."

Obligingly, I lifted the hem of my sweatshirt, just high enough to expose the waistband of my jeans, turned a slow circle. It went against all my training to present my back to an armed assailant, but he wasn't going to shoot me just yet.

Not without discovering what I knew — and who else knew it, also.

When I was facing him again, he gave a sardonic smile. "Don't know why that should surprise me — you always were so sure of yourself."

"With reason," I said coldly. "I caught you, didn't I?" *Twice.*

The smile lost some of its internal backing, became more forced. Not a memory he wanted to dwell on. His chin lifted on a taunt. "Tell me, Charlie — those reflexes of yours quick enough to dodge a bullet?"

"What does it matter?" I shrugged. "Epps has a bullet with your name on it, and you can't dodge that one for ever."

"Dodged it pretty good up 'til now," he said with satisfaction. His eyes were everywhere, I saw, as if expecting the Homeland Security man to storm in with a full SWAT team behind him at any moment. It took half his concentration away from me and I needed to use that while I had the chance.

I cursed the fact I'd left the SIG behind in New York, but I had set out to confront and detain, not to kill. The man in front of me may not have started out personally violent, but he'd certainly picked it up along the way. Who knows what else he'd had to do in order to survive on the run?

My heart rate had stepped up, but I let my arms dangle, kept my knees soft and my shoulders relaxed. Strangely, I felt no fear. I had no doubts that the man behind the gun was prepared to use it if he had to. He might even be looking forward to it, but if it was my destiny to die here, I was ready for it.

And I would not provide him with an easy kill.

"I hope you're not too attached to good old Roy Neese, because he's blown out of the water." I watched the information filter through the layers of nerves, tightening and tangling as it went. "*Roy Neese. Where* did you find that one? Doesn't quite have the ring of your old name, does it?"

As I spoke, I turned sideways, leant back and rested my elbows on the rusted steel handrail that bordered the walkway. I let my hands droop, and hooked one heel onto the lower railing, keeping it all very casual, relaxed. And all the while hoping he wouldn't notice that one arm was now half a metre closer to him, and I had a solid object behind me to launch from.

"Had to pick something." He flashed his teeth quick enough for it to be more grimace than grin. "Too many people in my . . . position go for names that stand out, for one reason or another. Or they keep a hold of their initials." He paused, as if not sure he should be telling me so much, but realising it didn't matter either way. "I used one of those random-name generators you find online."

"Clever," I agreed sedately, nodding. "I heard Epps sent you after one of the militia groups linked to Fourth Day. What happened — did being a double agent not do it for you?"

I kept my voice comparatively quiet, so the background roar of traffic overhead would make it harder to hear. And as I watched, he shifted his stance a little, unconsciously edging closer.

"You think I ever intended to spy on those crazy bastards?" he asked, almost incredulous. "Let me tell you, they do *not* take kindly to that kinda thing. And paranoid? They make guys like Epps look *real* trusting."

452

"He must have been, to turn you loose on a solemn promise to be a good little boy, cross your heart and hope to die."

He ignored the mockery in my tone and shook his head, the barrel of the Glock starting to drift downwards. "You just don't get it, do you, Charlie?" he demanded. "I'm hardly a blip on his radar. In fact, Epps is better off with me *off* of his radar altogether, because then he'll never have to answer for the errors he made in California. Errors that caused the deaths of his own people."

"The way I remember it," I said tightly, "that was down to you."

"Semantics," he dismissed. He paused, gave me a pitying look. "You really think I didn't know they were coming for me tomorrow? You think, even if I wasn't planning to be gone by then, that I won't be loose again a month from now?"

I tried not to show how hard that set me reeling, was suddenly glad of the railing at my back. "But you didn't know I was coming for you today."

He laughed. "You forget — I spent some time with you, Charlie, and you're one of the good guys. I had a feeling you might come with them, want to be the one who slapped on the cuffs with a self-righteous air. Didn't expect you to spring for an advance flight, though. You've been tailing me since — when? Saturday morning?"

So, my surveillance skills really did need improvement. "Friday night, actually," I said, as calmly as I could manage.

He smiled. "Should change your looks some, if you're gonna do this professionally. Once seen, never forgotten." His eyes suddenly narrowed. "Epps told me Meyer survived, so what's this all about, huh?"

The implications of his false assumption flashed through my brain as fast as the synapses could fire. For reasons of his own, Epps hadn't told him Sean was still in a coma.

So use it.

"You really don't know?" I murmured. "Never mind about me — you think *Sean* would be happy to let a little shit like you get away with taking him down?" I deliberately softened my voice still further. He leant close enough for me to smell his aftershave, strong enough to remind me that he was not a field operative, or he wouldn't wear something so distinctive in still air. I smiled. "You really think I'd come out here after you, alone and unarmed, for any other reason than as *bait*?"

I saw the convulsive jump of his Adam's apple. "Bait?"

I let my eyes slip past his face to a point behind his left shoulder. "Why don't you ask him yourself?"

His head snapped round, knees ducking his body as he turned, as if to avoid a blow. I kicked away from the railing and jabbed my knuckles hard into the rigid tendons at the back of his right hand. The hand sprang open immediately, a completely involuntary reaction. The gun clattered onto the planking and spun away behind him.

I followed up with a fast elbow to the throat, both to disable and to silence him. He crashed backwards,

454

scrabbling for the collar of his polo shirt as though the soft cotton was responsible for his lack of breath, and I realised I'd put all my pent-up rage and heartache into that single blow.

By the time he'd got his senses back under him, I'd picked up the Glock, checked the magazine and was pointing it in his direction. He shielded his head with his arms, palms outward and fingers spread, while he gulped for air and speech.

"Wait," he managed at last, rasping. "I'm on a boat — in the Riverside Marina. I have money on board! I can pay —"

"*Pay?*" I heard my voice crack, harsh and raw, and something else seemed to split open inside my head, my heart, and come pouring out like poison. "Do you honestly think there's enough money on a boat — on a whole fleet of fucking boats — to *begin* to make up for the damage you've caused?"

Smoothly, easily, I stepped back a pace, brought the muzzle of the gun up until the sights were aligned on the centre of his forehead.

"Charlie, wait! Please —"

"Too late," I said, and pulled the trigger.

CHAPTER
SIXTY-TWO

Twelve hours later, I found myself alone in a police interview room, having been temporarily relinquished by the Omaha Homicide detective who was in charge of the case.

On the scarred desktop by my elbow was a cup of tepid coffee. It had been barely drinkable when it was hot, and was even less so now. In front of me lay a yellow legal notepad with a few scrawled notes written on it.

I sat with my hands folded in my lap and stared back into myself, trying to work out how I felt about what I'd done.

Sean had once told me that killing without hesitation or fear was something you got used to. Something that got easier over time. That the danger sign was if you started to enjoy it.

I had not, I decided objectively, enjoyed killing the man pretending to be Roy Neese. It had seemed necessary and I'd done it, that was all.

And the fact remained that if I'd killed him months ago — right after he'd taken Sean down, while he was fleeing the scene with the weapon still hot in his hand — there would have been few questions asked.

But I'd wanted more, and I'd been naive enough to expect the justice system would provide it.

Not the first time I'd been wrong about that.

Behind me, to my left, the door to the interview room opened and I turned my head, expecting to see Detective Kershner return. Instead, it was Parker Armstrong who stood there, almost hesitant, as though he'd had to steel himself to face me. He closed the door quietly and moved further into the room, onto the opposite side of the table.

"Charlie," he said gravely. "You OK?" He seemed to ask me that a lot.

"Surviving." I shrugged, realised I couldn't read his eyes, and added carefully, "I didn't expect you to come."

"How could I not?" He paused. "The identity of the . . . victim has been confirmed?"

"Yes."

He closed his eyes a moment, rubbed his temple. "They gave me the gist," he said. "Single gunshot wound to the head, gun alongside him. Any chance it was self-inflicted?"

"Would be nice to think he'd finally developed a conscience, wouldn't it?" I said, regretful, "but you know as well as I do that's an unlikely scenario."

Apparently casual, Parker leant against the wall in the corner right under the camera, where its view was poorest. His gaze was on me fully now, intense to the point of pleading. "Why not?"

"The location of the body, for one thing," I said. "He was probably on his way to the little marina at

457

Riverside, where he had a boat moored. The walkway is neither one place nor another. Suicides tend to go somewhere specific, symbolic even, to do the deed. And the gun had been wiped clean."

"So he was murdered," Parker said flatly, the words almost forced out of him. "Could this be a random killing — unconnected to his . . . past?"

I shook my head. "I doubt it. From what Detective Kershner's told me of the crime rate in Omaha, it's a pretty safe town."

Parker sighed, as if he was trying his best and I was being deliberately difficult. When he spoke there was a trace of anguish underlying his even tone. "Why did you come here, Charlie?"

I met his gaze squarely. "Because certain information came into my hands about his location, and I knew Epps wasn't going to follow it up fast enough," I said. "I didn't want our boy to simply disappear again."

His eyes narrowed. "Well, that's for sure."

"A round to the head tends to make certain of that," I agreed, and saw the anguish turn to active pain.

"Charlie . . . What have you told them?"

"Everything," I said. *More or less.* "It would have been foolish to do otherwise. After all, it was all bound to come out sooner or later. Why hold anything back?"

He hid a flinch, not well. "You know I'll help you," he said. "Whatever it takes."

"Parker, trust me, I don't need your help." I spoke gently, easily, all the time acutely aware of possible listeners on the other side of the mirrored wall. "I assume Epps's boys have finally turned up?"

"Yeah, we came in on the same flight."

I nodded. "Better late than never, I suppose."

The door opened again and Detective Kershner hovered there, checking out Parker with a wary gaze. He was young, home-grown and relatively inexperienced, but sharp for all that. I had watched my step very carefully with him. His eyes slid to me.

"The department would like to thank you for your assistance, Miss Fox," he said formally. "We have your contact details in New York, should anything else come up, but you can go."

"Thank you." I stood up. "And good luck with this one."

He gave a wry smile. "We're gonna need it," he said. He paused, aware I wasn't quite a fellow professional, but I wasn't quite a civilian either. "Thought you'd like to know that Ballistics ran the weapon through IBIS and got a hit from an execution-style homicide about six months ago in California, thought to be connected to a militia group out there."

Parker's head snapped up. "Wasn't he supposed to be infiltrating a militia?" he said, puzzlement in his tone.

"That is my understanding, yes sir." The detective nodded. "Looks like they got wise to him, maybe followed him here."

Parker's eyes skimmed over me, thoughtful. "Yeah," he murmured. "Looks that way."

Kershner walked us out, flicking little covert glances at the pair of us as we went. I realised he'd checked up on both of us. This was probably the first time he'd met anybody with Parker's credentials, and was trying to work out what made us tick.

By the entrance, he shook our hands and left us. Parker jerked his head towards the door and I followed him out into bright sunshine. There was a light breeze, just enough to set the Stars and Stripes on the nearest flagpole rippling lazily. It could just have been something to do with the air conditioning in the building, but the air smelt sweet and clean outside.

Parker let us get as far as the front seats of his rented Chevy Suburban before he spoke again.

"I don't suppose you'd like to tell me what the hell just happened back there?" he demanded with a dangerous softness.

I leant back against the headrest and closed my eyes, feeling utterly exhausted. "I found the body," I said. It was easier to avoid telling the whole truth with my eyes shut.

"You found the body?" he repeated flatly. "Hell, Charlie, I get a call from Epps first thing this morning, telling me the guy was dead and you're being held by the cops out here." He shook his head a little and rubbed a frustrated hand around the back of his neck. "Do you have any idea what I thought . . .? What I *felt*?"

"I'm sorry," I said, and meant it. "But I was being interviewed as a witness. That's somewhat different from being arrested as a suspect."

I couldn't deny, though, that as I'd watched the last flicker of life expire from my target's eyes, I'd debated

460

on simply surrendering to fate and the police, in that order.

But, I realised I'd made the decision to overcome this before I'd even taken the shot. By stepping back, making it a non-contact wound, I'd avoided the inevitable blow-back mist of blood. I'm still not entirely sure what made me do that, other than some inbuilt survival instinct. A desire to distance myself from this crime.

Moments later, I'd wiped down the gun and dropped it alongside the corpse, walked back to my hotel forcing myself not to hurry. I didn't look back.

My clothes had gone straight into the hotel laundry, right down to the trainers I'd been wearing. Even though I was almost certain my sleeves had covered it, I scrubbed my waterproof Tag watch in the bathroom sink, left it to soak while I stood braced against the tiles in the shower for as long as I could manage.

Even so, I'd waited until the early morning for any possible remaining gunshot residue to dissipate before I retraced my steps towards the river. I confess that I was half expecting to see the police already on the scene, or the body vanished like part of some bizarre murder mystery.

Neither scenario played out. The body was exactly as I'd left it, with the exception of a couple of inquisitive seagulls. I ventured just close enough to verify the gun was still alongside him, then jogged to the nearest building and called it in.

The rest, Parker knew — or suspected.

They'd checked the time I arrived back at the hotel, but there was enough leeway with time of death for that to be inconclusive. As a matter of course, they also tested my hands and clothing for gunshot residue and found nothing, which had seemed to allay their immediate suspicions. I guessed the discovery of the murder weapon's unexpected provenance would do the rest.

Parker started the engine, dropped the Suburban into gear, and cruised sedately back towards my hotel without needing to be given directions.

"Charlie, why *did* you come here?" he asked when we were almost there, sounding weary.

"I told you," I said, keeping my voice even. "I wanted to make sure he didn't run again before Epps's people caught up with him."

"And that's all?" Parker persisted.

I could have lied to him. But I couldn't bring myself to do it. I twisted slightly in my seat.

"Do you really want to know?"

"I . . ." He sighed, and I saw his hands flex around the rim of the steering wheel. "No," he said at last, sounding more defeated than I'd ever heard him. "You should have told me. I would have come with you. This is not something you should have tackled alone. If I'd had any idea where you were, or what you were doing . . ."

"I thought you knew," I said slowly. "Why else the emails?"

He acknowledged my admission that I'd ignored his messages with a bitter quirk of his lips. "Your cell was

462

switched off. I couldn't reach you. I thought maybe you'd . . . decided to do something stupid."

And maybe I had. I shied away from going there. It was a dark corner I would not look into.

"Do away with myself, you mean?" I asked dryly. "You really think, Parker, after all the shit I've been through, I'd take the easy way out now?"

He pulled up outside the entrance to the Embassy Suites and glanced over at me, his gaze coolly assessing.

"It would have been the ultimate cruel irony, if you had," he said, and something in his voice sent my pulse buzzing, tightened my chest.

No. Oh, no . . .

"Why? What's happened?"

"If you'd opened those emails, you'd know," he said. He paused, a wealth of conflicted emotions in his voice, his face. "Sean's awake."

CHAPTER
SIXTY-THREE

Parker and I flew back into New York by scheduled flight, landing at Newark late that same evening. On the journey, I'd asked him over and over for more details about Sean, but he knew little beyond the bare facts.

He told me that Sean's brain activity had started to pick up on Friday afternoon, not long after I'd left the hospital. I wondered about the cause of that, whether the sound of a weapon being readied reached far deeper into his psyche than touch or smell could ever do. The memory of violence overcoming intimacy.

Parker received the call from the hospital not long after my text message came in. He'd tried to contact me, but my phone went straight to voicemail — hardly surprising as I'd switched it off before I left. When calling the apartment brought no response, Parker had Bill Rendelson check the airlines for a ticket in my name. Needless to say, there wasn't one.

Though he'd reported all this in a matter-of-fact tone, I could tell that was the moment he'd begun seriously to worry. He'd sent his first email that night, and kept sending them, from his PDA at Sean's bedside.

He relayed what the doctors had told him, that Sean seemed distressed, like a man trapped in a nightmare. His heart rate and temperature had soared, rapid eye movement increasing as he became more restless.

"It was like watching someone clawing their way out of the grave," Parker said, his voice hollow. "Like he was fighting for his life."

And I hadn't been there, fighting alongside him.

Instead, I'd been out committing cold-blooded murder in his name.

Through Saturday, as I'd tracked Roy Neese through his normal daily subroutines in downtown Omaha, Sean had become increasingly lucid, and increasingly disturbed. It was soon apparent that he recognised nobody around him and remembered nothing of how he came to be shackled to a hospital bed in a strange country with his body wasted and his mind in fragments.

And I hadn't been there to anchor him.

Now, as Erik Landers drove us in from the airport with blatant disregard for the posted speed limits, my heart was clenched tight in my chest. It didn't matter how many hours I'd sat by Sean's bedside during those three long months of his unconsciousness. All I knew — all *he* would know — was that I hadn't been there at the moment he needed me most.

I was wracked with a faithless dismay, stripped to the bone by guilt and fear, that by not being the first thing he saw when he opened his eyes, the memory of what we had would be somehow squandered.

And I hadn't been there to reinforce it in his mind.

465

"How much does he remember?" I demanded now. Alongside me, Landers dipped his eyes away from the road for a moment.

"Bits and pieces, mainly. He thought he kinda remembered me." He gave a downturned smile. "Thought we'd served together in Kosovo."

I swallowed. "And Parker? Did he remember him?"

And me? Does he remember me?

Landers' gaze flicked to his boss, sitting in the rear seat, as if being asked to tell tales. "Well, he was more kinda hazy on that."

"They're trying not to pressure him to remember anything, Charlie," Parker said gently. "It's the last year or so that seems to be the worst affected — the biggest blank. The doctors reckon his longer-term memories are clearer."

I twisted in my seat and exchanged a brief look with him. *He'll remember you*, Parker's eyes declared. I clung to that unspoken promise.

Landers dropped us outside the main entrance and I took the steps three at a time, galloped along familiar corridors with Parker at my shoulder. When I skidded to a halt outside the door to Sean's room, the figure of his nurse, Nancy, appeared in my path.

"Charlie!" she said, her face anxious. "I —"

But I didn't wait, ducking round her shoulder before she had a chance to give me an update.

For the first time, as I entered that room, Sean was half sitting up in his bed, eyes open and mostly clear. He turned to stare at us, slow and jerky, as if his neck would hardly support the weight of his head. I drank in the sight of him, greedy, needy.

All the way back from Nebraska, I'd prayed that I would not arrive and find all this had been a mistake, a false alarm. I had visions of walking in and finding him laid out as usual, those ridiculously long eyelashes fanning his cheeks, his body still and without animation.

Instead, there he was, shaky, weakened, but . . . *there*. And he would come back from this. We both would. I felt my eyes fill.

Sean's own eyes were very dark, his pupils huge as though still adapting to the light. His gaze swept across Parker, at my elbow, without a hint of recognition, then settled clumsily on me and he went very still.

I took a step forwards, hardly aware that Nancy had followed us in, had laid a gentle restraining hand on my arm.

"Charlie?" Sean said, his voice raw and croaky and incredulous.

I gave him a shy smile. "Hi, Sean."

He froze at the sound of my voice, a mix of frenzied emotions flashing across his face, chased on by a scowl. "What the fuck is she doing here? This some kind of joke?" he demanded. His chest heaved with the effort of breath and he had to swallow between sentences, as though speech was still difficult after long disuse. And at the same time I realised his accent was more pronounced than it had been, the last time he'd spoken. Now it was more like it used to be. Back when I first knew him.

Back when . . .

"Sean —" It was Nancy who went to his bedside, tried to calm him.

"Get Foxcroft out of here. I don't want to see her." He raked the nurse with a furious gaze, summoning up the energy with such effort it made him tremble. He turned on me with such intensity that I flinched in the face of it. "How could you think I'd ever want to see you again, after what you've done?"

EPILOGUE

"It's not that he doesn't remember you, Charlie," Nancy said. "It's just that he seems to remember you as . . . somebody else."

"No, he doesn't," I said dully. "That's the problem."

We were sitting in the small nursing station at the end of the corridor furthest away from Sean's room. I'm not sure if that was for my benefit or for his.

Nancy was at her desk with the seat turned towards me. The space was small enough that our knees were almost touching. She sat hunched forwards in her uniform, forearms resting on her thighs and pain in her eyes. Parker stood leaning in the doorway, face closed down.

"Who does he remember, Charlie?" he asked quietly. "What happened between the two of you?"

I put my hands to my face, pressing my fingers together as if to hold the words inside. They could not stay that way for ever.

All kinds of guilty associations had bolted through my mind at Sean's initial accusation before the last tattered shreds of sanity kicked in. No way could he know what I had just done. Not unless he'd been having an out-of-body experience. So, that meant . . .

I sat up, let my hands fall away and willed my eyes to dryness, like my throat. "He called me Foxcroft," I said. "That's who I was when we first met — in the army. I volunteered and passed my selection course for Special Forces training," I added, for Nancy's benefit. Parker had, after all, pored over my CV before he'd offered me a job alongside Sean. I glanced at him. His face still told me nothing.

"As for what happened, well, let's just say there was an element that didn't approve of the fairer sex moving into that particular branch of the military," I went on, unable to keep the bitterness out of my voice now. "And one night a group of them decided to demonstrate just how vulnerable female soldiers were. I —"

"You don't have to go through all this," Parker said tightly. "I know what they did to you, Charlie. Sean told me — some of it, anyways."

I shook my head. "But not all of it. We were . . . involved, back then. Shouldn't have been, of course. Sean was one of my training instructors. They posted him just before my . . . assault. By the time he came back, I'd been through court martial and I was well and truly out in the cold."

"Wait a moment, now," Nancy said, her own voice low with angry disbelief. "They attacked you, and *you* were the one who was court-martialled? Where's the justice there?"

I shrugged. I'd long since run out of indignant rage at the way things had turned out. The scars still lingered, but they were deep beneath the surface, a

470

blunt ache where once they'd been excruciating. The last thing I wanted to do was open them up to scrutiny again. "I tried to get in touch with him, while I was still in hospital, but the messages somehow never got through."

And when he did finally hear about what had happened to me, he was given a very different version of events.

"They told Sean I'd failed the course and when they tried to have me RTU'd — that's 'returned to unit' . . ." I said quickly, seeing Nancy's frown. I took a breath. ". . . well, that's when they said I'd started shouting about him taking advantage of his position. I believe the current term for it is 'command rape'."

I heard Parker suck in a quiet breath. "That's —"

"An ugly situation," I agreed. "I thought he'd abandoned me by refusing to answer my calls, appear in my defence at the trial. He thought I'd dropped him in it to try and save my own skin."

"How long?" Nancy asked eventually. "How long did it take before you both realised what had really happened?"

"About four years," I said bleakly. "At the time, the press got hold of it and had a field day. Certain misogynist elements of the powers that be used it as the perfect PR exercise to keep women out of combat roles." They hadn't been able to get rid of Sean so easily, so while I did my best to hide, they'd given him all the one-way missions, only to discover he was too bloody stubborn to die on the job.

471

"So that's when you changed your name," Parker said slowly, "From Foxcroft to Fox."

"Yeah, and it's pretty clear that Charlie *Foxcroft* is who Sean remembers now." I gave them both a twisted smile. "The girl who betrayed his love, his trust, and then ruined his career along with her own."

Nancy put her hand on my arm, fingers smoothing my sleeve. I stared down at them, noted the worn wedding ring.

"He'll remember the rest of it, Charlie," she said, but I heard the layer of doubt beneath the reassuring words. "Just give him a little time. He'll remember." When I looked up I caught the frown, quickly masked.

On the other side of the room, Parker's face was drawn, skin stretched tight across his bones. He loved me, I realised, but maybe it was the kind of love that only flourishes because it's unrequited, and the worst thing that could happen was for it to be given free rein. In the stress of the past few weeks, it had never crossed either of our minds that Sean might wake and simply not want me anymore.

I killed for a man who doesn't remember me except with hate. What does that make me?

Suddenly the years peeled back, leaving me stripped and alone and vulnerable. I looked up at the pair of them, utter despair in my voice.

"What if he *doesn't* remember?"

ACKNOWLEDGEMENTS

As ever, I am deeply indebted to various people who provided the necessary help, advice, encouragement or information in order for me to finish this book. Any deviation from the truth is entirely my own fault.

DP Lyle MD is my favourite medical guru, who was kind enough to give me advice about the realities of long-term coma patients; Crime Writers' Association member and fellow scribbler, Jason Monaghan allowed me to pick his brains about financial info and how to get away with the money; crime writer "Ninja" Kate Kinchen provided some important martial arts info; Dina Willner ran her eye over my New York scenes; and my UK copyeditors ran their eagle eyes over the whole thing.

Thank you to the members of the Warehouse Writers in Kendal, who read various scenes in no particular order and made plenty of valid comments.

I remain forever grateful to the remarkable team at my literary agents, Gregory and Company, including Jane Gregory herself, and my wonderful editor, Stephanie Glencross, who put so much time and effort into helping make this the book it is.

473

Big thank yous go to my UK publisher, Susie Dunlop and all the talented crew at Allison & Busby, and to all the sales and marketing people, and the bookstores and libraries on both sides of the Atlantic.

My husband, Andy, was as brilliant as always at keeping me going through the low patches.

Finally, Dina Willner was not just a test reader, but was also the winning bidder at the charity auction at the Mayhem in the Midlands convention in Omaha, Nebraska in 2009, to become a character in this book. As she was torn between having the character named after herself or her late mother, Caroline, I was very happy indeed to be able to find a place for both of them in this story. The auction was in aid of the Omaha Public Library Foundation, which buys children's materials for all branches.